Silent Hawk

first novel by Alfred Patrick

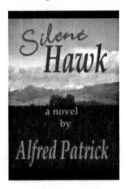

The Templeton family goes west and settles in the rugged and dangerous mining camp at Alder Gulch in the Montana Territory in 1863. They find the ruthless camp is besieged by murderous road agents and corrupt lawmen who are supposed to uphold the law.

Hezekiah Templeton, the teenage son, and his friend, Isaac, find the lawless camp filled with intrigue and adventure. They befriend and old Indian who is surrounded by mystical Indian Spirits, and discover their fathers' dangerous secrets which link them to the local vigilantes.

Hezekiah finds young romance with a saloon maiden, and encounters a fire and brimstone preacher and his weakness.

All these life experiences and tribulations become insignificant when Hezekiah's life suddenly takes a dramatic turn that thrusts him into manhood and changes his life forever

To the grand citizens
of Columbia City —
Choose your trail and
enjoy the ride.

Justice Beyond
The Trail's End

Alfred Patrick

Copyright 2011 by Alfred Patrick

ISBN 978-1-257-63426-2

To contact the author or to order 'Justice Beyond The Trails End' :

silent-hawk@comcast.net

allpatri@aol.com

Published in the United States of America

Printed in the United States of America

To my wonderful wife, best friend, and life-long love; I dedicate this verse, this book, and my life to you.

Bonnie, My Love,

If my life,
I had a chance to change,
Maybe, I'd be a cowboy
Riding on the range.
Perhaps, I might choose
to be a private eye,
Or seek the adventurous life
of being a government spy.
Possibly, a baseball pitcher
throwing a no-hit game;
If I had to do again,
It might not be the same.
But one thing I know for certain
 That I would never do,
Is change that part of life
Of always loving you.

Al Patrick

~Acknowledgments~

To all my family and friends, I thank you for your inspirational cheerleading, particularly when the flow bogged down (writer's block or brain freeze).

Thank you, Bonnie, my love, for allowing me to shut myself off, night after night, day after day, to complete my novel. I know I made you a writer's widow many times, as my fictional characters would drag me off to listen to their story. As always, I am indebted to you for being by my side, and offering your support and encouragement. You are my co-pilot that keeps me from crashing or being completely disoriented. I love you for all that you are and all that you have made me.

I need to give an enormous thank you to Natalie Tom for being a bright star, who gave me light and direction through the difficult finishing touches of the novel. Her insight, advice, and editing helped bring "*Justice Beyond The Trail's End*" to print.

Shanda Armstrong, thank you for providing a picture of your husband, Jason Armstrong, to use on the front cover of the book. Jason is my great-nephew. He and Shanda are the cowboy king and the cowgirl queen around the rodeos in Montana.

To all my readers, I can never thank you enough for your support and wonderful feedback on "*Silent Hawk*". I would never have attempted a second book if it were not for you.

Chapter 1

Joshua Parker and the remainder of the 36th Iowa Volunteer Infantry Regiment mustered out on August 1865 and they were sent north to Davenport, Iowa for their final wages. "The War Between the States" was over. Three years of suffering and death had fallen on the regiment. The hardened veterans who survived the war had to return to their farms, their families, and resume life as though nothing had ever happened.

Joshua was uncertain he could return to the life he had known three years earlier. He had always had the itch for more than the farm, and he was not sure what effect the three years of war would have on him. Maybe the itch would be gone, and he would be ready to settle down to the life he had known before the war.

Joshua stood at the railing of the dock in Davenport, waiting for the steamer due later in the day that would start him on his journey home--a home more distant in time than miles. He began recalling those earlier innocent days before joining the army and seeing the ravages of war.
****

Joshua Madison Parker, son of Elias and Meredith Parker, turned seventeen, on July 13, 1862, and he had never traveled more than twenty-five miles from the family farm. The farm,

1

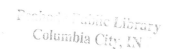

located halfway between Ottumwa and Fairfield, was no different from any other farm in southern Iowa in 1862. Life was a small circle to a young man with dreams and curiosities, and it was choking Joshua. Few people traveled in or out of his life, but when they did, they brought stories that were often beyond the imagination of one who had lived his entire life within that circle.

A couple of older boys, who lived nearby, had joined a volunteer regiment from Iowa a year earlier to fight in the "War Between the States". Folks called them heroes. With the circle ever tightening around Joshua, he decided to approach his father with his desire.

"Father, I want to join the Union Army. It's important to me."

His father looked up from the thrasher. "You're not eighteen."

"You could give your consent."

His father looked up again, only this time he looked annoyed. "First, your mother wouldn't approve. Secondly, see this field that needs harvesting? See that field over there?" He added, pointing in the opposite direction. "How are they supposed to be harvested?"

"I'll go next month. Besides Jonathan is only a year younger than me and Matthew and Mark are thirteen and almost fifteen. They can do more."

His father never looked up. "No! That's final, Joshua. Get the foolishness out of your head."

Joshua had seen the notice in town that they were asking volunteers to report to Keokuk by October 3, a Friday. Joshua had a dilemma. He was not sure he could rebel against his parents, yet the call was becoming too strong. There was nobody he could talk to about his predicament. He could not trust any of his brothers to keep their mouths shut, either by accident or on purpose. His older sister, Denise, would listen and would not say anything, but she was overly sensitive and he did not want to burden her.

Then there was Becky. Joshua and Becky were together, on and off, going on four years. Sometimes Joshua was certain

2

that two different people lived inside her body. On any given day, Joshua might find the sweetest living creature in the world, and then the next day, or perhaps even within the same day, someone else would show up meaner than a mother bear protecting her cub.

If he told the right Becky about his plans of joining the army, he was sure everything would be fine, unless the mother bear suddenly appeared. He shivered at the thought.

By mid-September, Joshua had made his decision to leave home and join the army. That was assuming he could convince the army he was eighteen. He had heard they were not particularly strict.

Joshua laid out his plans. He would leave very early the last Monday of the month. He would leave a note explaining his whereabouts and apologizing for going against their will. He would take the short cut across to Ashland Crossing, some seven or eight miles, and catch a barge heading south on the Des Moines River for Keokuk.

The Saturday before leaving was the Harvest Shindig. He would take the risk and tell Becky then. If the sweet Becky showed up, he envisioned her crying and pleading with him to stay. She would not know how she could exist without him. She would hug and kiss him. She would worry for his life and safety. He could imagine the perfect sendoff.

Of course, he would go to church Sunday. It would be disrespectful to his mother and father to leave Sunday. Besides, he needed a little assurance the Lord knew what he was up to and would keep a watchful eye over him. It was not as if he was going off to Bible school camp. He would spend Sunday afternoon with his family, perhaps the last Sunday...ever. He wondered if he could sleep between now and then.

****

The harvest festival had arrived. Joshua's plan to leave home and join the army was all bottled up inside him like a bad preserve ready to explode. Whether by choice or chance, he had not seen Becky since his decision to join the army. For the best, he thought, but today he hoped to tell her. He could not leave without telling someone his plan.

Becky had always been kind of pretty, or at least Joshua thought so. Her teasing curls always bounced playfully, and her round face with big, round, fluttering, green eyes and the pursed lips, always begging for a kiss, had always tantalized Joshua. He had kissed those puckered lips once, although it was a quick peck, and he was anxious to kiss them again, and maybe today, get to kiss them a lot.

Joshua was standing near the dance platform with his three brothers. His mother and father were off chatting with neighbors and his sister with her friends. It was almost ten, with the sun high in the sky, and he had not seen Becky arrive. Why was she not there? The panic that she might not come began to rush through him. He had waited two weeks for this day. If she did not come, it would ruin everything.

"They're getting ready for the three legged race," Jonathan said, slapping Joshua on the shoulder. "Come on, we can win it."

"No."

"Why not, grumpy?"

"Because."

"Because. What kind of answer is that?"

"Because I don't want to."

"Fine, I'll go get Becky to do it with me," Jonathan smugly remarked.

"She's not here."

"She just came," Jonathan said, pointing behind Joshua.

Joshua jerked his head to see. "Where?"

"You just answered the because." Jonathan began to laugh and ran off. "Wait up, Ben," he called to another boy.

Just one more reason to get out of here, Joshua thought as he watched his three brothers heading towards the race. Now where is Becky?

Joshua was beginning to give up hope for Becky's arrival when a voice behind him sent a tingle through his whole body.

"Hi, Joshua." Joshua stumbled on his own feet turning to face Becky.

Her pursed lips parted ever so slightly into a warm gentle smile. Her eyelashes fluttered. He could feel the sweat beads forming on his forehead. His body felt like butter in the hot sun. She looked better than he had ever seen her...in fact, so well, he was beginning to wonder if he was making a foolish mistake by leaving.

"Hi, Becky. I didn't see you come."

"We just got here. A darn old fox got into the chicken coop last night."

"You, you, well you look mighty smart, Becky."

"Thanks, Joshua. That's so kind of you." Her eyelashes fluttered and her lips were so puckered that it seemed like they were almost touching his lips. "Are you okay, Joshua? You look faint." Her hand reached out and stroked his cheek. It felt like fire.

"I'm fine," he quickly answered, his eyes never leaving her face. He wanted to shout with joy. The good Becky had shown up. It would be a great day.

Joshua was anxious to tell Becky his plans, but decided to wait to find that special moment...alone.

The young couple spent time wandering through the grounds. Joshua tried his luck at the pellet shoot and had a perfect score. Becky squeezed his arm showing her admiration. Joshua's body tingled again.

"Joshua, I saw how all the other boys looked at you. They were so jealous of you for being such a wonderful marksman."

They are jealous because you are with me, Becky, thought Joshua, not because I'm a good shooter. They know I have the prettiest girl at the festival. That's real good! Tell her that. She will probably kiss you right here.

"Becky, the reason the..."

"Look, Joshua," Becky interrupted, "they're starting the dunking throw. Hurry!" She quickly pulled him along. His romantic words were left dangling in the air like sheets on a line, never to be heard.

By mid-afternoon, Joshua could wait no longer. He led Becky away from the crowds and into a nearby quiet alley.

"Where are we going?" she kept asking.

Joshua stopped and faced her. "I want to tell you something, Becky, but you must promise not to tell anyone."

Becky's eyes brightened with curiosity, and her lips pursed, surely ready to kiss him once he told her the secret. "Of course, Joshua."

"Promise?"

"I promise. What's so secretive?" She moved closer. He felt her pulsing heat. Everything was going as planned.

"I'm leaving Monday morning to join the Union Army."

Becky stood several seconds looking at Joshua. Finally, she spoke as her eyes hardened. "I hope you're not serious?"

"Yes. Yes, I am. I wanted you to know. You're the only one I'm telling." Come on, throw your arms around me, Becky. That is the plan.

Becky stepped back. "You are not serious? Is this one of your horrible pranks? You know how I hate them, Joshua Parker."

"I am serious, Becky. I'm leaving very early Monday morning for Ashland Crossing."

"Joshua Parker!" she shouted, and then grabbed her face as though stung by a bee. Her voice became mournful, "I never want to see or speak to you again." She dropped her hands from her face. "Never!" The other Becky had arrived. She walked away in a huff, never looking back.

Joshua stood with mouth open, watching her. He might never get to kiss those lips ever again. Now he felt faint.

****

Joshua had only been to Ashland Crossing once. That had been some three years earlier when the entire family had journeyed to Ashland Crossing to see the new railroad that came all the way from Keokuk. They had been all disappointed when they left that day and no train had arrived, but father had still been impressed. "They're going to run those tracks all the way to Des Moines. People can travel half way across the state lickety-split."

Joshua was never sure how fast lickety-split was, but it had to be fast. His father said it often, like when they were sent out to do their chores. Perhaps the change in Becky, when he had told her his secret, would be considered lickety-split?

Joshua arrived at Ashland Crossing early Monday morning. He had checked the train prices but decided not to spend most of his money on tickets and had opted for the barge that was about to head south down the Des Moines River.

The barge rocked out from the pier and began moving slowly south, away from the circle, the family, and a protected way of life. For a moment, Joshua considered jumping from the barge and returning home, but he kept going. If he went back now, he thought, this is where he would be the rest of his life and he wanted more.

Joshua knew by now his note of his whereabouts had been found. He had left it on the kitchen table. He tried to envision the family's reaction--Mother and his sister would be crying, Father angry, and Mark and Matthew excited. He was not sure about Jonathan.

Joshua tried not to think about her, but his mind drifted to Becky. He wondered if she was still angry. He realized that she had a right to be upset with him. How else should she react to the news? His plan had been stupid. Now that was all behind him. A new life with adventure lay ahead. Joshua leaned over the railing and vomited. Maybe he should have spent the extra money for the train.

Chapter 2

$\mathcal{J}$oshua reluctantly walked the plank onto the steamer that would soon head south towards home. He promised himself this would be the last ride on the water. He immediately found a quiet spot by the railing, and waited for the steamer's departure. Jack Young, his best friend, followed Joshua to his secluded spot.

"It's all in your head you know," Jack remarked, tapping his head with his finger.

"Let me tell you, Jack, it's more than my head. Stick around and you'll find out."

"Umm, I think I'd rather see if any ladies are interested in a heroic soldier back from the war. Want to join me?"

"It's not funny, Jack. I really get sick."

"Sorry. So are you anxious to get home?" Jack asked, quickly changing the subject.

"I'm not sure. More than anything, I'll be glad to get my feet on the ground again in Burlington."

Joshua remembered the nervousness he had as he sat on the barge headed south three years earlier. Thinking back, he guessed he had good reason.

****

Joshua Parker lived seventeen years on the family farm, never having traveled more than twenty-five miles from home.

He lived a life of confinement; then in the fall of 1862, in less than one month, he left the family farm against his parent's wishes, traveled nearly one hundred sickening miles by barge to Keokuk, lied about his age and joined the thirty-sixth volunteer Iowa Infantry Regiment on October 4.

Life no longer was contained and predictable. People scurried. In the circle, only grouse scurried. Men with stripes on their uniform were constantly yelling commands. The more stripes they had, the louder they yelled. The new recruits marched all day and into the night: left, right, left, right. It seemed non-stop, yet Joshua could not learn to march. They yelled in his ear until he thought he would go deaf, but it only made his marching worse.

However, the one thing Joshua did well was shooting. "You're a natural, boy," was a common remark that he heard. How could one not be good, he thought, holding his newly issued Enfield rifle. He could never have imagined such a fine weapon. It was sleeker and finer to the touch than a woman's behind. He had no personal proof of that, but some of the men told him that is was true.

As if Joshua was not far enough from home, after training for a month, on a cold windy day in November, the men of the thirty-sixth regiment boarded steamers and headed down the Mississippi River. Joshua spent most of his time leaning over the railing. The regiment landed in St. Louis and attached to the thirteenth Corps and there, they continued drilling. Joshua's marching slowly improved, but his sharpshooting excelled. He figured his father would be proud of his shooting skills, but then his father would never know--the circle was now in the distant past.

One morning as rain drizzled over the staging grounds, Joshua received orders to report to the regiment's Sergeant Major's quarters. He was certain it was about his lack of marching skills and he was certain he would be returning home with a humiliating fanfare. He wondered who would enjoy it more, his father or Becky. He was very nervous when he arrived at the

Sergeant's quarters, and quite surprised to find a dozen other men mulling about, waiting for the Sergeant. Still more came, and by the time they came to attention, Joshua estimated eighteen to twenty men were present. Were they all there because of their lack of marching ability, too?

The Sergeant stepped from his tent. He moved with confidence and precision. He was a stout man with a large handlebar mustache and long, thick side burns. His uniform, with stripes from top to bottom on his sleeve, indicated he was no newcomer to the army, and Joshua was certain he could yell as loud as a tornado coming direct.

"Men," the sergeant began, his eyes carefully surveying each soldier who stood before him, "you may wonder why you have been called here today. Your superiors have observed you and they have determined that each of you have a very special skill that the army finds very beneficial. That skill, or at least your potential, is as a sharpshooter. Because of this skill, we are assigning you to the special sharpshooting unit. When you are finished with your training, you'll be able to shoot a horse fly off the rump of a mare and never touch a hair."

Someone behind Joshua interrupted, "Hell, I reckon I already can." Light laughter came from some of the men.

"Corporal, escort that man back to his company." The sergeant's face remained expressionless during the whole incident. The corporal left with the surprised soldier and silence fell on the unit.

After a pause, the sergeant continued, "Besides becoming the elite of the corps with your sharpshooting, we will also teach you the art of camouflage so no rebel will know from where the shot was fired. It will require grueling training and you will hate the instructors, but when your life hangs in the balance on the battlefield as well as the lives of your comrades, you will remember them as your nurturing mothers."

The men chuckled, but quickly quieted.

"We have also learned a valuable lesson here today that will also become an integral part of your training. You will listen and keep your mouth shut unless asked to speak. That will be all. Good luck, men, and may God be at your side during the trying times ahead of you."

The sergeant returned inside his quarters. Chills raced through Joshua as he listened to the sergeant's words. The future had become even more uncertain, complicated, and somewhat frightening.

The corporal informed the new unit to pick up their belongings and meet back there at fourteen hundred hours. That gave them a chance to eat, and perhaps say good-bye to any friends before returning to their new life.

While returning to their units, Joshua met Jack Young and Douglas MacKester, who also had reassignments with the sharpshooting unit.

Jack Young lived on a farm north of Ottumwa. He came from a family of fourteen children, ranging in age from eleven to thirty-one. Jack was eighteen and with the farm overcrowded, joined the army with little ado. Jack had met Douglas MacKester while they were traveling south by barge down the Des Moines River. They had arrived a day behind Joshua.

Douglas MacKester, called Doogie, lived in Ottumwa. He was nineteen and the son of a blacksmith. Doogie had worked in his father's forge for several years and combined with his Scots blood made him a rather large stout man, dwarfing Jack and Joshua, who were, in their own right, considered good sized.

The three were becoming good friends by the time they had returned for their new assignment. They had five minutes to find a bunk and store their issues.

First order of business for the men of the new unit was the returning of their new Enfield rifles. Joshua was dismayed at the loss of his beautiful weapon that he had babied. Then, three large wooden crates were carried out and opened. Two of the crates held Henry .44 caliber rimfire, lever-action rifles. As marvelous as his Enfield had been, the Henry rim fire was even better. The men were jokingly told it was a weapon you would load on Sunday and fire it all week. The third box contained Colt .45 magnum revolvers with holsters. Joshua loved the feel of the light sleek revolver as it slid effortlessly in and out of the polished black leather holster that he proudly wore on his hip.

The training intensified for the sharpshooting unit. Their schedule never altered due to the weather; in fact, the sergeant preferred the miserable elements. "More realism to the training," he stated. "It'll give you a little more sense of reality when you get into an actual battle, men. You'll be right at home when you're trying to sight up a Reb officer and the freezing rain is in your eyes and your fingers are frozen to the bone."

One morning, with no advanced notice, they were loaded up and headed south again. Everyone was sure this would be their first encounter with the enemy and most of the men sat quietly, looking straight ahead, each fighting resolve of their fears. Joshua understood.

They docked in Memphis, Tennessee. There had been no fight. It had almost been a letdown, since each soldier had locked his mind into the certainty of a battle. Yet each man gave forth a sigh of relief, but knowing it would come--only a matter of time.

From Memphis, they moved further south to Helena, Arkansas. The 36th was beginning to feel rather confident now. Moving so far south without a round fired, had the men speculating whether the war was nearing an end. Perhaps they would all see their families and soon. The toughest part of the war, thus far, had been the weather. It had been miserable.

In March 1863, the 36th became part of an expedition. They encountered their first exchange of gunfire, but again, it had been the elements--weather and terrain--that had created the biggest problem for the unit, leaving many severely ill.

They returned to Helena and began fortifying the city, expecting a major attack from the Confederate Army when the weather improved.

The generals had been right. On July 4, it seemed as if though the whole Confederate Army descended on Helena and the bunkered Union Army. Joshua along with several of the other sharpshooters had taken up strategic locations on rooftops throughout the city. Joshua was located on a two story building facing the wharves along the Mississippi River. The Gray Coats filled the river on every type of floating vessel imaginable. Joshua took bead on an early barge as it hit the dock. His sights centered on a young second lieutenant shouting orders. The young lieutenant stood bravely at the front with a swagger of confidence. Joshua's finger rested on the trigger ready to pull, but he hesitated for a moment. He wondered if the young lieutenant was a young husband and father, who would never see his wife or children again and the young family would be alone in this horrible time of war. Joshua blocked the thought, took a deep breath and pulled the trigger. The lieutenant grabbed his chest in pain and fell backward into the sack behind him. He never moved. Joshua's aim had gone true. The lieutenant was dead.

The chilling thought of a widow and fatherless children began to fill Joshua mind, but he shook the thought from his head the rest of the day. He fired often and with accuracy, but refused to count his hits. It was all that would help retain his sanity and perhaps allow him to pass through the Pearly Gates on Judgment Day.

The next day, as thousands of dead Confederate soldiers were gathered from the streets of Helena, Joshua began to reflect on his first kill. He wondered if there was some way he could find out about the young second lieutenant. He even located the barge where he had shot the soldier, but either the Confederates or the Northern burial brigade had taken the corpse.

****

Joshua sat by the railing, his mind returning to his current surroundings. They had journeyed for two hours away from Davenport, and he had not been sick once. In fact, he was feeling well enough to try to find his friend. Perhaps Jack had more women than he could handle, which was probably only one. A long time had passed, since Joshua had talked to a woman and certainly a much longer time since he had kissed one--much, much longer. Entertaining a woman or finding a nearby railing, suddenly became two overwhelming, but conflicting desires that struck Joshua. There would be no women in Joshua's future for the remainder of the trip to Burlington.

Chapter 3

$\mathcal{J}$oshua Parker and Jack Young disembarked the steamer at Burlington. Jack waved good-bye to three young ladies and their mother. Joshua headed for shade and leaned against the corner of a building.

Jack came over, squatted down and looked up at Joshua. "Are you going to make it, good friend? You're not looking too well."

"Glad you noticed. That, my friend, is the last time I'm getting on anything that moves on water. The absolute last time."

"I'm starving. Think you can hold it down?" Jack asked, showing concern.

"I'm starving too. Let me tell you, I'm empty inside. Let's find a nice place and have some home cooking. I'll be okay shortly."

They left the wharf and found a restaurant with a delightful aroma spilling out into the street. Noticing their uniforms, several people welcomed them home. It all felt good to Joshua until one older couple stopped by their table.

"We're glad you're home," the man remarked, a faint smile on his lips. "I overheard you were with the 36th and our son was with the 36th. Did you know Mark Brenner?"

The couple anxiously watched the faces of the two men. "I don't believe so," Joshua said. Jack shook his head. The couple's faces showed their disappointment.

"We received a letter in March of sixty-three. That was our last letter," the woman said.

"I'm sorry. There is still more of the 36th coming. We'll pray for you," Joshua said.

The couple thanked Joshua and Jack, and left, their expressions somber.

"You know," Joshua said, his hand clenched on his coffee cup, "I only wrote two letters the whole time I was gone and the last one was the day we mustered out. I hope my family got the letters. Actually, I might even beat the last letter home."

"I only wrote three letters," Jack added. "I guess a person forgets that the family might be worrying back home. I'm sure they heard some horrible stories about what was happening."

"We left them high and dry about how we were doing," Joshua added. "But then, I never got any letters from home either. I really didn't expect much, though, and I doubt if any mail could find us. The first reb that I killed was a young lieutenant, and I often wondered if he had a wife and children and imagined them receiving news of his death. I guess that will always stay with me. They weren't bad people. They were like you and me with families and dreams. Just to think how many died on both sides is sickening--no matter who won."

After they finished their meal, they purchased horses, and with excitement building, headed west for home.

The ride felt good. There was no timetable to keep, no commands given, and no enemy trying to kill them. It was just a quiet ride with a friend, and friendly people acknowledging them as they passed. To Joshua, it was one of the best feelings ever. It was even better than Becky's kiss, but then that was so long ago, he rather forgot how it did feel. Once he arrived home, everything might be different. He did not even want to think about that now. He was going to enjoy every moment of his trip home, and he was in no hurry.

Jack's voice interrupted his thoughts. "You still plan on going west one day?"

"Sure am. I'll wait until I get home to decide when, I guess."

"Have any ideas how to get there other than facing west and start walking?"

"I had thought about trying to get a job with the Pinkertons, but while we were in Davenport, I saw a building with the sign U.S. Marshal Office on the front window. I'm thinking that might be the best way to go west. I think being a U.S. Marshal would be exciting."

"Well let me know, we can go together." Jack paused for a moment before adding on, "You don't think Becky will change your mind?"

"No!"

"That sounds a little too definite to me. You still have feelings for her don't you?"

"No! And I don't want to talk about her anymore." Joshua had been surprised that Jack had hit upon a sore spot. He had been sure that Becky was behind him.

"Alright. No more said." Jack laughed.

Joshua laughed, trying to put the thought behind him and, at the same time, to convince Jack that Becky was not important. He knew he had failed on both accounts.

****

"You still coming with me to Ottumwa to see Doogie's family?" Jack asked as they left Fairfield and were nearing Batavia.

"Definitely. It's the least I could do for a very good friend. I would never forgive myself if I didn't."

"I just hope they received word," Jack said, shaking his head. "I wouldn't want it to be like the poor couple in Burlington. I don't want to be the one to drop the bad news on them."

"Yeah, I never even thought of that," Joshua commented. "That would be terrible. I just hope we can say something that will give them some comfort."

Under the circumstances, Joshua knew it would be difficult to meet Doogie's parents for the first time, but Jack, Doogie and he were the absolute best of friends. He wanted to share some of the later moments in their son's life--moments that could make them laugh, or make them burst with pride.

He rode in silence as he remembered the horrible days of the expedition that crushed the 36th and ended their days as a functioning unit.

****

It was March 1864 when the 36th attached to the 7th Corps departed from Pine Bluff, Arkansas on a campaign to the Red River in Louisiana. They immediately encountered skirmishes upon departure, but then the Confederates, laying in ambush, caught the seventh Corps as they were crossing the Little Missouri River. After numerous assaults, the Confederates finally withdrew, but 7th Corps had taken heavy casualties, and they had fallen way behind schedule with their supplies running dangerously thin. They re-routed to Camden in hopes of restocking from the local granaries and mills. They found the retreating army had destroyed the mills.

A supply train of two hundred wagons was to return for additional supplies at Pine Bluff. The 36th, along with other regiments, were assigned to escort the wagons. Once again, the weather made progress difficult and the enemy was constantly attacking and retreating. They rested on Sunday. When the army started to move again, they placed scouts on the roads: front and rear. The 36th sharpshooters were scouting the rear, moving silently along each side of the road about a mile behind the main train. Suddenly the sound of rifle fire became prominent. Joshua, along with the sharpshooting squad, hurried toward the onslaught of gunfire. As they approached, they witnessed a mass of Confederate gray attacking the Union battery from both sides. They moved to each side and set up position for firing from the rear of the Confederates. The Confederates were in strong number with the Union Army taking heavy casualties. The 36th sharpshooters continued their attack from the rear until noticed, and the Confederates began sending troops in search of their attackers. Joshua, Jack, Doogie and another soldier by the name of Henry, moved jointly through the forest and then the tall grass to find another advantage point from which they immediately began firing on the Confederates from another angle. The return fire became heavy as the Rebels began to fire in their general direction. The four men moved again, but suddenly Henry went down. The three remaining men grabbed Henry and dragged him with them until Henry fell silent. They stopped for a moment in disbelief. They had felt untouchable, but now they were aware of their vulnerability. They said a quick prayer for their fallen comrade, then proceeded to another location and resumed firing until the confederates had discovered their new location.

Then it happened, Doogie went down. He lay on the damp swamp ground, bleeding from his back. His words were weak. "Tell my mother and father I love them for me, will you?" His eyes closed. Joshua and Jack knew they could not bring Doogie with them. With tears in their eyes, they took one last look at their friend as he lay in the tall grass, wondering if his body would be found and buried, and then as trained soldiers, moved on to another location.

The rest of the day and night was like a bad dream. As Joshua and Jack continued to hit and run from the rear, they were becoming acutely aware of the outcome of the battle in front of them. Then the firing stopped. Their comrades who were still alive were now prisoners.

Seeing the futility of their continued efforts, Joshua and Jack, with heavy hearts, moved out during the night and returned to Camden where the remainder of the 7th Corps was camped. The 7th Corps realized their failed expedition, and returned to Little Rock. The war virtually ended for Joshua and Jack as they were relegated to guard duty for the remainder of the war. Joshua and Jack had fought with everything they had and returned with only sorrow for their fallen comrades. Joshua at a lone moment cried for Doogie and he was aware that Jack had also. They promised each other they would find Doogie's parents and tell them his last words.

****

As Joshua returned to reality, he became aware that Jack had been watching him. "I sure wish Doogie was coming with us," Joshua remarked. "The three of us were like those three musketeers one reads about."

"So what shall we call the two of us?"

"I don't know. I'm sure somebody will figure it out one day."

They laughed and headed on toward Ottumwa.

****

They arrived at the home of Doogie's parents in the mid-afternoon, but decided to wait until evening to ensure both parents were home. It was a visit where Mr. and Mrs. MacKester would need the support of each other. The two friends rode through town and saw the forge where Mr. MacKester worked. To their delight, they found a vendor selling crawfish at the waterfront. As evening approached, both men grew silent. Joshua was trying to prepare what he would say.

"Jack, I think we need to lie in at least one instance."

"You mean about his body being left?"

"Definitely that. I still have nightmares about whatever happened to his body. I'm not sure the Rebels would ever have found Doogie unless they were searching for us. I hope they did and buried his body."

"You have anything else you think we should avoid?"

"Not now, but we need to be sure we read each other's words and not mess up. It'll be hard enough on them as it is."

They rode back to the MacKester house. "I hope they're through eating," Jack commented. "I guess there's never a good time to deliver bad news like this. Darn, I just hope they already know."

The two young men knocked on the door. A dim light burned inside assuring them someone was home. A small, frail woman in her fifties answered the door. Her hair, once dark, was

20

mostly white now. Her face was drawn and her soft eyes filled with sadness. When she saw the two men in uniform, her face brightened.

"Hello, boys."

"Good evening, Mrs. MacKester," Jack quickly answered. "We hope we didn't come at a bad time."

"No, not at all. Did you know our son?" Her eyes beckoned for a favorable answer as she stood straighter.

"Yes, we did. We were all best friends," Jack quickly added.

"Come in, please," Mrs. MacKester said, stepping back. They entered and she quickly showed them to the parlor. "I have water heated. Would you care for tea?"

"Thank you. That would be nice," Jack said.

"I'll get my husband. He's in the shed out back." She hurried away.

"They know," Joshua said with a sigh of relief. "I feel better about this already."

"Me, too. I was getting pretty nervous."

"Nice place. I don't really see Doogie living here though," Jack commented looking around. "I guess being in the army changes a person, being away from home and all."

"I think you're right," Joshua responded. "I've wondered how I will be around the farm when I get back. If the family will see much difference in me from three years ago."

"I'm sure. Heck," Jack said, "I just wonder if my family will even notice I'm home." Jack chuckled at his own humor. "I'll be kind of like a raindrop in a rain storm."

Joshua smiled and held his reply as Mr. MacKester entered the room. He was quite the opposite from his petite wife. He was large, more so than Doogie. His hair was dark and strung about on his head. His eyes were deep set and dark but he still carried a kind-looking face.

"Hello, gentlemen. I understand you knew our son." His voice was strong.

He extended his brawny hand.

21

"Yes, sir. We knew him well. He was our very good friend. By the way, I'm Joshua Parker and this is Jack Young. We were all in the same sharp-shooting unit."

"I remember those names in his letters. He thought kindly of you. Please be seated," he said, gesturing to their chairs.

"Nice fall weather we're having," Jack commented, making small talk until Mrs. MacKester returned.

"It's good to be back in Iowa. I'll take the snow here to the freezing rain in Arkansas any day," Joshua said.

Mrs. MacKester returned with a tray of cups and a pot of tea. "I'm sorry I took so long," she said. "I guess at my age things move slower." She smiled politely and poured the tea. When she finished she sat next to her husband.

Joshua watched the couple for a moment. They were so different in stature that it seemed almost comical, except given the reason they were there, kept the mood somber. "I would like to say first about your son, Mr. and Mrs. MacKester, he was an upstanding and brave soldier." Joshua cleared his throat and went on, "You can be very proud of him. He was always a gentleman, acting in the finest manner. He often spoke kindly and highly of both of you. He was our dearest friend and we, like you, are deeply saddened by his death." Joshua looked at Jack. He nodded for Joshua to continue. Joshua watched the couple before him. Their eyes were tearing and Mrs. MacKester touched a kerchief to her eyes. "Doogie's last words to Jack and I were, 'tell my mother and father that I love them'." Mrs. MacKester began to sob openly and Mr. MacKester put his arm around her. Joshua took a deep breath. "I want you to know that although Doogie died in the field of battle, he was given a decent burial; one deserving of a brave soldier, good friend, and a loving son."

Joshua and Jack sat quietly as the grieving couple held each other. Mr. MacKester looked up. "We thank both of you for coming here today. I know you have families that are anxious to see you, and for you to take the time to give us some comfort is a very special deed on your part."

22

Jack and Joshua spent the next hour reminiscing with the MacKesters, and then excused themselves. "You boys are welcome here anytime you are in town. Please stop by," Mrs. MacKester said as the two war veterans mounted their horses. They waved good-bye and left.

"Went well," Joshua commented.

"That was a great job you did, old friend. I was quite impressed. I never knew you had it in you."

"Think so, huh. I hope it helps the MacKesters. I know it makes me feel much better."

"You're right," Jack replied. "I feel better myself."

Joshua figured visiting the MacKesters might have been the easy task. Now he was going home to face an unknown situation. The next day, when he and Jack parted ways, his stomach was churning with anxiety. It almost felt like he was on a barge somewhere in the middle of the Mississippi River.

Chapter 4

After leaving Jack in Ottumwa, Joshua had more time to dwell on his return home. He was sure his father would still be angry with him. He anticipated his mother had long since gotten over her anger. The brothers would probably not care much one way or another. His sister would be glad to see him. Becky was definitely a variable. She had been very upset with him. Joshua was not certain himself, how he wanted Becky to react when he arrived home, and that was the underlying problem. He still had that tingle for her, he guessed, but he also knew that she could be the stake that could tie him down and dash his dreams of going west. He supposed sometimes he could be less than a good person, but he knew it would be very unfair on his part if he came home, and led Becky into thinking he was home for good and then left again. He had to be careful not to repeat his selfish blunders.

Heading south from Batavia, he passed by the grounds where the Harvest Shindig was held. He wondered if he would go this year. Everything seemed so uncertain. He dreaded arriving home, and yet he was anxious to see everyone and to discover where he stood with the family, and of course with Becky. He was drawing ever closer. He could see Becky's house off in the distance and in another mile, he would be able to see his old home.

When Joshua spotted the family farmhouse, he spurred his bay into a gallop. As he rode down the lane to the house, he noticed that some crops had been harvested, but there was still more to do. He would help. He would work hard and try to amend his disobedience. He had to make things right.

He pulled in the reins in front of the house. In a distant field, he could see four figures harvesting the grain. He would ride out there later. It would probably be his father and his three brothers.

The door swung open and Denise raced towards him. "Oh praise the Lord, You've returned Joshua to us." Tears streamed down her face. Denise was her usual wonderful self as Joshua had expected. She hugged him and kept crying, "I'm so happy you're home safe." She grabbed him by the arm and started dragging him toward the house. "Mother, Mother, Joshua is home. He's really home."

Mother appeared at the front door. She was crying and wiping the tears with her apron. She said nothing, just grabbed him and held him, her body shaking from sobbing. Joshua was in no hurry to have her let go. She deserved whatever she wanted. He had not done right by her as a son, leaving without saying good-bye and then only writing twice in three years. Joshua squeezed her while fighting back his own tears that wanted to rush from his eyes. Finally, she stepped back and cupped her hands to his face. "You've aged beyond your years, Joshua. I can't imagine the horror you've been through. Come in and let me fix you something to eat, you look so skinny. Don't you think so, Denise? You look half starved."

The three laughed and cried their way to the kitchen. The kitchen remained as Joshua had remembered it, both in sight and smell. It was then that Joshua saw a figure standing at the open back door. The light shining through made it difficult to determine who it was. The person stepped forward.

"Becky," Joshua burst out. "What are you doing here?"

The room fell silent. Mother and Denise nervously looked from Becky to Joshua. Joshua was aware of the sudden awkwardness in the room and he was aware of a change in Becky. Her eyes were neither the vibrant green, nor did her eyelashes flutter the way Joshua had remembered, and her lips were not puckered, ready for him to kiss. They were...were...well...plain. Maybe it was the second Becky. Maybe that was all that was different. However, she did not look angry or perturbed. She looked different.

"Hi, Joshua."

Even her voice sounded plain.

"Becky, I didn't think you would be here."

"Why not, I live in the other house out behind here. You didn't notice it when you came in?"

"What house? I don't understand."

Denise stepped forward. "Of course you wouldn't know," she said, trying to remain calm. "Becky and Jonathan got married about a year ago."

"Married." Joshua looked from face to face. His first thought was it was a prank to get even for all he had done, but no one was laughing.

"How'd that happen?"

"We fell in love." Becky spoke with a hardened determination in her voice.

"Congratulations." Joshua knew the word did not come from his lips with the sincerity that it should have, but he did the best he could. Trying to regain his composure, he turned to Mother, "I guess Father and my brothers are out in the field? I saw them as I was coming in."

"Yes, but won't you eat first?"

"Let me go say hello to them. Mother, how will Father react when he sees me?"

Her look became distraught. "I know he'll be glad to see you, but he may act a little different at first. He took your leaving pretty hard, honey."

Joshua nodded, walked past Becky and out the back door. He had to get away from the house, but facing Jonathan and Father was not his desire either.

26

As Joshua slowly made his way to the field, his mind flip-flopped, between greeting the men of his family, and what had just happened in the house with Becky. He had not even considered Becky being married and certainly not to his brother. It was difficult to conceive now what had happened, as it would have been if he had found out while he was away. So why was he upset? This was exactly what he needed--freedom. His father had Jonathan on the farm. They had built a second house for Jonathan and Becky. He would only be in the way, he suspected, and now he had no fear of Becky tying him down. He was free. He had to get that through his head. Yet somehow, it did not set right. He wanted to be able to make the choice, not have it shoved in his face.

Matthew was the first to see Joshua, and without hesitation, dropped his pitchfork, and came running to Joshua. Now sixteen, three years had changed Matthew considerably in stature and facial makeup. He grabbed Joshua in a bear hug and they tumbled to the ground, laughing. "We got your letter about a week ago that you were coming home. It's great having you back, big brother."

Joshua stood up and brushed himself off. "Thanks, Matthew. It's great having a reception like that."

Mark arrived. He was all smiles. He had also grown considerably in three years, now almost eighteen. He was more formal, shaking his brother's hand. "Glad to see you, Joshua. You look like you made it through the war in good order."

"I did. I was one of the lucky ones."

"Daniel Kramer got killed and Peter Delway got shot up pretty bad and has to walk with a cane."

"That's really tough. One of my best friends was killed, too. It's not easy."

"Father could never understand why you left," Matthew added, still sitting on the ground. "He said you were too young to go off and die."

"Guess I better get over there and face the music."

All three grinned. "You heard about Jonathan and Becky?" Matthew asked as they made their way through the harvested field.

"Sure did."

"Mad?" Matthew probed.

"Why would I be mad?" I left, and Becky's not my slave or anything."

"You sound mad," Matthew continued.

"Shut up, Matthew!" Mark clamored. "You don't know when to keep your mouth shut."

"Still a pest, aren't you, little brother," Joshua quipped, as he grabbled Matthew's hat and hit him with it.

They were all laughing by the time they arrived where Jonathan and their father were working. The men stopped and watched the three arrive. Joshua greeted Jonathan formally. "Hello, Jonathan. Good to see you."

"Same here, Joshua. Glad to have you home." They shook hands.

"Congratulations on your marriage."

"Thank you."

Joshua did not want to say any more to Jonathan, partly because he was not sure what to say, but mostly because he wanted to turn his attention to his father.

"Hi, Father."

"Joshua." They shook hands.

That was it. That was the entire conversation with his father. They stood for a moment looking at each other. He turned to Jonathan. "Let's see if we can finish these stacks before quitting time."

"See you all later," Joshua said and started back towards the house. He did not turn back to see if anyone was watching.

He guessed he had brought it on himself. He had hurt everyone in the family, which now included Becky, by taking off, and joining the army against everyone's wishes. He did not go directly back to the house. He needed time alone and chose the rocky knoll behind the farm buildings, where his imagination gave him the world as a small boy.

Joshua was convinced his father had chosen not to consider him as a son anymore. A traveling salesman selling medicine for whatever ails you would have received a warmer and more respectful greeting than his father had given him. The greeting that he had received was far worse than he had ever imagined. If not for his mother and Denise, he would have left immediately. With the harvesting season almost over and winter coming on, work would become scarce. His final army pay would only last so long, and how could he stay in the same house with his father who apparently despised him?

An hour passed before Joshua came down from the knoll. He saw his mother watching him from the kitchen window. She had been there all the time. When he entered the kitchen door, she continued to stare out the window. Joshua knew it was to hide her tears. Denise stood behind her, hands on her shoulders. Denise smiled as he entered.

"Amazing how much Mark and Matthew have grown. I hardly recognized them," Joshua said, sitting at the kitchen table.

"I'm sure they have since you've seen them," his mother said, only glancing toward him. "They are good boys. Pranksters, sometimes, though," she added, forcing a smile. "Joshua, he'll come around. Please understand and give him time."

"Sure, Mother. I know I hurt him. Can I put my stuff in my old room for the time being?"

"With Jonathan not there, the room is all yours," she said.

"Thanks."

Joshua went upstairs and walked into his old room. He and Jonathan had always had to share the bed, along with most everything else that was around. He guess it would only be appropriate that he now had Becky. The room was as it was when he left, except emptier, with all of Jonathan's things gone. He went to the window and looked out over the rolling hills. He could see the new house that Becky and Jonathan called home. Becky was in the window presumably unaware that Joshua was watching her. He wondered if she was truly happy. She did not seem herself when he had seen her earlier. Maybe she married Jonathan out of spite for him. He hoped not, for her sake, and for Jonathan, too. The marriage stuck in his craw, but he really did not want to wish anything bad on either of them.

Joshua became aware that Becky had left from the window. He was about ready to retreat to the bed to rest for a while when he saw Becky come from the house and head for the cooling house. As she approached the cooling house, she paused and looked toward the window where Joshua stood. She then disappeared inside. She had been aware of him watching her all the time, and was it his imagination or was she encouraging him to come to the cool house with her? His mind was racing. Against his better judgment, he decided to follow her. He quietly went downstairs, out the front door, and walked quickly to the cool house. He stepped inside and felt the blast of cool air hit his sweaty body.

Then Becky was before him. Obviously, she had made herself more presentable than when he had seen her earlier. Had she done that for him or had he caught her at the wrong time earlier? Her eyes were brighter, and there were her lips pursed, teasing his whole being. Be careful, Joshua, he kept telling himself. You know this is not right. Neither spoke as they moved closer. What was he doing? He could feel his groin aching for her.

"What brings you in here?" Becky asked.

"I was feeling a bit warm and I remembered how good it always felt in here."

"It is a pleasant place to sit for a spell. I wish I could stay longer but I have to get this butter and finish baking a fresh apple pie for Jonathan."

He had come so close to making a fool of himself and creating an unforgiveable scene. What kind of beast was he?

As Becky was ready to step from the door, she turned, "Joshua, I noticed a hornets' nest up in the eave."

"Oh, okay, I'll take a look."

30

She continued looking at Joshua. "By the way, Joshua, you're looking quite handsome. Just as I remembered, except a little more dashing now."

Her lips were pursed. He had not been wrong. She was tormenting him and she knew it. He had to keep his head solidly on his shoulders to ensure the rest of him minded its own business.

****

Joshua received word later in the afternoon that his hopelessly innocent mother had invited Jonathan and Becky for supper. The tension would already be enormous with his father sitting at the same table with him, but now with Jonathan and Becky, it would be unbearable.

Joshua had fallen asleep on the bed, but awakened when he heard the men washing up on the back porch. He headed downstairs, knowing supper was about ready. He could smell the roast beef coming from the oven and the sweet smell of buttermilk biscuits. The aroma made him forget the torment he would soon be facing at the supper table. He paused before sitting. He had been gone a long time and did not want to upset the seating arrangement that had been in place since he had left. His mother quickly realized what he was pondering, took him by the arm, and sat him between Mark and Matthew. Perhaps she was more aware of the situation than he had first thought. It was the perfect spot for him except now Becky was directly across from him and Jonathan was next to her. Joshua felt the burning of Jonathan's stare as though keeping an eye on his big brother.

Joshua glanced toward his father, who was staring ahead as though he was the only one seated at the table. Once all the food was on the table and everyone was seated, his father bowed his head, the rest followed. He said the Lord's Prayer, and then began filling his plate. The conversation picked up.

"Looks like we'll finish the harvest by Friday, maybe sooner," Father stated. "I have a good crew here. Thank you. We can all enjoy the shindig Saturday."

"That's great," Joshua added.

The room became silent. All eyes looked to Father for a reaction, but there was none. It was as though he had not heard Joshua.

Joshua considered excusing himself, but instead, began eating without looking up from his plate. He knew his position in the family from the early onset of his return. All that had happened since his return made the decision of his future much easier. Perhaps it's all for the best, he kept telling himself.

Joshua had intended to offer his help in the fields, but considering the previous day's encounter chose against the useless offering. Instead, he decided to spend the day visiting with Mother and Denise. They were anxious to hear about the three years he was gone, and he wanted to catch up on all the news in the circle.

Joshua spent an enjoyable morning listening to the gossip and news in the area. Mother and Denise were also asking about his life. He tried to avoid much of the death and misery, but sometimes it was out before he realized it.

About mid-morning, Becky arrived at the house. She quickly joined everyone at the table and quietly listened and watched Joshua. He was painfully aware of her eyes never leaving him and he wondered if the others were noticing. Unfortunately for Joshua, Becky was looking her best. During the three years while he was away, Becky had developed from a flirtatious girl into a seductive woman. In the past, there had been nothing wrong with her body; but her face was always what enchanted him, but time had changed all that. He had remembered the term some of the men used in the army, 'she has fully ripened'.

Near noontime, the women excused themselves and began preparing for the noon meal. Joshua went to the barn, cleaned the stalls, and put out fresh straw. He decided that in the afternoon, he would clean the corral and pick some apples that were becoming ripe in the orchard. He would try to make himself useful in spite of his father.

After the men returned to the fields, Joshua told Mother his plans and found a couple buckets and headed for the orchard. He was enjoying the quietness and the thought of being somewhat useful. As he was stretching for an apple at his fingertips, a voice sounded behind him, very close behind him, "Hi, Joshua."

The same tingle from years past raced through him. Without turning, he continued reaching for the apple. "Hi, Becky. What brings you out here?"

"Would you believe to get some apples?"

Joshua refused to look. He knew she was so close that if he moved at all he would bump her. "Why not. It's an apple orchard. If you like I can bring you some when I finish."

"That's sweet of you, but I can help."

"As you wish." Joshua moved forward trying to put some distance between them, but she followed close behind. "How is the married life with Jonathan?" he asked, wanting to remind her that she was married to his brother.

"Old. Don't get me wrong, he's a wonderful husband. Very attentive."

"I'm glad he's a good husband. I would feel terrible if my own brother wasn't."

"Aren't you going to ask me why I married him?"

Joshua could feel her moving closer again. He quickly stepped away and turned. "I figured it was none of my business. I assumed you married him because you loved him."

Her eyes saddened. "All those years growing up, I always assumed that one day I would marry you, Joshua. It had always been my dream. I used to pretend we were married when we were together. You never knew that did you? In fact, the day that you told me the horrible news, I was pretending that day. I thought it was the best day of my life and then in an instant, you turned it into the most horrible day of my life. The day you left, long before daylight, I sat at my window and cried. I couldn't stop crying. It wasn't until my mother came looking for me that I spoke of your secret. It was the most horrible thing in my life not being able to share the heart-breaking news you placed on me.

Jonathan consoled me for the next six months. I think I might not have made it, if it were not for him. After a year, he asked me to marry him, and I, without hesitation, said, 'yes'. He knows I still love you, Joshua. Did you know that? I try to be a good wife for him. He's a wonderful man, but I can't stop loving you." Tears filled her eyes, but she did not cry. "I can live with the thought that I would never have you, but not with the agony that I'm a failure as a good wife, because I love the wrong man."

Joshua stood dumbfounded. He had created a horrible mess because of his self-righteousness. He had walked away from the circle, fulfilling his dreams and desires, but leaving behind lives destroyed and mutilated by his selfish decisions. Moreover, to make it worse, it was too late to correct the wrong. The damage was beyond repair. So many lives were altered by his reckless decisions.

"I didn't know all this, Becky. I was only thinking of myself. I wanted out of here. I wanted to see more, to live more."

"I would have run away with you and gone to the ends of the world with you, Joshua, but you never asked...never gave it a thought. You honestly could not tell how much I loved you? Maybe I was at fault, not outwardly telling you my feelings. I just assumed you felt it."

"Becky, three years ago, I was self absorbed in my pity of being tied to the farm. I did have feelings for you, but when a boy is seventeen and has those feelings, they become very confusing. There were a lot of feelings roaring through my body."

Becky smiled. "I know. I could tell. I would go home and giggle about how you would act. That was always part of my dream for us to be married. Those special moments alone."

"I'm sorry, Becky, for what I've done to you. I realized I had done wrong as I floated on the barge down the river that day towards Keokuk, but I couldn't convince myself to go back. I wish I had now and maybe I could've done everything right and not have hurt so many people."

Becky stepped forward, placed her hands around Joshua's neck, and kissed him. The kiss, filled with passion, lingered for what seemed an eternity. Joshua struggled with his feelings, unable to push her away and afraid what would happen if he embraced her. He did neither and stood with his hands at his side. Finally, when she stepped back, she looked into his eyes. "I would still run away with you on a moment's notice, but I know you would never ask. I will always love you, Joshua...always. I just hope I can find some of that love for Jonathan, perhaps like one finds new love after a previous love has died."

Becky turned and left, not looking back. Joshua sat on a stump as tears filled his eyes. He could never forgive himself, not only for the way he left, but also for returning and reopening the wounds that were trying to heal. In a sense, he needed to die. It would be the only decent thing he could do.

****

After his conversation with Becky, Joshua knew that staying on the farm would be impossible. Even though mother, sister, and some of his brothers had been glad to see him, he realized it would be best for everyone, if he left. It was the only way to restore order within the family. As long as he remained under the same roof, tension would exist.

The next morning, after the men had left for the fields and before Becky had arrived, he sat with mother and Denise. "I need to see if I can find work before winter sets in. I'm thinking of going to Ottumwa. There is a better chance there and I can check with Doogie's folks. You remember, I told you about him. I want to see if they know of any jobs."

Both nodded. They knew what he said was true, but he was sure they knew the need for him to distance himself from the family. Life could never be the same.

Becky never came by that day. Joshua hated himself, but he wanted to see her. He could not get the kiss from the day before, out of his mind. His body ached for her touch, yet he knew he could never go near her. He would commit a mortal sin that would devastate everyone. A sin that could never be rectified.

That evening, Becky and Jonathan did not join the rest of the family. Joshua announced his plans of going to Ottumwa to look for work. Matthew voiced his disapproval. "I want you to stay here. I want you to take me hunting."

"That sounds like fun. Maybe I can come to visit on occasion and we can go hunting," Joshua replied with a joyful air. He would miss the delight of Matthew, but it just was not to be.

****

Joshua left the next day without much ado. He had said good-bye to the men before they headed for the fields, and a tearful good-bye to his mother and Denise. As he mounted, he cast a glance towards Becky's house, but he did not see her.

It was not until Joshua had left Batavia, that the places with memories of Becky were behind him; however, it did little to clear his mind of her. He tried to think about his new life in Ottumwa and what it might bring, but he kept imagining what it would be like if she were with him. He had told Becky that at the age of seventeen his feelings were confusing. He was twenty now, and nothing had changed, except the confusion had worsened.

By day's end, Joshua arrived in Ottumwa, found a cheap room and settled in for the evening. He ate the last piece of fried chicken his mother had given him and stared out the small window of his room that overlooked the river, the same river that had taken him away three years earlier.

By morning, Joshua's head was becoming clearer. He hoped that the distance he had put between he and the family would begin to clear the air at home. His feelings were secondary.

He was excited about finding work and at least for the time being a new way of life. The dream of going west still remained inside him, and in the spring, he was determined to begin the journey.

By noon, Joshua had found work--splitting firewood. The owner promised him work through the winter and that was all Joshua wanted. The job was hard and the pay was not much, but working felt good. His life was turning for the better and he hoped it was becoming better back home. That was about all he could do to correct the wrong he had done.

By week's end, Joshua visited the MacKesters. They were delighted he was in town and insisted that he move in with them and have Doogie's room. It would delight them and they knew that would be what Doogie would want.

"My room is paid up through next week."

"Just let it go," Mr. MacKester said. "No cost for you here."

"Absolutely not. I would have to pay room and board if I move here."

"If that's the only way you'll come, then okay. But not much."

"We'll see. I'll be here next Sunday when my rent is up."

Chapter 5

$\mathcal{F}$all gave way to the cold winter days. The cold generated new business for Joshua's boss, who in turn gave Joshua more work, and because his wood splitting skills were continuously improving, his wages were improving also. In addition, any free time Joshua did have, he would help Mr. MacKester at his forge.

Joshua also enjoyed living with the MacKesters. They were always friendly but never pried or forced themselves on his time. Also, Joshua always made sure he kept letters going home on at least a monthly basis. He journeyed north once, when the weather permitted, to see Jack. Jack, feeling the confinement of the large family, was also anxious to leave for the west. In early February, they sent letters to the U.S. Marshal's office in Davenport, and then eagerly waited for a reply.

The long awaited letter came for Joshua in April of that year. The letter was from the U.S. Marshal of Iowa, Peter Barstow, stating that he would be in Des Moines the last three weeks of May and would be available to interview Joshua Parker for the position of Deputy Marshal of United States of America.

Joshua immediately contacted Jack Young about the letter. Jack had received a similar letter and they made plans to head north to Des Moines by May 15. There was little sense in delaying what could be the biggest day of their lives.

The two anxious men arrived in Des Moines amidst a heavy downpour. Even with their slickers, they were soaked to the bone when they arrived at the office of the U.S. Marshal. They introduced themselves to a man sitting in the front lobby, who directed them to hangers for their slickers and hats, and chairs to wait while he notified Marshal Barstow of their arrival. He disappeared into a private office behind him. Several minutes passed before he returned. "Marshal Barstow will see you now."

The marshal rose as the two drenched men entered the room. He grinned. "Looks like Des Moines greeted you boys rather rudely. Please be seated, gentlemen."

"Sorry for our appearance," Jack responded.

"Don't worry about it. Caught in a rainstorm will not determine whether you become part of the force of the U.S. Marshal. The fact that you two were diligent enough to brave the weather says a great deal. Let's get some coffee, so you gentleman can warm up." He rose and went to the door and asked for coffee. When he returned, he stood behind his desk. "I decided to interview you gentlemen together. Reading your resume's and with the understanding of your friendship, I could well imagine the outcome will be the same for both of you. So, Joshua, why do you want to become a U.S. Marshal?"

"There are several reasons I suppose. Maybe some are the wrong reasons. I want the adventure. Before the war, I spent my entire life on a farm down south of here. It's a respectable way of life, maybe the most respectable there is, but I wanted a life with adventure. Secondly, I would like to receive an assignment out west. There is a lot of new country to see and be a part of. I also love firearms and from my resume', you can see I can use them if necessary. And lastly, I feel I can help protect the law-abiding people from those who choose not to abide by the law."

"Okay, Joshua. So Jack, you agree or disagree with any of part of what your friend has just said?"

"I hate to sound unoriginal but I concur totally with Joshua. I might add it would be an honor to serve as a U.S.

Marshal just like it was an honor to serve in the Iowa Volunteer Infantry."

"From your resume's, I had already decided to begin processing your applications, but I had to see you in person, just to verify my original decision. I see no reason to change my mind. We're always looking for good men. I will send your applications on, and I have no doubt your applications will be approved. However, it may take months or a year before you receive your final approval. With that said, I have some news that may not satisfy you now, but one has to start somewhere. I will have to assign you to Iowa. After six months or a year, you can ask for a transfer further west. What I am doing though, is recommending your first assignment be Sioux City. That will put you as far west as Iowa goes. It's rugged in Sioux City. The weather can be the worst, and it is the frontier. However, having said that, the worst element in Sioux City is Marshal Harley Broker. He will be your boss. I'll let you evaluate him for yourself, but just beware. It is the same warning I would give someone that was facing a rattler. He has been in Sioux City a long time and that is probably where he will die because everyone wants to keep him as far away as possible. With that, I wish you gentlemen good luck and I am sure my congratulations are not premature. I hope your wait for an assignment will not be too long."

"Thank you and we'll be ready," Jack exuberantly replied.

"Good. In addition, might I recommend the Parson Hotel about two blocks from here. Stick around for a day or two until the weather eases up. Roads will probably become flooded around here anyway."

Joshua and Jack left the marshal's office that day with jubilation. Their dreams were coming true. Besides, how bad could Marshal Harley Broker really be?

****

Their assignment for Sioux City, Iowa came late August, 1866. They were to report to Marshal Broker by September 30 of that same year.

40

Although Joshua had written and received letters from home, he had not returned for a visit and it had been almost a year now since he left. He decided to would return and say good-bye, perhaps for the last time. He would stay two days. Any longer could create problems.

****

Joshua had chosen to spend Saturday and Sunday visiting home. He arrived late Friday afternoon. Joshua's arrival was as he had expected. The three people that Joshua remained keenly aware of were his father, Jonathan and Becky.

Joshua was pleased to see Jonathan and Becky happy; they seemed to have resolved their inner battles and found a new bonding of their love. He hoped he was right, because he did not want to leave home feeling he was to blame for their unhappiness.

Saturday night after supper, Joshua sat on the front porch with Mark and Matthew. Jonathan and Becky had gone home and were coming back later with an apple pie.

"So what's Sioux City like?" Matthew asked.

"Not sure till I get there, but it's I guess it's pretty rugged."

"Indians?"

"Yeah, but I'm told they're peaceful."

Joshua looked up. His father had come onto the porch. Mark jumped up from his chair for Father. Father mussed Mark's hair and sat down.

Matthew continued his questioning. "How far is it?"

"Not sure, but it's as far west as you can go in Iowa."

Joshua heart jumped when he heard his father's voice. "Does your assignment have any particular length of stay?"

"No, Father. I'll be there until I ask for a transfer or I receive a new assignment. I'll probably be there at least a year."

"Please write to your mother regularly. She worries about you something terrible. I keep telling her if you made it through the war, you know how to keep yourself safe, but it doesn't help, so please write."

"I promise. I know I did poorly in the army. I am sorry for that."

"Are you going to church with us tomorrow, Son?" Father asked.

"Sure am, Father."

"Good. I guess Jonathan and Becky are here with the pie. We better get in there if we want a piece." Joshua saw him smile for the first time in a very long time. Joshua knew he could leave now with some peace of mind. However fragile it might be, a bond had redeveloped between him and his father.

Sunday in church, Joshua thanked the Lord for his family, and the peace that had miraculously come to all of them. He sang louder that day than he had ever sung in his life.

Monday morning, everyone was there to say good-bye. Father had said the crop could wait harvesting for a couple hours. A lump settled in Joshua's throat as he waved to his family amongst tears and smiles. As he looked back for the last time, he doubted in his mind, if he would ever see them again.

Chapter 6

The two new deputies arrived in Sioux City by late September. The last of the golden leaves were falling to their winter bed, and the fall chill was becoming evident as the two deputies rode into town. They had spent half the trip discussing Marshal Harley Broker, and upon their arrival were still not convinced that Marshal Barstow had not been exaggerating about the old marshal.

"There is only one way to find out I guess," Joshua commented as they rode up in front of the small building with the sign, 'U.S. Marshal Office and jail'.

"I still can't believe he's as bad as Marshal Barstow says. Nobody could be that bad and be a marshal," Jack quipped.

"Let's find out," Joshua responded as they dismounted. "You want to go in first?" Joshua asked, and then burst into laughter.

People nearby stopped and watched the two new deputy marshals make their way to the door.

"Look at all the people staring," Jack remarked, stopping short of the door. "I'm guessing Marshal Barstow was right."

"I'm not taking that bet," Joshua answered, looking about. "Good afternoon," he shouted to everyone watching.

All the by-standers turned and went about their business, except for one older man that came forward. "Good afternoon, young fellers. Are those U.S. Marshal badges you're wearing?"

"Yes, they are, thanks for noticing" Jack said, holding his badge so the old gent could see. "This is our new assignment here in Sioux City."

"Just what we need here," the old man replied with disgust, "more of you no count fellers hanging around here."

"I'm sorry you feel that way," Jack said, showing dismay. "We'll show you that we're going to be good for the community."

"We'll see," the older gent stated matter of fact and shuffled off. "Sure enough, we'll see."

Joshua and Jack looked at each other and shrugged their shoulders. "Okay, let's get this over with," Joshua said and opened the door.

An older balding man sat behind the desk, hunched over spooning some unknown concoction into his mouth. He never looked up as he rhythmically continued shoveling with sounds of slurping, snorting and smacking done with loudness beyond the imagination. His gun belt lay piled on the desk and his badge next to it.

On the far side of the room, an Indian squaw stood silently watching the marshal consume the contents of the bowl. She seemed unconcerned by the marshal's eating habits. The marshal finished, tossed the spoon into the bowl and pushed the bowl away. He looked towards the squaw. "Good as usual, Morning Flower."

Morning Flower without expression, nodded, scooped up the bowl and left. The marshal smiled. "I have no idea what her name is, but she's kind of pretty and I just thought Morning Flower sounded good. She responds to it, so I guess everybody's happy. Now, I presume you are my two worthless sidekicks that good old Peter sent me."

"Yes, sir. I'm Joshua Parker and this is Jack Young. We're ready to get busy with our duty here."

"You are, huh. What did Peter tell you about me?"

"Not much, sir," Jack quickly responded.

"You keep calling me sir; I'm going to have your behinds marching up and down in the street. If you want to be soldiers, go

44

join the damn army. Call me Harley for all I damn care, but don't call me sir. It makes me feel like I've got to take care of you like...like some damn...whatever. Anyway, whatever Peter told you that you're not telling me is probably true. Some people around here find me to be a little crusty. I think that's the word they use. Those people don't know me. The ones that know me say I'm rotten through and through." He started to laugh, and then stopped. "They don't tell me that. Any questions?"

"What kind of trouble do you encounter around here, sir...uh, I mean Harley?" Jack asked.

"Trouble. You mean like lawlessness, wild Indians, bank robberies, killings? That sort of stuff?"

"Yeah," Jack responded.

"I was going to take my little afternoon nap, but I think it's my duty to show you fellers around, besides it could be a might more interesting. Your revolvers loaded?"

They both nodded. "Good," Harley said, "I can leave my weapons here. Ready, men?" Harley opened the door and walked out onto the wooden sidewalk. Joshua whispered to Jack as they started to follow, "I think the marshal is having some fun with us, Jack."

Jack turned, and looked at Joshua as though a shovel had smacked him in the face. "He is?" He called out to the marshal, "Marshal, we know you're having a good laugh at our expense. We get it."

The marshal stopped and slowly turned. His eyes looked hard, and then slowly a wry smile appeared. "Good. Damn time you figured it out. I can go have my nap now." He returned inside. Joshua and Jack started back inside when their saddlebags and bedrolls flew out the door. The marshal closed the door without a word.

They had just received their introduction to Marshal Harley Broker. The two deputies picked up their belongings and started down the street. The older gent they had met earlier approached them. "The hotel down the street a piece has some

45

rooms that are room and board by the month." He eyed the two deputies up and down and moseyed on.

Day one had barely started and Joshua was already anxious to leave.

Chapter 7

During the first days in Sioux City, it became obvious that the first order of business was trying to repair the damaged relationship between the U.S. Marshal Office and the people of the community. The new deputies painfully sensed that the men outside the law had a higher stature with the community than they did. Except for the old gent, no one was anxious to speak to them.

The old gent always seemed to be nearby wherever Joshua and Jack were. With formal introduction to the old man, they hoped he could give them valuable information about the community and surrounding area. When they approached him, he looked at them with great suspicion. "What do you want? You're not going to arrest me are you?"

"Why would we do that?" Jack replied. "We just thought we should introduce ourselves since we'll be seeing each other from time to time."

"Are you sure you're not going to arrest me?"

"Absolutely not," Joshua replied.

"Okay, I guess. I'm Daniel P. Crawford. Some call me Dan. Most call me crazy. I'm not though."

"I believe that to be true," Joshua responded. "You look like a smart respectable citizen of this community."

47

"I could tell you stories that would make your skin crawl. Some of them about the marshal, but nobody around here wants to listen. They tell me I'm crazy, but I think it's because they're scared."

"One of these times soon, we'll sit down and listen to those stories. We promise. I'm Joshua and this is Jack."

"People are scared of you like they are the marshal."

"They have no reason to be frightened of us. We're here to help," Jack said, sounding disappointed and frustrated.

"They'll come around. You boys seem nice enough."

"Thanks, Daniel."

Joshua and Jack had convinced the first resident of Sioux City; only several hundred more to go.

****

The first snow fell early October and the temperatures were beginning to stay below freezing for longer periods. Marshal Barstow had been right about the weather in Sioux City and Marshal Harley Broker. The two deputies had already decided that come spring they would apply for a transfer, but in the meantime, they wanted to serve as protectors of the law and the citizens of Sioux City. The problem was no one wanted their help, and their boss did not want to be bothered with them. They decided they would have to do it on their own and maybe convince the folks in town that they were useful.

One cold October night, as the deputies were making their rounds about town, they heard gunfire from one of the saloons. When they went inside, they found one of the young locals had drank too much and was letting off some steam. They promptly took his revolver and escorted him to jail to sleep off his drunk.

Joshua and Jack dragged the local drunk to the jail and opened the door. When they carried him inside, Marshal Broker was laying on the cot in one of the jail cells. He sat up; his eyes were those of a madman.

"What the damn hell are you doing? Get him out of here!" He pointed his finger at the two surprised deputies. "I don't want my life interrupted by you two, bringing a drunk in here. This is

48

my place. This is where I live. You want to arrest him, take him to your place. Let him sleep it off there. Now get out!" The marshal kicked a nearby chair in disgust.

Joshua, Jack and the drunk left. The deputies stood in the cold night air trying to resolve their dilemma.

"Any ideas?" Jack asked, hanging onto the drunk who had passed out now.

"We have his revolver and I don't think he's in any condition to hurt anyone now, but if we leave him in the street, he'll freeze to death."

"Let's find out where he lives," Jack suggested.

They proceeded down to the saloon, dragging their first arrest with them.

"Anyone know where he lives?" Jack called out.

The patrons looked at them amused. "About five or six miles out of town east of here," the bartender answered.

The deputies carried their problem back into the street. "I guess we have one choice," Jack said.

"Not our room?"

They swore that would be the last time they made an arrest of a drunk.
****

As winter progressed into January, as the temperatures continued to drop and the snow continued to fall, the deputies spent more time in their room. The community did little towards warming up to the two men, although the deputies tried to befriend them. The first Sioux City citizens to take to them were the fancy ladies at the brothels.

Joshua knew he would never forget the first time he decided to fall to his wantonly ways. The young woman, rather pleasant to the eyes, dressed in sheer clothing, led him up the stairs and to a room filled with dainty frill. She had laid him on the bed, pulled off his boots and suggested he undress. He did as she watched.

"I love good young men," she said as she pushed him back on the bed and crawled on top of him.

He nervously wrapped his arms around her and placed his hands on her behind. The thought of his Enfield rifle came to mind.

When Joshua left that evening, the winter in Sioux City seemed a little more tolerable.

****

Jack Young was a good friend. One could not find a better friend, but by the end of January, with cabin fever and all, Joshua was beginning to find his very good friend was starting to get under his skin. Living in the same tight quarters could become too much, even if he was your best friend.

"Jack, we need to do something about our living conditions," Joshua said staring out the window.

Jack sitting upright on the bed looked over his newspaper. "Like what?"

"Like this. Nothing personal, but I am tired of looking at your ugly face all the time. I want us to get separate rooms. We'll just have to figure out a way to afford it."

"Thank you!" Jack shouted, throwing down the newspaper. "I have wanted this for a very long time, but I was afraid of hurting your feelings."

"You're kidding? We've been suffering all this time, because we didn't want to hurt each other's feelings? From now on, we need to speak our mind. Friends should be able to speak their minds."

Jack looked curiously at Joshua. "Yeah, I suppose, but let's not get carried away. Is something else bothering you?"

"No. How about you?" Joshua responded hesitantly.

"No."

"Well, I'm glad that's settled."

By the end of the week, each had their own rooms. Joshua was feeling a little better with his assignment now, having his own room and the ladies down the street. If only winter would end.

****

Spring did arrive...late. By the end of May, the rivers and streams were overflowing from the melting heavy winter snows and the torrential spring rains. Moreover, where there was not water, being knee deep mud seemed to prevail. Every able body in town, including Joshua and Jack, spent long hours sandbagging to help whoever was in need.

After a week, the skies cleared and the floodwaters subsided. In addition, along with the easing of nature's elements, the townsfolk began to look upon the two deputies differently. They had worked elbow to elbow with the people of the community to save the town. Perhaps they had been wrong with their suspicions of the newcomers.

Joshua and Jack began to enjoy their new status. People greeted them on the street and even one of the young women about town seemed to be turning sweet on Jack. Without any encouragement, Jack began to pursue the opportunity for a romantic relationship.

Joshua, satisfied with a more casual relationship with Molly, a young lady at the house, steered clear of a more meaning relationship. He did not want to encounter another Becky situation. He was determined to fulfill his dream of going west to the new unchartered territories. He wrote a letter asking Marshal Barstow for a transfer. Not surprising to Joshua, Jack decided to wait. Joshua, though disappointed, understood. Love could be a dominating factor in one's decisions.

July arrived with the discovery of a possible horrific secret involving Marshal Harley Broker.

Chapter 8

On a late Saturday afternoon in July, Jack was away courting his steady woman friend, Hester. Joshua, feeling a little bored, saw Daniel passing by. Daniel had not been hanging around the deputies as much lately and Joshua wondered if the old man felt neglected.

"Daniel," Joshua called, from a bench in front of the hotel.

Daniel stopped and looked about him with calculating suspicion. He eyed Joshua for a moment and began to move on.

"Daniel," Joshua called again. "You want to sit and chat for awhile?"

Having someone call him over and chat was obviously something foreign to the elderly gent. He was about ready to scamper away as fast as his old legs would carry him.

Joshua figured he had one sure way to convince the old man to come over. "Wait, Daniel. I wanted to ask you about your secrets."

Daniel stopped dead in his tracks and looked around him. Slowly he began to come towards Joshua, all the while casting suspicious glances around him.

"Good afternoon, Mr. Daniel P. Crawford."

Remembering his full name obviously pleased Daniel. "Good afternoon, Marshal. You remembered our talk."

"Sure did. Have a seat."

Daniel made one last glance up and down the street before sitting on the bench next to Joshua.

"Daniel, I remember you saying you had secrets about the town, even Marshal Broker."

"I do, Marshal. Horrible secrets. They say I'm crazy, but I'm not, Marshal."

"Is he mean to you?"

"No, I stay away from him like everyone else. It's the half-breed sisters at the edge of town."

"How many are there?"

"There were four and their squaw mother. First the mother disappeared without explanation, then about a year ago last spring, when the waters were high, I saw the eldest leave the marshal's office crying and yelling to him that she would not do his dirty deeds anymore. It was late and I was the only one around. I saw him follow her and threatening to do harm to her sisters if she didn't come back. I never saw her again, Marshal. I think he killed her and threw her body into the river."

"You think the marshal killed her? That's a strong accusation. How can I ever prove it?" Daniel shrugged his shoulders. "You said she would not do his dirty deeds, any idea what that means?"

"Sure, Marshal. I think he forces them by threats to come to the jail and does bad things to them or something like that. He also makes them cook for him and do whatever he asks. By threatening them, they're his slaves."

"How old are these sisters?"

The youngest is probably twelve or thirteen. The oldest was probably seventeen or eighteen at the time she disappeared. I could be wrong. It's kind of hard to estimate an Indian's age. They live a different life, even the half-breeds."

"You think he does dirty things with even the younger ones?"

"They all have their turns late at night and they aren't bringing any food with them."

53

"Anything else?"

"I think he hurts them and hurts them bad sometimes. I've seen them leave all slumped over crying and they can barely walk."

"Why didn't you tell me sooner?"

"You didn't seem interested. I wasn't sure if you was with him, or frightened of him, or think I'm crazy like everyone else."

"Sorry for ignoring you. I had no idea."

"So you believe me?"

"I believe you believe what you said and I don't think you are crazy. Let me know if you think of anything else or see something. Is there any particular day or time I should be watching for the rendezvous?"

"I'd say once or twice a week, well after dark."

"Thanks, Daniel. I promise Jack and I will investigate what you have said."

Daniel left, his eyes darting from side to side as though suspicious that someone was following him.

Joshua shook his head. What a strange fellow, he thought. Joshua had to determine whether Daniel's story about Marshal Broker had any validity or whether they were only wild thoughts. People did say he was crazy. Maybe Daniel was busy telling stories about Jack and him. Joshua scrunched his face at the thought.

When Jack returned later that day, Joshua relayed the frightening story that Daniel had told him. Whether their career was at stake or not, they agreed to begin an investigation.

"We'll have to stake out the office I guess. We can take turns," Joshua suggested.

"We'll need to follow the marshal when he goes out sometimes during the day. I'm curious what he's up to anyway," Jack added.

"So how did your Saturday afternoon go with Hester?"

"Nice. Really nice, Joshua. I'm really beginning to take a liking to her, and I think Hester is also taking to me."

"Sounds pretty serious, Jack."

"I'm not rushing. Not sure I want to give up going further west and I'm not sure Hester would go with me."

"I had the same feeling after the war and Becky. It's just my brother fixed my problem."

"So what do you think you would have done if Becky had been available?"

"Don't really know, but that's all in the past now, and I'm over it. There was just too much water under the bridge for anything to ever happen between us. I'm happy with where I am."

Jack nodded and dropped the subject.

"About tonight," Joshua said after a period of silence. "I'll watch the jail. I think a little past midnight will be sufficient."

****

The first week passed without incident. The young sisters came and went with the meals for the marshal and usually once a day the marshal would take a walk around town or down along the river, but nothing out of the ordinary.

Joshua and Jack were beginning to think they had been deceived into the whole story about the marshal. Maybe Daniel was just a crazy old man with an imagination beyond his control. They decided to give it another week.

It was a Tuesday evening when the youngest sister, or so Joshua believed to be the youngest, left the jail after serving the marshal his evening meal. She was obviously upset as she hurried back towards her house outside of town. She had not been inside very long, just long enough for the marshal to eat. Joshua concluded Marshal Broker had said something that upset her. Maybe tonight was the night he had been waiting for all last week.

Joshua remained tense as he waited through the evening. At least the weather is pleasant, he thought, as a cool breeze from the river brushed through the balmy evening.

Sometime after ten, Joshua sat up with a start. The young Indian girl was making her way towards the marshal's office. She was crying as she tapped on the door. She paused for a moment, then hesitantly pushed the door open and went inside.

Joshua quickly moved closer to the window on the side of the marshal's office. He could not see in but it would be the best place for him to listen. He could hear the girl pleading, "No". The marshal was not saying anything but Joshua could hear him grunting. Then the girl began to scream and Joshua heard a smack.

Joshua could not refrain himself any longer. Something terrible was happening inside. As he rushed to the front door, he saw Daniel watching from across the street. Joshua tried to open the door but found it locked. He stepped back and rammed the door with his body-once-twice-the door gave way.

As Joshua fell inside, he saw Harley lunging toward the desk for his revolver. His gun was breaking leather as Joshua regained his balance.

"How dare you, you bastard," Harley shouted.

Joshua fell to the floor as Harley began firing. Joshua rolled and came up with his colt in hand. He fired. Harley grunted and fell back, falling into his chair.

"Drop the gun, Marshal," Joshua called.

The marshal raised his weapon to take bead on Joshua. Joshua fired again hitting Harley just as the wounded marshal fired. His bullet hit the floor just inches from Joshua's head. Joshua rose to his feet, his revolver ready to fire again, but the marshal sat motionless in the chair, his revolver on the floor. He looked at Joshua with the look of a defeated man.

Joshua looked to the open doorway of the jail. He could see the young Indian girl naked, her hands bound together and tied above her to the jail bars.

Joshua grabbed Harley's gun, hurried to the girl, and began untying her. She was sobbing uncontrollably. She had a whiplash across her back and Joshua saw the small whip lying on the floor next to her. Without acknowledging Joshua, she quickly dressed and ran from the office. Somehow, Joshua thought, he would have to find a way to talk to her and her sisters, but for now, he would let her have the solitude with the only ones she trusted.

Jack arrived about that time. Daniel had gone to his room and told him what was happening. "Looks like I'm a little late," Jack commented as he looked at Harley lying back in his chair barely alive.

"I'll fill you in, but first we need to take a look at the marshal."

Harley waved his hand to indicate, no. "Hand me my revolver and leave for a moment. That's my final request."

Joshua and Jack looked at each other. Joshua hesitantly handed the marshal his revolver, and the two deputies left the office, closing the door behind them. Shortly, a shot fired from inside the office. They returned inside and found the marshal dead on the floor.

A small late evening crowd had gathered outside, mulling about trying to find out what happened. Joshua stood at the front of the jail. "Marshal Harley Broker has died from an accidental self-inflicted gunshot. That is all the information that is available."

"We heard several shots fired," someone from the crowd shouted.

"Perhaps it was an echo. I've given you all the information available. Please go on about your business."
****

Joshua and Jack buried Harley in an unmarked grave. No one came. Daniel watched from a distance amongst some trees.

"We need to get information about Marshal Broker to Marshal Barstow," Joshua remarked as they left the cemetery. "We can send a letter or one of us can ride south to telegraph him. I know they are putting up lines from Council Bluff, but I'm not sure how far they've come."

"I can go," Jack offered.

"Let me go," Joshua replied. "I don't have a Hester waiting around, and besides I want to check on the status of my transfer."

"I guess I can start doing some marshal work now that we have a jail," Jack said, taking a deep breath.

"It might be a shock to some of the old drunks around town," Joshua added with a broad grin.

****

Joshua traveled fifty miles to find the nearest telegraph office. He sent a message to Marshal Peter Barstow in Davenport.

'Marshal Harley Broker dead from accidental self-inflicted gunshot wound. Everything under control. Send status of Joshua Parker transfer request.'

The next day the reply came.

'Marshals Parker and Young proceed as usual. Transfer request being processed for Parker.'

Joshua returned feeling disappointed by the telegraph reply of being processed, which could mean days, months, or years.

****

Although Sioux City became more tolerable with Marshal Harley Broker gone, Joshua remained anxious for word of a transfer. He watched his friend become more involved with Hester as summer ended and winter set in. In January, the expected announcement arrived. Jack came home on a January Saturday, a broad smile on his face.

"Joshua, I'm getting married. I asked her this afternoon and by darn, old friend, she said, yes."

"Congratulations, Jack. I know you'll be happy. Hester is a good woman." Joshua was happy for his friend. He knew Jack would eventually marry Hester, therefore he had already prepared himself to leave Sioux City alone. Yet, he was still saddened and disappointed that he and his best friend would soon be departing ways. Of course, he assumed he would eventually receive his transfer.

The wedding would be mid-June. Joshua wanted to be there for his friend, but he also wanted to leave sooner from Sioux

City. He decided not to fret, because fate would choose the outcome anyway.

Late February, the long-awaited letter came. Joshua had received his transfer papers. '*Joshua Parker to report to Cheyenne in the soon to be new territory of Wyoming by August 15, 1868.*'

Joshua was anxious to leave but he was happy he could stay for his friend's big day. Winter dragged on, but Joshua knew each day would bring him closer to fulfilling his dream.

In April, Joshua helped Jack build his home. The weather constantly interfered, and Jack became concerned whether he could finish the home before the wedding. If not, the newlyweds would have to live with Hester's family. They finally got a break in the weather in May and with help from family and friends, the home was completed before the wedding.

The wedding day arrived with joyous celebration. Joshua watched his friend beam with happiness. Jack had found his dream. Joshua hoped that his happiness was in Cheyenne and that he was not chasing a dream that would never materialize...that perhaps he was only a dream chaser.
****

Joshua shook hands with Jack, and then mounted his horse. They spoke few words as Joshua prepared to leave. The many years of friendship, good and bad, had said everything that needed saying. They knew how each other felt.

Joshua felt an emptiness as he rode away that day, glancing back and waving at Jack and Hester. The ride this time would be very lonely.

Chapter 9

Joshua Parker arrived at the outskirts of Cheyenne on a hot August day, 1868. There was no breeze or clouds to soften the scorching hot day. He first saw Cheyenne from a small bluff overlooking the young town, in the new Wyoming Territory. The town was sprawling with tents that intermingled with newly built structures, and stretching along the new settlement, like a snake bathing in the hot sun, were the tracks of the Union Pacific Railroad.

Joshua looked over his new home for a short time and then decided to find refuge from the withering heat of the afternoon sun. He found the coolness of a nearby stream and favored camping there for the night. The willows and greenery along the banks offered a lush paradise to the scorching, barren terrain he had faced for past several days. He settled in for the evening. Over the past several days as he approached his new home, he had felt an increasing nervousness, but now that he was here, seeing it so near, a sense of calmness filtered through his body. He ate early and lay back against his saddle. He listened to the ripple of the stream nearby, waiting for darkness to come on a long summer day. His mind drifted back to Iowa and his family. He had left with a clear heart, but the torturing words of Becky that day in the apple orchard still left lingered in his mind. He sincerely hoped she had found happiness and complete love with Jonathan. He presumed the torment of wondering would always be with him.

It had been difficult to say good-bye to his good, close friend in Sioux City, but he knew Jack was happy there with Hester. Joshua was about to fulfill his dream and only hoped he could find his happiness in Cheyenne. He wondered if he was just a restless soul on an endless search for something that he would never find. Tomorrow he would begin that search.
****

Joshua rose early the next morning, anxious to see and feel his new home. It was still early as he rode into Cheyenne for the first time. His eyes scanned the streets as he looked in awe at the vibrant young town. The dust-laden streets were bustling with early morning activity from the street vendors, wagons, horsemen, and those on foot. People were everywhere, some seemed to have a purpose, others standing around as though waiting for something or someone. The shops, many being tents, were open for business and from the apparent crowds, were doing well. New building construction was prevalent everywhere-- some brick and mortar, some wood. Joshua wondered where all the wood came from for the projects, having seen little more than brush and scrub trees coming into town.

Saloons were in abundance and already open in the early morning hour, filling the air with the sounds of shouting, music, and laughter. Joshua wondered if the saloons ever closed, thinking it would probably serve better if they did not, he thought; otherwise the rowdy patrons and drifters would end up in the street creating mayhem.

Joshua had received notice not to expect any organized law in the settlement or surrounding area. He would be the first, although vigilantes had left their mark. He possessed the authority to hire two deputies for jail duties and general functions. As he looked over the street around him, he speculated on the difficult task of finding two reliable and available men. In addition, he had to find a place to live and locate a structure that could serve as a jail. Considering the number of tents, he presumed that durable wooden, or brick structures would be extremely difficult to find. With all the difficulties he faced, the biggest would be establishing some semblance of law and order in all the chaos. With certainty, he felt he would wish for Sioux City many times during the next few days and probably months.

He chose to keep his presence unknown for a few days while he tried to sort out his options and hopefully some solutions. He wanted to observe the town for potential problems, support, and help.

Joshua also was aware that far more land was under his jurisdiction than just Cheyenne. His orders indicated the jurisdiction ran west to the Laramie Range, south to Colorado, east some fifty miles inside Nebraska and north to Bear Creek and along Horse Creek. Fort Laramie would handle anything further north.

As life began in Cheyenne for Joshua, an argument and fight ensued nearby as he rode down 16th Street. The two men, quite intoxicated, had no visible weapons, so Joshua ignored the brawl rather than expose his presence. For now, he would have to choose his encounters. Besides what would he do with the drunks if he arrested them? He cringed at the thought, remembering Sioux City.

Joshua found two hotels and chose the one that looked cheaper. He would look for a place with room and board later, but for now, he needed to settle in and begin performing his duties. The hotel lobby was small with a small clerk desk and two wooden chairs to the side. He imagined the chairs' limited use, they looked quite uncomfortable and there was little else in the lobby to make one feel welcome.

The clerk was small but when he stepped behind the counter, he suddenly grew a foot, enabling him to look down on his potential customers. His eyes stared down with disdain at Joshua.

"Can I get a room?" Joshua asked.

"One night?"

"Probably not, but I'll renew each morning until I leave."

"As you wish. That will be one dollar."

"One dollar for one night?"

"Yes."

"What if I rent for a week?"

"Four dollars."

"Give me a week."

"As you wish."

Joshua laid the four dollars on the desk, and noted to himself to check the hotel across the street. Maybe he had made a poor decision. The clerk collected the coins and looked them over before handing the key to Joshua. As Joshua walked past the clerk, he commented, "Nice stool, Shorty."

Joshua settled into his room and then set about finding a stable for his faithful bay that he had purchased in Burlington. He returned to his room and spent the remainder of the daylight hours relaxing. The room was hot and stuffy, but it was a break from the hot sun and dust that he had dealt with for the last several days. He wondered if it ever rained. He had spent two weeks waiting for a rain cloud to relieve the heat while traveling here.

By evening, the new marshal had found an eatery, ate supper, and then walked about the streets, taking note of saloons, card clubs, brothels and the like that he anticipated he would be dealing with in the days ahead. Unfortunately, he concluded, half the businesses in Cheyenne seemed to be of questionable virtue.

The next morning, Joshua decided to ride north a short distance to see some of his jurisdiction outside of Cheyenne. He had seen the east on his arrival to Cheyenne.

Joshua ate breakfast and headed for the stable. He walked straight to the stall where he had left his horse and tack. He stopped and blinked his eyes. He looked around thinking he was mistaken where he left his horse. His horse, saddle, blanket and bridle were gone.

Joshua questioned the stable worker who was nearby. He grunted he wasn't responsible. Joshua grabbed the pitchfork from the useless worker and shoved his U.S. Marshal badge in his face. "You get the word out that by noon, my horse, saddle, blanket and bridle had better be tied in front of the Westman Hotel. I can spot my horse and my saddle a mile away. I will have anyone hanged if I catch them with my horse." He threw the pitchfork into the pile of hay and left the stable. The first thing that came to mind was his rope was gone too. He would have to borrow a rope to hang someone.

Joshua returned to his room. His anger grew as he paced back and forth. He had not wanted to let everyone know a marshal was in town this soon, but he figured it was his only chance of getting his horse back.

At noon, Joshua left his room and headed downstairs. The small clerk stood respectfully away as Joshua passed. "Good afternoon, Marshal," he said with a subdue tone in his voice. The word was out. His days of being inconspicuous were over. A marshal was in town...a horseless marshal no less.

Joshua walked outside into the bright sunlight. Looking through squinted eyes, he casually looked at the hitching post in front of the hotel. Tears of joy filled his eyes. There was his horse, saddled and ready to ride.

It was at that moment, Joshua wished he had a pouch of tobacco to open, pour the tobacco into a paper, pull the tie string with his teeth, roll the cigarette, light his match on his trousers, light up the cigarette, and smoke it before strolling to his horse. He wanted anything that would allow him to be nonchalant about noticing his horse, and not being surprised to find him there. That is what he wished, but Joshua had no tobacco, could not roll a cigarette, did not have a match to light it, and would probably choke trying to smoke it. Instead, he could feel his feet move as though on air like a ballerina, prancing towards his horse. He just hoped it looked better than it felt, because he knew many eyes were watching him at that moment.

Chapter 10

Once the stolen horse incident passed, Joshua set out to find reputable citizens of Cheyenne who could help him establish a jail and find jailers to mind it. His first days in Cheyenne convinced him the tasks might be monumental.

While riding down 17th street, Joshua noticed a small sign in the window of a small wooden structure, which read, 'The Rocky Mountain Gazette'. A newspaper could help direct him to the upstanding citizens in town, if in fact there were any.

Inside, he found a middle-aged man with graying hair and beard. He was busily writing at his desk. The man looked up and immediately spotted the marshal's badge. "So you're our new marshal." He quickly rose and came to Joshua, extending his hand. "I'm Thomas Prescott, editor and owner of this little newspaper."

"Joshua Parker. I arrived yesterday from Sioux City, Iowa."

"Glad to see some law here. We've been trying to get a new mayor and find a sheriff here for some time with little luck. Our old mayor was like a tick, felt a little heat and ups and leaves."

"In honesty, right now it's a little overwhelming. I need to figure out something for a jail and I need to find a couple good men that can work as jailers and general help. My first day has not given me an abundance of hope."

Thomas smiled. "Word is around town you had some difficulty earlier. The good news though, people were quite impressed with the speed that you resolved the problem."

"It was definitely getting off on the wrong foot here, but what is done is done."

"I might have some good news for you. I do have an idea for a jail. It wouldn't be a place you would want to keep hardened criminals; but I think it would do for the drunks and rabble-rousers. As for a couple good men, I think I know a couple young men that are available. Stop by tomorrow morning and I might have some answers for you. Of course I would expect a favor in return."

"If you can help me, how could I say, no?"

"Once you're settled in, I would like an interview."

"Interview me?"

"Whether you know it or not, you are big news around Cheyenne. Better get used to it. And be careful out there, we don't want the new marshal getting shot by some young slinger trying to make a reputation."

"Thanks for the advice. I'll do my best to stick around for a while."

Joshua left the Gazette feeling better about the status of his job. He could probably never control Cheyenne and its wild style, but possibly corral it a bit.

****

That evening when Joshua brought his horse to the stable, he found the stable hand and gave him some advice, "Listen. If tonight my horse, saddle, or any of my belongings turn up missing, someone will be shot. If I can't find the thief, you will be his replacement. There will be no hanging, it's too much trouble. Just one shot." Joshua pointed between his eyes. "Bang. This is not an idle threat. Understand?"

The stable worker nodded nervously. Joshua left the stable that evening, feeling assured his horse would be there in the morning.

Joshua had supper at the Red Rock Cafe, one of the few eateries that was not in a tent, and spent the next two hours walking the streets. People acknowledged him, but none tried to befriend him. For now, he thought, that was probably best. He ignored the drunks and their outlandish behavior. He did not want anything to befuddle his life at that moment.

When Joshua returned to his room, he decided he would start collecting the weapons of the drunks and the rowdy types that were endangering others, but he would wait on arresting them until he had a jail or at least an adequate place to detain them. He would not have a situation similar to the one he had in Sioux City with the drunk. If he had to hold someone, maybe he could handcuff them to a lamp pole or if they gave him too much trouble, the train tracks. He could not do all for all, but at best some for some.

Joshua fell asleep to the loud sounds in the street of yelling and music blaring. They were the sounds of his new home, and he would be hearing them for some time to come. This was his dream of what he wanted, and if he could not find happiness here, there was nowhere else for him to go.

The new morning returned the hot sun to Cheyenne. At least the higher elevation had cooled the night, Joshua thankfully concluded. With confidence, Joshua had breakfast before going to the stable to check on his bay. Still he breathed a sigh of relief when he saw his horse and tack where he had left them.

A different worker from the previous night was working, but obviously, Joshua's message had reached him. The worker leaned on the handle of his fork, obviously pleased. "Your horse and saddle are here, Marshal. He's in good shape. I just fed him and gave him water."

Joshua smiled. "Thanks. Keep up the good work."

Anxious to see if Thomas Prescott had had any success on his projects, Joshua headed for the Gazette. He had not walked far when a man excitedly shouting, approached him. "My friend needs help. I'm afraid he's dying."

"You need a doctor."

"There is no doctor. Please help."

"I'm not a doctor."

"He is cut up bad, Marshal."

"Cut up? Where is he?"

"At our tent. Please hurry."

The tent was located about a quarter of a mile away on Pioneer. Joshua tried to get information as they hurried along, but it was difficult to understand the man. Apparently, the victim had received his monthly pay and was robbed on his way back to the tent. There were three or four men, carrying knives, that robbed him. They had badly cut him over his face and body.

When they arrived at the tent, Joshua found the injured man had lost a considerable amount of blood and the wounds lay weeping and open. "Isn't there a doctor around?" Joshua asked. "He needs to be taken care of by someone who knows more than me."

"I don't know of a doctor," the friend replied, slowly shaking his head.

Joshua, realizing he was only a block and a half from the Gazette, decided to see if Thomas could help him once more. "I'm going to see if I can find a doctor."

Joshua arrived at the Gazette and found Thomas talking to a young woman in back. Thomas, seeing the urgent expression on Joshua's face, excused himself and came up front.

"Sorry to interrupt, Thomas, but I have a bit of a pressing emergency. I'm looking for a doctor. I have a man who has been badly cut up and has lost a lot of blood."

"There is Doc Stuart, though I heard he was in Denver buying supplies for his new office." He turned to the woman who was now standing in the doorway.

Joshua had paid little attention when he arrived, but now noticed the elegant woman before him.

She nodded. "I'll go," she said, "just let me get my bag."
She returned to the backroom.

Thomas looked back to Joshua. "Jennie is a pretty good
nurse. She's mended quite a few in need."

"That's great. She's going to be facing a bad looking job.
A bunch of thugs worked him over pretty badly with their knives.
They must have done it for pleasure, because they could have
robbed him without a hitch."

"Unfortunately, those type do exist," Thomas added. "By
the way, I think I have a suitable place for a jail not far from here,
and I have a couple fine young men who are interested in working
for you."

"That's great. I owe you."

Thomas smiled. "You sure do. Remember the interview."

Jennie returned from the back with a black bag. "I always
come prepared," she said as she moved to the door.

As they hurried down the street, Joshua introduced
himself, "By the way, I'm Joshua Parker, U.S. Marshal. This is my
third day here."

"I knew who you were. I've heard quite a bit about you
already."

"From Thomas?"

"From him, but also several others."

"Really. I heard Thomas mention your name as Jennie."

"Jennie Peterson. I work for Thomas at the Gazette."

"Yesterday he never mentioned you. I guess he didn't
want me hanging around too much."

Jennie smiled. "My mother always warned me to beware
of smooth talkers."

"You're the first that ever described me as a smooth talker.
I usually trip over my own tongue."

Joshua felt disappointed when they arrived at the tent.
He had immensely enjoyed his conversation with Jennie.

Jennie hurried inside and immediately took charge. She
quickly examined her patient's wounds, checked his vital signs,
and began stitching several of the more prominent wounds, then

dressed and bandaged all the injured man's wounds. Joshua, the injured man, and his friend watched her in awe as she quietly did her business. When she finished, she stood up and smiled.

"I think you're going to make it," she said to her heavily bandaged patient. "You need to take care of yourself, though. You've lost a considerable amount of blood and if you get up and move around you'll probably collapse in a heap on the ground. Keep the bandages on and I'll check on you tomorrow. I hope we've avoided infection in any of the wounds. As I'm sure you are already aware, these cuts are going to be painful and I'm sorry to say they will remain painful for several days."

Jennie turned to Joshua. "I can find my way back."

"I'm sure you can, but you're not going alone."

As they walked back to the Gazette, Joshua continued their conversation. "I was impressed with your mending skills. How did you become so good?"

"My father had a trading post about five miles from here on Crow Creek. My mother was always patching somebody up. I remember the worst was a skin dealer coming in. A brown bear had attacked him. You thought that man back there was bad. I was nine years old then, but I remember it vividly. When mother was finished with him, most of his body had bandages, and the man was drunk. She poured the better part of a bottle of whiskey down him while she worked on him." They both laughed.

When they arrived back at the Gazette, Joshua politely shook her hand. "Thank you. The man probably would have died with my care."

"You're welcome, Marshal Parker."

"Please call me Joshua."

"Okay, but in public, I would prefer to call you marshal."

"All right, at least for now. I have to get back. I need to get to the bottom of this crime and arrest someone. It was too brutal to ignore. Time to render some justice."

They said good-bye and Joshua returned to the tent. He sat down next to the victim. "Looks like Jennie did a pretty good job of fixing you up. For the records, what's your name?"

"Mason. Lewis Mason."

"Lewis, I need your help. I need you to tell me who these men were that attacked you."

"I didn't see them, Marshal."

"How many? Were they old, young, dark hair, anything?"

"Sorry, Marshal, they attacked me from behind."

"You know who they are, don't you?"

The man did not answer and would not look at Joshua.

"If these men walk away from this, they will continue to harass you, your friend over here, and every other poor soul that walks around this town. Each time they will become more aggressive. They just might attack Jennie, the nice lady who fixed you up. Think about it. Remember her beautiful face? What if they cut it up for pleasure? Think about it, Lewis. Think about it."

Lewis looked to his friend. "What should I do, Silas?"

"I think the marshal has a point. I think you need to tell him. They'll come back after you time and time again if they think they can get away with it."

Lewis looked back to the marshal. His eyes showed fright but his voice was strong and determined. "There were four of them. Two brothers, Eli and Amos. Don't know their last name. There's Joel Baker and Solomon Blackman. I think Solomon is kind of their leader or at least the one looking for trouble. People are afraid of them. They all carry bowie knives and know how to use them, and they enjoy using them."

"Where can I find them, Lewis?"

"Probably at the Lame Horse Saloon or one of the brothels. They're probably busy spending my money."

"Thanks, Lewis. I hope to even things up a bit and maybe get your money back."

"Be mighty careful, Marshal. They're mean and good with their knives."

"I'll heed your advice. Thanks."

Joshua headed for the Lame Horse Saloon. His nerves were on edge. Perhaps his biggest fear was the unknown. He had very little familiarity with knives, particularly when used in a fight. Obviously, they were very proficient with them. Could his Colt match four Bowie knives? He guessed he would find out very soon.

Joshua stopped across the street from the saloon. Relying on his skills he learned in the army, he carefully laid out the different situations that could occur once he entered inside. He watched the saloon, seeing who was coming and going. The long walk and the hot day were making Joshua perspire. He stepped into the shade. He needed to be sure the sweat did not get into his eyes and that his hand not sweat to endanger his drawing or firing of the Colt.

Joshua slowly moved across the street. He could hear loud voices and laughter from inside. He made one last check of his revolver, walked to the saloon door and entered. He moved to one side of the doorway to ensure no one came in behind him. For the next few moments, it was as though the world had stopped. The room became quiet as the patrons started to become aware of Joshua. Everyone was looking his way. Joshua did a quick surveillance of the room. Three men at the corner table were already gathering their chips in anticipation of trouble. Two other men sat at a table closer to the bar. The bartender was moving out of any line of fire. That left four men standing near the bar. They all carried belts with a Bowie knife and each had a revolver, an older issue from before the war. The knives were obviously their weapons of choice.

Joshua looked for any blind spots in the room where someone could go unnoticed. There was one other door visible near the back. He checked to see where the sun was shining that might cause momentary blindness if any move might put him in direct line with it. Once he was familiar with the saloon, he moved toward the four men at the bar. He stopped some twenty feet from them. At least he was far enough away that they would have to throw the knives to do damage and yet, he was close enough that he could fire his revolver with deadly accuracy.

"Solomon Blackman?" the marshal asked.

"What about him?" the largest of the four men asked.

"You Solomon?"

The man looked around. "Maybe he's out back relieving himself." The others laughed.

The marshal, not wanting to play their game, ignored the remark. "You boys seem to be having a good old time pretty early in the day. Maybe you've come into some money."

"None of your business whether we did or didn't, Marshal. Especially you being alone and all."

Joshua removed his revolver from his holster and rested his arm on the bar. "I reckon alone depends on how you look at it." The four men's eyes hardened. The smiles were gone. "You see, I'm here because it was a might unfriendly what you boys did to a nice fellow last night, and I've come to settle up."

"And how are you planning to do that, Marshal?"

"Two ways. I want all the money returned, maybe with a little interest. That would be kind of you boys. Second, I want your weapons. How I plan on doing that will depend on how well you boys respond. I can arrest you if you do well and you go off to jail and wait for the circuit judge to come by for a trial, or I can kill you and haul you off to boot hill."

Solomon turned to the others. "He'd arrest us and put us up in his fine jail." The others laughed.

Joshua removed his hat and scratched his head. "Darn, you're right. Never thought of that. Reckon I'll just have to kill you." He cocked his gun.

"You can't just kill us."

"I think I can. There are four of you. I've got six rounds here in my Colt and by all accounts I'm a pretty good shot. I can't give you any references though. You see, they're all dead."

They all began removing their revolvers and knives and placing them on the bar. "You're not a lawman. You're nothing more than a hired killer."

"You may be right. Lucky for you, you were smart enough not to find out. Now my first problem, I only have two handcuffs, so here is what we'll do. I want you to pair off and cuff your right hand. This way one will be looking forward and one backwards. You can walk that way with some trouble, but it'll be mighty difficult to run."

The marshal and his four prisoners left the saloon, and headed for the Gazette. The new marshal in town would need to find out where his new jail was located. Joshua had four gun belts and four knife belts slung over his shoulder. The prisoners, handcuffed in pairs, fought over who would walk forward and who would walk backwards, all to the delight of the throng of onlookers.

If anyone had remained unaware of a new marshal in town, it would soon come to pass. The marshal had made a statement to all the ruffians, thugs, and no counts that he was serious on cleaning up Cheyenne. However, with the statement, he also knew it would increase the danger, either from newfound enemies wanting revenge, or just those threatened by his presence. Yet, perhaps the biggest threat would come from those who sought to build a reputation, and might see the marshal as a challenge. His bluff had worked twice since his arrival in Cheyenne, but the day would come when somebody would call his bluff. He hoped he would be up to the task.

Chapter 11

Thomas Prescott fulfilled his promise by making the old empty mayor's office into a jail for the new marshal in town. It had two rooms and fortunately, the back room had no window. They made a small slit in the door to view the prisoners and a small opening at the bottom of the door through which to pass food and drink. The door was fortified and a lock put on the door. It would have to do until workers could improve the situation. A desk and four chairs were about all that was in the outer room.

Thomas had also found two young men to work for Joshua. Joshua, satisfied with Thomas' judgment, put the two men to work. Joshua had to feel good about the two new assistants, having the same names of his brothers--Mark and Matthew.

The new jail of Cheyenne was officially in business with four prisoners and two jailers. Joshua received information that a circuit court judge was arriving in a week to hold court. If a jury found his four prisoners guilty, they would send them to Colorado, since Wyoming did not yet have a state prison.

The town, only days before, had no formal law. Now it seemed everyone needed help from the marshal, which quickly became overwhelming. He set up a register so people could write down their name and address and their problem. Joshua tried to go in order, but had to prioritize situations that needed more immediate action. The problem with the register was a large number of those needing help could not read or write so Mark and Matthew had to spend much of their time writing down the information.

Unfortunately, the trivial day-to-day operation of the jail and office consumed a great deal of Joshua's time rather than bringing law and order to Cheyenne. Adding to his problems, Joshua received word that the circuit court judge had been delayed indefinitely due to an Indian uprising. The marshal had a growing concern with finances for his new office and jail. The money was not arriving regularly and his expenses kept increasing with the four prisoners to feed and salaries of his two jailers. In addition, he wanted to avoid mixing the disturbing the peace prisoners with the four thugs in his one room jail.

Most of the complaints received by Joshua involved someone taking or trying to take someone else's property. Joshua would take the names and information, promising to give it to the judge when he arrived. The other places that required considerable and immediate attention were the numerous saloons, brothels and card clubs. The beating of the women in the brothels became a high priority and the marshal had no problem arresting and placing the assailants in the same room with the tough elements. He just hoped the judge would arrive soon. The occupancy in the jail had become dangerously full with the poor conditions, and it was becoming a powder keg ready to explode.

When the judge finally arrived, Joshua handed him the workload of cases to handle, and breathed a sigh of relief. The judge reviewed the list. "Marshal, you've been busy. I'm not sure I can get to them all. I'll telegraph and see if I can get an extension or have another judge come as soon as possible. I suppose I'll have to hold court in one of these miserable tents again."

"You start with that and I'll see if I can find something better." Joshua wanted to keep the judge happy.

The most important case was the four thugs who had knifed Lewis Mason and stole his money. Joshua rounded up Lewis, his friend Silas and Jennie to testify.

While at the Gazette, Thomas approached him about the interview for the paper.

"I don't know if I have the time," Joshua responded.

"I understand," Thomas replied. "I just hate telling Jennie you said no to an interview with her. I know she'll be disappointed."

"Jennie's the one that wants to interview me?"

"Yes. She asked if she could. She occasionally does articles for the paper that interest her. She has written some very impressive works."

"She asked to interview me?"

"She did. She said she thought the people of Cheyenne would like to know their marshal better."

"Okay, maybe I can find a little time. Just let me know where and when and I'll try to break loose for a while."

"Glad to see the change of heart, Marshal. Any particular reason?" Thomas grinned. "I'll let her know you said, yes. She'll be pleased, I'm sure."

This was Joshua's first interview. The thought of an interview had never entered his mind. Being alone for some time with Jennie clouded his thoughts. Perhaps he resembled a buffalo herded towards a cliff, knowing what was ahead but for some reason unable to stop. If she wanted, she could probably cut him to shreds, and then publish the interview for everyone to read, or at least those who could read. He was being ridiculous. Jennie was not the vulture type feeding on someone else's misery. Still he felt mighty nervous. He wanted to make a good impression on her, since she seemed like someone that he could take a real liking to in the future.

The next day, when Joshua returned the prisoners to the jail from court, Mark handed him a note that he had received earlier in the day. "It's a note from Miss Peterson from over at the Gazette," Mark said excitedly.

Joshua took the note. Again, he wished he had a tobacco pouch. He tried to be casual, but found himself opening the note in haste.

Marshal Parker,

I understand you have given your consent for an interview with me on behalf of the Rocky Mountain Gazette. I might suggest Friday evening at my family residence for supper at five and the interview reasonably thereafter. If this meets with your approval, please reply by Thursday P.M.

Sincerely,

Jennie Peterson

When Joshua finished reading the note, he turned quickly, catching Mark staring at him. Mark quickly looked away.

"Is there something wrong with my back?" Joshua asked.

"I don't think so, Marshal."

"Why were you gawking at it then?"

"I'm sorry, Marshal. I didn't mean to."

"Come on, Mark, can't you tell I'm just having fun with you?"

Mark smiled. "Yeah, sure, Marshal. I knew that."

"I need your opinion though, Mark. Jennie, uh, Miss Peterson wants to interview me for the Gazette this Friday at her family home. It would be for supper and then the interview."

"Wow! I mean that's great, Marshal...Isn't it?"

"Sure...or at least, I believe so. My dilemma is whether I should give my answer in person or should I have you deliver the message for me?"

"I'll go, Marshal."

"From your reaction, I'm sure you would, but I'm not sure I could trust you."

"You having fun with me again, Marshal? She'd never be interested in me, and besides I think she's got a fancy for you."

"I think you may be reading too much into things, but I do hope you're right. Now, should I be a little reserved by having

78

someone else deliver the note for me? I don't want to be too bold and if I rush over and deliver it in person, it may look that way."

"Marshal, I'm no expert with how women think. In fact, they confuse me, but my opinion is to deliver the reply in person. If you're interested in Miss Peterson, let her know. It's not too bold and I think she would be pleased."

"You are wise beyond your years, Mark. I am going to take your advice. Are you sure there is nothing wrong with my back?"

Mark laughed heartily, slapping his leg.

Joshua entered the Gazette trying to be nonchalant, but he knew he was doing a poor job of it. Obviously, Thomas noticed too. "Looking for Jennie, I suppose?"

"Yes, I was. I wanted to respond to her note she sent me yesterday."

"I hope it's a positive reply, but then that's none of my business. She'll be back shortly. Sit down if you have time and I'll pour you a cup of fresh coffee that I just made."

"Thanks, I'll take you up on that offer."

Joshua sat down and began to look nervously around the room. Usually his visits were rushed and he never really took the time to see the details. Thomas returned with the coffee. "Don't tell her I told you, but Jennie is quite excited about the interview."

"I guess I'm more nervous than anything. I'm not sure how personal she'll be."

"She'll probably ask some tough questions, but she is fair and not a reporter who is only looking for a big story. I think you'll enjoy it. I need to get some things done in back so if you'll excuse me, Jennie will be here any moment."

"Yes, please, do what you need to do. I'm enjoying the quiet moment off the street."

Jennie arrived a few minutes later. Joshua felt a surge rush through his body when he saw her, a feeling he had become accustomed to when she appeared. She was dressed rather conservatively with her hair neatly tied in a bun. Although she attempted to hide it, her beauty still shone through.

"Good morning, Marshal Parker."

"Good morning to you, Miss Peterson."

From the backroom, Thomas watched the two young people for a short period, then smiled, and went back to his project.

"I received your note earlier today about the Friday supper and interview."

"Good," she responded with a pleasant smile.

"Friday at five would be fine, but I do need directions."

Thomas stepped from the back at an opportune moment. He obviously had overheard their conversation. "Marshal, how are the two young men working out for you?"

"Splendid. I couldn't be happier. They've been a big help."

"Good. By the way did I tell you that Mark is my son, and Matthew is my nephew?"

"No, you did not. I suspect that was on purpose, Thomas."

"Perhaps. I didn't want any outside influence on your determining their worth."

Jennie was smiling, listening to the conversation. "Perhaps Mark or Matthew can give you directions to my home," she replied. "Have a good day, Marshal." She walked past Thomas into the backroom.

Thomas smiled. "Enjoy Friday, Marshal."

Joshua left, feeling a little foolish. Perhaps Mark had been looking at a big target on his back. The thought of the buffalo reappeared in Joshua's mind.

****

Friday came with feet dragging. Joshua was uncertain and confused about how he felt...kind of in the apple-orchard-with- Becky feeling. He was anxious to be with Jennie and away from the hubbub of their previous encounters, yet meeting the family and then the unknown of the interview left Joshua unsettled.

80

Joshua arrived in front of the well-kept, two storied, whitewashed house. He drew a deep breath, and dismounted, his eyes riveted to the looming door. He stepped onto the long porch and knocked, unsure what unimaginable experience lay behind the door. He nervously rubbed his hands, waiting for the door to open. When it did open, he almost choked. Standing before him was Jennie, but not the same Jennie he had seen at the Gazette. She was dressed in an elegant, light blue, floor length dress covered with delicate lace. Her sparkling dark hair lay vibrantly on her back and shoulders. Her face radiated, her eyes shone and her lips were slightly parted in a soft smile. He removed his hat.

"Good evening, Marshal."

"It's Joshua now, remember?"

"Of course. Come in Joshua."

Joshua stepped inside, his eyes never leaving her. "You look very pretty this evening, Miss Peterson."

"Jennie, remember?" she reminded him, her gentle smile broadened.

"Yes, yes I do," Joshua replied. He hoped the nervous blush he felt was not showing.

"I don't want to sound rude, but I need to have you leave your gun at the door. My mother is a stickler about guns in the house."

Joshua removed his gun-belt and hung it on a post next to another one. "You look so elegant, Jennie, I feel underdressed."

"Not at all, Joshua. I'm sorry if I made you feel that way. Perhaps I was overzealous with my wardrobe. I did it for...well I just did."

You did it for me, I hope, thought Joshua.

"Come in and meet my family." She placed her arm in his and they headed for the front room. He wondered if she felt his body shiver at that moment. She felt and smelled so good. His mouth suddenly went dry.

They entered the parlor. There were three people in the room. Jennie led Joshua to the older woman seated in a chair.

"Mr. Parker," Jennie said, "this is my mother, Mrs. Peterson. Mother, this is Marshal Parker."

"I'm sorry, Marshal. Perhaps my daughter, Jennie, forgot our names. I'm Margaret."

"Joshua."

"Hallie. Joseph. This gentleman is Joshua, the marshal of our fine town. Joshua, these people are Hallie, my daughter and her husband, Joseph. Joshua is the young man that Jennie brought home for us to meet."

"Mother, I'm interviewing him tonight after supper."

"I know, Jennie. You don't need to keep reminding me. I haven't forgotten."

Hallie and Joseph crossed the room to the others. "It's nice to meet you, Joshua. Welcome to our home and our town."

Joseph extended his hand, "I hope your first days here have not been too trying. I know Cheyenne is not the most congenial place."

"It's had its moments, but I'm doing well."

Hallie excused herself to finish supper. Jennie followed.

"Joshua," Margaret said, looking at him seriously, "sometimes my Jennie tries to be too formal and reserved, and it just makes her look stuffy and snobbish. She is not. Don't judge her too quickly. She is a sweet caring person.

"Margaret, it is my fondest desire to know your daughter better and I never doubted her being a gentle caring person. I saw her at work mending a man who had been badly cut by the knives of thugs."

Margaret took Joshua's hand. "Thank you. I believe you will not regret it."

Hallie returned and announced that supper was ready.

The nervous anticipation that Joshua had felt earlier, left as he found his meal very enjoyable and the table conversation pleasant and rewarding. He had almost forgotten about the interview until Jennie rose from the table and made the announcement. "If everyone will excuse the marshal and me, we have some work ahead of us."

Joshua excused himself and followed Jennie. The buffalo and the cliff flashed through his mind. They entered a smaller, more lavish room. Joshua presumed it to be the library, although he was not certain, because he had never been in a house that had one. The room had a polished dark wood desk with two matching padded chairs. The wall behind the desk had a bookcase full of books.

"My favorite room," Jennie commented. "Make yourself comfortable," she said, pointing to one of the chairs. She picked up a pad and quill and sat in the other chair next to the desk. "Hallie will bring us coffee shortly."

Joshua smiled. "Sounds good." He had never had this good an opportunity to look at Jennie. Normally a commotion or emergency had taken place when Joshua was around Jennie and it made it difficult for him to observe her. He knew he was staring, but tonight he felt he could. With the interview, she would be finding out information about him, so he was going to know more about her.

"If you're ready, I'll begin. Your full name please."

"Joshua Madison Parker."

"Where were you born and raised?

The questions continued, and Joshua answered them with ease. Then a question arose. "What have you found in Cheyenne that sets the community apart from others?"

Joshua thought for a moment. He was risking a perfect evening, but he had to chance it. "Two things. First, the young vitality of the town. With all the problems that a new community might encounter, Cheyenne seems to rise above the problems, and I believe in the near future, it will be a community to be reckoned with in the new west." Joshua paused.

"And the second thing you mentioned."

Joshua shifted nervously. His eyes stared directly into her eyes. "The second thing is actually the first. In my opinion, Jennie Peterson sets this town apart from anywhere else."

Jennie stared back, her quill dangling in her hand. Her lips parted, but no words came out.

"Shouldn't you be writing all this down?"

"I, uh, I," she murmured, setting the quill down.

"I had to tell you, Jennie. I find you very attractive, intelligent, interesting, and a good person through and through."

"Thank you, Joshua for those kind words. I'm speechless."

"If you don't realize that you are the person I described then perhaps you do have one fault. You are not very observant."

"I guess that concludes the interview. I had intended that to be the last question." She rose quickly. "Thank you, Joshua, for the interview. I presume the paper will publish the interview next week. I hope you find it acceptable."

"Jennie, I'm sorry if I was out of line."

"No. I'm just not very good at accepting compliments. Forgive me if I seem to be rude. I'll show you out. I'm sure mother has retired."

Jennie walked Joshua to the door. "Tell all your family I enjoyed meeting them and thank them for the enjoyable supper. The food and conversation were very special to me."

"You're welcome, Joshua. Thank you for the interview."

Joshua nodded and left the porch. Just as he was about to mount his horse, Jennie called to him. "Joshua." He stopped and looked at her. "Thank you for the compliment. It was very nice of you and I am glad you said it."

Joshua walked back to the foot of the porch. "Jennie, would you like to go for a ride Sunday afternoon?"

"Yes, that would be nice."

"What time would be good for you, Jennie?"

"How about two?"

"Two would be fine. Good-night Jennie." I truly enjoyed the evening."

"Me, too. Good-night, Joshua."

She waved as he rode away. He looked back but she had already returned inside. It was the best evening of his life, he thought, and with any luck, it would be one of many.

Chapter 12

oshua left in the best of spirits from the Richardson ranch after the interview, but when he arrived at his hotel, he found nothing but smoldering ashes. The hotel and two adjoining buildings had burned to the ground. All his possessions except horse, saddle, revolver and rifle were gone. With nothing left by the time he had arrived at the hotel and no place to go, he rode over to the jail. Matthew was on duty asleep on the cot. Joshua pounded on the door to wake him so he could unbolt the lock.

"I guess you saw what happened to your hotel?"

"Sure did. Any idea what caused it?"

"No. Mark came by and said some people were speculating that maybe someone was trying to get even with you, or chase you out of town."

"Damn, Matthew, don't tell me that. That'll just make me mad and I'll become some ornery cuss and go around shooting people."

"No. You wouldn't do that."

"Probably not, but I really don't want people gunning for me. It can make for a darn miserable stay and I'm not going anywhere. Actually I don't have anywhere else to go."

Matthew laughed. "Yeah, and besides, Mark said you and Miss Peterson kind of got a liking for each other."

"I think Mark is getting ahead of himself."

"So you admit you like her."

"Sure. How could a person not like Miss Peterson? I'm sure you do."

"Okay, I'll drop the subject. I suppose you'll want my cot."

"Actually, yes. Take the rest of the shift off and I'll cover for you here tonight."

"Thanks, Marshal." Matthew left. Joshua lay on the cot and thought about Jennie. She was beginning to consume his thoughts. Could he be falling in love? Surely not this soon, but he did have to admit, he could hardly wait until Sunday.

****

Saturday, Joshua found a haberdashery and purchased two new shirts and a pair of trousers. The fire had motivated him to do things he had previously avoided, like buying new clothes and moving to the jail.

Saturday night was a busy night, mostly contending with drunks. The Bowie knife prisoners were still in the jail, awaiting transfer Tuesday to the Colorado prison, so Joshua just confiscated guns and assorted weapons and if they had money, purchased them a hotel room for the night.

Sunday morning, Joshua was exhausted from Saturday night, but even so, he was anxious for his afternoon with Jennie. She had spent all that time interviewing him and learning every detail of his life, and now it was his turn to find out more about her. Having met her family, he knew a little about what made her the woman she was, but he wanted to learn more...a good deal more.

Joshua arrived at the Richardson ranch shortly before two. Joseph was saddling Jennie's horse. Jennie was still preparing for the ride and she would be down in a few minutes. Margaret was rocking on the front porch and her broad smile showed her pleasure to see Joshua.

"I hope you two have an enjoyable afternoon. I think both of you need a break from your hectic lives and to focus on the personal things in life. Don't tell her I told you, but she hasn't shut up about you since Friday. 'Did you know Joshua did this, or the marshal did that'?"

"Thanks for the insight, Margaret. I'm often unsure about where I stand with Jennie, so sometimes I remain on my heels, afraid to go forward."

"I can see why a courting young man might feel that way. As I've said, she can be a little stuffy, but honestly I think you, above anyone else, are breaking down that barrier and it makes me one happy mother."

"What are you two talking about?" Jennie asked as she came through the door."

"Weather and Cheyenne," Joshua quickly responded.

Margaret smiled. "My, you two make a handsome couple. Pretty snazzy for just going for a ride."

"Mother, you are not going to embarrass me. I'm onto your clever shenanigans."

Margaret winked at Joshua as Jennie headed down the steps. He smiled.

Jennie suggested a ride on a trail that soon led them through increasing foliage and greenery. They found a peaceful meadow with a stream winding through it. The couple dismounted and walked for some distance before they found a nice sized boulder for sitting. They watched their horses leisurely grazing on the green grasses, each gathering their thoughts.

"I wish this land was mine," Jennie remarked. "It's so peaceful."

"The idea is appealing. We'll have to keep that in mind."

Jennie looked at Joshua a bit, taken back by his remark, but she decided not to comment on it. She knew it was a treacherous path to travel and she was not sure she was ready to pursue it.

"I suppose the winters here are pretty bad."

"They are. Lots of snow and sometimes so frigid and long, one thinks it'll never end. Cattle and livestock starve and freeze. The perils of winter around here can be very frightening."

"Maybe I'd better enjoy the heat while I have it. And I think I had better get a nice big stove put in the jail."

Jennie smiled. "I think that would be wise, Marshal."

"So, Jennie, tell me about yourself, your family and your life up to now. I think I deserve a chance to learn about your life. You certainly know a good deal about mine."

Jennie leaned back against the rock, thrusting her body forward, showing its delightful curves, beckoning him to take her in his arms. Instead, he let his eyes feast upon the wonder before him.

Jennie seemed unaware of the thoughts racing through Joshua's mind as she began telling her story. "I mentioned before that Father had a trading post east of where Cheyenne is today. He and Mother originally came from Washington County in western Pennsylvania. They moved to St. Joseph, Missouri sometime after 1840. That's where I was born. Then my uncle and father decided to move to Colorado when gold was first discovered, so about fifteen years ago, we followed a wagon train west. They soon discovered that gold mining was not producing as they thought it would, so they set up a trading post for people passing through heading south and west. That's how we made it here. Father died ten years ago. Mother took all the money she had and bought the ranch. When Joseph married Hallie, they purchased more land and that's how the ranch came about."

"So what about you? How did you become so intelligent?" Joshua inquired.

"Thanks for the compliment. Mother always insisted I have the best schooling that was around. Besides, she was always an avid reader and self-taught scholar. She won't let on, but she knows a lot about a lot."

"What are your dreams, Jennie?"

"Family I guess. The family I have, but also a family of my own. I think that's God's plan and I like it."

"How did you meet Thomas?"

"When he moved here a year ago, Mother was quick to introduce herself and then me to him. It was a natural find I guess with his paper and Mother's interest in anything with publishing."

Jennie sat up. "Here I am, doing all the talking."

"Am I complaining? I want to know everything about you."

Her eyes captured his. "Stop being such a gentleman. You put a woman at a disadvantage."

"I never knew that. I'm glad you told me."

"I gave up one of the secrets of a woman. Shame on me. Now you must give up a man's secret."

"Okay, this is a personal one though." Joshua paused, debating whether to continue. "I have an overwhelming urge to kiss you."

She looked at Joshua with a start. "That's no secret. I knew you wanted to do that a long time ago."

"You did. So what was going through your mind if you knew that?"

She smiled mischievously, "What's taking him so long?"

Joshua's throat tightened. He could hardly speak. "Jennie, I want to hold you and kiss you so much." He reached out and brought her willing body into his arms. Their lips met and fire raced through his body. He knew this was the woman; the soul that he wanted in his life forever.

When he relinquished her lips, she lay contently in his arms. They spoke few words, only shared thoughts of a new love that was blossoming in their lives.
****

Margaret Peterson stood at her second floor bedroom window, watching the return of her daughter and the marshal. She had sensed that a budding romance was growing between the young people, but as she watched them return from their afternoon together, it became obvious that love had seized them. As the young marshal helped Jennie slide from the saddle, they stood close, looking into each other's eyes. They did not kiss, but the slowness of his release of her told more than words could ever reveal.

Margaret smiled, gave forth a sigh and closed the curtains. How marvelous young love can be, she thought, to not only the soul, but also its beauty through an old woman's eyes.

****

Joshua returned to the jail, now called home, after leaving Jennie for the day. Even the bleak jail with its pungent smell could not dampen the exhilaration that filled his heart. He now knew where he wanted his life to go. He had found the key-- Jennie. He was beginning to understand the feeling of his good friend, Jack. Fulfilling one's dreams and desires was not where one was, but who was there beside you.

Monday brought good news, as two U.S. Marshals arrived to take the recently found guilty prisoners south to the Colorado prison. This cleared the jail for any new prisoners Joshua might arrest. He had some additional construction done so that he could have three small cells in back, allowing him to open the door to the jail without fear of attack. He also had a partition and bed put into the outer room to offer some privacy and a little more comfort. He ordered a potbelly stove so that when winter came to Cheyenne, he would not freeze to death.

Joshua began to fulfill a promise he had made to himself. He wrote a letter home and one to Jack Young. He would try to write once a month.

****

Marshal Parker sat at his desk, opened the Rocky Mountain Gazette and looked for the article written about him by Miss Jennie Peterson. It was another moment when he wanted that tobacco pouch. Mark and Matthew were sitting across the room watching him, waiting for his reaction.

Joshua looked up from the paper. "Don't you two have anything to do?"

Mark leaned forward in his chair. "No, sir. The place is swept. There are no prisoners this morning. The log is current. I haven't heard of anybody getting killed last night. No, sir, we are just sitting here waiting for some law-abiding citizen to come along and ask for help and we know the first place they will look will be here. But we'll take care of it if something does arise so you go ahead and read the paper, Marshal."

"Have I mentioned that you two get on my nerves?"

"Yes, sir, you have...and often, I might add."

Joshua got up, went into the back, and sat down on a bunk in one of the cells. He opened the paper. There it was, the first article ever written about him. He would send a copy home and one to Jack. That would impress everyone. Well maybe he had better read it first. Just because Jennie was falling in love with him, she still might put her professional side ahead of love. Would she do that? Read the paper and find out. Moreover, how did he know she was falling in love with him? Go on, Marshal, read the article. Wait, I need a cup of coffee. Joshua went to the front. There was no coffee. "How come there's no coffee? You said you had nothing to do."

"Marshal, you just told us yesterday to only make one pot in the morning and that was all. You said it was too darn hot for coffee after nine."

"Do either of you smoke?"

"No."

"You should." The marshal returned to his cell, picked up the paper and began to read the article.

Article written by Miss Jennie Peterson

   Last month, an U.S. Marshal came to Cheyenne, the first law officer the town has had since its inception. Joshua Parker, a Civil War veteran, has been an U.S. Marshal for two years. His prior service was in Sioux City, Iowa.

   Since his arrival, the marshal has resolved a horse-stealing incident, made numerous arrests and helped convict four assailants for assault and robbery, while handling numerous other disputes.

   The residents of Cheyenne can be thankful for having such a man of the law in their midst. One can be certain that the law-abiding people of Cheyenne can feel better about justice coming to our fine community and those who choose to live outside the law will find their lifestyles severely repressed or obliterated.

The Rocky Mountain Gazette would like to welcome our new citizen, U.S. Marshal Joshua Parker.

Joshua left the cell and came out front. The two young assistants watched Joshua carefully as he headed for the door. He turned to the two men. "I'll be back shortly. I'm going to buy some tobacco." He left. As he stepped into the street, he fought back the urge to jump and click his heels. He decided rolling a cigarette would attract less attention.

Chapter 13

Fall in the new territory of Wyoming ended abruptly in '69. November brought the first Wyoming blizzard of the year. All the warnings received and all the preparations made by Joshua seemed grossly inadequate. It was the blizzard of all blizzards. The temperature plummeted, the wind blew and the snow kept coming...straight across, filling every crack and crevice.

Joshua used the jail cells to store his woodpile. He figured if anybody had been shot in the streets that they would have to lie there until the storm was over. He stockpiled supplies and used his new potbelly stove for heating food and heating his body. In the beginning he would go outside and remove the snowdrifts from his door, but later decided if anyone wanted in, they could remove the drifts themselves.

By the third morning, Joshua was beginning to feel guilty about the dereliction of his duties and began pushing his way into the storm. It did not take long for him realize that he was about the only fool forging their way in this weather. Several of the saloons, whorehouses, and card clubs appeared open and bustling with business, but little else. He decided to check on his horse, and was relieved to find it protected from the elements and enough feed to last a couple of days.

Joshua returned to the jail without guilt and promptly stoked the fire in his stove. He could relax until the storm passed.

Next morning, the snow had stopped falling, and the wind had subsided. The temperatures were still well below freezing, but at least one could be relieved that there was still a sun, although it was highly doubtful whether it still worked.

Normalcy began to appear as people shoveled their way out of their hibernating holes. Wagons rumbled down the street again, street vendors resumed setting up shop, and fresh horse dung was once again littering the streets. Businesses were open and customers were coming out in numbers to restock their supplies. Joshua checked along alleys to make certain no one had frozen to death. He walked to the Gazette and found Thomas busily working. He had a deadline to keep and had already lost a couple days. There was no sign of Jennie, so Joshua decided to check the ranch to ensure everyone had survived the storm. Besides, Joshua had become accustomed to seeing Jennie on a regular basis at either the Gazette or the Richardson ranch, and felt a little deprived.

The snow was deep, and in places very deep with the snow drifts, but steadily, Joshua made his way to the ranch. Jennie and Hallie were near the barn. Jennie was swinging an axe with all her might, trying to break the ice in the water trough. Hallie was tossing hay from the loft with a pitchfork. Joshua quickly dismounted and rushed to their aid. "Where's Joseph?" Joshua asked Jennie as he relieved her of the axe.

"He's out taking count of the cattle and moving them as needed to better feed."

"Where can I be most helpful?"

"I think we are about done here. We have all the animals and chickens around here safe and taken care of for now."

"All right, I'm going out to see if I can help Joseph." He kissed Jennie on the cheek, waved to Hallie, and left.

Joshua passed several longhorn cattle on his way out to find Joseph. Their lean bodies stood hunched and covered with frozen snow and ice. A short distance later, he found Joseph bringing a dozen head of longhorns back towards the other cattle. He waved as Joshua rode up to him.

"Morning, Joshua. What brings you out on such a splendid day?" He grinned.

"Thought I would check on things here at the ranch. The ladies said you were out here and they were finishing up there."

"The storm sure raised Cain around here. I'm still missing a dozen. I'm worried their carcass is under some snowdrift. I found two dead so far. If you'd do me a favor and move these back with the rest, I'll take another pass through the area and see what I can find. There's a draw over there I want to check. They might be protected in there, or they might have gotten covered by a drift."

Joseph rode off, his horse lumbering through the deep snow, while Joshua moved the stray cattle up to the rest of the herd. He waited for some time and then saw Joseph coming with six more cows.

"Found these," he said when he arrived. "Found another carcass. Still missing five. I'm thinking they're a lost cause."

The two men moved the cattle to a windblown slope with some grass exposed and headed back to the house. They found the women huddled around the stove, trying to get warm, but they quickly started administering to two frost bitten toes that Joseph had received while out searching for the cattle.

"I found three dead and there are five missing," Joseph explained to Hallie. "Could have been worse, I guess," he said, turning to Joshua, "but usually we don't start losing too many until January and February. This storm was brutal for November. Might be slim pickings for the rustlers come spring." He laughed.

For five months, there was little relief from the relentless weather. Everyone had grown weary. The ranchers lost more livestock than normal. Shortages became commonplace. Railroad workers had an abundance of idle time. Cheyenne was becoming a haven for drifters. Then finally, the much-needed spring arrived.

After the long winter, spring delivered new life to the countryside, reawakened the people of Cheyenne and renewed the spirit of Joshua Parker. Spring brought one other important aspect to Marshal Parker's life--the town of Cheyenne hired a sheriff, and he in turn hired deputies. The new sheriff assumed control of the jail as one of his new duties. The sheriff hired Mark and Matthew as jailers to ensure continuity of the transfer. With relief from several of the time demanding functions, and often minuscule tasks, Marshal Parker began to assume a greater role of tracking hardened criminals in his territorial jurisdiction.

The disadvantage of his new role meant traveling more and further distances, which greatly reduced his opportunities to court Jennie. Often, the only brightness of the long winter days and nights had been the time he had spent with her. As soon as he left Jennie, he wondered when he could see her again. By spring, he knew that he was helplessly in love with the woman.

On a bright sunny day in early May, when Joshua knew Jennie was at the Gazette, he headed for the Richardson ranch. He wanted to receive permission from Mrs. Peterson to ask for her daughter's hand in marriage. He could no longer talk himself out of making the commitment for life.

Joshua felt relieved when he found Mrs. Peterson rocking on the front porch when he arrived.

"Good afternoon, Joshua."

Joshua nervously strolled up the front steps. "Good afternoon, Mrs. Peterson."

"Mrs. Peterson is not here."

"Pardon?"

"Are you looking for Margaret?"

"Gosh, I'm sorry. Good afternoon, Margaret."

"It's a pleasant surprise to see you, but Jennie is at the Gazette."

"I know she's there. Actually, that's why I'm here." Joshua paced in front of Margaret.

"I see. Yes."

Yes?" Joshua looked at Margaret blankly.

"Yes, you may ask for Jennie's hand in marriage."

"You knew?"

"With your bouncing around here like a bee, I knew something was up and you not wanting Jennie around, it was easy to draw a conclusion."

"Thank you, Margaret."

"For the life of me, I wondered what took you two so long to consider getting hitched. All winter long, you two have been running around here like ducks looking for water. When you planning the big day?"

"I thought maybe August."

"August! What's wrong with July or even June? Next week? August." She shook her head in disbelief. "For the life of me."

"I didn't want to rush Jennie."

Margaret burst into laughter. "I'm thinking Jennie would be happy with yesterday."

"Okay, I'll talk to her."

"Are you going to ask her tonight?"

"I thought I would."

"You better do it soon before you drive yourself and everyone else crazy, prancing around here like a bull moose looking for its cow."

"I'm not that bad." Joshua laughed.

"Look in a mirror sometime."

"Okay. I guess I'll be going. I need to get out of here with a little self pride."

"Sorry, but I need to keep the pressure on or nothing ever happens."

Joshua returned to town feeling excited and beaten. No one could ever match the resourceful wit and cunning of Mrs. Peterson...Margaret. He knew it was best to concede defeat early on and walk away with fewer bruises to the ego.

Awaiting evening, Joshua spent the afternoon walking around town. He had to keep his thoughts away from the big event. For whatever reason, the streets and saloons remained relatively calm for a Saturday. With the jail now under the watchful eye of the sheriff and his deputies, Joshua did not even have the jail to monitor. He decided to take a long ride outside town before preparing himself for the ride that would change his life forever. Of course, that was assuming Jennie said, "yes".

The ride did little to settle Joshua, but at least he kept his bottled up emotions to himself, and did not irritate those around him. Eventually evening came, and Joshua rode to the ranch. Margaret had told Jennie that Joshua would be by so that she could make herself presentable when he came.

Jennie greeted him and they walked to the parlor where everyone was seated. After a few minutes of polite conversation, Joshua and Jennie went for a walk.

"Mother said you had stopped by today."

"Yes, I forgot you were at the newspaper today."

"I always work Saturday."

"Actually, I'm not very good at lying."

"Lying. What do you mean?"

"Jennie, I've been in love with you for some time. You're on my mind all of the time." He held her delicate hand with his sweaty hand. "I think and I hope you feel the same way."

"Of course I do, Joshua."

"Would you marry me, Jennie? I want us to spend the rest of our lives together."

Jennie gasped, placing her hand over her heart and smiled. "I hoped one day those words would come, but for some reason I wasn't expecting them tonight. Yes, Joshua, of course I will marry you."

He brought her into his arms and they kissed, their bodies woven together as one. There would be no change of heart from that moment forward. In that moment, Joshua's future lay out before him like the sunrise of a new day, and it felt good. They returned to the house with the good news to a joyous household. Margaret, although quiet now, sat with a smile that spread from ear to ear.

When Joshua left the ranch that evening, he knew exactly what he must do. He would begin his search the following afternoon.

****

By the following week, the wedding date had been set for Saturday, July 24, 1869, for Miss Jennifer Peterson and Marshal Joshua Parker. Jennie wanted a small simple wedding that would be at the ranch. Joshua agreed with all the details; he just wanted to be married to Jennie.

On Saturday afternoon, two weeks after their announced engagement, Joshua took Jennie on a ride to the broad meadow where they had first kissed. Joshua had remembered how much Jennie loved the meadow and it had become very special to him, also. It had been the beginning of their blossoming romance.

Jennie took a deep breath, and then spoke, her voice so soft and gentle. "I always love this place, but this time of year, everything is green and fresh and the wild flowers are in bloom with all of God's glory."

"I remembered how much you liked it here and I became fond of its beauty too, but mostly because of you." Joshua turned and stared for a moment at the meadow, then turned back to Jennie. "I have a little surprise for you Jennie. An early wedding gift for you."

"You always surprise me. What is it, Joshua?"

"Close your eyes."

Jennie closed her eyes and giggled. "I feel like a little girl."

"Are you ready?"

"Yes. Hurry up. I can't stand the excitement."

"Okay, open them."

Jennie opened her eyes and looked around. "What? Where's the surprise?"

"You're looking at it. Don't you like it?"

Jennie turned to Joshua with a confused look. Joshua was smiling from ear to ear. "I bought this meadow and the surrounding land for you. This is where I want to live the rest of my life with you, Jennie."

"You bought this? This is going to be our home?" Jennie jumped to her feet and began dancing round and round until she staggered with dizziness. She stopped and ran to Joshua, who had been watching her with delight. "I love you," she hollered, throwing her arms around his neck. "Thank you, my darling. This is the most wonderful gift you or anyone could ever give me." She turned and gazed out over her new home-to-be. "I want to change our wedding plans." She turned to Joshua. "I want to have our wedding here in the meadow, our new home."

Chapter 14

$\mathcal{T}$he word spread about the new home that Joshua and Jennie would have after their wedding. The problem was that there was no house. Each Sunday afternoon, family and friends arrived at the meadow and soon a house began to take shape, and then a barn. By mid-July, with just over a week before the wedding, the meadow had a house, a barn, and a corral. The newlyweds would have a home to spend their wedding night.

Everything was set for the wedding when Joshua received word that a horse thief and murderer by the name of Hiram Willis was held up in a small settlement of Elk Springs just inside the Nebraska border. Joshua had 8 days until the wedding. It was a two-day ride out and two-day ride back.

Joshua stopped by to tell Jennie his plans. After pleasantries with the family, the young couple strolled through the garden. Jennie's eyes never left Joshua's solemn face.

"What's wrong, Joshua? I know something is bothering you."

"I have to go to Nebraska tomorrow. I should only be gone four or five days. I just don't want you worrying about me not getting back for the wedding."

"How dangerous is the trip? I know I shouldn't ask. Let me rephrase. Be careful and come back to me. We can change the wedding date, but I only have one man that I love."

"I'll be careful. I promise. Now that I've found happiness with you, I have all the reason in the world to be careful."

"Good. I love you so much, Joshua and I can't help worrying about you."

"Maybe I should give up being marshal."

"No. That's who you are. I would never want you regretting such a thing because of me. I'll have to learn to be brave."

"We can talk another time about our future. I just want you to be happy."

"I am, Joshua. You have no idea how happy I am." She reached up and kissed him. He pulled her tightly to him in a long embrace.

As Joshua rode away that evening, Jennie wiped the tears from her cheek. "Please, Joshua, be careful and come home to me."

The marshal had received word about Hiram Willis from an old timer named Charlie, who had lived in Elk Springs. The night before he left, Joshua found Charlie. Together they sketched a map of the settlement, and identified where Hiram lived and hung out in town. Charlie also made Marshal Parker aware that the small town had become a haven for those outside the law or wanted to be in hiding for some reason. To snatch one from amongst their midst would be like taking a hornet from its nest without upsetting the whole nest.

Joshua left early the next morning, taking an extra horse with him. He knew he might not have time to find a horse for his prisoner on their escape. He brought an extra ammo belt for his Colt .45 and one for his rimfire rifle. Even with all the ammo, it was his intention not to fire a shot, but bring his prisoner out without another person in town knowing what had happened.

Joshua arrived outside of Elk Springs as planned on the evening of the second day. He found an isolated bluff at the edge of town and compared the layout of the town to his map, making sure there were no mistakes on the map. He looked at the sketch of his intended prisoner, and then waited as darkness began to spread over the settlement.

In the evening, most of the lights and activity of the town were centered in a one block area on the main street. The marshal located the hotel where Hiram stayed, based on the information he had received from Charlie. It was located at the nearest end of

Main Street. He would determine if Hiram was in the hotel before beginning his search through town. The task would be difficult without arousing any suspicion. The prevailing problem that the marshal faced, he did not know who would be his enemy and who would look the other way. Unfortunately, the problem was significant and his life would depend on the unresolved answer.

The marshal left his extra horse outside of town. He rode into town with no fanfare, and got a room at the same hotel where Hiram was staying. He rented his room with no apparent suspicion. He spent a half hour in his room, and then returned downstairs to the clerk.

"Any place still open where I can get a bite to eat?" Joshua asked.

"Yeah, the grub house usually stays open late for the drunks. Food not too good, but it's filling."

"I heard an old riding acquaintance was here in Elk Springs. You ever heard of Hiram Willis?"

"Hiram? Yeah, he was around. Wasn't paying his bill, so I kicked him out. I was a little worried he might come back and shoot up the place including me, but I haven't seen him since he left."

"How long ago was that?"

"Ah, let's see. Um, day before yesterday."

"Any idea where he would go?"

"Why you so interested in a no count like him?"

"To be honest, he owes me money, too."

The clerk smiled. "He's a worthless piece of life, that's for sure. He used to hang out at the *Dead Man Saloon*. If he wasn't paying up there, they probably up and killed him. They're a rugged bunch down there. You go in there you might be finding trouble."

"Thanks for the warning. If I find Hiram, I'll see if I can get your money, too."

"Be mighty appreciative. My boss is never too happy when I let a no count leave me hanging."

"Have a good evening," Joshua hesitated waiting for a name.

"Carl."

"Have a good evening, Carl."

"The marshal headed for the Grub House to fill his hunger and perhaps find more information on Willis. The clerk was not a concern for the marshal.

The marshal passed the Dead Man Saloon on the way to the Grub House. From the open door, the saloon was not much more than a small room. There was a short bar some six feet long and a half dozen tables. The room looked crowded as the marshal slowed to look inside. He was unable to determine if Willis was there.

When Joshua entered the Grub House, he immediately knew he had made a mistake. The place was dimly lit, probably to hide the filth. A couple drunks were the only occupants besides a cook and waiter, which was one and the same. Joshua ordered some beans and salted pork, thinking it could not be ruined too badly, but he was wrong. The clerk had been right about the food. He was hungry and forced himself to finish eating, passed on a second cup of blackened something they called coffee, and left. The meal was probably going to be the most dangerous part of his trip. If he lived through it, and he still was not sure he would, he could survive anything.

The moon had drifted behind some clouds, leaving the street very black, as the marshal stood in front of the Grub House, checking the street for people and other places open for business. He could see another saloon about six doors further down the street. He decided he would check this one first. It might be easier to verify if Willis was there.

The place was a little larger than the other saloon, but it too, was a dismal place. About a dozen patrons were present along with a bartender who was drying glasses behind the bar. At least the glasses received attention with a wash was the first thought that came to Joshua. He felt a little more comfortable about the place when he noticed half the customers did not wear

104

gun belts. He moved to the end of the bar where he could keep the door and all the patrons in full view. He received a few casual glances, but no one seemed particularly interested in him. He ordered a beer and slowly sipped from the mug. Only one person even resembled the sketch he had of Hiram Willis but from the man's actions, looks, and carrying no visible weapon, Joshua concluded, he would not be someone who would be hiding from the law. The bartender stood nearby watching Joshua.

"You looking for somebody?" he asked.

"Not particularly," the marshal replied. "I get around quite a bit and I was just looking for any familiar faces to chaw about old times."

"And what would old times be?"

"Trail driving out of Texas and east of here in Nebraska and Kansas."

"Most of the boys in here live in these parts. I think the Dead Man down the street is what you're looking for. They got plenty of drifters there."

"They bother you up here?"

"Not much. I think most of them would rather not have their whereabouts known, so they stay to themselves."

"I know a few like that," Joshua said, smiling. Joshua finished his beer. "I think I'll turn in for the night."

The bartender nodded and Joshua left. If Hiram Willis were still in town, he would most likely be at the Dead Man Saloon. He headed back down the street, first passing the Grub House. The smell and thought churned his stomach. He came upon the Dead Man Saloon. Dangerous or not, he had to go inside. Either he would find Hiram there or his trip would prove wasted.

The marshal's biggest concern entering the saloon was the crowded environment that would leave his backside exposed and the inability to draw and fire his revolver. He would be more vulnerable than he would normally allow himself. He would have a quick beer, while checking the saloon for Willis, then leave. He hoped no one would recognize him from passing through

Cheyenne. Other than ordering a beer from the bartender, he spoke to no one and there was little attention given to him. He presumed drifters passed through town on a regular basis and everyone kept to their own business. Joshua spotted a drifter sitting with two other men that he believed could be Hiram Willis. He took his beer and moved towards a poker game at the next table, allowing Joshua to have a better look at the man in question. The man had a several day growth on his face that made it difficult to compare him to the sketch. He watched the game for one hand, but then became concerned when one of the players in the poker game began to watch him as though he was somehow affecting the game. Joshua moved back and began to move along the table past his suspected fugitive. He spoke to a nearby man.

"Hey, is your name Hiram," Joshua paused. The suspect showed no interest.

"No. Why do you care?"

"You sort of look like a cowboy I rode with a couple years back. Sorry I bothered you."

The man grunted and the suspect still showed no interest. Joshua finished his beer and left. Other than having a firsthand observation of the town perhaps for another time, his trip had produced nothing. He returned to his room and spent a restless, anxious night. He had a concern that someone may have recognized him or was not happy with his snooping around.

When morning arrived, Joshua left in a hurry. He wanted to be gone before anyone knew it. He picked up his second horse he had hidden outside of town and headed west for Cheyenne. He had not found his target, but he had left town in an undamaged body. That had to be worth something.

Joshua was about five miles out of Elk Springs near the Wyoming border when a burning sensation hit his shoulder just as rifle fire rang out. Joshua slumped and tried to stay in the saddle, but after a quarter mile, he fell to the ground. He rolled to some brush for cover and managed to pull his revolver. His intuition had been right. Somebody had considered him trouble. He had been wrong about when they would try to take him out.

Somebody wanted him dead. He hoped they were happy with their shot and would not come looking for him. He did not feel like a hide and seek gun battle right now. His shoulder was throbbing with pain and the fall had not done his body any favors. He was also aware he was losing blood and it would not be long before he might lose consciousness unless he could attend to his gunshot wound.

For a moment, his mind turned to Jennie and her concern for his well-being. He had promised her his safe return. He had not kept that promise, but he was determined to survive his setback and return to her. He had a wedding in five days.

The marshal could hear hoof beats approaching. He dropped low behind a bush. The hoof beats slowed then resumed. Joshua was uncertain whether the rider had been friend or foe, but he was in no position to challenge him. He laid there quietly for some time. The bleeding had slowed with him at rest. He hoped the unknown rider had not found his horses and taken them. The sun became warmer as it moved higher in the sky. With the blood loss and the hot sun, Joshua began to lose consciousness.

The marshal was uncertain how much time had passed when he heard a rustling sound coming closer. He shook the drowsiness from his head and had his revolver raised and cocked, ready to use. He could not believe what he was seeing. His bay had never looked as good as when his head appeared over the brush. The second horse was nearby, having followed the bay back to his rider. Joshua believed the gunshot had made a clean hit and had passed through his body. He found an extra shirt in his saddlebag and bandaged his wound as well as possible. He needed to get started. He had remembered a small cow town probably ten miles away. He hoped to reach it before nightfall and perhaps get some help for his wound.

Joshua had thought he might encounter travelers along the road, but none came. Several times, he started to slip and his loyal horse sensing a problem with its rider would stop and allow Joshua to regain his composure in the saddle. The sun was beginning to set after the long daylight June day when Joshua spotted a building in the distance. As he rode up to the ranch house, a man with a rifle came out and a woman and three children followed.

"I was shot some ten miles back and I was wondering if I could get some mending done. I won't bother you. I'm Marshal Parker."

The man set down his rifle and hurried to help the marshal from his horse. He quickly helped Joshua inside and lay him on a blanket on the floor near the hearth. The husband and wife immediately began heating water and tearing rags. "We'll fix you up in no time, Marshal. Looks like you took a pretty good hit."

The man and woman worked diligently on him for the next half hour. "Better get him something to eat, Emma. We need to get some strength back into him. Ten miles you said. That's a long ride when you're smarting."

"Many times I thought I had reached the end. Thanks for taking me in."

"A real pleasure, Marshal, besides you can't just leave somebody to die. My name is Hal Brandon."

Joshua had some broth and bread and then fell into a sleep.

The daylight shining through the window awakened him. The woman was standing at the kitchen counter when Joshua called to her. "Ma'am, what time is it?"

She turned and smiled. "Near noon. You really were out of it."

"I have to try and get going. I'm getting married Saturday."

"Where you getting married?"

"Cheyenne."

"Could be a problem for you. You slept all day yesterday. This is the second day."

"What day is it? I'm confused."

"I think Tuesday, but you're in no condition to travel for at least two days."

Joshua started to get up, but fell back onto the blanket. His head spun. "I can't see."

"You're weak, Marshal. You need to lie there. Besides you get up and start moving, you're going to open up that wound again and start bleeding and next time it might well kill you. You need some venison soup I've made. Get some strength back in you so you can get on back to your girl and get married. She might want you in good shape on your wedding night, Marshal." She laughed. "She just might you know."

The marshal ate some soup, and then feeling exhausted, decided to lie down. He immediately went to sleep. When he awakened, it was still daylight. He was feeling a little better. He figured he would leave tomorrow. That would be Wednesday. The man came over to him.

"You sure are getting your rest. Slept another whole day."

"What! What day is it?"

"Late Wednesday afternoon. Emma says you're getting hitched Saturday. I'm thinking the good Lord doesn't want you to get married, Marshal. You're a couple hard days ride from here and that's if you're feeling a might better than you are, Marshal."

Joshua knew the Hal was right. In his condition, he would never make it on time if he made it at all.

Thursday morning, Joshua was feeling better, but when he tried to stand up, he staggered to a nearby chair and fell exhausted into it. If he did not leave now he would never make it to the wedding...his wedding.

That evening, Joshua sat helplessly thinking about what he had done to Jennie. Then an idea came to him...almost a slap in the face. He looked at the farmer across from him. "How far away are the train tracks?"

"About five miles. There's a station at Sandbar, some ten miles from here. You ain't thinking about riding that contraption are you?"

"Yeah I am. It can get me from here to Cheyenne lickety-split."
****

At daybreak Friday morning, Hal Brandon hitched up his buckboard, loaded the marshal in the back and headed out for Sandbar. They arrived three hours later. It was eight and the train was due in around noon, but the agent assured Joshua that it was never on time. He could expect it sometime in the afternoon. The train arrived at four and left at five. It would take six or seven hours with stops...not exactly lickety-split, but it sure beat riding a horse. There might not be any sleep, but God willing, he would make it to his wedding.

Joshua thanked Hal and as the train pulled away from the station; he waved to a bewildered man, who was shaking his head in disbelief at the iron contraption rolling down the tracks.

The train rumbled slowly up the tracks towards Cheyenne. Joshua leaned back and felt relaxed as he headed toward his Jennie waiting for him to hold her in his arms. Suddenly the train ground to a halt. Word came down through the cars that the tracks were damaged. A repair crew would come in the morning. The train would not arrive in Cheyenne until after noon tomorrow at best.

Joshua clutched his face in his hands. He would be late for his wedding. He sat up with a start. The conductor was passing through the car.

"Sir," Joshua clamored.

"Yes."

"How far are we from Cheyenne?"

"Perhaps six miles."

"How far from the tracks to the road into Cheyenne?"

"About a mile up the tracks, we cross the road."

"I need to get my horses off the train. I have my wedding I need to be at tomorrow."

Chapter 15

$\mathcal{J}$oshua had to proceed very slowly on horseback along the railroad tracks. Normally he would have led his horse until he reached the road, but his physical condition made it impossible. He hoped to be in Cheyenne by sunup. It would give him plenty of time to ready himself for the wedding. He would hate showing at the altar in his current physical condition, although if necessary, he would. He would not miss the wedding and the beginning of his future with Jennie. He would like to catch a little sleep, too, but he feared lying down. He might sleep right on through another day.

The stars glittered brightly in the sky, so Joshua assumed it would be a pleasant sunny day for the wedding. At least something was going right. He assumed Jennie and everyone else was fretting his whereabouts, not only for the wedding, but if he was all right. He hated doing this to Jennie. He knew how much she worried about him. He once again questioned his selfish decision to continue as marshal. He knew she would rather he be a rancher like Joseph, but that was why he ran from Iowa. Jennie understood that, and she placed his happiness ahead of her desires. Did he have the right to subject her to his reckless and dangerous lifestyle?

As the sun cracked the horizon, Joshua was riding down 19th street of Cheyenne. He had arrived back in time to clean up, get the bandages on his wound changed, let everyone know he was back in town, and get married. He had kept his word...barely.

First, Joshua rode by the jail, hoping to find Mark or Matthew on duty. He wanted to get the word out he was back. When Joshua walked in, Mark stood up, his mouth hanging open.

"Morning, Mark. You act like you've seen a ghost."

"By golly, I think I'm looking at one. Have you looked at yourself lately? What happened, Marshal?"

"I ran into some problems, but I'm back and ready to get married."

"Does Jennie know you're back?"

"No. You're the first to know. I was hoping you could pass the word to the ranch that I'm back."

"Sure. They're going to be mighty happy to get the news. My relief will be here shortly."

"Thanks. I need to start getting ready. I hope Doc is in town to mend my wounds. I wouldn't want to make my bride do it before we head down the aisle."

Mark laughed. "I reckon that wouldn't be right, Marshal. What do you want me to tell them?"

"I'm back. You had better warn them I was shot, but that I'm okay and I'm getting ready for the wedding. Don't make it sound too bad. You know how I look, but I hope in a few hours, I'll look better. Okay?"

"Okay, Marshal. I'm glad you're back. We were all worried."

Joshua headed to his room. He would prepare his wardrobe, and then track down Doc. He had to keep moving. If he closed his eyes for one minute, he might never open them for a week. Once he made it through the wedding, he could sleep then. No, he couldn't. It was his wedding night. Maybe lying in bed with Jennie would revitalize his weary body.

Joshua carefully laid out his clothing that he would wear. There was a knock at the door. Thomas stood at the door with Doc.

"How'd you know?"

"Get in there and sit down," Thomas said with authority. "Mark and Matthew are like two Paul Reveres out there. We were beginning to think we had lost you. You're not looking good, Joshua. Can we save him, Doc?"

"Only if I do my best, but who is going to save him from himself? Whoever dressed your wound probably saved your life. They cleaned it up and helped stop the bleeding. You came mighty close to packing it in, Marshal...mighty close. Are you sure you're up to today?"

"I have no choice. I made a promise to the one I love and I'm damn well going to keep that promise."

The doctor turned to Thomas. "Get him some cooked liver. We've got to get him nourished." Doc looked back at Joshua. "When's the last time you've eaten? You can't do this to your body and expect any good from it. I'm going to tell Jennie to treat you like a six-year-old child, because that's the way you're acting. You could still die. You're not through this yet, Marshal. Then what favor would you be doing for Jennie?"

The doctor had struck a chord with Joshua. He had been so intent on just the wedding that he had ignored any consequences beyond today.

Over the next two hours, Joshua cleaned up, dressed and choked down some liver under the watchful eye of the doctor. Time was drawing near to leave for the ranch. The decision was made, without Joshua's input that Joshua would ride to the ranch with Thomas and his wife in the buggy, with Joshua's horses tied to the back. He needed to conserve all his energy.

With everything happening over the previous days and hours, Joshua had little time to be nervous about the wedding. His only concern had been whether he would make it to the wedding. The ride to the ranch now gave him ample opportunity to become nervous. The nervousness that should have been there for the last eight days suddenly came roaring through his mind and body like demons after a lost soul.

"Are you all right, Joshua? You're looking peaked," Thomas called out from the front.

"A little nervous, I guess. I'll be fine," he lied.

When they arrived at the ranch, Joshua was taken to the edge of the garden and seated. "We have about half an hour yet," Joseph commented, hurrying to Joshua's side. "Sit here and rest. Glad to see you here even though you're not in the best shape."

"Is Jennie upset with me?"

"She's been upset for a couple days in all honesty. Not with you though. She's been worried sick. She broke down and cried for half an hour when she found out you were back. She wanted to see you when you arrived, but Margaret said absolutely not and risk bad luck for the marriage. She said it would make that moment all the more special when you two met at the altar."

Mark came running up with a glass of water. "Here's some water, Marshal. It'll help wash down the liver that's coming in a second."

Joshua looked up. "I'm not eating any more liver."

Mark began to laugh. "The word is out about you and the liver. Everybody is enjoying the story immensely.

"I swear, Mark, some day I'm going to get even with you."

"You learned how to roll that cigarette yet? It might be a good time to have one." Mark walked off laughing boisterously.

Joseph put his hand on Joshua's shoulder. They're signaling us it's time. Shall we take our place?"

Joshua nodded. "Were you nervous when you got married, Joseph?'

"Definitely. I think it's a requirement of the groom."

The crowd was not large, but it felt like a thousand eyes were on him as he and Joseph made their way to the altar. Everything looked beautiful. Jennie had put forth such an effort for their wedding and he had just shown up...barely and in poor condition. He would have to do better in their marriage...much better.

114

Joshua watched Mrs. Peterson...Margaret being escorted to her seat. Then Hallie came down the aisle and stood across from him. She smiled at Joshua. He turned and watched Thomas bring Jennie down the aisle towards him. She looked so beautiful and her radiance emitted a glow of love and happiness.

Jennie came to him and her arm slid into his. The moment he had waited for had arrived, giving him an exhilarated feeling that he had never felt or imagined. The vows came with a commitment of love as one for all eternity. Each word filled their hearts with the love of the other, and then the minister said the words that two people in love receive with great joy, "I now pronounce you husband and wife. You may now kiss the bride."

Their lips met in the passion of love, and then Jennie's lips felt empty, her arms felt empty. Her new husband was slumped motionless at her feet. She screamed, "Joshua!"

Chapter 16

"Joshua. Joshua. He's coming to. Joshua."

Joshua's eyes opened to blurred figures hovered above him. All he could distinguish was Jennie's voice. "What happened?" he mumbled.

"Jennie's kiss knocked you out," a voice called out and laughter followed.

Slowly his vision returned and Jennie's soft, sweet face stared down at him. "I'm sorry, Jennie."

"Don't be," Jennie whispered. "Don't be. I love you for trying after all you've been through." She bent and kissed his lips, then his cheeks, forehead and back to his lips. "We're married now. I could never be happier."

"Me, too. I just wanted it to be perfect."

"It was."

"Where am I?"

"In our bed." She smiled.

"But I never got to carry you over the threshold."

"We'll have plenty of opportunities for that. Rest."

"No." He sat up and fell back. "Wow, feeling dizzy."

"Rest for awhile, and then maybe you'll feel like getting up."

"Don't let me sleep through the party. Wake me within the hour. Promise?"

"I promise. No more than an hour."

"I want to see you more in your wedding dress. You look like a grand princess."

Jennie put her fingertips to his lips, then his eyelids. "Rest."

As Jennie promised, she awakened Joshua in an hour. After sitting up for several minutes, they made their way outside to the reception.

"You did a wonderful job making everything so perfect, Jennie," Joshua said gazing at all the decorations.

"You gave me the setting, Joshua. I love our new home."

Joshua sat in a chair, while Jennie stood next to him. Everyone came by congratulating them.

Later in the evening after all were gone, the newlyweds sat on the sofa holding hands. Jennie's eyes glistened with happiness. "Are you happy, Joshua? I mean really happy like I am?"

"I am, Jennie. This is by far the happiest day of my life. The first time I kissed you here in the meadow is the second happiest day. Each day I've spent with you has been wonderful. My life is all about you, Jennie, and it will never change. I promise."

They kissed and it lingered for some time. Jennie stood. "I know you said you wanted to see me in my wedding dress, but I think it's time you see me in something else."

"What is it?"

Jennie gave him a teasing kiss, smiled and left the room. She giggled from embarrassment as she dressed in her wedding night evening attire. She combed out her hair and stared in the mirror. She took a deep breath. "Here goes," she whispered and started for the living room to her anxious husband.

She stepped in front of the sofa. "Well, do you..." She blinked and her mouth fell open. Her new husband was sound asleep. She smiled and covered him with a blanket, pulled off his

boots, and laid his legs up on the couch. She gently kissed him. "Another time, my darling."
****

Joshua awakened to bright sunlight, and the sound and smell of frying bacon. Realizing he had fallen asleep on his wedding night, he started to jump up, but fell back from the sharp pain. At a more careful pace, he rose and headed into the kitchen. Leaning against the kitchen door, he watched Jennie, with all her beauty, standing at the stove. How lucky, he thought, I have this view for the rest of my life. He finally spoke, "Good morning, my darling."

She turned. "Good morning, darling. How are you feeling?"

"Embarrassed. I'm so sorry about last night." The newlyweds came together and kissed. "I'll make it up to you," he said meekly.

"I know you will. I'm glad you were able to get a good night's rest. I worry about you."

They kissed again. Jennie jerked away. "My bacon!" She hurried back to the stove.

Joshua watched her. It was too perfect. "Next Sunday, let's go to church. I've got a lot of thanking to do and it's been a long time...a very long time."

Jennie placed their breakfast on the table. "Of course. Mother will be happy to hear that."

"She probably thought you were marrying a heathen."

"Not at all, just a young man trying to be independent and doing it all on his own."

They laughed, held hands and said a prayer.
****

The newness and bliss of their first days of marriage showed no signs of wearing off. In fact, quite the opposite was happening as Joshua's health improved.

After two months, reality began to set in. Elk Springs was troubling to him. First, he did not find Hiram Willis. Charlie, who had originally given Joshua the information, was in disbelief that Hiram was not there. The most troubling was that somebody had tried to kill him as he left town. He had given no one any indication he was the law. None of them he talked to seemed interested who he was or bright enough to figure it out. Yet somebody shot him.

Joshua felt the need to return. A blatant sore continued to fester in his territory and the law needed to eliminate it. He had taken an oath to uphold the law of the land to the best of his ability. Jennie urged him to wait until he could have the adequate force to clean the town, but Joshua knew that the force would never come. It was too remote and too far west for the political arm of Lincoln to reach that far, and to the Wyoming politicians, it was Nebraska. If Joshua did not react, then there would be no one to respond to the needs of the town.

Joshua constantly reviewed the wanted posters sent to his territory. Occasionally he would identify someone from the posters, but he never found anyone on the poster that he remembered from that night in Elk Springs. He was beginning to feel restless, spending most of his time assisting the sheriff in Cheyenne.

Joshua finally made the decision to return to Elk Springs. This time he would go as Marshal Parker. If someone had tried to kill him, at least one person knew him as a marshal and it seemed senseless to return undercover. He had to be extremely careful, but the only way to get rid of the hornet's nest in his territory was to disrupt it. He believed good folks who lived in fear of their town would eventually leave it as Charlie had done.

This time he would have to spend a few days in Elk Springs. The days leading up to his trip were solemn. Jennie tried to remain cheerful, but Joshua could read the fear in her eyes. They spent a great deal of time going for quiet walks, or in the evening, they would cuddle on the sofa in front of the fire.

When the morning came for his departure, Joshua held Jennie for several minutes before mounting his bay. Jennie did not cry, but tears filled her eyes. He rode away, often looking back and waving. Jennie walked down the lane following him until he disappeared from sight.

Jennie was such a gentle and tender loving woman, yet her inner strength was as durable and mighty as a mountain. Joshua wondered how he deserved to receive such a blessing, to have Jennie as his lifetime partner.

****

Jennie watched Joshua disappear from view and returned to the house. She had spent much of her life watching a loved one ride away. Her father, constantly traveling, would leave the three females to operate the trading post. Mother always remained strong in front of the girls, but Jennie had seen her mother cry silently when she thought she was alone. Jennie knew there was always danger in the isolated outpost. Many times, she watched her mother chase some wandering heathen away with the shotgun pointed at his face. Other times Indians would prowl around the outpost and Mother would leave something outside, hoping to appease them while she, with her two young girls, remained barricaded inside. She had learned to live with loneliness, but the fear always remained that a loved one would not return.

Jennie cleaned up the breakfast dishes and walked to the rock where she and Joshua first kissed. She knew then he was a marshal that would be performing dangerous duties and would spend a considerable time away from home. She had hesitated falling in love with him because of that, but she fell in love anyway. She could not have stopped falling in love with Joshua Parker any more than she could have stopped a train with her bare hands. Nevertheless, with all her fears and anxieties for the well-being of her man, she would not want her life any other way. She loved him and for good reasons; the most important, he loved her back. Moreover, with all the outward toughness that he showed as marshal, he was gentle, kind and caring toward her.

Jennie cried alone, sitting on the rock, and recalling the special memories. She wrapped her arms around herself and pretended he was with her. She had to remain brave for Joshua.

****

Joshua rode into Elk Springs with bolstered confidence. Any sign of fear would only endanger his well-being. He arrived late afternoon. The streets were relatively empty. Joshua presumed most folks had gone home for the day with suppertime approaching and it was still a little early for the nightlife of the wilder side. He checked into the same hotel where he had stayed on his prior visit. The same clerk, Carl, was there and looked surprised when he saw Joshua's badge. Joshua felt assured Carl had not sent the message to his attempted killer.

"I guess I know why you were looking for Hiram the last time you were here, Marshal."

"Have you seen him since?"

"No. I heard he moved on south into Colorado. Only hearsay though."

"Heard anything about somebody taking a shot at me the last time I left?"

"No. I never heard anything like that. You think it was Hiram?"

"At the moment, I have no idea, but I'd like to find out. It might make me feel a little better about my health."

"If I hear anything I'll let you know. It's good seeing the law around here. It's getting a little uncomfortable for decent folks. I don't particularly know anything about those that's moved in here, but you know they're not worth a lick of salt."

Joshua dropped his belongings in his room and found a stable recommended by Carl for his horse. He located an eatery that proved far better than the Grub House. He returned to his room for the night. He tried to make himself visible enough that the word had spread about a marshal in town. He placed a chair to the door to ensure an extra level of safety while he slept.

In the morning, the marshal ate breakfast, and then moseyed about town making his presence known to the merchants. During the day, the town appeared almost as normal as other small communities did, except there seemed to be fewer people about doing business and friendliness was not in abundance. There were more drifters and less-desirables hanging around than you would find in most small towns. Joshua hoped he could change that. He needed to get the cooperation of the local good folks. It was not a job one man could do alone. Joshua had found help for a seemingly hopeless task in Cheyenne, and he needed that same help here.

The marshal started by introducing himself to some of the merchants and made mental notes as to which ones he felt might offer assistance. He found a telegraph office to send a telegram to Jennie and the officials in Lincoln if needed. The marshal also found two abandoned buildings for a jail if he made any arrests.

Carl at the hotel, offered names of those who would help unless they were too frightened. "People in these parts are afraid, Marshal. They fear payback if they create any problems with the riffraff around here. I think you'll also find that most people know very little about the ones who have moved into their town, just that they're no good."

"That's my concern if I just run some of them out of town. They'd come back as soon as I left and would probably take it out on the fine citizens around here. I need to get the worst jailed, convicted and sent off to prison or if need be, put them six feet under. If I can rid the town of the worst, the others might leave on their own. Of course, they'll go somewhere else, but at least it'll relieve the people here. If I can identify the worst and determine why they're on the run, and from where, I can go after them. What I might need from the folks here is a posse to keep the others at bay, while I handle the few."

"It might be difficult, but I think some may help. I'll see what I can do, Marshal. We're all sick and tired of the way it is now."

That evening Joshua studied each of the two dozen posters he had brought with him. The men were wanted for bank robberies, train robberies, cattle rustling, and murder. Each was dangerous; each could end the marshal's life.

Next morning, the marshal strolled around town speaking to the merchants and townsfolk. He hoped to build confidence in the people and it gave him a chance to look more closely at the

122

drifters hanging out around town. On his morning rounds, he identified two of them and on his return to the hotel confirmed them with the picture on the poster. Zack Rollins--murder and John Brassard--train robbery.

The fourth day in Elk Springs, Joshua sent a telegram to Jennie to let her know he was fine and not in any danger and everything was going as planned. That evening, Carl informed him that several citizens had repaired and reinforced one of the buildings to serve as a jail. There was still a question whether any of the townspeople would be willing to serve on a posse to assist the marshal in a time of need. Joshua decided he could wait no longer. He would look for Rollins and Brassard in the morning and with some luck, arrest them. He wanted to hopefully do it during daylight hours when more citizens would be about town, would see the arrests, and would encourage them to get involved.

At daylight on day five, the marshal began his sweep of the street looking for a familiar face from his posters. The first he found was John Brassard wanted for train robbery. The marshal noticed Brassard in the Grub House and waited for him to come outside. As he stepped outside, the marshal stepped behind him with revolver drawn, "This is Marshal Parker and you're under arrest. Drop your gun belt slowly, John Brassard." The outlaw, taken by surprise, offered no resistance, and he was immediately taken to the makeshift jail.

The marshal knew that this would be his last surprise arrest. Word would spread quickly among the fugitives.

Marshal Parker immediately notified the Nebraska authorities of his arrest and informed them that there may be more. He needed help to have the prisoners escorted east to the prison in Lincoln.

Joshua's problems began late that afternoon. He was standing in the doorway of the general store when a ringing voice called out to him. "Marshal, come out into the street."

The marshal saw a gunslinger standing in the middle of the street waiting for him. Ambush! His immediate sense told him there were more. His eyes scanned the street. At least two

123

more waited in the shadows on the walk across the street, and he caught a glimpse of the reflection of a gun barrel from the stairway leading to the whorehouse. The outlaws had banded together, the one thing Joshua did not want to happen. He laid out a scenario. He could not step out into the street. He focused on the gunman in the stairwell. From his position, he could move to a vantage point behind the pole and take a shot with his rifle, immediately drop and roll down the steps that gave way to the alley. From behind the steps, he would go after the two across the street and then worry about the lone gunman in the street. His chances were slim that he could get all four men, and he wondered if there may be others hiding from view.

"What do you want the marshal for?" Joshua called out.

"I think we need to settle some things, Marshal."

Without hesitation, Joshua moved quickly towards the pole. He had a good view of the man on the stairs. His eyes had already lined up the target before he had raised his rifle. The air was still, making it ideal for firing with accuracy. With precision quickness, he raised his rifle and fired. The man hollered and fell forward rolling down the stairs. Joshua dove for the stairs as gunfire rang out around him. He rolled down the steps and immediately had his rifle aimed where the two men across the street had been waiting. He saw the one running for cover and fired. The outlaw fell to the boardwalk. He was not dead but temporarily out of action. The second man across the street had disappeared, so Joshua turned his attention to the dazed man still standing in the street. Joshua fired and he fell to the ground, his revolver never leaving the holster. The wounded outlaw across the street was trying to crawl to safety. Joshua fired again and he lay motionless. He still had at least one gunslinger unaccounted for on the streets. It was about that time when a sense of relief swept through him. The missing outlaw came out from the alley with his hands up and two of the local men behind him with their revolvers drawn. The townsfolk were taking their town back. Joshua knew his job here would be much easier going forward.

All they needed was for someone to take the lead and others would follow.

Before Joshua left the next day, he had made two more arrests. He had also received word from Lincoln that someone would be sent to pick up the wanted men.

Joshua immediately telegraphed Cheyenne and told Jennie he was safe and was coming home. She had worried long enough.

Chapter 17

Three Years Later

Jennie waited nervously for Joshua to return. It was nothing new for her. Over the last three years she had waited for her husband's return on trips that she knew each time could be his last. She knew some were more dangerous than others were, but something could go wrong on any of the trips, and it could mean death for Joshua. Today, the return from his trip meant more than usual. She was pregnant. She had waited a week to tell him as the excitement and nervousness kept building. She knew Joshua would be pleased. They had discussed having children for two years, but for whatever reason, God chose to have them wait. Now the time had arrived.

Jennie began her morning chores, which included feeding their chickens, pigs, horses, and half dozen cows of which two needed milking. She enjoyed her daily routine. She still occasionally worked for the newspaper, but she spent most of her time at the ranch. She loved her home. Each time she left it, she could hardly wait to return to its serene, peaceful beauty. She only wished Joshua could spend more time with her at their home. He always seemed to hate leaving, and she prayed that one day he could and would stay there with her. They had discussed adding more land and someday he might be ready to leave the marshal service. Jennie would not press him on it. She would wait until he was ready.

Later that afternoon, Jennie sat on the front porch sipping a cool glass of tea when a familiar rider approached the house.

"Joshua," she shouted and ran to greet him.

He slid from his horse and she embraced him with all her strength. "I love coming home to you," he said, kissing her repeatedly about the face. "It makes all those lonely days almost worth it."

"I always miss you so much, Joshua. You are my gallant hero returning to me."

"And, I returning to my beautiful princess."

"How was your trip?"

"Without incident. Prisoners delivered as promised. It helps with the new prison in Laramie. I just hope it can keep them locked up. So new, their procedures are a little lax, I'm afraid."

"Sit and I'll get you some tea."

She hurried off and returned shortly with a glass of tea. He sat on the swing and she slid in next to him. "Joshua, I've been so anxious for you to return."

"I can tell, and I'm happy for that." He kissed her gently on the forehead.

"Joshua, I'm pregnant." Her face was aglow as she looked into his eyes.

"Pregnant! Oh, Jennie, that's great. That's wonderful." He threw his arms around her and began kissing her. Suddenly he pulled away. "I've got to be more careful with you."

"Joshua, I'm not that fragile. You had better not stay away from me. I need more loving now than ever before. In fact," she smiled, "I think I need some special attention now."

"In the afternoon?"

"I'm sure it will run into evening."

Joshua swept Jennie into his arms and they disappeared inside. The evening chores would have to wait.

****

Joshua remained at home for the next two months. He was very attentive to his expectant wife. Jennie bathed in the luxury that he bestowed on her, but after two months when he told her he had to leave for two or three days, she almost welcomed the breathing room. It would give her a chance to move freely, without Joshua underfoot all the time.

The next morning after Joshua left, Jennie rose and began her morning chores. She was not feeling very well and when she finished the chores, she decided to go inside and lie down for a while. She was barely able to climb the back steps, and as she entered the house, she was overcome with terrible pains and cramps in her mid-section. Everything started going dark as she reached for a chair.

****

Mark had promised Joshua that he would come by and check on Jennie every day. Fulfilling his promise, Mark rode up the following afternoon to the Parker home. He knocked on the door, but no one answered. He went around back and found no one in the barn or barnyard. He knocked at the back door. No one answered, and then he heard a faint cry from inside the house. "Jennie," he shouted, "are you all right?" He heard the faint cry again. He pushed open the door and ran inside. He found Jennie lying on the kitchen floor. "Jennie, what happened?"

"I think I'm losing my baby," she said, tears rolling from her eyes. "Can you get me to town and the doctor?"

"Of course. I'll team up the wagon. I'll be right back."

Shortly, Mark returned and carried Jennie to the wagon. He had placed straw in the wagon and covered it with a blanket. He placed another blanket over the distraught Jennie and started for town, carefully avoiding the rocks and bumps in the road.

As the wagon slowly moved towards town, Jennie kept repeating, "Joshua is going to be so disappointed."

Mark was concerned the doctor might be out of town or unavailable so that when the doctor answered the door on their arrival, Mark breathed a sigh of relief.

128

"Doc, I have Jennie Parker in the wagon. She thinks she has lost her baby and she's lost a lot of blood."

They carried her inside and Mark waited in the outer room while the doctor and his wife attended to Jennie. He paced the floor for a few minutes and then decided to go to the press and get his father.

Thomas looked up when his son entered the building. "What's going on? You look half frightened out of your wits."

"It's Jennie. I found her this morning on her kitchen floor. She'd miscarried and was lying on the floor in a pool of blood. I've got her over at Doc's now."

Thomas wasted no time closing shop and the two men hurried to Doc's office. In a few minutes, Doc came from the back room. "She's going to be okay. She did lose the baby and she did lose quite a bit of blood, so she will need some tender care for several days. She said Joshua was out of town for another couple days."

"She can stay at our place," Thomas offered, "but I'm sure the family will want her to stay at their ranch until Joshua gets back. Poor thing, she had wanted to have a child for so long, and she was so happy to be pregnant. It's going to be devastating for her."

"She's worried about Joshua," Mark added. "That was all she kept repeating as we were coming to town."

"That's Jennie," Thomas remarked. "She's an angel for sure."
****

Jennie lay in bed, tears flowing from her eyes. She wondered if she would ever be able to have a baby. Joshua would be so disappointed in her if she could not give him a child. He might even feel resentful and leave her. Their vows were 'for better or worse,' and she had made the worst. She was not worthy of his love.
****

Joshua returned from his three-day trip and found the house empty. The dishes were still in the sink, which was unlike

Jennie to leave them to go somewhere. He had noticed two of the horses and the wagon were missing when he arrived. She could have taken it somewhere, maybe to town for supplies. Then he saw the floor stained with blood. His heart fell. Something had gone dreadfully wrong. He raced from the house and headed for the Richardson's place. He hoped they would know what had happened.

Joshua found Hallie coming onto the porch as he dismounted. "Where's Jennie?" he shouted, racing towards Hallie.

"She's here with us. She had a miscarriage day before yesterday, Joshua. She lost the baby."

"How's Jennie?" Joshua asked with a strained voice. "How's Jennie?"

"She's doing okay. She just needs rest."

Joshua started to move by Hallie. "Joshua, wait." Joshua turned. "Joshua, she is quite depressed. She thinks she let you down. She's even worried that you will leave her."

"How can she believe that? She's my entire world." Joshua fought back the tears. He wondered what he had done or said that would ever make her believe he would react that way.

"She's very disappointed and sad about losing your child. Just show her your love and she'll come around, I'm sure."

Joshua nodded and went inside. He hugged Margaret. She looked at him with sad eyes. "She needs you. Go to her," was all she said.

Joshua went into Jennie's room. Her eyes remained closed as he quietly walked to her side. She opened her eyes and smiled at him.

"I'm sorry, I didn't mean to wake you." He bent and kissed her gently but Jennie's arms went around his neck and pulled him tight to her. Joshua could feel her crying as she held him. She held him for a long time before releasing him. She wiped her eyes.

"I'm sorry, my sweetest. I know how much the baby meant to you."

"Don't be sorry on my account, Jennie. The most important thing in my life is you. I want you to get well. You must not blame yourself. I should have been here. Jennie, my wonderful angel, I love you. Please, just get well." Joshua leaned over and kissed her.

Joshua sat next to her and held her hand. They quietly stared at each other, until her eyes closed. Joshua stayed for some time, holding her hand, and then left the room. As the door closed, Jennie opened her eyes and tears rolled down her cheeks.

"What did the doctor say about what happened? If I had been there maybe she wouldn't have lost the baby."

Hallie moved forward and squeezed Joshua. "No one should be blaming themselves. Doc said something wasn't right and it was God's will."

"At least I could have been there."

"Perhaps. However, life takes people apart from time to time. We do the best we can, Joshua."

Joshua moved to a chair and sat down, holding his head in his hands. He looked up. "Did Doc mention about future babies?"

"He said there was no reason she couldn't have children in the future," Hallie answered. "One can never be certain."

"I need two more years I figure to save enough money to turn our place into a ranch that can support us. Then I can make a real life with Jennie and our children. I've spent my life risking my neck in the name of justice. I need to bring that justice home to my family." Joshua felt embarrassed about his speech. "Sorry for my going on."

"It sounded good to me," Hallie responded. "Have you told Jennie what you just told me?"

"No. I wanted to be sure that it would happen. We had talked about me leaving the marshal service, but there was nothing for certain. I guess I should tell her my plans though. I will when she feels a little better."

"I think that would be the best healer she could have. It'll make her feel better."

"You're right. When she wakes up."

****

Jennie awakened as the late afternoon shadows spread across the room. She had lain there for half an hour when the door opened and Joshua entered with supper on a tray. His smile relieved the tension she felt. Maybe everything would be all right. She had to believe that.

"I brought you some good cooking from the kitchen. You can feel safe, I didn't do the cooking."

Jennie laughed, and then grabbed herself with pain.

"Sorry. I need to be more careful with you."

"You are being perfect. The laugh was well worth the pain. Before I eat, I need a kiss."

Joshua kissed her gently and then carefully placed the tray on her lap.

"Tomorrow, I want to get out of bed and I would also like to go home. I want us to be together...alone. I realize more than ever how much you mean to me."

"I guess I realize it more than ever how much you mean to me. I always knew, but today brought it all to the front. Sometimes we take things for granted. There is something I want to tell you." He scooted his chair closer. "I've been thinking about it for a year or more but was afraid to tell you in case things didn't go as planned. But I realize now, it is a dream we should share together and if it doesn't happen we will share the disappointment together."

Jennie had stopped eating and was intently watching Joshua. He took her hand. "I figured in about two years, we will have enough money saved to expand our place and I can leave my job as marshal, and we can ranch our little place, together. I know it would make you happy."

"Listen to me Joshua. I love you for who you are. If quitting as marshal is not what you would want, then I would not be happy. I don't want you to change and if being a rancher would change you, then don't become a rancher."

"Jennie, this is what I want. I want to be with you more. I hate it when I leave for days on end. I hate it when I can't hold you at night. I hate it when I awaken in the morning and you're not there. Being marshal was what I wanted until I met you. Now being marshal is no longer what I want. I just want to spend my time with you."

"As long as you're sure that's what you want. We have a couple years to think on it anyway."

"Good. That settles that. Now eat before everything goes cold."

Chapter 18

Marshal Joshua Parker received a telegram from the Lincoln Marshal's office that the notorious and ruthless Harrison Brothers were believed to be in his territory, and heading south towards Colorado. He immediately prepared to begin a search, not wanting them to slip through the noose of the law once again. They were considered extremely dangerous. The brothers had killed on several occasions, the last being a sheriff in Kansas. They had avoided capture for many years. The Harrisons had come out of Illinois ten years earlier having already built a reputation. They moved between states and territories, wreaking havoc and terror on the citizens and businesses they encountered. Joshua had seen their wanted posters when he was in Iowa and now he had the opportunity to end their string of robberies and killings.

Once again, Joshua kissed Jennie good-bye and rode off. By spring, he would be turning in his badge, and there would be no more good-byes, and leaving his beautiful wife alone. However, for now, he had to focus on the danger that lay ahead. He headed southwest towards Colorado, where the Harrisons had been seen heading in the direction of High Peak, a small community near the border.

The three brothers apparently always rode alone. Tinch was the older brother, and ran the gang with an iron fist. Rumors

134

had it, because of Tinch's strict rules and keeping the younger brothers in line, kept the three outlaws out of jail. Hank, the second brother, had the reputation, to be the sadistic one of the group. Although none of the brothers hesitated to kill or maim man or woman, Hank usually carried the acts further. Jasper was the youngest. He joined his older brothers after they had left Illinois. Rumors had it that he was the spirited one and the most difficult for Tinch to control. He wanted to live life on the high road and be damned if he was killed or captured.

Joshua arrived in High Peaks in the late afternoon. He received information that in fact three men fitting the description of the Harrison brothers were in town and had been in the High Peak Saloon most of the day. Joshua found the saloon and began evaluating the surroundings. Most of the town was within a stone throw. The town, built during a brief gold mining rush, was mostly deserted now because very little gold had ever been found in the area. This made the town an ideal hideaway for outlaws like the Harrisons, as there was little activity coming in or going out of town. The marshal speculated that half the population of High Peaks must be at the saloon. The saloon sounded very busy and Joshua decided to be patient and wait before confronting the brothers. It would be too dangerous for him and too dangerous for the innocent bystanders if he approached them inside. He figured the longer they remained in the saloon, the more liquor they would consume, reducing their ability to resist arrest. Besides, he would have more control in the empty street than in a crowded saloon.

The marshal found a nearby alley where he could comfortably wait and watch for the brothers. People came and left the saloon, but the brothers never showed. Time slowly passed and darkness began to set in. Joshua wished he had kept his pouch of tobacco to help pass the time. He started becoming troubled. Perhaps the brothers were not inside, but he did not want to approach the saloon door, fearing he might give away his benefit of surprise.

Just when Joshua had convinced himself to risk approaching the saloon door, he recognized the youngest brother, Jasper, appearing in the lighted doorway of the saloon. He staggered across the wooden sidewalk, sat down on its edge, and leaned against a pole. He sat with his head cupped in his hands. Joshua knew it would be easy enough to take Jasper in his current condition, but he needed to wait for the two older brothers to appear.

The marshal did not have long to wait. Within a minute, Hank the middle brother, staggered through the doorway. Apparently, he found great pleasure in his little brother's condition. He stood behind Jasper, laughing and prodding him with his boot.

Tinch, the oldest brother, stuck his head out the door. "Are you two fixing to have another drink, or ya gonna' stay out here all night?"

"Yeah, in a minute," Hank hollered back. "Jasper thinks he can't keep up with his two brothers," Hank began laughing and staggered to Jasper's side and sat down, putting his arm around his brother.

Joshua watched the events unfold before him. If Tinch would follow the lead of his two brothers and sit down next to them, it would create the perfect opportunity for him to apprehend them. The brothers would be at a distinct disadvantage sitting all together. "Come on, Tinch," Joshua mumbled. "Take a break and sit down with your brothers."

However, Tinch did not seem to want to cooperate. He disappeared back inside the saloon. "Dang," Joshua grumbled. Shortly, Tinch reappeared with a mug of beer in his hand.

"If you two ain't joining the party, then by damn I'm bringing the party out here," Tinch said, holding up his mug and staggered alongside his two drunken brothers. He put the mug to his mouth. The beer spilled over and ran down Tinch's chin, but he seemed unconcerned or unaware.

The marshal knew it was time to make his move. The situation would most likely not improve and it could deteriorate quickly. Joshua removed the Colt from his holster and replaced it with his second revolver that he had been carrying in his waistband. He quickly moved across the darkened street towards the saloon and the unsuspecting brothers. Joshua had moved within twenty feet of the brothers when he called out to the drunken outlaws, "I'm the United States Marshal and you are under arrest. Put your hands in the air."

All three brothers' heads snapped to attention as though a bucket of cold water had been thrown in each of their faces. Jasper and Hank started to get up. "Stay where you are or I'll shoot," Joshua commanded. Tinch remained frozen as though unwilling to drop his mug of beer.

Joshua moved a little closer. It appeared the surprise attack had been successful. Joshua took a deep breath. "Tinch, you first," Joshua ordered. "With your left hand, reach across and remove your revolver and toss it out in the street."

Tinch hesitated. "Now!" Joshua shouted. Tinch slowly did as he was told, still holding on to his mug with his right hand. "Good," Joshua remarked and looked to Hank. "Do like your brother and toss your revolver out here in front of you."

It was at that moment that Jasper decided he was not going to allow the marshal to take them into custody. He reached for his revolver. "Stop!" the marshal shouted. The youngest brother chose to ignore the command. Jasper's revolver was just leaving his holster when Joshua fired. Jasper fell back onto the sidewalk.

The two older brothers immediately turned their attention to their wounded young brother. Hank whirled back towards the marshal. "You son-of-a-bitch killed my little brother."

"He left me no choice," Joshua responded. "Now do as you were told and with your left hand remove your revolver and toss it on the ground."

Hank glared for several seconds, uncertain whether to obey the marshal's command or follow his brother's fate. Slowly he removed the revolver and tossed it into the street. Joshua gathered the revolvers and had the two surviving brothers lay on the ground as he handcuffed them. He gave instructions for someone to remove the dead man from the street and take him to the town undertaker. Joshua led the two brothers to an unused jail in town and settled in for the night. He would face considerable danger over the next twenty-four hours until he had the two killers safely locked up in the state prison in Laramie.

****

Early the following morning, Joshua escorted the two prisoners out of High Peaks and began the journey to the new state prison in Laramie. He wanted to make the trip in one day. An overnight trip would create added danger of an already dangerous trip with only the marshal escorting the brothers.

By late afternoon, the brothers were continually complaining that they needed a rest. Although there were still several miles to journey before reaching Laramie before nightfall, Joshua found a small stream and decided to stop for a short period. He knew a stop was needed, but he made the stop more for the horses than the two brothers.

Shortly, an argument ensued between the two brothers, then a fight. Joshua sat back and watched them roll around on the ground. After some period, they stopped and sat up. Joshua leaned forward. "You boys think I'm some kind of idiot? I'll tell you what, the one that gives me the best argument comes with me and I'll gladly shoot the other one."

"Go to hell," Tinch mumbled. "We eat your kind up and spit them out. Go to hell."

"Yeah, I'm sure you do. Now get your behinds up, we're moving out."

Shortly, they were on their way to Laramie.

****

After Marshal Parker had booked and relinquished the two prisoners to the prison, he found a hotel for the night. He was feeling relieved that the brothers were now behind bars, but a nagging concern about the Laramie prison holding the two killers behind bars until their conviction and hanging was troubling. It was a relatively new prison with escapes in the past and they now had two notorious, ruthless men that would not hesitate to kill. The other worrisome concern for Joshua was their threat as he left them at the prison. "We'll get even with you for killing our brother and putting us here. They can't hold us and when we get out, we'll come looking for you, Marshal." Joshua did not take their words as an idle threat, remembering their eyes filled with hate and their voices ringing with revenge.

Chapter 19

Joshua had been home less than two weeks after arresting the Harrison brothers, when he received word from Fort Laramie, north of Cheyenne, that reports came of rebellious Indian activities northeast of Cheyenne along and into Nebraska. Fort Laramie was asking the marshal if he could investigate the reports rather than sending troops unnecessarily into the area and exacerbating the volatile situation. He hated going, knowing the task would take at least two weeks and he wanted to spend more time with Jennie.

Once again, Joshua prepared to leave, and once again, he promised that by next spring, he should be ready to retire as U.S. Marshal. Jennie kissed him with a lingering kiss and held him unusually long. He looked into her eyes.

"Everything will be okay, I promise," he said as he mounted his horse.

"I know. Just be careful."

As Joshua rode away, he could feel an inner force trying to pull him back. He could not shake that feeling the entire day as he rode northeast.

****

Jennie watched Joshua leave, wiped away the usual tears that appeared when he left, and sat on the porch step. The closer he came to retirement, the greater the fear consumed her each time he left. It was like tempting fate each day he remained a marshal. Something inside her was screaming for him to stop now. Although she was not sure, she believed she was pregnant again, having the feeling the last two or three days. She had not said anything yet, not wanting to create false hope and make his leaving more difficult for him.

Jennie shook off the blues and began the day's chores. She had to keep busy when Joshua was gone so not to worry or become lonesome. She would visit her mother and family later in the day.

****

Marshal Parker arrived noon of the third day at Shelby Flats, just inside the Nebraska border. It was a flat grazing land and Joshua had seen numerous livestock coming into town. He headed to the sheriff's office where he found Sheriff Hanson. The sheriff was a tall lean man with a large bushy mustache. He was friendly and very willing to provide information about the problems taking place in the area.

"Seems some of the Indians have strayed from the reservation and are raiding the ranchers' cattle and horses."

"How do you know they're Indians?"

"Not sure, except the rustlers' horses haven't any shoes."

"Nothing else?"

"Well, nobody around here has seen any strangers hereabouts."

"Anybody tried tracking the rustlers?"

"Yeah, sure, but they lose the tracks after awhile."

"You say they. Have you had a chance to try and track them?"

"No. I'm just taking the ranchers' word."

"Okay. The army at Fort Laramie wants me to check into this. They don't want to stir up any unnecessary trouble in these parts with the Indians or the ranchers. In the morning, I would like to talk with the ranchers who are having problems."

"I'll arrange that," the sheriff offered. "I contacted Fort Laramie myself, not wanting any problems. All it would take is for someone to get killed for all hell to break loose around here."
****

The overcast sky hid the full moon, shrouding Laramie in heavy darkness. The silhouette of the prison cast an imposing sight to anyone passing nearby, but unknown to those outside the walls a deadly escape was taking place.

Tinch and Hank Harrison stood over a crumpled jailer's body that lay in a pool of his own blood. Hank kicked the body for enjoyment. "Feels good to get revenge on these pigs. I'm hoping we can get a few more before we leave."

"I'm sure we will," Tinch added. "Then we can start looking for that worthless marshal who killed our brother and put us here."

"That'll be the greatest pleasure I've ever had, well, except for maybe that feisty little filly in Springfield, who thought she was too good for us. Too bad we had to get rid of her. She would have made a nice travel companion...soft and all." Hank stood still thinking of his past conquests.

"We'll find another one, maybe two, one for each of us, but first, we need to get out of here," Tinch said as they moved from the cell into the hallway.

As the other prisoners slept, the two murderous brothers made their way along the passageway to the door that would take them one-step closer to freedom. The two escapees peered through the small barred window in the reinforced door. Two unsuspecting guards were playing cards at the table. The brothers looked at each other and smiled. "We'll create a commotion and when they come through the door, I want the fat one," Tinch remarked. "He's given me too much trouble."

"Either is fine with me," Hank answered. "I'll enjoy sticking any of the pigs in here."

The two brothers started yelling and banging on the nearby cell bars and then slid back out of sight. The commotion irritated the other sleeping cellmates and they started shouting.

The two guards immediately grabbed their weapons, peered through the door window, then opened the door and rushed into the secured hallway. Tinch and Hank caught the guards by surprise from the back and ripped their makeshift knives across the throats of the two helpless guards. They fell to the floor gasping, and then laying still as the blood oozed from their wounds.

The other prisoners began yelling for their release by the Harrisons, but the brothers had no interest in helping the others escape. They grabbed the revolvers and rifles of the dead guards and headed toward the exit. They knew they were close to freedom, perhaps the silent killing of a couple more guards and they'd be free...free to terrorize the territory and free to hunt down Marshal Parker.

****

By early morning, the news of the escape reached the warden. He formed a posse, but with two saddled horses reported missing in town, the warden knew the chances to find the two Harrisons were thin. The murderous brothers would do whatever was necessary to make their escape, including murder. By late afternoon, the posse had returned without any clues as to where the two killers had gone. They had disappeared, but the warden had no doubt that the brothers would reappear, leaving murders and robberies in their wake.

****

Marshal Parker, along with Sheriff Hanson, were making their rounds to the nearby ranches that had reported missing livestock. They were all helpful, but angry, feeling confident it was caused by Indian raiders. Joshua assured them he would investigate and asked them not to do anything rash that would start a renewed conflict with the Indians.

Marshal Parker found an old trail abandoned by a rancher. The trail was days old but Joshua carefully followed it. Apparently, the rancher was quick to blame the Indians and had put little effort in the search for the actual thieves. The marshal was fully aware it could be Indians, but he needed to be certain before he made his report to Fort Laramie.

The first trail went cold and Joshua returned to Shelby Flats. Told of a more recent stealing of livestock, Joshua began his search of the new trail the following day. A growing confusion kept feeding the marshal's mind. They were almost one hundred miles south of the Pine Creek Indian Reservation. Why would a few renegade Indians travel so far to rustle livestock? The new trail left by the rustlers proved to be much easier to track. The rustlers had headed north as though heading towards the reservation but after some fifteen miles turned east. Joshua set up camp for the night. Although Joshua could not prove anything yet, he was convinced someone out here was running a herd of rustled cattle. Joshua's concern was that the herd might already be moving towards the stockyards of Omaha or Kansas.

****

Jennie awoke feeling sick, and it was overcast and raining, but she still felt excited for the new day. She knew she was pregnant. She was a little disappointed she would have to wait at least a week to tell Joshua. The anticipation to share the news with him was bubbling inside her. She prayed that this time she could see her pregnancy through and deliver a happy, healthy baby. It would fulfill the last part of her perfect dream. Joshua would be through as a U.S. Marshal and be home for good when the baby arrived. Everything was coming together perfectly.

Jennie looked out her kitchen window and saw Mark riding up the lane towards the house. He was her guardian angel when Joshua was away.

"Hi, Jennie," Mark called out, still sitting in his saddle.

"Good morning, Mark. Won't you come in for coffee?"

"Can't this morning, Jennie. The sheriff is meeting with the mayor this afternoon. He wants his deputies mulling around and looking busy during the meeting. I think he is trying to impress the mayor and town officials. Of course that is between you and me."

"Of course. Just don't tell your father, he might put it in the paper."

Mark laughed. "I'm sure he would. So everything is okay out here?"

"Everything is fine. Thank you for checking on me. It makes me feel safe and special."

Mark smiled. "You take care, Jennie." Mark tipped the brim of his hat and rode off.

****

Sheriff Towson nervously paced in his office. He was concerned that the mayor and his colleagues were not happy with the results for Cheyenne. There had been little progress in cleaning up the town and the sheriff was going to have to explain the reasons to the mayor and committee that afternoon.

Fred Grissom from the telegraph office opened the door disrupting his thoughts. "Telegram for you, Sheriff."

The sheriff took the piece of paper. "Thanks, Fred." Fred nodded and left. The sheriff opened the note. "*Prison break at Laramie night before last. Harrison brothers escaped. Five jailers killed.*"

"Dang!" the sheriff remarked, shaking his head. Reckon they're half way to New Mexico by now, he reasoned. They sure won't be staying around here. He wadded up the paper and threw it in the trashcan. He returned his thoughts back to the afternoon meeting.

****

"Good morning, stranger," the storekeeper greeted Tinch Harrison. The general store was at the western edge of Cheyenne. Hank Harrison stood outside with the horses.

"Good morning to you, mister. We're needing some tobacco and shells for this Winchester and revolver."

"I think I can take care of that."

"Hey, I heard my old friend Marshal Parker lives around these parts."

"He sure does," the storekeeper called out from the back of the store. "He and his lovely wife live on a nice little spread about two miles up Willow Spring Road, but I think you're out of luck. I heard the marshal is out of town for a while."

"Too bad, I guess I'll have to catch him another time." Tinch replied, making note of where the marshal lived.

The storekeeper put the ammunition and tobacco down. "Okay, will that be all?"

"I think so. Say does that well out back work?"

"Sure does. Gives out good water. I had it dug extra deep so I could always have good cold water."

"Think you could get me some? My canteen is dry."

"Sure, mister."

Tinch called out to Hank, "Bring the canteens around back."

"Huh."

"You heard me."

The storekeeper and Tinch went out the back door. The storekeeper lowered the bucket. Tinch removed his knife and thrust it into the back of the bent over storekeeper. He pulled the bloody knife out and rammed it again into the gasping man. Tinch grabbed the storekeeper and pushed him over and down the well. "Thanks for all your help." Tinch laughed. Hank was just arriving. "Let's load up our saddlebags with some supplies and get out of here."

"What about the water," Hank asked.

"It just went bad," Tinch said, wiping the blood from his knife.

****

Joshua's second day out proved beneficial. He discovered a draw used to keep the cattle while other cattle were being rustled. Unfortunately, the cattle were gone. They had been driven eastward and then south towards the Union Pacific Railroad. The cattle rustlers were obviously not Indians. They had several days, probably a week or more head start. Joshua decided he needed to notify Sheriff Hanson at Shelby Flats and notify Fort Laramie. He would never be able to catch the cattle drive before they arrived at the railroad and if he did, he would be badly outgunned. Perhaps Sheriff Hanson could notify the proper authorities along the railroad and capture the thieves. Besides, his most important task now was to prevent a flare up between the Indians, ranchers, and the army.

Joshua hoped that after he gave his findings to the appropriate people he would be free to return home to Jennie.

Chapter 20

$\mathcal{M}$arshal Parker returned to Shelby Springs and informed Sheriff Hanson of his findings. The sheriff immediately began contacting the ranchers to form a posse and head south. Joshua said he would telegraph the marshal in the area in hopes of stopping the rustled cattle before shipment on the railroad. He also needed to send a telegram to report his findings to the army in Fort Laramie and to telegraph Jennie that he would be heading home. He knew she would be pleased that he had finished early and would be home soon. Of course, no one was more pleased than he was.

****

Jennie hoisted a bucket of water from the well and started for the house. The fall day had become quite cool. She wondered if a storm was brewing. She worried a storm might delay Joshua's return. She was anxious to tell him the good news that she was carrying his child.

In the distance, Jennie could see two riders approaching. Her first thought was that someone was coming to deliver bad news about Joshua. Her stomach knotted. However, as they drew closer, she did not recognize either rider, and something about them gave her a bad feeling. She hurried inside, set the bucket of water on the table and retrieved the rifle from the rack on the kitchen wall.

Jennie had learned to use the rifle as a child and Joshua had taught her how to shoot more accurately, but she still did not feel comfortable holding the weapon in her hands.

Jennie hurried back to the front of the house and peered out the window. The two men, strangers to Jennie, pulled up some fifty yards from the house. Their appearance made Jennie shutter. They looked like hardened drifters riding their horses hard as though they had been in a hurry. They sat on their horses for some time talking between them. After a short period, one of the men called out. "Anybody home? We're looking for work."

Jennie was sure they were trying to determine the situation. She did not want to answer them and make them aware that only a woman was at home. She was afraid if she did not answer, they would decide to ransack the house. "My husband and the hired hands have everything under control and we don't need any extra help."

The two strangers conversed between them for a moment, and then the one spoke. "We'd like to rest our horses for a few minutes and give them water if that's okay."

Jennie tried to sound not frightened. "Suit yourselves."

The two men dismounted and led them to the side of the house where the water trough was located. They stood casually by their horses and chatted, before one started moving to the back. Jennie hurriedly moved to the kitchen window. She turned away embarrassed as he relieved himself. She returned to the front window. The second man had disappeared. She returned to the kitchen window thinking the second man had joined the first man, but neither man was there. Panic began to set in. Her initial deduction of the two men had been right. They were up to no good. She moved from room to room, window to window, but could not see either man. It was then she heard the chickens. One of the men must be near the coop by the barn. Now she needed to locate the second intruder. She looked out front but saw no one. She quickly moved to the back. A shot rang out, then another.

Both shots came from somewhere out front. She was sure it was a diversion. She waited at the kitchen window. Then she saw movement as the man in the rear made his way along the corral fence. For an instant, the man appeared in the open as he moved from the corral towards the house. Nervous tears filled Jennie's eyes but she kept her sight on the intruder. She squeezed the trigger and the rifle blast echoed through the house. In the same instant, the intruder went down with a yelp. He slowly crawled to cover. He was not dead but appeared to be out of commission for the time being.

Jennie quickly moved to the front window and peered cautiously at the front. There still was no movement. Where had the other man gone? She hoped the wounded man would remain disabled. She thought she heard the floor of the back porch squeak. As she rushed to check in the rear, the front door busted open and the second man with revolver drawn rushed in and knocked Jennie to the floor. The man kicked the rifle from her hands and then kicked her in the jaw. Jennie fought to stay conscious as the man kicked her in the stomach.

He reached down and grabbed her by the hair, yanking her to her feet. He dragged her onto the back porch where the other man lay bleeding.

"Looks like you did a pretty good job mangling my brother. That's not going to make him happy, honey. I'm thinking he's going to be pretty hard on you once he begins to feel a little better." The man laughed. His brother lay groaning on the floor. "Why in darn hell did you let her get a shot off on you?"

"Shut up, Tinch. I'm hurting pretty bad, and I need some patch work here."

"We've not only caught the marshal's wife here, we've taken in quite a looker here, Hank. I think we've found ourselves a nice little filly to take the place of the one we got rid of. Yes sir, she's going to do just fine. Sorry I kicked you in the face, honey. We sure don't want to mess up that nice looking face." Tinch pulled Jennie to him and kissed her hard. Jennie tried to pull away but it just tantalized Tinch that much more. "I can't wait," he said, releasing her, "to get a real taste of you, my pretty one."

Tinch shoved Jennie to the floor next to Hank. "Patch my brother up so we can get out of here. And you better do it right or you'll regret it, mark my word." He pushed Jennie. "You better get started, you pretty little thing."

"I need my bag," Jennie said looking at Tinch with tears in her eyes.

"Bag. You a nurse?"

"No. I just have a bag."

"Where is it?"

"In the hall closet."

"Well, let's go."

Tinch pulled her to her feet and they went to the closet where she retrieved the bag. She wished she had the foresight to carry a weapon in the bag, but unfortunately, she did not.

Jennie quickly set about looking at his wound. She would have killed him if her shot had only been two inches up and to the left, she thought. He had lost quite a bit of blood and he was in definite pain, but all she could do was clean the wound and patch it up. With luck, he would die in a short period. She had never thought so vilely of a patient.

Tinch paced behind Jennie, as she worked on his brother. "What's taking so long? You trying to stall until someone gets here to save you? Let me tell you, pretty little one, if anybody shows up, they're dead. Now would you want that?"

Jennie kept working and did not reply. "Answer me!" Tinch shouted. "Are you worth someone getting killed over you?"

"No," Jennie answered. "I'm just trying to save your brother."

"You hear that, Hank? She's trying to save you. When's the last time someone tried to save you? Mamma wouldn't even have tried." Tinch laughed. "Here you got this pretty little thing trying to save you so you can have her when you're feeling up to it. That's what I call being nice."

"Sure is," Hank grunted in pain. "Her hands are so soft and gentle. A mighty nice find for sure."

Jennie straightened up. "I've done everything I can do."

"I hope it's enough for your sake, little one. I would hate to take revenge on you if something happens to my brother. Your husband has already killed one of my brothers."

It was then that Jennie realized that these men were the Harrison brothers that Joshua had talked about capturing, but he had delivered them to the Laramie prison. They must have escaped. Surely someone would come checking on her at the ranch knowing Joshua was the one that had put them away.

"We need to get going," Tinch said after Jennie had finished with Hank. We stick around here and some damn posse is going to come looking for us."

Tinch tied up Jennie and went to the barn to saddle her horse. Jennie had mixed feelings. She knew they would kill her if they left her, but she feared for her life, and perhaps worse, if they took her with them. These men were ruthless and would have no mercy about what they would do to her. She just hoped that someone would capture them before they had a chance to do anything horrible to her. Joshua would not be home for days.

Tinch returned with a saddled horse for Jennie and grabbed a winter coat for her. "Don't want my little filly to get cold," he said wryly. He tied her hands and led her outside to the horse. He helped hoist her into the saddle, while his hand groped her beneath her skirt. "Feels damn nice," he said. "Looking forward to some time with you, honey."

Tinch helped his brother on his horse and they headed out. No one had arrived to save her from a despicable and uncertain future. Jennie knew she was at the mercy of two vicious men who had no remorse for anything they did and they would particularly enjoy the fact they were doing it to the marshal's wife, the man they so despised.

****

Deputy Mark Prescott turned down the lane towards the Parker house. He usually checked on Jennie in the morning but had another obligation today. He was glad he had waited though, since he had a telegram to deliver to Jennie from Joshua that had come in late that day.

Usually before he had reached the steps of the porch, Jennie was there to greet him, but not today. At first, it alarmed Mark, but decided he was arriving in the afternoon, and Jennie was probably not expecting him. Perhaps she was taking a nap, leaving Mark uncertain on how he should proceed.

Mark tapped lightly on the door. There was no answer. He walked around to the back of the house to try the back door. He stepped up on the back porch. "What the heck is going on?" he shouted as he saw the blood on the porch. He pushed through the unlocked door and rushed inside. "Jennie!" he shouted. "Jennie, Jennie," he called moving from room to room. He saw some bloodied rags and more blood on the kitchen floor.

Mark made a quick check of the barnyard and barn. He found a horse and saddle missing. He tried to analyze what had happened. Had Jennie injured herself and was riding for help? There was an awful lot of blood for that to happen, especially being able to saddle her horse. Had she injured herself and maybe Joseph happened by and was taking her for help? That was possible. He decided to ride to the Richardson ranch first. He hated to unnecessarily frightening them, but the well-being of Jennie was the most important. He could go by there and it would not be too far out of the way to town.

Mark rode by the Richardson ranch but Jennie was not there, nor had they heard from her. Joseph rode to the Parker house in case Jennie returned from some place unknown. Mark rode on to town. He hurried into the sheriff's office with the news.

"Sheriff, I was just at the Parker place and Jennie was gone and there was blood all over. She's not at the Richardson ranch. Something has happened to her."

"I've just received word that Hal Stenner from the general store west of here turned up dead in his well. He was stabbed. I'm concerned it's the Harrison brothers."

"But they're in prison," Mark responded.

"Were," the sheriff replied. I received notice they escaped night before last. I thought for sure they would get plum out of these parts, but I guess I misjudged their evilness. They might just go looking for the marshal since he helped put them away and killed their brother."

"When did you find out?"

"Yesterday morning."

"And you didn't put the word out?" Mark was so angry he wanted to hit the sheriff.

"No. At the time, it was not on my priority list. Like I said, I thought they'd be long gone."

"We need a posse."

"I would agree," the sheriff responded, "if we knew where to look."

"We can't just sit here. If they have Jennie, her life is in serious danger. And we don't know if that's her blood or not."

"Tell you what, Mark, I will deputize a couple good men and you can take them north with you. I'll take a couple men and go south. I'm sure they won't head back towards Laramie from where they just came. I'll have someone check east a ways and see if they could have gone that way. You can leave tomorrow morning. You can travel much quicker than the Harrisons and Jennie, particularly if someone is injured. After three days if you don't catch them, you'll be wasting time, so come back here."

Mark nodded and left the office. He needed to cool his heels. When they found Jennie and this was all over, Mark had already decided he could no longer work for the sheriff after what he had done. Mark headed for home and began preparing for his ride in search of Jennie, but first he would give the horrible news to his father.

Chapter 21

Joshua was anxious to return home, but he wanted to make a little detour to visit with Hal and Emma Brandon. They had saved his life and he wanted to thank them and see if there was anything he could do for them.

"Nope," Hal had said. "I reckon we've got everything we need and then some. Am sure glad you made it though, Marshal. You weren't looking a bit too well when we left you. Got married too. You're a pretty tough fella."

Although it had delayed his trip home a few hours, he was glad he had stopped. He decided he would catch the train back to Cheyenne and make up the time. He hoped the train would do better keeping its schedule than last time.

He sat comfortably in a passenger car as the train pushed west into Wyoming. If things went well, he could be home two days early and surprise Jennie. His nostrils flared as his imagination brought the sweet scent of Jennie to him. He could feel her gentle softness coming to him. He had never thought he could love her more than the day they married but somehow his love for her grew stronger with each passing day.

A voice startled Joshua from his daydream. He opened his eyes. The conductor stood over him. "You feeling okay, Marshal?"

"Oh, yes sir. Feeling great. I'm heading home to my lovely wife."

The conductor nodded and moved on. Joshua reddened. What facial contortions had he been making?

Joshua arrived in Cheyenne early in the darkened morning. He decided to have breakfast and not frighten Jennie by showing up in the dark. He took care of his bay and had him ready to ride. He found a small eatery that had just opened and went inside for breakfast. He was apparently the third customer as two men sat nearby chatting. Joshua placed his order and sipped his hot coffee. His mind was on riding home in an hour. He could hardly wait as he looked at the clock--quarter to five.

"Posses are looking for her everywhere." Joshua's ear pricked up as he heard the comment from the next table. "They think it's the Harrison brothers. A tough bunch I hear."

Joshua swung to face the men. "I couldn't help but overhear your conversation. What is it about the Harrison brothers and posses?"

The one man had a stunned look as he stared in disbelief at Joshua. "Marshal!" he exclaimed. "You haven't heard?"

"I've been out of town."

"Your wife, Marshal, she's been kidnapped. They think it's the Harrison brothers."

A cold chill raced through Joshua's body. The words rang unbelievable. The Harrison brothers were in jail. Jennie was at home waiting for him. All this could not be true. He stood up. "Are you sure? It can't be true."

"I'm sorry, Marshal. I think it is, tho'."

Joshua raced out the door. He thought about riding to the sheriff's office, but knew no one would be there this early. He rode to the jail, but no one was there. Of all times, not one prisoner was in jail so that a jailer would be on duty. He started for home. He had to find out if Jennie was gone. He could not believe it. He was convinced the man had been mistaken. The Harrisons were in jail. He had seen it for himself. His stomach was on the verge of convulsions. What if it was true? Jennie would be at the mercy of two of the worst men imaginable. What would they be doing to her? Joshua began screaming and crying as he raced toward home. "I'll kill you son-of-a-bitches so unmercifully when I catch you," he screamed.

Joshua rode up in front of his house and dismounted before his horse had stopped. He raced up the porch and inside. "Jennie!" he screamed, but there was no answer. He raced up the stairs. No one had slept in the bed. The reality that the man's words had been true began to lay heavy on Joshua like a hot iron. He wanted to collapse on the floor in defeat, but he knew that it would not help Jennie. He had to find out what was going on. He needed information.

Joshua raced back outside and mounted his horse. He spurred his bay forward. The Richardsons could tell him what was happening. Joseph and Hallie would know.

Joshua rode into the Richardson ranch at a full gallop. Hallie saw him coming and was on her way to meet him as he dismounted. "Is it true, Hallie?" Joshua called as he raced to Jennie's sister.

"Oh, Joshua, we're so frightened," she exclaimed throwing herself into his arms.

"I overheard the news from a man in town. He said something about the Harrison brothers had kidnapped Jennie, but they're supposed to be in jail."

"They broke out, Joshua. Killed several guards and escaped. They think the Harrisons have Jennie. We don't know if the blood at the house is Jennie's or one of theirs."

"Blood! I didn't even notice any blood. Where is Joseph?"

"He's with Mark and a posse going north. The sheriff has a posse headed south too."

"I'm confused about the times. When did Jennie disappear?"

"Mark went to the house in the afternoon, day before yesterday and he found her missing and the blood. They found the body of a storekeeper that same morning just west of

Cheyenne. Mark and Joseph left with a posse early yesterday morning headed on the road to Chugwater."

"They're not going to take a main road with someone injured and holding Jennie as a hostage. I don't understand how come Mark or the sheriff didn't protect Jennie when the word was out about the Harrison's escape."

"Mark didn't know. He's madder than a hornet, because the sheriff received word of the escape the day after the breakout and didn't tell anyone."

"What's wrong with that man? How could he be so stupid?" Joshua grabbed his hat and beat it against his leg. "I've got to start looking for Jennie. I need to go home and prepare for a rough trip. I'm so scared for Jennie right now. How is your mother?"

"She is just sitting there quietly. You know that's not like her."

"Tell her I love her. I need to start looking for Jennie. Tell her I'm going to find her and soon."

"Okay. Where are you going to look, Joshua?"

"I'm thinking if they're on the run, they're going to head for the badlands in the Dakotas. A lot of low life head there."

"You be careful."

"Don't worry about me. I'm going to find Jennie, Hallie. I'm going to find her, bring her home, and never leave her side again. I swear." Joshua's eyes filled with tears as Hallie began to sob. They hugged and Joshua left.

Chapter 22

Joshua Parker left his bay in the pasture for the trip. His companion was aging and he had just completed a long journey. He needed two fresh horses that would give him speed and endurance. He loaded one horse with supplies, brought an extra rifle and revolver with plenty of ammunition for his arsenal. Also included amongst his weapons was a bowie knife that he had confiscated from an earlier arrest. He had wisely stored most of his weapons under the floor in the bedroom; otherwise, the Harrisons might have taken the cache with them.

Joshua looked for any clues that might help him. He decided the blood was from one of the Harrisons. Jennie's black bag was gone and it appeared she had used it before they had left the house. It would only be Jennie attending to one of their wounds and not one of them attending to her. Also, spent shell casings lay strewn on the floor in the house; most of the blood was on the back porch. Joshua also noticed one of the Harrison horses had a missing shoe. That could be very beneficial in tracking the Harrisons and Jennie.

It was early afternoon when Joshua spurred his roan into a gallop and never hesitated to look back at his house. It meant nothing until he had found Jennie and returned her to it. Anguish and hatred filled his body and heart. Revenge was the only thought on his mind. Neither brother would ever return to prison. They had set their fate. He would track them to the ends of the world with only two ending options--they were dead, or he was dead. The only variable was finding Jennie. He prayed he would find her well and rescue her from the terrible clutches of the two ruthless killers.

Joshua felt confident which route the brothers would take. They would head north to the lawless and desolate badlands of the Dakotas. Also with the recent gold discovery in the Dakotas, they might find the riches would be an easy prey for their unscrupulous undertakings. They would stay off the main road to the gold country. Since the brothers were injured and Jennie was their prisoner, they would want a less traveled trail. The trail that best fit their needs ran along the Nebraska border. Joshua estimated the brothers had at least two days start on him. He could travel much faster than the brothers, especially with one injured, but with such a time difference, it might allow them to reach Goshe's Hole before he did. It could be difficult to find which one of many routes they might take from there. He would take another trail further west, but still east of the main trail. It was a much easier route to travel. Once convinced he had traveled north of them, he would cross over, and then turn south and meet the brothers head on. He could catch them by surprise, knowing they would be looking over their shoulders. The risk would be moving over too soon. He had to watch carefully for the shoeless horse.

Joshua stopped and analyzed the tracks where the two trails split at Lodge Pole Creek. It appeared he had been right: the lesser used trail to the east had three relatively new horse tracks, and one horse was missing a shoe. They had stopped to water the horses, but only one set of boot prints showed. They probably had left Jennie on horseback and perhaps if one of the brothers was injured, he, too, remained on horseback. Joshua knew that shortly the trail would become more difficult to follow as it headed into rockier terrain. He would continue with his original plan. To travel more quickly, he would take the more heavily used westerly route.

Joshua finished watering his horses and stroked their necks. "We've got some hard riding ahead," he said as he hitched his boot into the stirrup and swung into the saddle. He checked the sky. Rain clouds were gathering in the west. Rain could slow his progress, but he had no choice, he would have to keep going. His mind remained ravaged with the thought of revenge, but he had to keep his senses about him. Any wrong decisions or erratic behavior could cost Jennie her life.

The desolate trail only worsened his grief. Now all his time was devoted to thoughts of Jenny. How frightened she must be. She loved life, but now she faced the portal of hell. His memory brought the laughter of Jennie to his ears like a mirage of a man in thirst of water in the desert. He feared he might go crazy before he could find her.

Joshua rode late into the day, arriving at the rim of the plateau. He decided to wait until morning to maneuver down the rugged slope into the valley. He found a ranch house with an old man agreeing to his staying in the barn. The need to rest his horses and the difficulty of traveling at night were the only reasons that stopped him. Joshua barely slept, his mind never leaving the thoughts of Jennie and detailing the plans on saving her. A coyote howled in the distance added to his loneliness of not having Jennie by his side.

****

Jennie closed her eyes and tried to shut out the pain and fear that griped her. She had traveled for three days since the Harrison brothers took her captive. The binding on her hands had rubbed her wrists raw and riding in the rough terrain had left her body exhausted and aching. A noose was around her and tied to the saddle horn of the horse ridden by Tinch. The fear of falling off was great with the rugged terrain and her hands tied, limiting her balance. She also feared that at some point the two heathens would begin assaulting her. They had thus far used all their energy in making their escape. The younger brother, Hank, sometimes rode alongside Tinch and they talked, often laughing at their humor, but usually Hank rode alongside or behind Jennie. She would often see Hank looking her up and down like a vulture waiting for the right moment to attack its helpless prey.

Jennie worried about the baby inside her. She feared for her unborn child. The kick by Tinch to her stomach and the endless riding across the terrain was endangering the baby. Thinking about losing another child brought tears, but she gritted her teeth with determination. She was not going to allow her heartless captors to defeat her. She would remain strong and wait for Joshua to find her. She knew in her heart that he would come.

Jennie tried to overhear the two brothers' conversation, hoping to get a hint of their plans, but soon realized that they did not have a plan except to head north to less controlled territory. She also tried to observe and memorize the terrain around her, sure that it would help her, should she escape.

Jennie became aware that Hank was having more difficulty as they traveled. The wound was obviously affecting him. There was fresh blood appearing on his shirt. The wound might be her salvation from the two men. If Hank worsened or died, it would increase her chances of escape from just one abductor. In addition, the wound would keep Hank from attacking her if it consumed his thoughts.

The sun began to settle on the horizon and the fall shadows strung out across the landscape. Hank rode past Jennie, groaning as the jarring intensified the pain of his gunshot wound. Jennie strained to listen to the conversation between the brothers.

"Tinch, we need to stop. This bullet hole is killing me," Hank spouted angrily.

"All right damn it, I'll look for a place to stop," Tinch responded angrily. "If you had been more careful about letting the woman get a shot off, we wouldn't be in this mess."

"Go to hell! You hide your hind end behind a building while I do the moving in on her. Fat chance of you getting shot."

Tinch looked straight ahead as though he had not heard a word that his brother had said. Hank dropped back alongside of Jennie.

"So bitch, I suppose you feel good about putting a hole in me? Well don't. Your day is coming. When we're done with you, you'll beg us to kill you and we will, slowly." Hank began to scream. "Do you hear me? Do you, bitch?"

Jennie did not look at Hank as her body shivered. She did not doubt his threats. She knew he was capable of anything.

The three had ridden about another half hour in silence. Tinch stopped and turned in his saddle. He called out to Hank, "There are some lights from a cabin up ahead. Stay here and I'll check it out. Think you can keep an eye on your friend back there?" Tinch laughed.

"Go to hell. Just get us some shelter so I can get some rest."

Hank took the rope from Tinch and Tinch galloped off toward the cabin. Jennie feared the pent up anger in Hank might cause him to take the opportunity to hang her, except it would probably be too quick a death for him, and she knew Hank feared his brother.

About ten minutes after Tinch had left, there were two blasts of gunfire, and then the countryside grew quiet. Hank sat up, stretching to see what had happened. About five minutes later, Tinch appeared on a crest and waved for Hank to come on in. Hank smiled. "Some bastard met his maker." He began laughing.

Jennie's heart sank. Life to these soulless men meant nothing. She shivered, knowing that it included her own.

Chapter 23

The following morning, Joshua arose and was on the trail before daybreak. He needed to determine how far he had to ride to ensure he had moved north of the Harrisons and Jennie. If one of the brothers was injured, it would certainly slow their travel. If he did not remain vigilant, he might cut over too soon and if they were north of him, and he headed south, he could lose their trail indefinitely.

Joshua reached the valley floor and made his way north. Once on the valley floor, he was able to move more quickly. The number of travelers lessened as he headed north. He figured with late fall, most people had settled for the winter. The few he met, he would question them whether they had seen Jennie and the Harrisons. None of the southbound travelers had seen anyone fitting their descriptions.

Joshua crossed Horse Creek. With his progress, he hoped to reach Bear Creek by nightfall. He knew of an abandoned farmhouse where he would be able to stay and with the weather becoming colder, he wanted a break from its frigid fingers. By the following evening, he planned on crossing to the other trail, and from there, he would head south unless he found tracks of the horse with the missing shoe. Every moment he began to question his judgment, fearful he had guessed wrong and would lose track of the murderers that had his Jennie.

The farmhouse was a welcome sight as Joshua reined in his horse and slid from the saddle. A cold wind began to chill the evening air, leaving little doubt that a northern storm was brewing. The abandoned farmhouse left few comforts, but Joshua was able to start a fire in the fireplace and warm his chilled bones. He knew the following days would become more difficult with the worsening weather, but he was more concerned about Jennie traveling in the same weather. He worried about what attire she might be wearing and if it would protect her from the cold. He prayed for her safety. What horrible things was she encountering? He hoped he had the skill and judgment that could soon save her.

By the next morning, the weather had worsened. Joshua anticipated snow by nightfall. Snow on a trail always increased the danger of travel, and he feared for Jennie on the lesser traveled trail.

Early on in the day, he met a couple of drifters heading south. "Morning," Joshua called out. The two men nodded their acknowledgement without speaking. "Seen two men and a woman along the trail?"

"Can't say we have," one answered. They were not friendly and kept moving. Joshua tried to analyze their behavior. Maybe they were only suspicious of him, but he felt they were hiding something or running away from something. For now, Joshua had no interest in pursuing trouble with the two men. It would only slow his efforts to find Jeannie.

"Thanks, anyway," Joshua replied and started past them.

After they had passed, one of the men called back to Joshua. "I reckon I should warn you. We spotted some stray Indians a few miles back. They looked like they were up to no good."

"Any sign of their trouble?" Joshua asked.

"No, just a warning," he called out as they hurried on.

They had wasted little time and were too far down the road for Joshua to ask any other questions. They seemed very nervous about the Indians. Joshua was doubtful whether he was getting the full story. They were acting guilty and Joshua wondered if they had provoked an incident with the Indians.

The marshal had never received word of any problems with Indians this far south. The Arapaho were generally peaceful. Maybe some of the young braves had decided to put on some war paint and create some ruckus. He was concerned for not only his safety, but also slowing his pace north and his rescue of Jennie.

Joshua rode with extra caution. His rifle lay across the saddle and his revolver readily exposed on his hip for easy access. He had no idea how many Indians he would encounter, their attitude, or even their whereabouts. He had not passed any other travelers coming south since the two drifters that had warned him. He thought about waiting for other travelers coming north, thinking larger numbers would provide extra safety. He quickly discarded the idea, thinking he might have to wait for hours or even days before anyone came. He could not afford such a luxury. He had no time to waste. Every hour could be essential for the safety of Jennie. He decided to forgo all precautions; they were slowing him down.

Joshua planned to turn east by early afternoon. This would place him some five to ten miles north of Indian Springs. He was feeling more comfortable that the Indian warning had been erroneous when he spotted smoke billowing skyward around the bend. He moved off the road and to higher ground to observe the cause of smoke. He found a smoldering wagon. There was little left of the wagon except its charred frame. There was no sign of life or death, just the wagon. He moved closer, but still found no sign of life.

"Hello," Joshua called out. "Hello. Is anyone here?" There was no response. "This is U.S. Marshal Parker. Is there anyone here?" With still no response, Joshua readied to leave when a young woman, clothes torn and her face filled with fear and distress, appeared from the side of the road.

"Marshal," she cried out. "Can you help us?"

The marshal jumped from the saddle and hurried to the young woman's assistance. "You said us. Are there more?"

"My younger sister. She is too frightened to come out."

"I had a report of Indians creating mischief in the area. Did Indians do this?" Joshua asked.

"No. Two men attacked us, drug us to the side of the road, and then had their way with us. They were brutal, Marshal. My poor sister, she's so young." The young woman began to sob, clutching her face. Joshua was uncertain whether to take her to his arms, fearing she might react poorly to a man's touch, but when he did, she fell helplessly to him.

"Let's go attend to your sister. Do you know if she is physically well enough to travel?"

"They burned our wagon and took our horses."

"They didn't take your horses. I think I saw the two men about three hours ago south of here and they didn't have any extra horses. They may have chased them off and maybe I can find them, but first, let's check on your sister."

The young girl, mid-teens, was near an emotional breakdown. Her clothes were badly torn, exposing much of her body to the cold. Her face was scratched. She sat in a ball on the ground, weeping. The terrible sight of the girl before him tore at Joshua's heart. Her older sister, probably mid to late twenties, held her, and the two young women sat and cried together.

"Stay here," Joshua said. "I'll go look for the horses."

Joshua soon found the horses nearby and brought them back.

"Where were you headed?" Joshua asked when he returned to the young women.

"To the family ranch north of here some ten, fifteen miles."

"If you're up to traveling we can be there before nightfall. I'll make sure you arrive home safely." Joshua knew he had to take them, but his heart ached at the thought of delaying his rescue of Jennie. Maybe the Lord would watch over Jennie while he helped the two women in dire need.

"Yes, we're ready to travel. Thank you," the older female replied. "We're so grateful for your help."

Joshua placed the two women on his horses with the saddles and Joshua rode one of their horses. As they started out, he kept thinking he should be moving east now, but as they moved north, he knew he could not abandon the women.

"I'm Marshal Joshua Parker," Joshua said as they began the three or four hour journey to the ranch.

"I'm Elizabeth Fuller," the older sister responded. "This is my sister, Julia."

Julia never looked towards them or responded in any way. She continued to stare straight ahead, as she had since they had started. It was as though life around her had become nonexistent, Joshua thought. Perhaps it was the only way for her to keep the horror of the attack away. Maybe when they arrived home to familiar surroundings and loved ones, she would begin to feel better.

Although Joshua's heart went out to the two young women, he could not help but feel the frustration of the change in plan that was slowing his search for Jennie. He feared each moment was endangering the life of Jennie and certainly adding to the torment that she was encountering.

"Out of curiosity, Elizabeth, what brought you and your sister out here alone on this road?"

"My husband and I were living outside of Cheyenne. Julia was living with us for a while. My husband was killed in an accident, so Julia and I were returning to our family ranch north of here. It was poor judgment on my part trying to make it back alone. Poor Julia, I'll never be able to forgive myself."

"You can't blame yourself. Life doesn't always give us simple choices and we do the best we can."

"I'm so glad you came along, Marshal. It was one stroke of good luck for us."

"I'm glad, too. I just wish it wasn't two bad incidents that caused our meeting."

"Two?"

"My wife was kidnapped by a couple killers who are trying to get revenge against me. I'm trying to catch up to them."

"That's horrible. And you stopping to help us is slowing you down. You must go on. We'll make it by ourselves."

"I'm not leaving you. You need the comfort of protection. Maybe you can help me though."

"How's that, Marshal?"

"I assume you're familiar with this area around here and I'm not. Maybe you can give me information on different routes, places where one could hold up, things like that."

"I can help you somewhat, but when we get to the ranch, my father would be a wealth of information. In fact, he has several ranch hands that could help you look for your wife."

"That would be a big help, but unless someone had dealt with people like I'm chasing, it would be too dangerous for them. The information would help enormously though."

Elizabeth smiled. That was the first smile he had seen from her. Joshua knew the horrible ordeal would never go away, but he believed her strength would allow her to recover and build a good life. His concern was Julia. She was struggling and having enormous difficulty with what had happened. He wondered when he rescued Jennie, which of the two women Jennie would resemble. Jennie was strong and he was sure it would be Elizabeth. He had to believe that.

Joshua learned that the Fuller ranch ran along a small creek that dumped into Horse Creek. A road ran southeast along the creek from the ranch and intersected the route that Joshua believed the brothers were taking. This would mean he would come in further north than planned, but perhaps for the best. He had lost precious time helping the two Fuller women. He hoped to find out at the Fuller ranch, other routes the brothers might take. It would mean disaster for Jennie if he missed them because they had taken a different route.

The uncertainty was driving Joshua mad. He needed to return the two women safely to the ranch and resume the search for Jennie. Everything that mattered in the world depended on finding her. He would never leave his beautiful angel alone and unprotected again.

****

Bound, Jennie sat silently in the corner on the floor of the cabin. She tried to maintain control of her emotions. She had seen the body of a man a few yards from the cabin. She wept for his soul. Her body ached and her insides left her doubled with pain. She feared she had lost her unborn baby. She had been so anxious to tell Joshua that she was pregnant when he returned from his long trip. She wondered if the child was a boy or girl. She mourned for its life, taken before it had a chance to feel, see, or hear life around it. It would miss all the simple pleasures or the chance to love.

Each moment, became more difficult for her to go on, but the love and the need for Joshua's arms around her would help her to endure all the agonizing pain. She could endure; she would endure.

Hank lay on a cot not far from her. She could see he was suffering badly from his wound. If he died, she wondered how the older brother would react. She had been the one that shot him and Tinch might find it to his liking to take revenge out on her.

"I need someone to take care of my wound, Tinch," Hank moaned. "It's hurting bad and you can't just let me die."

"What the hell do you want me to do?" Tinch growled. "You got yourself shot and now you want me to fix you up. There's probably not a doctor within fifty miles of here." Tinch threw up his hands. "We probably got half the country looking for us and here we sit on our behinds, just waiting for them to come along and pick us off."

"Maybe we can head towards Chugwater. They might have a doctor."

"I reckon we're a good twenty-five miles from Chugwater and there's damn good reason we're not near it. There are too damn many people there to recognize us."

"So you're going to let me die to save your neck. What kind of brother are you?"

"Shut up, Hank! Let me think." Tinch turned, his eyes focusing on Jennie. He walked briskly to her, seated on the floor. He grabbed her arm and yanked her to her feet. Jennie thought her body would come apart as she groaned with pain. She could hardly maintain her footing as Tinch dragged her across the floor to the cot where Hank lay.

"You're going to fix my brother. If he dies, you will pay dearly for it, bitch. Do you hear me?"

"She's not a doctor," Hank said, his face scrunched with pain. "It was her fixing me that's left me like this."

"I'm not going to chase around looking for a doctor and we can't stay here. We need to get a move on. She'll have to do." Tinch turned to Jennie. "You better fix him right." He shoved Jennie to the floor next to the cot. Jennie screamed with pain. Her insides felt like they were coming out of her. She began to gag. Slowly the agony began to settle, and she wiped the tears from her eyes.

Jennie stared down at Hank. Usually his face was set with the look of a killer, but at this moment, the face looked like a small child begging for relief from his mother. Jennie removed the bloody rags covering the wound. The horrible stench made her gag. The wound was badly infected. Unless Hank saw a doctor and removed the bullet, Jennie believed he would die. She methodically began cleaning the wound the best that she could. Hank was moaning with pain, his body remaining tense.

Jennie turned to Tinch. "I need hot water and clean rags," she demanded. Tinch stared at her with surprise. "If you want to save your brother, get a move on. We can't be wasting time." Tinch hesitated, unsure how to react to a woman suddenly making demands on him, but he finally began following her orders.

Jennie examined the wound more closely. The bullet remained lodged inside. She knew the bullet needed removing to let the wound start healing and to control the infection, but she would not be the one to do that. She had to try to reduce the infection and the bleeding to keep Hank alive. She had to keep

171

him alive so that she could stay alive. She had become certain of that. She prayed to be rescued, and soon.

Tinch brought some clothing of the dead man that he found in the cabin. They were hardly clean, but she would use the hot water to clean them the best she could. "How's the water?" she asked.

"Give me a minute," Tinch responded angrily. "I've got the fireplace going. Stop being so demanding or I'll slap the breath out of you."

"It's your brother," she replied coldly.

"Yeah, and you better be treating him like he was your brother for your own sake."

It appeared to Jennie that the bleeding had stopped since their arrival at the cabin. Losing so much blood had weakened Hank, but the infection would kill him.

"How's it looking?" Tinch asked as he brought some water.

"Not good," Jennie responded without looking at him for a reaction. "The wound is badly infected. We need to stay here until the infection is better and he regains some strength from the loss of blood."

"We're not sitting around here. Somebody is going to show up here. The whole territory is looking for us. You have until tomorrow morning to make him ready for traveling."

"That's not enough time," Jennie argued.

"It is and it will be. Get busy! You're wasting time."

Jennie decided to make a stronger argument later. Tinch would not listen now. Maybe in the morning he would reason with the need to stay longer. She placed the rag into the hot water. It burned, yet the warmth flowed through her, giving her some relief to her tormented body. As she applied the cloth to the wound, Hank flinched.

"Take it easy," Hank groaned.

"Shut up, you whiner. I'm doing the best I can," Jennie replied, anger consuming her.

Hank started to rise up in response to her remark, but fell helplessly back in pain. "Damn Hank, quit being a little girl," Tinch added. "She hardly touched you."

"Shut up, damn it," Hank said, writhing in pain as Jennie applied another hot rag.

Jennie worked diligently for the next hour. Her back ached from tension and continuously bending over working on Hank. Her stomach knotted up in pain and all her limbs were sore and weary. Finally, she fell back against a post. "That's the best I can do for now," she said. "He needs rest and I'm sure I'll have to keep cleaning the wound."

"We're leaving tomorrow. Nothing has changed," Tinch replied in a cold raspy voice.

Hank seemed a little more relaxed. Jennie sat down closer to the cot. She closed her eyes, but Tinch tying her hands to the post interrupted her moment of solitude. She closed her eyes again, and fell asleep through all the pain.

Chapter 24

$\mathcal{J}$ennie awoke to a frigid cold. Her hands and feet ached from the rope tied around her wrists and ankles and then to a post. It was still dark, but a glimmer of light in the lone window in the cabin offered the first sign of daybreak. Everyone appeared to be asleep. She tugged at the rope to no avail. She tried shifting her position to relieve her aching body, but her movement was very restricted.

Jennie remained awake, when about half an hour later, she heard Tinch begin to move and grumble. He slowly stood up, stretched, glanced toward Jennie, and without speaking, walked over to where Hank lay quietly on the cot.

"Hey Hank, you dead?" Tinch hollered.

Jennie's heart jumped at the words. Tinch kicked the cot. Hank moaned.

"We're heading out this morning. I'm not wasting any more time, damn you." Tinch looked down at his motionless brother. He angrily turned and headed for Jennie. He began untying her without speaking. Once she was free, he grabbed her by the hair and began hoisting her to her feet. She screamed with pain. He pushed her shivering and throbbing body towards the cot. "Get him ready to travel. We got to get out of here!" Tinch bellowed.

Jennie looked down at Hank. His eyes were half closed, but his overall complexion looked somewhat better. There was no outward appearance of blood on his new wrap. Jennie slowly removed the bandage. The wound showed little bleeding, at least externally. The infection had improved slightly, although the wound was still festered, swollen and bright red. She could only imagine what his insides were like.

"I need more hot water to clean the wound," Jennie called out.

"Damn it, woman, stop being so demanding. Somebody for sure is going to see the smoke from the fire, and it'll end up getting us killed, and I'll make sure you go down before me." Tinch banged around the cabin, continuously complaining as he started a fire and heated a pot of water. He brought the pot of water to Jennie. "How is he?" Tinch asked with a threatening tone.

"Perhaps a little better, but we need at least another day here."

"Hell no!" Tinch yelled, kicking a nearby post. "Ouch, damn." Tinch hobbled around momentarily. "I told you no more time. We're leaving this morning."

Hank opened his eyes. "Listen to her, will you," he pleaded. "I reckon I'm still in a lot of trouble here, Tinch."

"Listen, Hank, if we stay here, we're sure fire in a heap of trouble. You know they're out in force looking for us for killing all those guards. And for sure, that Marshal Parker is flipping around the countryside like a tail after a horsefly, looking for his pretty one. It's like a hornet's nest around here and we need to get our behinds out of here. We get to the Dakotas, we can relax, but until then, we got to keep moving."

"I thought we wanted to get even with the marshal for killing our little brother?"

Tinch grinned. "Hank, we are getting even with him more than if we killed him. We got his pretty one here, and you get better, you can have her as much as you want. Can you think of a better way to get even with the marshal? And if we get tired of her, we'll sell her to the Indians. Then we'll go find the marshal and kill him, but before we kill him, we'll tell him everything we did to his pretty little honey. Can you think of a better way to get even with the marshal?"

"You're right, Tinch, but I don't want to die first. I'm hurting bad."

"This little thing is going to fix you right up. She knows she better keep you alive."

Jennie dipped the cloth in the hot water and gently rubbed it on her face, letting the heat sooth her aching temples. She tried to shut out the horrible things Tinch was saying about her and Joshua. She knew he was not boasting idly what he wanted to do to get revenge. She dipped the rag again and placed it on the back of her neck. She sat there feeling the gentle flow of heat penetrate her very soul. She was startled back to reality by Tinch's booming voice, "Hey bitch that water's for my brother. Get busy!"

Jennie left the warm rag on her neck and tore another rag. She dipped it in the hot water and began cleaning Hank's wound. Tinch stood over her watching, as though doubting her sincerity of helping his brother.

"That's it, honey. You fix old Hank up and we'll take turns repaying you." Tinch walked away, his laughter continued for some time as he began gathering supplies to leave.

Jennie fought back the urge to jam the rag into the wound. She wanted her patient dead more than anything, but for now, she had to keep him alive to save herself. At moments like this, she wondered if it was worth the effort. Hank was watching Jennie and from his nervous eyes, she presumed he could see the hate and anger in her face, and remained quiet.
****

Joshua and the two Fuller women arrived at the Fuller ranch late that evening, well after dark. Even with the delays, Joshua had arrived at his northerly location in three days of travel. In the morning, he would head east to the fork of the road where he expected the Harrisons to be traveling and then head south. He hoped they had not reached the crossroads yet.

The ranch was quite elaborate for the Wyoming territory. The house and horse barn were large, and he had been told by Elizabeth that the ranch covered several miles.

Tears flowed and anger grew as Elizabeth, clutching to Julia, unraveled the story of her husband's death, their desperate journey home, and the horrifying encounter with the two merciless drifters.

Joshua was introduced to Syd and Martha Fuller. They were very appreciative of his rescue of their daughters, but when Elizabeth told her parents of the atrocious situation Joshua was facing, Syd immediately offered support.

"I've got some good men that can help and I'm certainly available," Syd responded.

"I'm not going to endanger you or your men, but you could help by spreading the word from here to Nebraska to be on the lookout for the two killers and my wife, Jennie. I'm sure which trail they are coming north on, but in case I miss them, I would like to know where they are heading. Tell everyone to stay clear of them, because they are ruthless and will stop at nothing."

"I can certainly make that happen. First thing in the morning we'll get started. You need a good night sleep and we have a guest bedroom."

"I can't imagine how a bed feels anymore. Thanks. I plan on leaving before daybreak."

"We'll be ready and ride with you until you head south," Syd offered.

****

By mid- morning Tinch had saddled the horses, and he had helped Hank onto his horse. He untied Jennie and led her to her horse. The day was cold and a sharp wind cut across the rolling grasslands as they rode away from the cabin. Tinch was impatient by their slow progress as Hank rode slumped in the saddle, appearing half-dead.

Jennie was suffering from the cold and pain. Her clothing was not sufficient for the weather and her body ached from all the beatings and kicking she endured.

Jennie overheard Tinch talking to Hank, "Listen to me Hank, we get north of Fort Laramie and I know a place we can hold up for a few days. We can't stick around here."

Jennie was not familiar with the territory that well, but she was sure it was a couple more days of riding, and she questioned in her mind whether Tinch even knew of a place they could stop. She believed Hank could not take two more days of travel without seeing a doctor and getting a great deal of rest. She knew if Hank died, her life would worsen until Tinch killed her. Tinch would keep his promise.

****

Joshua, Syd, and three Fuller ranch hands headed out in the early morning before daybreak. They had arrived at the fork in the road near Horse Creek. Joshua waved his thanks and headed south following the trail that ran along Horse Creek. He had to ride cautiously from this point forward, uncertain when he might encounter the brothers and Jennie. He wanted the surprise element on his side. He laid his rifle across his saddle in front of him and had his revolver ready for use. The encounter with the Harrison brothers could happen in minutes, hours, days, or the unthinkable--they were on a different trail. It was a chilling thought.

Chapter 25

$\mathcal{B}$y mid-afternoon after leaving the cabin, Jennie no longer was concerned about Hank. Her own well-being was in doubt. She could barely stay in the saddle. Several times, she caught herself drifting from consciousness. The cold wind ripped at her sparsely clothed body. She knew if she did not find shelter soon she would die from the cold, and her insides felt like they were coming apart. She was sure Tinch had done some serious damage when he had kicked her.

Perhaps Tinch was feeling the cold, but for whatever reason, he decided to hold up at an old abandoned wickiup, located down an embankment about a quarter mile from the road. Tinch gave his brother the more sheltered part of the deteriorated hang to, and tied Jennie to a tree next to the wickiup, which offered little shelter.

Some two hours after arriving at the wickiup, Jennie awoke by Tinch hollering, "Wake up, Hank! Damn you, don't up and die on me."

Jennie tensed from fear. Her body felt frozen to the icy ground.

"Hey bitch, I need you to take care of my brother."

"I'm tied here," Jennie answered angrily. "Remember."

Tinch untied Jennie and dragged her by the hair inside the wickiup alongside of Hank. She was so numb by now that she could hardly feel any pain. "He better not die. I'm telling you, he better not die."

As soon as Jennie reached the side of Hank, she knew he was dead. His face was white and his body cold.

"How is he?" Tinch inquired leaning over Jennie.

Jennie wanted to say, "He's dead and you killed him you self-indulging idiot," but she knew better. "Get back and give me some room," Jennie demanded. She had to buy time. She tried to determine a means of escape, her only chance to live.

Tinch was standing three feet behind her. She had just this one chance. With all the remaining strength in her, she swung around, fist clenched and hit Tinch in the groin. He groaned and fell backward to the ground, his body bent in pain. Jennie crawled to her feet and began to run. Her legs collapsed and she fell, face first to the frozen ground. She tried to stand again, but her body could not make it. She began to crawl, anything to get away. Then a boot slammed into the middle of her back. She fell flat to the ground, the air gushing from her lungs.

Tinch kicked her in the ribs to roll her over on her back. She lay with her eyes closed, waiting for a click on his revolver and the end to her life. Slowly she opened her eyes. Tinch towered above her. "You let my brother die. I gave you fair warning."

"You killed him! You killed your brother." Jennie did not care about the consequences of what she said. It could not worsen her situation. "That makes you the lowest of all mankind. Killing your own blood."

"Shut up!" he screamed. "I loved my brother. It was your job to keep him alive, and it was you that shot him, bitch."

Tinch walked to a nearby fallen tree and sat on it. He was quiet for a considerable length of time, first looking at his brother, then at Jennie. Finally he spoke, his voice almost calm. "I'm giving my brother a decent burial and you're going to dig his grave."

"How? I have nothing to dig with."

"Perhaps your hands if you can't find any sticks." Tinch smiled. We still have a few daylight hours and all night if we need it." Tinch looked around. "Over there would be nice." He grabbed Jennie and dragged her half walking, half crawling, to an area near some barren willows. "This'll do just fine. Start digging." He laughed, sounding like a mad man. "This is for you, Hank. A delicate flower digging your grave. A least you'll get something from her."

Jennie sat helplessly on the ground. The ground was frozen, yet she knew it was not an idle threat from Tinch. She found a nearby pointed rock that she could grip. The work was slow. Her body ached in spite of the numbness from the cold. Tinch lay against a nearby log and watched Jennie. She would give an occasional glance waiting for him to fall asleep. As she dug, she planned the best way to escape if the opportunity arose.

To sneak away by foot would be the easiest, but she would be unable to go far and Tinch would surely discover her in the grassy land around them with so few places to hide. Even if she were able to hide from him, she would not be able to survive very long in the cold and so little clothing, especially in her deteriorated condition.

Jennie considered the horses. She could ride one and chase the others away. She wasn't sure she could mount and stay mounted.

Her other choice was to try to get the rifle that rested on the log some three or four feet away from Tinch. If Jennie could get to the rifle and kill Tinch, it would permanently remove him and give her a moment's pleasure too. Even after killing him, she still had to make her way to some hospitable location, and she knew that would be very difficult considering her unknown and unfamiliar whereabouts in her much weakened state.

Jennie decided she would go for the rifle. She would worry about everything else when Tinch was dead.

Two hours passed and Jennie had dug a hole about a foot deep. She saw Tinch's head dip towards his chest for the last time.

She waited a few minutes and he did not move. She slowly stood and steadied herself. She had to move quietly without stumbling and she knew in her current condition that would not be easy.

With each step, Jennie thought she would fall, but slowly she moved ever closer towards the rifle and her freedom from one of the most despicable men in existence. Tinch had not moved and Jennie was within six feet of grasping the rifle. Suddenly one of the horses snorted and kicked, causing a reaction from the other two horses.

Tinch jerked and sat up with a start. Jennie grabbed for the rifle, hoping to grasp it before Tinch was aware of what was happening. Just as she had the weapon in her clutch, Tinch grabbed the rifle and yanked it from her hands. He was still on the ground and Jennie tried to wrestle the rifle from his grasp. Fighting Jennie off, he stood and backhanded her across the face, knocking her to the ground. "You damn whore, you're going to pay for that, but first you're going to finish digging that grave." He kicked Jennie. "Get up!" She got to her feet and staggered back to the hole.

Jennie finished the hole at two feet. "Maybe you'd like one for yourself," Tinch remarked as he dragged his brother to the shallow grave. "Keep the varmints from picking apart your tender little body." Tinch laughed and grabbed Jennie's behind. "I think I could use some of that later. You know, to help ease my sorrow because you let my brother die. I think Hank would like that. You know, even feeling a might poor, he had a hankering for some sweet time with you. It's too bad for Hank. I would have shared, but now I'll have to keep you all to myself. I'm sure the marshal won't mind." Tinch's eyes turned cold. "But first little one, I need to teach you a lesson you'll never forget, so you don't try a dirty deed on me again. Next time you try to sneak off or kill me, you'll think twice, remembering the teaching I'm about to give you. I just hope I don't mess up your pretty little face."

Tinch grabbed a rope from a saddle and tied Jennie's legs together. "Mighty nice," he said, throwing her skirt up to her thighs. "I hope there's something left after this lesson." He left to get a horse.

Fear gripped Jennie. She knew something horrible was about to happen. In moments, she may be dead or wish she were. Tinch returned with the saddled horse. He fondled her breasts and ravaged up her skirt before tying the rope around the saddle horn. "I wanted to see what was for supper," he said. "Getting a little hungry." Tears flowed from Jennie's eyes. The fear coupled with the humiliation was destroying her will to live.

"First things first," Tinch remarked. He mounted and looked back at Jennie. She watched the barbarous man as he smiled at her. Tinch started the horse slowly as Jennie slid across the frozen rocky soil. Then he spurred his horse into a gallop. Jennie screamed and begged for mercy. Suddenly the screaming stopped. Tinch reined in the horse. Jennie lay silent. "Guess that's enough if I want any supper." He slid from the saddle and walked back to the still and silent Jennie. "Damn, I hope I didn't kill her." He bent over and saw a faint breath. "Aw, still warm for supper." He untied her legs and carried her back to the wickiup where he tied her. "Going to give Hank a nice send off then I'll be back for a feast like one of those kings."
****

By late afternoon, Joshua had become concerned that darkness would force him to camp for the night. If he traveled after dark, he might miss the threesome if they had camped somewhere off the road for the night. In addition, there was the added danger of being surprised by the brothers. His being killed would not help Jennie.

The trail looked almost abandoned since he had started south along Horse Creek. From lack of recent tracks, apparently no one had come along in several days. This was good news for Joshua. The brothers and Jennie had not reached this point thus far. He still worried that they had abandoned this road for another and he would miss them all together. They could have traveled further east into Nebraska. He now wondered at what point he should abandon his southerly movement. The further south he rode without finding Jennie and the low-life brothers, the more he was beginning to regret he did not stay on the road and follow them. Maybe he could have overtaken them. He was still glad he had the opportunity to rescue the Fuller women, but with all that, Jennie was his entire reason for being here. He had to find her or all else was pointless.

Suddenly Joshua's blood curdled. A woman's scream echoed through the crisp air. "Jennie!" Joshua screamed. He spurred his horse forward trying to follow the horrifying screams that continued to fill the countryside and rush into every part of Joshua's body. He was closing in on rescuing her, but the thought of what was happening brought tears to his eyes, as he continued to spur his horse toward the screaming. Then the screams stopped. He slowed his horse, trying to determine where they had been coming from. He had mixed feelings when the screaming stopped. It made it more difficult to find her, and why had the screams stopped. He stopped and listened. As violent as the sounds had been only moments ago, now only an eerie quietness. He was so close, yet so far from rescuing Jennie. Where was she? He edged forward, carefully peering into the trees and underbrush. If Jennie would only call out his name, so he could locate her.

****

Tinch placed the last rock on Hank's grave. "Hank, you should have stuck around. We could have raised a lot of hell in the Dakotas. And the marshal's little filly, you could have enjoyed her a lot. In fact, I think I'm going to have a little enjoyment now. I got so mad at her, that I damn near killed her. I guess I better lay off for a while. I don't want to lose her. She's going to take good care of me and if she doesn't, I'll sell her to the Indians. So long, Hank. I'm going to miss you. It was good while it lasted."

Tinch turned and headed towards the wickiup. "Here I come," he called out to Jennie, a broad grin appearing on his face.

Stepping from the brush some thirty feet away, Joshua stood facing Tinch, revolver drawn. Tinch stopped, surprised and

184

confused. He had certainly not expected anyone, especially the marshal.

"That had better not be Jennie in that grave, Tinch," Joshua said with anger in his voice and his face filled with hate.

"Well if it isn't the marshal."

"Where's Jennie?"

"Jennie. Do I know a Jennie?"

"You're a dead man, Tinch." Joshua cocked his revolver.

"You can't just shoot me. A marshal has to bring his prisoner in. You shoot me and that would be murder."

"You are badly misinformed, Tinch. I can bring you in dead or alive. That is my choice and I think you know what my choice is. I'm not here as a marshal, but a revengeful husband that would want nothing more than watch you die. Besides, why would I want to drag you all the way back to Laramie? You made some people there very mad, and I reckon they'd just hang you anyway, so why should I miss out on the fun of killing you myself"

Tinch realizing the marshal would not hesitate to pull the trigger, glanced towards the wickiup to distract the marshal. Joshua looked in that direction. Tinch seizing on the opportunity, reached for his revolver in his holster. Joshua, realizing Tinch's attempted trick, cleared leather and fired twice. Tinch fired aimlessly once as he fell to his knees. Joshua fired twice more and Tinch fell motionless onto the cold frozen ground.

Joshua nudged Tinch to make sure he was dead. He prayed the grave was not Jennie's. "Jennie," he called out.

A faint woman's voice came from the wickiup, "Joshua. Is that you, Joshua?"

"Jennie, I'm coming!" Joshua shouted. "I'm coming." Tears filled his eyes as he ran to the deteriorated structure. He hurried inside and looked with horror at his Jennie. Her frail body lay on the ground, her hands and feet tied, her body half exposed to the frigid elements, and her face bloodied and bruised. "Oh, Jennie," he cried as he unbound her hands and feet. He took off his coat and covered her frozen body. He clutched her into his arms. "Jennie, you're safe now. I'm going to take you home and never leave your side again. I love you so much."

Her lips quivered as she spoke. "I love you. I'm glad you came. I knew you'd find me."

"Oh, Jennie, I'm so sorry this has happened. I'll do everything I can to make it up to you."

"It's not your fault. Please don't blame yourself. You came and saved me. That means everything to me."

"I'm going to get blankets for you. I'll be right back."

Joshua returned with blankets and wrapped her in them. He immediately gathered wood for a fire. Once, he had the fire going, he prepared some broth for Jennie, then held her in his arms. Jennie's back and the back of her head were badly scraped, but at least, there was no new bleeding. There was little else Joshua could do to help her now. After the wickiup warmed up, he decided he would use Jennie's black bag to find some ointment to put on her wounds. Getting her warmed and nourished had been his top priorities.

Joshua spent the night keeping the fire going, feeding broth to Jennie, and holding her in his arms. He could feel her frail weakness and see the desperate hold on life in her sunken eyes. He feared the worst for her. She had encountered more than anyone should, yet she still was fighting for life. He would give up anything and everything for her recovery and return to the Jennie that he had known.

Joshua had hoped by morning that Jennie might be able to travel so he could seek proper medical care for her. However, as dawn broke on the horizon, he knew he could not move her. He would wait another day, but could not wait any longer. She needed attention. She lay quietly in his arms, speaking few words. She did say something inside her was not right.

Joshua spent the day devising a means to allow her to travel. They were more than a day away from the Fuller ranch where she could rest comfortably while he sought help. There was a small community southwest, but he doubted they had a doctor. He was not even sure what a doctor could do for her, but he had to find help.

Joshua knew Jennie was not well enough to ride. He was certain if he made a basket to pull behind the horse, it would be much too rough on her. He decided he could make best time and make her the most comfortable if he wrapped her in a blanket and carried her in the saddle with him.

By nightfall, Joshua could see Jennie was growing weaker. He knew in the morning that he would have to transport her to help. There could be no more waiting. The night seemed eternal. Joshua held Jennie the whole night except when he rekindled the fire.

Morning came. At the first sign of light, Joshua bundled the frail body of Jennie in a blanket and saddled his horse. He carried her to a rock where he was able to hoist himself into the saddle with Jennie in his arms. Slowly they began the tedious journey towards civilization.

Joshua kept whispering to her, "Jennie, I'm taking you home. We will live a long life together."

Jennie would occasionally open her eyes and the hint of a faint smile would appear. Even in a moment when her life was uncertain, Jennie would show the gentle, giving side of her. The ride was torturous and relentless, but Joshua kept going. At times, he thought his arms could hold her no longer, but he reached inside himself and kept going. Jennie would do whatever was necessary for him. He knew that beyond a doubt.

It was afternoon when Jennie opened her eyes. Her lips quivered as she spoke, "Joshua, darling, I want to stop. I know the end is near. I want you to hold me. There are things I want to say. I want us to be at peace when the end comes. I want you to hold me in your arms like old times. It's my wish."

Joshua could hardly control himself at that moment. She had said what he knew but would not admit to himself. He did not want to give up. He wanted to beg her to go on, but he knew she was right. Their last moments together should be in each other's arms; speaking words, that each wanted the other to hear.

Joshua found a small draw surrounded by foliage, giving them some shelter. The heavy brown grasses helped soften their final bed. He placed a blanket over the bushes and one in the grass, giving them some shelter and a place to lie.

As they lay in each other's arms, Jennie looked longingly into Joshua's eyes. "Thank you, my darling, for giving me my last request. You were always so good to me."

"Jennie, I spent so much of my life trying to find happiness. When I met you, my search was over. You have given me everything."

"I wanted to give you a child, Joshua. I wanted to so much. I was carrying a child, but I lost it during this ordeal. I'm sorry I didn't give you a lasting celebration of our love."

"Oh my dearest Jennie, I promise you, your love alone will be a lasting remembrance that will be with me until we meet again."

They lay quietly for some time; occasionally Jennie would open her eyes and smile, assuring Joshua that she was still aware of his closeness. Darkness had settled when Jennie opened her eyes and whispered, ""I'm being called, Joshua. I can feel it. I must say good-bye, my Darling. I love you." She closed her eyes.

"No, Jennie. No. Please don't leave me. I love you. How can I go on without you?" She never answered. Her body relaxed. Joshua clutched her in his arms and sobbed. He could never imagine such a wrenching pain that rushed through his body. His mind could not grasp that his love, his life, was gone. She deserved more. She deserved a full and happy life. How could God cheat her of what she deserved?

Joshua's body and mind became numb as he held his lifeless Jennie through the night. Everything around him disappeared; Jennie in his arms was all that existed. Time passed without notice before he became aware of the sun rising...it was the first day without Jennie. Every sunrise and every sunset would be without her. How could he face all those countless days and nights?

Chapter 26

$\mathcal{J}$oshua decided to take Jennie to the Fuller ranch. He hoped they would agree to her burial at the family plot. He knew of no public cemetery anywhere in the region, and he did not want to bury her in some isolated terrain where her grave would become obscure to civilization.

Joshua methodically prepared to leave. There were no thoughts directing his body. Except giving Jennie a decent burial, there was nothing left in his life, no future. He could not imagine what he would do next. Where he would go? There was nothing. The home that he and Jennie had built their lives around, the land they were so enchanted with over the years now was no more than a reminder that Jennie was gone. He could not even imagine looking at it, let alone living there. He'd had times in his life when he felt helpless, but nothing like now.

Joshua wrapped Jennie in blankets and for the next several hours held her in his arms as he began the long journey to the Fuller ranch. He arrived in the afternoon as the sun shone brightly in the southwestern sky. How ironic, he thought, now the sun was out when he had struggled to keep Jennie warm during those last hours. He clenched his teeth in anger. Everything seemed to be wrong.

189

Joshua slid from the saddle, holding Jennie close to him. Martha and Elizabeth came onto the porch. "I was too late," Joshua said, his voice barely audible as he tried to control his emotions.

Both women came down to him. "I'm sorry, Joshua," Elizabeth said. "If it weren't for..."

"No, don't do that," Joshua interrupted, knowing Elizabeth was about to blame herself. "I do have a request though," he continued.

"Certainly," both women answered simultaneously.

"I don't want to leave Jennie alone. She deserved better. Would you mind if she was buried here?" His voice broke and tears appeared in his eyes.

Martha quickly answered. "Of course, Joshua. We would be happy to have her buried here."

"Thank you, it means so much to me."

Syd arrived from the barn and helped Joshua with Jennie. "We'll prepare Jennie for burial, Joshua. I'll have the help build a nice casket for her. You need rest and I'm sure something to eat."

Leaving Jennie was difficult, but Joshua knew the Fuller family would take proper care of her. He retired to the guest bedroom and rested for a couple hours. Later, when he returned downstairs, the family had prepared him a meal of much needed nourishment, and except for Julia, they all gathered around, giving the grieving Joshua needed comfort.

Having not seen Julia since his returned, he inquired to her well-being," I hope Julia is all right?"

A look of concern was on everyone's face. Syd spoke," In all honesty, she's having a very hard time. I hope in time the dark shadows of that incident will lessen for her. We're just not sure what to do for her. We've all tried to talk to her, but she is so withdrawn. I know it's been hard on Elizabeth, too," he said nodding in her direction, "but she's trying to deal with her nightmare." Syd paused, before continuing, "We shouldn't be burdening you at a sorrowful time for you. I'm sorry for going on like this."

"Don't be sorry," Joshua replied. "We all need to help each other when we can, and you folks have been good to me. That's what good people do."

"Amen to that," Martha quickly added. "Good people have long arms to reach out to those in need."

Although the conversation was a good healing medicine for Joshua, he finally excused himself and retired to his room. He had doubted he could sleep, but the absolute weariness of the past week overwhelmed his body and mind and he quickly fell into a deep slumber.

Joshua awakened himself in the darkness of night when he reached for Jennie and she was not there. He lay there for a while unable to rid the torment in his mind that she would never to be there again. He rose and sat, staring out the window. The stars and full moon shone brightly across the still and quiet countryside, casting a surreal silver glow about it. Everything seemed unreal. He hoped that he would awaken from the never-ending nightmare, and find life full of joy and happiness with Jennie, as it was not long ago. He should not have trusted a future filled with wonderful dreams for Jennie and him. It was all a lie. It had betrayed him. Had Satan intervened and stolen God's gift to him? Is that what had happened? Surely, God could have prevented the devil from taking the gift He had given Joshua. There were never answers, only gnawing unanswered questions. Yet he knew answers would not be enough. Without Jennie, nothing would ever be enough. When the dirt covered Jennie, what would he do? Perhaps he would stand there until he died. How could he walk away? Walk away and go where? To what? Returning to his and Jennie's home would never be a possibility. He hated the place now. It was there that the horrendous brothers had abducted and battered poor Jennie. Besides, it had always been Jennie's home more than his. He had allowed himself to travel and leave her there alone. No, he could never return.

With his face cupped in his hands, Joshua envisioned the beautiful face and smile of Jennie. That was all he had left. He sat helplessly alone until the light of a new day broke on the horizon.

Another day filled with anguish and uncertainty. Another day, he would have to face a solemn future without Jennie.

****

The morning brought the somber task of burying Jennie. Joshua had tried to force his mind not to imagine what he knew was going to happen. However, when the time arrived, and he viewed Jennie for the last time, he felt a sense of tranquility. Jennie, robed in white, looked peaceful with a look that told Joshua that the angels had already taken her to a place where she would be happy. A place, Joshua thought, that looked like the meadow that she dearly loved. She was home. "Someday, we'll be home together," he whispered.

At the grave, among the maple trees, Syd read from the Bible. The world seemed to disappear around Joshua as he stood by the gravesite, only Jennie and he existed for that last moment. Joshua was unaware that Syd had finished, and was surprised when his hand rested on Joshua's shoulder. "She's at peace now," Syd said and motioned the others to leave Joshua alone.

"I'm going to miss you Jennie. I can't imagine life now. I know you're with the angels. You looked so beautiful, I believe you have become one of them." Joshua knelt and prayed, "Please Lord, give me strength, give me some understanding and direction in life."

Joshua paused, turned and headed for the house, wiping his eyes. She was gone...gone forever.

Joshua informed the family he was going for a ride to help clear his head. He found the ride did little to ease the agony and pain, but he was grateful to be alone and did not have to sit with the family and conceal the building emotions that filled him. He wanted revenge for what had happened to Jennie, but the brothers were dead. How could he fulfill his revenge for what was done to Jennie? He felt he had fallen off a cliff with nothing to grasp on to, as he drew closer to the ground below him. He needed a purpose. He needed something to grasp on to before it was too late.

Joshua returned late to the house and sat with the family for a while, so not to be rude. The family had offered their home, their family burial plot, and their warm, caring selves to him. After a period, he excused himself and went to his room.

Joshua awakened early, washed and went downstairs. Martha and Syd were sitting at the kitchen table, drinking coffee. They greeted him and Martha immediately poured Joshua a cup of the hearty brew.

"How'd you sleep?" Syd asked.

"Quite well. Better than I expected."

"For good reason," Martha commented. "A few good nights sleep in a soft bed and you'll feel much better."

"I appreciate the kind offer, Martha," but I'm going to be heading out tomorrow. I have to take care of some business.

"As long as you know you're welcome to hang around," Syd offered. "Maybe find some peace of mind."

"To be honest, Syd, I feel like a bear coming out of hibernation, except the bear is looking for food and I'm looking for reasons. I need to find a reason to go on; a reason why what happened, happened. There are so many reasons that I can't understand, that sitting around is going to drive me crazy."

"Son, be sure you're looking for answers and not ignoring the answers that are already there. Traveling won't necessarily give you answers, Joshua, but only lets you hide from them."

"I understand, Syd, and I do appreciate your insight, but I can't sit around. I need to justify my existence. I need to understand why Jennie was killed so brutally. I need to justify your daughters' brutal attack by two vicious men. I need to even things up. I need to do something, Syd. I can't sit here. Anger would fester inside me and consume me, as a plague would destroy a city."

"Joshua, you're a good man, and I understand the anger that can fill someone when their loved ones have been put through the horrible perils of life. I know that feeling with what happened to my two girls. But I can't right the wrong. If I could kill the two men that did this to my girls, I would. However, even if I did, I know it won't give my two girls their innocence of life back. I know they'll forever feel the scars of that day, but what I can do is give them love and respect that will hopefully lessen the pain."

"That's good for you, Syd, but your girls are alive to give them the love they need. If Jennie were still here, I would never leave her side. There would never be anything more important. My confusing problem is I don't have Jennie to give all my love to, and the men that did this to her are dead, and I can't do any more to them. And that leaves me empty. All my feelings are pent up in me and they have no way of escaping. I feel I could explode sometimes. That's why I need to keep moving, searching, trying to find something." He apologized and excused himself. He did not mean to sound so hateful.

Joshua spent most of the day at Jennie's grave, saying his good-byes. He hated the thought of leaving her, but staying and seeing her grave every day while he did nothing, would continue to build the anger and frustration inside him. He had to ease the hate and frustration, the agony and grief, the loneliness--all the emotions beating at him--all demanding his thoughts.

The first thing Joshua had to do was carry the bad news back to Cheyenne. It would be difficult telling the family and all her friends. Maybe, he thought, by the time he arrived in Cheyenne, he would have gained a little strength and composure, and possibly some insight. At least he had a short-term plan. Without that, he would ride off aimlessly through the territory. He was also going to turn in his U.S. Marshal badge, one that he had taken so much pride in wearing. He even considered returning to Iowa and family, leaving the west to those who still had a reason to be here. However, it would be selfish to do that. He had disrupted the lives of his family once; he would not do it again.

The early morning brought good-byes from the Fuller family and Joshua headed west towards Chugwater, where he would catch the Cheyenne-Black Hills road south. In departing, he could not get his mind off the distant gaze of Julia. She was showing no signs of recovery. Joshua wondered what could be done that would lift her out of the deep doldrums and uplift her spirits to give her the desire to live. There had to be something. If the two vile rats that ravished the bodies and souls of the two young women could be brought to justice, perhaps their pain and suffering would lessen. It would benefit the women, society and give him a purpose. There were other criminals, too, who had forced themselves on the good citizens of society that needed removal.

The countryside was quiet and still as Joshua pushed his way west towards Chugwater, with only the sound of leather against the leather of the saddle, hoofs crunching in the snow and an occasional snort from the horses. It allowed him the uninterrupted time to begin putting together a plan with a future that now had a purpose. If he could benefit society by removing the unscrupulous individuals that terrorized the good citizens, he would have a purpose. He could never fulfill his desire for revenge against the Harrison brothers; he had to accept that. However, he could hunt down those who were of the same wretched mold, not in the capacity as a U.S. Marshal but as a free-lance bounty hunter. The bounty hunter was not limited and impeded by the strictness of law and the oath of the U.S. Marshal, or the limitations of territory, or available time, but most of all the limitation on the means of capturing the fugitives. A bounty hunter did not have to give the Harrison brothers another opportunity to pillage society. Perhaps, Jennie would still be alive if a bounty hunter had captured the brothers. As a bounty hunter, Joshua would not have to give the filth of society another chance to kill and maim.

Joshua's ride out of Goshe's Hole was mostly a steady incline for thirty miles with occasional rugged terrain as he moved towards Chugwater. An increase in altitude of over one thousand feet also brought on the chill of a decrease in temperature. He rode hard, changing horses often, in hopes of arriving in Chugwater by the end of day.

Chugwater had grown rapidly, serving as a layover station for the increased number of travelers headed north with the discovery of gold in the Black Hills. The traffic this time of year was less with the winter, but there were still a few dreamers, who believed a claim awaited them, and the freight wagons continued, hauling much needed supplies to the flourishing encampments to the north.

Darkness was settling in when Joshua looked down from a rise overlooking Chugwater and the creek that ran alongside the town. The burning lamps of the town gave off a comforting sign of civilization and the opportunity to warm and feed the body, but unfortunately, it did little for the anguish in his mind and soul.

Chapter 27

$\mathcal{J}$oshua found a room for the night and left his badge, quartered his horse in a nearby stable, and then found an eatery close by. After his meal of beef brisket, he finished his cup of coffee and watched the patrons coming and going. Many were freighters, hauling supplies north to the gold fields, but there were other men headed north, thinking the find of riches was an arm's length away. The foolishness of dreams, Joshua thought, they turn into despair. Never again would he fill his mind with such nonsense. Besides, with Jennie gone, there were no dreams worth keeping.

Joshua left the eatery and headed for his empty hotel room, dreading a night with only the memories of Jennie. He could almost feel her holding on to him as they walked along the darkened street. He passed a saloon, hearing the laughter inside. He wanted to laugh again. He enjoyed those carefree moments with Jennie. She gave him the happiness of life that he never had when she was not around.

Joshua stopped and watched through the well-lit window. Maybe one drink, he thought. I'll have one drink to relax me, and then I'll go back to the room. He opened the door and stood there for a moment. No one seemed to notice him. It was as if he was not there in body, only in mind. There were probably two dozen men sitting at the tables or leaning on the bar. Some were playing cards, but most were there for the drinking or chatting with the three women working there. Two of the women dressed in bright, brassy attire, while the third woman dressed in more elegant street attire. In fact, Joshua reminisced, she was dressed similar to Jennie the night of the interview.

Joshua made his way to the bar. The bartender continued conversing with some other men, but finally strolled down to Joshua. "What's your choice, mister?"

"A shot of rye and a beer would be fine."

The bartender grunted and set about fixing the order.

The last time Joshua had done this was when he and Jack would spend a night on the town in Sioux City. He could use his old friend about now. They had depended on each other for so long. He wondered if Jack was happy. Had his life taken any bad turns? Maybe he would go back to Sioux City. That could be one possibility for him, although he would only disrupt Jack's life with his problems.

Joshua was surprised his shot and beer were empty, and ordered a second round. When the rye and beer came, Joshua immediately drank the rye. He turned and looked around the room. Some of the patrons had left, but the bar was still crowded. He sipped his beer, watching those around him. He had been unaware of two hard looking men with their guns hanging on their hips as though they used them often. He wondered if they had been there when he entered or had they come in without him noticing. Either way gave Joshua an uncomfortable feeling that he had not made himself aware of the two men. If he had been wearing his badge or one of the men recognized him and carrying a grudge, it could have been a problem. He was letting his emotions control his mind, endangering his life. He tried to pull his thoughts together. How could he get control of himself?

Joshua finished his beer and ordered another rye and beer. This would be the last. The two gunslingers had begun talking to the well-dressed woman in the saloon. She tried to ignore them, but they became more persistent in their attempt to receive her full attention. Joshua was calculating whether he should intervene in his condition and come to her rescue, when suddenly the bartender shouted from behind the bar, "You boys are through in here. Time to leave." He held a shotgun pointed their direction. Everyone near the two men quickly moved away. The men hesitated, but the bartender was steady and showed no signs of weakness. "Now!" he commanded. The two men left, grumbling as they went.

Joshua realized the precarious position he had placed himself by consuming so much alcohol. If the bartender had not stepped in and taken control of the situation, what could he have done? He placed the beer down and left. Jennie would not have wanted him drinking himself into a stupor.

When Joshua arrived at his room, he sat at the window and watched out over the street. People were going about their business; no one out there cared that Jennie was gone. Each had their own lives to deal with at that moment. For some, it was good and their future prospects looked favorable, and perhaps for others, they faced the same sorrow he felt, finding life but a mere passage of time until it ended.

****

Joshua rode into Cheyenne. He dreaded passing the terrible news to family and friends who had always held Jennie in high esteem. She was a giving, unselfish and caring woman to all that knew her. They enjoyed her friendly manner, her intelligent conversation and her contagious smile. She was so much to so many, and now he had to deliver the news that she was dead. He had failed to save her. How could one say that with words that were not abrupt and cold?

Joshua felt his first stop had to be the Richardson ranch. This would be the hardest for him, trying to soften the pain for Margaret and Hallie. Until now, it had been a selfish concern about his pain and loss, but a mother and sister would also feel immense grief. He hoped he would find Joseph first, and tell him so he would be there to give strength to the women.

Joshua arrived at the lane leading into the Richardson ranch. He could see the lights on inside, as twilight set in on the high plateau. Normally it was a warm, welcoming sight. He wondered what they were doing. Were they sitting in the front room wondering and discussing whether he had found Jennie and was bringing her back to them? Had he saved the woman he loved and cherished, the woman he vowed to protect? He took a deep breath and rode slowly down the lane, saying a prayer under his breath that he could be strong enough, yet gentle enough to give them the news as best as possible.

Joshua reined in his horse and slid from the saddle. He immediately unhitched his gun belt and tied it to his saddle. Somehow walking into the house before removing his weapon seemed harsh, thinking a Bible in hand would be more appropriate. He climbed the porch steps and hesitated before going to the door and knocking.

Joseph answered the door. The look on his face immediately reflected the expression that Joshua showed. Joshua shook his head. Joseph stepped back. "The women are in the front room."

The men solemnly made their way to the parlor where Margaret and Hallie were sitting opposite each other. Hallie looked up, "Joshua!" she shouted, jumping to her feet, and then seeing the expression on the two men's faces, fell back into her chair. "No," she sobbed, "please tell me everything is all right."

Margaret looked up from her chair, her eyes searching for something other than bad news. She never spoke. Joseph took Hallie into his arms as she began to cry mournfully. Joshua moved to the side of Margaret and took her frail hand into his hand. "I'm sorry, Margaret. I found Jennie and she was still alive. She fought for life. She had the will, but not the strength to go on. She died peacefully in my arms, and I buried her at a family plot in Goshe's Hole, well north of here. I tried, oh how I tried, but it just wasn't enough." Joshua's voice began to break. "I'm sorry."

Margaret squeezed his hand. "You have no idea how much it means to me that Jennie died peacefully in your arms. That is such a blessing. That is the way life in this world should end." Her eyes filled with tears, but she never cried.

Hallie came to her mother and squeezed her. They never spoke, but Joshua knew that communication between them was deeper than words could say. When they parted, Hallie looked to Joshua for answers. He knew they would want to know what happened. He wasn't sure how much to tell them. He did not want to make their agony worse than it had to be at this moment.

"It's all right, Joshua...if you're not ready to talk about it," Hallie said, watching Joshua's eyes.

"No, it's not that, Hallie. I just don't want to create any more anguish for you and your mother. I know how hard it is."

"Joshua, we need to know," Margaret added. "We'll never heal wondering what took place the last couple of weeks."

"Let me get you coffee," Hallie said, moving to the kitchen. Joseph followed her, thinking she might need a good cry away from everyone.

"How are you doing?" Margaret asked when they were alone.

"Okay," Joshua replied, his hands clasped.

"Joshua, don't lie to me. I can see it all over your face, in your voice, your mannerisms. You are not okay. Let your feelings out." Margaret stood up and put her arms tightly around Joshua. "We are family and it's important to share emotions and thoughts at times like these. It'll help you, Joshua, and it's part of the healing process for us."

"Margaret, you, Hallie and Joseph are gentle people, just like Jennie was. My feelings right now are filled with so much anger; I don't think it would be fair to spew them on you folks."

Hallie and Joseph had returned while Joshua was talking. Hallie set the coffee down and listened to Joshua as Joseph stood by her with his arm around her.

"I'm angry too, Joshua. I'm sure we all feel the unfairness that such a wonderful person like Jennie would be put through such horrifying trials."

"You don't understand. I am so angry with the Harrison brothers for what they did, angry with myself for letting it happen and not finding her in time. I'm angry with every thug out there with his killing and mayhem. I'm angry with God for letting this happen to Jennie. There are no logical answers and all I want is revenge." Joshua turned away, embarrassed with his outburst.

The other three looked at each other. "Sit Joshua," Hallie said, "and drink your coffee before it gets cold. Maybe we can talk in the morning. We are all absorbed with sorrow. Tomorrow would be better."

"Sorry," Joshua answered. "Perhaps you're right, tomorrow would be better." However, Joshua knew that another day would not change his feelings. Several days had done nothing to help. Time was not the answer.

****

Joshua spent most of the night awake, but waited until he heard others up and about before he came downstairs in the morning. His feelings had not changed, but he knew he had to do a better job controlling his emotions. He had done exactly what he did not want to happen.

Joshua was surprised to find all three of the family members in the kitchen. Hallie was at the stove fixing flapjacks and bacon. The enjoyable aroma filtered through Joshua like a cure-all-tonic. Margaret and Joseph were at the table, drinking coffee and discussing the fall weather when Joshua walked in.

"I didn't realize everyone was up," Joshua commented, "or I would've come down earlier."

"We were trying to be quiet," Joseph responded. "I'm sure you were exhausted from such a hard ride from the north."

"I was. Maybe I didn't realize how tired."

Joseph rose. "I'll pour you some coffee. Made it myself."

"Thanks. I can use it."

"Breakfast coming up in a minute," Hallie added.

Joshua was aware that Margaret had remained unusually quiet. He was apprehensive he had said far too much last night. He struggled to find something light to say to her, hoping to ease the tension...at least with her. "So, Margaret, am I at risk, drinking Joseph's coffee?"

Margaret smiled. "I don't want it to go to his head, but it is quite good."

"Try this," Joseph said, placing a steaming cup of coffee in front of Joshua. "The best thing about this cup is there is a bottom." He laughed. "That's assuming you make it that far."

Hallie served breakfast and while they ate, only made general, light conversation.

After they finished washing the breakfast dishes, everyone went to the front room. Joshua knew they were anxious to hear the details of Jennie's death. He owed them that much. As they said, it was part of their healing process.

Joshua sat next to Margaret, and Joseph with Hallie across from them. As he began, he was attentive to each face, careful not to reveal more than perhaps they were ready to hear. He explained his plan that he undertook, deciding where the brothers would be heading and their route. He explained his plan to outflank them because of their two-day head start. He told of his encounter with the Fuller women and his delay by escorting them home. That delay, he told them, could have delayed his finding Jennie. He would always wonder if that might have caused Jennie's death.

At that moment, Margaret gripped his hand. "You did what was right, Joshua. You are too good a man to have left them in such a deplorable situation. I shall never question your judgment on that decision." Joseph and Hallie nodded in agreement.

"Thank you for those kind words, but I'm afraid it'll always haunt me." Joshua took a deep breath, stared away from everyone for a moment and then resumed with the difficult part of the story, finding Jennie. "She was so frail and battered," he said, his words just above a whisper. "I wrapped her half frozen body with the blankets and started a fire. I fed her broth, hoping she would regain some of her strength. I held her, and kept talking to her. I kept telling her to keep fighting for life, how much I loved her, and that I could not go on without her. She would from time to time open her eyes and tell me she loved me and thanked me

for everything I had done for her. How much I had done for her."
Joshua began to lose control. "It was all that she had done for me,
everything she meant to me. After that night and the next day, it
became obvious that her strength was not improving, and I made
the decision that the following morning I would move her to
somewhere more comfortable for her, and that maybe I could find
a doctor. The next day we left for the Fuller ranch. I carried her in
my arms as we rode slowly towards the ranch. I knew at our
slowed pace, it would take the entire day and into the night, but I
knew I had to find a better place for her to ever recover. About
half way, she asked to stop. She told me she was about to leave
me and wanted me to hold her and we would talk until she
passed. I agreed to her wish as much as I wanted to keep going
and try to save her. I didn't want to give up, and I didn't want her
to give up. Now I'm glad I stopped. I know now she would never
have made it, and that period of time we had together before she
died was like the Lord had brought us such peace and tranquility
beyond one's imagination."

Margaret and Hallie began to cry outwardly. "That's what
I needed to hear, Joshua," Margaret said, her words coming in a
jerking sound. "Oh thank you, Lord," she called.

Joshua held Margaret's hand, unsure what else he should
do. As her crying subsided, she looked at Joshua with her face set.

Suddenly her words became calm. "I want you to listen
carefully, Joshua. I know the anger you are carrying. I
understand. It would be easy for me to be angry and fill my heart
with hate, but I must find forgiveness in my heart for the souls of
those two men. If I don't, I'll have the same tortured soul that they
must have." Her eyes were riveted on Joshua's eyes. "I want you
to find the same forgiveness, Joshua. I want you to find happiness
again. Jennie would want that more than anything for you.
Please try, Joshua. Please."

Joshua listened in disbelief. How could Margaret, Jennie's
mother, ever forgive the terrible things those wretched men had
done to her daughter? There was no forgiveness in his heart for
them, only hate. Joshua looked to Joseph and Hallie to see if they

agreed. They said nothing, their faces showed only remorse, leaving Joshua confused as to their thoughts. Joseph obviously knew that Joshua was upset. He rose. "Let me bring us some more coffee."

Hallie stood. "I'll help," she said.

"No," Joshua said, "Let me help him. Relax, Hallie, you made a delicious breakfast and you deserve a moment."

Hallie, aware of Joshua's state of mind, nodded. "Thank you, Joshua."

Joshua walked into the kitchen. Joseph had his back to him, pouring the coffee.

"Tell me, Joseph, is it me? Am I the only person that has no forgiveness in my heart? Is it only me that is so bitter?"

Joseph turned. He hesitated before he spoke. "Joshua, I'm not sure I will ever find it in my heart to forgive like Margaret feels she needs to do, but I hope she does find the strength. Apparently, it's what she needs before she can ever accept her daughter's death. I hope I can find some acceptance if not forgiveness. I think I need it to help Hallie."

"You have Hallie, and the responsibility to help her. But that's my exact problem. I don't have Jennie. Those despicable men took my Jennie away." Joshua's voice cracked. "I hate them. I hate their souls. May their souls rot in hell!"

Joseph started toward Joshua, but Joshua raised his hand. "Will you tell Tom, and all the others waiting for information on Jennie, what happened? Give them my apologies, but it'd be best if I saw no one for a while. I'm going to head for Colorado. I've got some business I need to attend to."

"Of course. When will we expect you back?"

Joshua shook his head. "I have one thing I need to do, and beyond that I don't know. I really don't know."

"Joshua, please take care. I know you're hurting. Don't do anything rash, and remember our door is always open to you, and inside there'll always be good coffee and someone to listen."

"Thanks."

Joshua immediately packed his saddlebag, and gave his good-byes.

Margaret held Joshua by his arms. "I'm sorry, son. I didn't mean to upset you. With time, we shall mend our broken hearts together. For now we all need a little time for mourning and remembering." She rose up and kissed his cheek. "May God be with you during these painful times."

"Thank you, Margaret. I hope you find the healing that a mourning mother deserves."

Joshua left and headed out from the ranch. He felt as though the walls were crushing him. When alone, he had to answer to no one.

Chapter 28

𝒥oshua rode through Cheyenne and headed straight for Denver. With respect for the U.S. Marshal Office, he chose to turn in his badge at a U.S. Marshal office rather than notify by telegraph. He had always taken pride in his career and wanted to leave with honor. However, the badge no longer allowed him to fulfill his new challenge.

Joshua knew many did not hold being a bounty hunter in highest esteem, but it was what he needed to get results. His goal was to find every vile murderer and low life and bring them to justice, and he would consider death as much a viable justice as a trial.

Joshua had contemplated turning in his badge in Laramie to the U.S. Marshal located at the state prison, but considering it was the prison that had allowed the Harrison brothers to escape and kidnap his Jennie, he decided against it.. His feelings toward them were strained at best and he did not want to have a confrontation. He wanted to finish his business of resigning, collect any new information they had on wanted fugitives, and be on his way. Life had become that simple to him--keep his mind on the need to render justice...feel satisfaction...get revenge.

****

Joshua arrived in Denver and found the U.S. Marshal office. When he entered, he was surprised at the elaborate setup. The outer office had three desks, personnel were using two, and in the back room was the marshal's desk. The office had curtains over its large plate glass windows. Attached to the office by a short passageway, was a stone jail with bars. Maybe he had never set his goals high enough for his office. He had been delighted when he received the potbelly stove.

Joshua's awe of the room was interrupted by a voice, "Good morning, Marshal, may I assist you?"

A young thin man with a fine line mustache was standing before him. He wore a suit that snugly fit about his chest. Maybe I should have made Mark and Matthew dress like that, he thought.

"Yes, sir, you certainly can. Is the marshal in?"

"He will be back shortly. I will tell him you're waiting. May I have your name please?"

"Joshua Parker, out of Cheyenne."

"Oh yes. I will tell him as soon as he returns. Please make yourself comfortable." The man pointed to some overstuffed chairs near the large window facing the street.

While Joshua waited, he continued to stare in amazement at the room. The desks were of fine wood. His desk at the jail had been nothing more than a wooden crate with two sides knocked out. Joshua was surprised when a figure suddenly blocked his vision of the room.

"I'm Marshal Cranston," the large man growled. He almost sounded disgusted that he had to talk to Joshua. Joshua wondered if he and Harley had been friends at some time in their lives.

"I'm Marshal Parker," Joshua responded, not wanting to give any more information than he had received. Joshua already felt irritated talking to the man. At least there would be no socializing.

"Zachery said you wanted to see me?"

"Yes I do. Perhaps your office might be more suitable." Joshua was going to resign with a little more dignity than hand his badge to Cranston in the middle of the outer public office.

Without another word, Marshal Cranston turned and headed for his office. Joshua assumed he was supposed to follow. Marshal Cranston walked straight to his desk. Joshua followed him inside, closed the door and sat uninvited in one of the chairs.

Marshal Cranston leaned back, placed his hands across his stomach, and began tapping his fingers as though counting out the seconds until Joshua left. Joshua had not wanted to, nor planned to be neighborly, but the thought of irritating Marshal Cranston was just too tempting.

"Weather's been getting a might chilly, wouldn't you say?"

"Expected. It's that time of year." Marshal Cranston's fingers were beginning to move more rapidly.

"You're right there. There was some snow in the pass getting here from Cheyenne, but it hasn't laid in too heavily yet. Good thing for me I guess."

"Could snow three feet in a day and you might not get back 'till spring."

Sounds like a hint to hurry up, Joshua determined. "Have you been in the area long?"

"Ten years. You said you had business?"

"Yes. I'm sorry if I'm keeping you from capturing some bad guys...or do you have a rendezvous date with one of the ladies over at the ...what was it called, I saw it coming in...Bernice's Ladies."

"What the darn heck you up to, Parker?"

"I was just trying to be friendly. You're acting like your boots are too tight."

"I've taken away from my busy schedule to see what I could do for you, Marshal Parker. Now if we could get down to business."

"Actually Marshal, I came to resign and turn in my badge. I kept having doubts, whether I was doing the right thing, but since meeting you, I know I am. So here is my badge, Marshal."

Joshua laid his badge on the table. "Don't forget, my name is Joshua Parker. And if you don't mind, I'll be stopping by your elaborate wanted board out front. If there is anything I can do to help, just let me know."

The marshal stood, listening to Joshua but never replying. Joshua started to extend his hand, just long enough to have the marshal respond by starting to extend his, and then Joshua dropped his. "Never mind, I don't want to take up too much of your time. Have a good day."

Joshua left the office. He needed that pouch of tobacco about now. He could stand at the door of the marshal's office, slowly roll his cigarette, light it up and casually take a puff before ambling on towards the wanted board. Instead, he paused at the doorway, and then feeling stupid, headed towards the board. He had to practice being lackadaisical.

The number of wanted posters that he had not seen surprised Joshua. He assumed there might be a few new ones that he had missed during the recent days, but somehow he seemed to be out of the loop on most everything concerning his office. He received little information or instructions, and no one ever visited him. He reasoned no one would care or miss him now that he was gone. He wanted to kick something, really bad. He chose the polished desk that the clerk was sitting behind to release his frustration. The clerk jumped to his feet in disarray.

"It needed to be broke in a little like a new saddle," Joshua said as he strolled towards the door. It was a small satisfaction, but at least it was something.

****

On his return to Cheyenne, the first thing Joshua wanted to do was visit the Gazette and see Thomas. He felt guilty for being rude and not bringing the news firsthand about Jennie. He had been a long time friend of Jennie and he deserved more than Joshua had given him.

Thomas looked up from his typeset when Joshua entered. Thomas grabbed a rag and wiped his hand as he hurriedly came to the front. He grabbed Joshua's hand and threw his other arm around him. "I'm so darn sorry, Joshua," he said. "She was an angel. I miss her beyond belief and I cannot imagine what it is doing to you."

"I can't seem to function, Thomas. I've turned into an angry beast of some sort. I can't seem to get my head straight that she's gone and I'm suppose to go on with life. I'm sorry I didn't come personally to tell you the news."

"That's fine, Joshua. Joseph told me you were struggling. I understand."

"It's like I want to kill somebody, but both the brothers are already dead. I can't go near the sheriff's office. He might be the one I kill. I want to get even with the Laramie prison for allowing the Harrisons to escape, but I know they lost many good men, too. I can't seem to make things square, or even things up."

The front door opened and an elderly man stuck his head inside. "When's the next edition coming out?"

"Tomorrow, Arthur." Arthur nodded and closed the door.

"The paper was due out today, but I have an article on Jennie and I've been struggling to find all the right words I want to say. Normally I don't have this problem. Jennie always said I could write about anything at anytime. If the poor thing only knew."

"I'm sure it's difficult. I don't know how you can even do it. Another bit of news, I resigned and turned in my badge yesterday."

"Sorry to hear that. We need someone good like you around here."

"I'm not leaving and I'm not giving up going after the criminals."

Thomas eyed Joshua curiously. "You're becoming a bounty hunter?"

"I am. I had too many restrictions as a marshal. I can go anywhere, anytime and bring them back using my rules."

"Be careful, Joshua. As a warning, I've seen more than one bounty hunter end up outside the law and eventually having a bounty on their heads."

"Thanks for the warning, but it's something I feel I have to do."

"You know Mark and Matthew want to see you. They both resigned from the sheriff's office after the blunder the sheriff made with the telegram about the Harrisons' escape."

"I knew how angry Mark was. I'd never be able to work for the man after that either. I'm sorry it all didn't work out for them."

"Aw, they'll be fine."

"I'm staying at the Rollins if you need me. I'm not sure how long I'll be in town. Weather may play a factor on that. Thanks for being a good friend, Thomas."

"It was my privilege."

****

Dan Barnes leaned back against the hitching post across the street from the National Bank. He had been watching it for two days. It would be an easy target. Tomorrow, his two partners and he would clean the bank out. The three men had started their lawless spree in Kansas. They had remained in the Kansas and Nebraska area until they killed a teller at a bank robbery near Lincoln. They began moving west through Nebraska and into southern Wyoming. From there they had plans to head north into the lucrative mining camps of the gold country in the Black Hills of the Dakotas.

Taking the bank in Cheyenne would be an easy pick for the Sagebrush Gang. That was a name given to them in Kansas when the newspaper there said they just disappeared into the sagebrush.

Coming west, the Sagebrush Gang had split to remain less conspicuous, with Dan Barnes coming west through southern Nebraska and his two partners taking the more northerly route of Nebraska. They had a disappearing reputation and Dan was determined to keep it that way. The partners had arrived yesterday. Dan learned about their stupid escapade coming south when they had raped two young women. Dan, angered by their lack of brains, sent them straight to the hideout that they planned

212

to use after the robbery for a few days. They would wait there a few days until things cooled down before heading north. If his partners would keep their noses clean and follow his plans, Dan figured they could continue their robberies indefinitely.

****

After leaving the Gazette, Joshua retired to his hotel room and began sorting through all the posters he had accumulated in Colorado. He slowly looked at each paper, and then laid them in different stacks on the bed. Some were older and in different territories. They were less likely to be around Cheyenne and the surrounding territory. Some had pictures or drawings, adding an added possibility of recognizing them. Others were ones that he had captured earlier, or someone else had captured. Three of those posters were the three Harrison brothers. Joshua felt fortunate that there were no pictures on their posters. He angrily ripped each one to shreds and threw the pieces in the trashcan. He was nearly through the entire stack when he came upon a poster with a drawing. The drawing had a likeness to one of the two men that he had met on the road north in search of Jennie, one of the men that had raped the Fuller women. He was a member of the Sagebrush Gang out of Kansas and Nebraska. They were wanted for murder. He found two more posters, without drawings, of the Sagebrush Gang. More than likely, he figured, one of the two other posters was the second rapist. If the rapists were two members of the Sagebrush Gang, where was the third member? Other questions persisted: where were the two men heading? Were they meeting up with the third member?

Joshua laid the three posters of the Sagebrush Gang apart from the others and headed for the Red Rock Cafe. He would inquire at the different saloons to see if anyone had heard anything or had seen a stranger resembling the drawing.

The nightly rounds of the Cheyenne saloons produced nothing for Joshua concerning the Sagebrush Gang. He became convinced his wild search for the members would not produce any results, and he decided to go ahead with his original plan and head north to the badlands of the Dakotas and the gold fields. He was certain he could stay busy there for some time.

He would pack and prepare tomorrow, and weather permitting, he would leave early the following morning.

The next morning, a loud pounding on the door awakened Joshua. He rolled from his bed, slipped his revolver from his holster and crept to the door. "Can I help you?" he called out.

"We're here to help you," a familiar voice called out.

"Just a minute, Mark, I've got to get my pants on."

Shortly, he swung open the door and came face to face with two broad grins. "How you doing, Marshal?" Mark asked as he and Matthew stepped inside.

"A few moments ago I was sleeping and I was doing fine," Joshua replied with a grin. The exuberant youth did wonders to his withered soul.

Mark sat on the bed and Matthew sat back in the lone chair in the room. Mark was quick to get to his point. "I talked to my father and he told me what you'd done...you know, about giving up the badge and becoming a bounty hunter. We want to join you."

Joshua rubbed his hand through his hair. "The answer is, no."

The smile dissipated from their faces. "Why not?" Matthew asked, now leaning forward.

"First of all, Thomas would kill me personally if I led you two into something like this. Get it straight, both of you, this is not a venture for the light-hearted. Secondly, this is personal. This is something I need to do for myself."

The two young men remained silent. Mark looked behind him to where Matthew was sitting, then back to Joshua. "Okay, Marshal. We'll respect your wishes," Mark said, as both men stood. "I'm really sorry about Jennie. She was a great person and I miss her a lot."

"Yeah," Matthew added, "I'm really sorry, Marshal. She was one of the best."

"Thanks, guys. Jennie was the greatest. And I do appreciate you trying to look after me, but this is something I've got to do for myself."

The two young men started shuffling towards the door.

"Wait," Joshua said. "Let me get dressed, wash the cobwebs from my eyes and I'll buy you two breakfast."

"Darn right," Mark quickly responded, his smile returning. "We sure are going to miss you, Marshal."

"Yeah we will," Matthew added.

"Good. I'll miss your ugly mugs, too. And stop calling me marshal."

"Yeah, sure, Mr. Parker."

Joshua grinned. "You two will never let up. You're like a two headed snake, coming at me from all sides."

The two young men burst into a hearty laugh. "We'll see you out front, Mr. Parker, so you can prettify yourself," Mark chided.

"Get out," Joshua ordered, kicking at Mark's rear end as they left.

As Joshua readied himself, he thought how much he enjoyed the two young friends and if he had them with him, they would help ease the gnawing loneliness he constantly felt. However, he knew that there would be dark moments in his quest; moments that he would not want to expose to his two young friends. He would only be self-serving if he allowed them to come along, and besides, this was something he needed to do for personal reasons.

As promised, Mark and Matthew were waiting out front when Joshua came down from his room.

Mark immediately began his taunt. "So it took you all that time to get ready and I don't see where it has helped one iota."

"You're not getting under my skin, Mark, so give it up," Joshua responded as they moved towards the eatery.

As soon as they were seated, Mark became serious. "Have you been over to the sheriff's office yet?"

"No, and I won't either. I might end up killing him if he rubbed me the wrong way."

"Know the feeling," Mark responded, biting his lip in anger. "I'll never get over his arrogant self-serving decision to ignore the telegram because he was so busy trying to make points with big-wigs around here."

"That's something I've had a real hard time with since I've been in Cheyenne. Politics is everywhere. I never got into it. That's one of the reasons I decided to quit as marshal. I would rather do it on my own without all the elbow rubbing that goes on."

The server took their order and left. The three sat quietly for some time before Matthew spoke. "So you're leaving tomorrow?"

"Tomorrow, unless these storm clouds bring in a whopper."

"Remember, we're still available," Matthew offered.

"Yeah, we are," Mark added.

After breakfast, Joshua parted ways with the two friends and began preparing for his trip north the following day. He had to admit, the couple of hours with Mark and Matthew had helped take his mind off his sorrow and he regretted that he would be leaving them behind, but he would not change his mind. Joshua looked to the sky. Storm clouds were moving in from the northwest. Joshua scrunched his face. His trip would not be a pleasant one.

Chapter 29

Joshua was ready to leave for the Dakotas--his supplies purchased, his horses shoed, and his good-byes done, except stopping at the Richardson ranch on the way out of Cheyenne. He walked into the Red Rock Cafe for the last time, or at least for a while, and settled in the corner for supper and to read the day old Gazette. He began to scan the paper for the article about Jennie when a man ran by on the street shouting about a hold up at the National Bank.

Joshua jumped up and hurried out into the street. Another man was shouting about the robbery. Joshua raced to the bank a block away where a crowd had gathered. The sheriff and a deputy arrived at nearly the same time as Joshua. The sheriff immediately found the teller who was working at the time of the robbery, and started asking questions. Joshua listened as he stood nearby without interrupting.

"There were three bandits," the teller said excitedly. "They all wore masks. They demanded the money..."

"How much?" the sheriff asked.

"I'm not positive, but I think at least fifteen hundred. I'll need to count for sure."

"Go on," the sheriff asserted.

"Well, of course I gave them the money. They all had guns. They left on horseback. I followed them into the street and I saw them turn north down Hill.

The sheriff looked up. "Anyone else see the men?" No one answered. It was at that moment that the sheriff saw Joshua. He nodded, but said nothing. He looked back to the teller, "we'll see what we can find. You had better tell Mr. Haskins. He's not going to be happy."

"Certainly not," the teller responded. "I already have someone on the way to tell him."

"All right, I guess we're finished here," the sheriff said casually, "let's go Henry."

Joshua watched them leave. The teller remained, still anxious to tell anyone that wanted to listen to his hair-raising story. Joshua approached him. "Hi, I'm Joshua Parker."

The teller eyed him, paused for a moment, and then spoke. "You're the marshal, aren't you?'

"I was. Not anymore. I resigned recently. Mind if I ask you a few questions?"

"Yeah, go ahead, Marshal."

"Thanks. For formality, your name is....

"Jacob Franklin."

"Jacob, you said they were all wearing masks, so I assume you never got a good look at their faces?"

"No, but the one holding the gun on me while I was getting the money had a big scar on his forehead. The other two bandits were standing near the door."

"You were alone in the bank?"

"Yes. Sidney always leaves about half an hour before closing."

"Always?"

"Yeah."

"So they had probably been staking out the bank and knew you would be alone. Ever see any strangers hanging around the bank?"

"No. Wait. Wait. Now that you mention it, yesterday Sidney asked if I knew the man was that was standing across the street. He said he had been there for some time and had noticed him the day before. I was somewhat busy at the time so I paid little attention to the man, but I would imagine Sidney got a good glimpse of him. I've sent for him also, so he should be here shortly."

"You saw them turn down Hill?"

"Yes."

"Could you describe the horses?"

"It was getting dark. They all looked dark in color."

"Were the men tall, short, skinny, or heavy-set?"

"The two men guarding the door were both tall and slim looking. The one with the gun pointed at me looked shorter and somewhat stout looking. Actually kind of like the man Sidney mentioned outside the bank."

Joshua reached in his pocket and pulled out the three wanted posters he had tucked away, carefully unfolded them, and showed them to Sidney. "Does the drawing or descriptions of any of these men here fit the robbers last night?"

Jacob carefully read each sheet of paper, looked up and shook his head slowly. "They could perhaps. It's just hard to say, and the drawing, I can't tell. I don't think it was the one with the gun held on me."

"Okay. You've been a big help. Thanks, Jacob."

"Why didn't the sheriff ask me these questions?"

"I don't know, Jacob, you'll have to ask the sheriff. Maybe he had an important meeting with the mayor and city officials."

The next morning as Joshua had breakfast, the eatery was abuzz with the robbery from the night before at the National Bank. Joshua listened to the usual speculation about the bandits, how much they robbed, and where they had disappeared to in the night. He quickly dispersed the idle chat and speculation, but his ears caught an interesting conversation at a nearby table. "I saw three riders heading out in a hurry shortly after dark. Struck me odd they turned onto the old Potter road. Nobody takes that road anymore, especially in an all fired hurry."

Joshua paid for his breakfast, picked up his cup of coffee and moved over to the table where the man with his story sat with two other men. He was an older man with a white scraggly beard, and a weather beaten, wrinkled face from many days of exposure to the weather. His eyes were dark and small.

"Mind if I join you? Your story has me interested," Joshua said.

Obviously, the old man was pleased as a broad smile spread across an otherwise stern looking face. "Sure can. I got no claim here," he responded.

"My name is Joshua Parker." He extended his hand.

"Cal," he said, grasping Joshua's hand. "This is Walter and Hugh," he continued as he slowly released Joshua's hand. Joshua acknowledged the other two and turned his attention back to Cal. I overheard what you said about three men in a hurry heading down Potter road. I've been here for several years and I don't remember any Potter road."

"You're the marshal, aren't you?"

"Not anymore, I resigned."

"Oh." The old man paused as though digesting the information, then without further question, continued. "I'm not real sure if Potter road is the right name, but it was the only one I ever heard. Not used anymore. There are three or four abandoned cabins back there. The road is overgrown. Last night, these three men were in one heck of a hurry and turned off on the old road. If they hadn't been in such a hurry or hadn't chosen that road, I might not have even paid a lick of attention to them."

"Did they look like they were coming from the bank that was robbed?"

"No. Actually they were coming from almost the opposite direction."

"Maybe circled around."

"Darned if you're probably not right. They could have. Cut over on Hill and turned back."

"So the cabins are empty now?"

"Yeah, pretty sure. Rufus moved about a year ago. Not sure why people move out and not sure why they moved in. I guess they're trying to find something they ain't got. A small creek out that way, and some small rocky knolls. Can't raise much out there but rattlers." Cal laughed.

"Did you get a look at the riders or horses?

"Moving too fast and dark to see the riders very good. The horses were sorrels I think. The one rider did look at me for a flash as they went by. I thought maybe he'd come back and shoot me, but I reckon they were in too big a hurry."

Joshua pulled out his wanted posters. "Recognize this one?" he said pointing to the one with the drawing.

"I think I do," Cal responded quickly. "I wasn't sure I got a very good look at the rider, but he's the one. I'm pretty sure."

Joshua's heart leaped. He was closing in on the scoundrels that raped the Fuller women. "Thank you, Cal" he said excitedly and almost leaped from the table. He quickly nodded to the other man and left the building. The trip north would be on hold for a few days.

Joshua immediately went to the stable, saddled his bay and headed for the hotel. He took two Colt 44 revolvers and his Winchester, and plenty of ammunition. He would certainly not capture them because he had an inadequate arsenal.

Joshua wasted no time riding to where he was supposed to find Potter road. As he headed towards the location, he wondered how the Sagebrush Gang out of Nebraska and Kansas would know about Potter road. Someone had given them the information: either willingly assisting them, or unknowingly. Whichever, Joshua figured someone in town had, had a good look at them. However, for now, he would follow the clues he had, which seemed reliable.

Snow had fallen overnight, but Joshua spotted the indention of horse tracks leading into an area overgrown by brush, weeds and grass. Joshua dismounted and made his way on foot for a short distance. A road obviously had existed there in the past, but like Cal had mentioned, had been abandoned for some time. He remounted and followed the rutted trail. Joshua wondered how the three riders found their way in the darker evening light. They had traveled the trail before their get-away.

As he moved further down the road, he was able to determine horse tracks going in and coming out of the area. His eyes carefully scanned the area, watching for a possible ambush. Joshua was convinced they were still in there somewhere, because the freshest tracks were the ones going in.

Joshua had been on the road for about a mile, when he came to a bend in the road about one hundred yards ahead. He moved off the road until past the bend to be sure he maintained the element of surprise on his side. As he came around the bend, he spotted an old cabin ahead with the roof half caved in and it was obviously empty. As he moved back towards the road, he could see the horse tracks continuing beyond the deserted structure.

About a quarter mile further, Joshua spotted a structure set one hundred feet back from the road, mostly hidden by aspen and brush. Joshua retreated from the sight of the building and crossed the road to the same side as the structure. He studied the layout of the terrain. Anyone inside the building, from its vantage point, could spot someone approaching along the road for some distance, making it an ideal hideout. Although uncertain that the cabin was even occupied, Joshua approached it with extreme caution. He could feel his blood pumping, thinking he might be close to finding the two rapists of the young women. Capturing the heathens, dead or alive, could help ease the torment of the two women, and benefit all of society.

Joshua decided to circle behind the building to a small knoll. From that location, he could better determine if the building was occupied, and if so, how to approach it. This would allow him to maintain the element of surprise.

He crossed a small stream, making a mental note that in a month it would be frozen solid. Once behind the knoll, he left his horse, and made his way by foot to its crest. He kneeled and looked over the cabin one hundred yards ahead. He could see a light billow of smoke coming from the chimney, assuring him it was occupied. Joshua had no way knowing it was the bandits occupying the cabin, but he had to assume it was. A second structure, the barn, was about fifty to one hundred feet behind the cabin. The horses would probably be hidden there.

Joshua decided to ride a short distance beyond the cabin, leave his horse and come in by foot from the opposite direction of his arrival. He could follow the small stream, partially lined with barren willow and small shrubs, giving him some coverage and hopefully their attention would be in the opposite direction.

Joshua found a small draw to hide his horse that was far enough away that any sounds his horse might decide to make could not be heard from the cabin. He removed his rifle from the saddle holster, checked to ensure it was loaded, slung the ammunition belt around his head and shoulder and made his way towards the cabin. He moved slowly and cautiously along the sparsely covered streambed. The snow crunching under his feet seemed to echo loudly through the cold winter air.

Eventually, Joshua arrived about fifty feet behind the barn. From there, he crept the remaining distance to the barn and peered inside through a crack in the logs. It was dark inside and his vision was slight. There were at least two horses, but he could not even tell their color. He found a larger slit, but his vision of the horses was more inhibited.

The barn door faced the back of the cabin and only small scrubs stood between the barn and the cabin. A feed trough was near the barn and a well was closer to the cabin. Both could offer protection once he reached them.

Joshua moved to the edge of the barn. He was bent low and ready to make a dash to the old feed trough, when suddenly the back door of the cabin opened and a man stepped outside. Joshua swung back behind the barn. He took a deep breath. Slowly, Joshua peered around the corner. The man had his back to him, relieving himself. He finished and turned, looking directly in Joshua's direction. Joshua's heart leaped. It was one of the men

Joshua had passed. He was looking straight at one of the despicable rapists. His first impulse was to kill the lowlife where he stood, but it would put him at a disadvantage with the two remaining outlaws inside.

The man spit and called out to the ones inside. "The horses are acting a little spooked."

"So why you telling us?" a voice shouted back from inside the house. "Go check it out."

The man grumbled something and pulled his revolver from its holster. He started for the barn, and then stopped. "It's too cold out here for this," he mumbled aloud, and headed back for the cabin.

Once the man returned inside, Joshua moved like a stalking cat to the feed trough. He settled behind the trough and reviewed his surrounding from his new location. He decided the rotted trough would offer very little coverage if a gunfight ensued. Forty-four caliber bullets would penetrate the rotted wood with ease. Although it would be twice as far to the side of the cabin than to the well, he chose the side of the cabin because the well would leave him vulnerable with nowhere to go. The side of the shack had no windows or doors, but he figured the dilapidated structure would allow him to listen to the conversations inside.

Swiftly, Joshua raced for the side of the cabin. The back door opened. Joshua lunged out of sight alongside the building. A voice rang out, "Sitting around here is making me crazy. I'm beginning to feel like a bull penned up next to some heifers."

"Quit complaining," a voice inside responded. "We've got the law off our back."

"They could show up here anytime and we're goners for sure."

"If they were going to show, they'd be here by now. We sit tight a couple days and ride out of here one by one and no one is the wiser. Especially with the law around here, dumb as a rock."

An abundance of laughter split through the chilled air. "Yeah, I know, but we've got all this damn money and here we sit.

I've been told the gold country has all these ladies aching to please us."

"Ladies!" They're all whores, Jake." Laughter started again.

"Who cares? I've got the money to spend if we ever get there."

"Maybe we'll find our two ladies again out on the road."

"That would be nice...really nice. I liked the way the little one begged. It really excited me."

"That was stupid," the third man said. "That's the kind of stupid stuff that'll get us caught and hung."

"It was worth it, Dan. Both were so deliciously young and tender."

"Nothing is worth getting hanged."

"Calm down. I think you could use a soft woman for a night, yourself."

Jake returned inside.

Joshua's anger was at a high pitch, listening to the horrendous discussion of Elizabeth and Julia, but he had to maintain control. Elizabeth and Julia's moment would come soon.

They were not leaving for another day or two. Joshua needed to force their hand and get them outside in the open. The wind was beginning to pick up and Joshua did not want to be sitting out in the cold, waiting for them. He regretted not taking down one of the men when he had a chance.

Joshua looked around him. About twenty feet behind him was a small draw. He could cover the front and back of the house by moving along the indentation. He quickly moved to his new location. He could toss a rock on the small front porch. The thud would perhaps draw them outside. He shook his head. It was a poor scheme.

Joshua started scheming for another idea. His eyes fixed on the barn. He needed to unsettle the horses. At least one of the men would check on them, hopefully two. Joshua could lie in wait in the gully and pick them off as they came outside. He gathered several rocks and began to pelt the barn roof. After the third stone, Joshua could begin to hear movement inside the barn, and then the horses began to kick and whinny.

"Bart, check out the horses. Something's got them spooked."

"Why me? Jake, why don't you go?"

"Because I end up doing everything. It sure the hell is your turn."

"Alright, I'll go, but someone cover me. There seems to be a lot of bears around here. I thought they were supposed to be in hibernation by now."

"I'll protect your rear end. Let me get the rifle."

Joshua settled in and took bead on the backdoor. His finger rested lightly on the trigger. The door opened and the first man stepped outside. It was the second rapist. Joshua's pulse increased. He had the no count in his sights, all he needed to do was squeezed the trigger, but he waited. Shortly the second man appeared. It was the third missing outlaw. He glanced in Joshua's direction. A large scar was across his forehead. He was the apparent leader. Joshua decided to bring him down first. The first outlaw was in the middle of the open space between buildings. Joshua aimed and fired. The outlaw dropped where he stood. He never felt a thing, Joshua thought. Joshua immediately turned to the exposed outlaw, whom had turned in shock to see his comrade on the ground. Before he could regain his senses and move, Joshua fired again and he fell in the snow. The man grabbed his leg in pain. He tried to rise, but Joshua fired again, hitting the other leg. The man lay motionless, moaning. Joshua did not want to kill the man yet. He had to know why he was going to die.

Joshua turned his attention to the third man still inside the cabin, the other rapist, Jake. He was the one that enjoyed Julia begging him to stop. He would certainly know what he did before he died.

"Come out," Joshua called. "You're alone now."

There was no response. Joshua waited in the draw halfway between the front and back. He waited a few more seconds, reloading his weapons. "Times up. Throw out your weapons and come out with your hands in the air."

There was a short pause before the man replied. "Okay, I'm coming out the back."

The thought decoy immediately raced through Joshua's mind. Why would he mention back. Joshua moved closer to the front, yet still able to watch the back.

A rifle slowly appeared at the front door and then Jake. Joshua fired and Jake dropped the rifle, clutching his shoulder. Joshua, with revolver in hand, moved swiftly towards the wounded rapist.

"Don't shoot," he begged.

"You're Jake?"

"Yeah."

"Remember me?"

Jake only looked confused.

"I know you remember the two young women who were so young and tender. The ones your friend over here and you so viciously raped."

Joshua motioned Jake to the back of the cabin. Both men looked at Joshua in fear.

"For whatever reason, I'm going to give you a chance to live. A chance you never gave those young innocent women. Did you know one was a young teenager? Of course you did, but you could care less. Only for your own personal pleasure. You couldn't care less what it did to those poor young women."

Neither man spoke, only staring helplessly at Joshua.

"I'm going to give you a chance to draw."

"My shoulder's been hit. I can't. I need a doctor."

"You'll die as you stand then, and for you," Joshua said, looking at the other man, "there is nothing wrong with your shooting hand.

"I remember you. You're the marshal we saw on the trail. You can't just shoot us," Bart said, as he lay on the ground.

Joshua showed a broad smile. "You're wrong on two counts, you worthless bucket of horse dung. First, I'm no longer a marshal. Second, I wouldn't even care if I was." Joshua pulled the wanted poster from his pocket. "Wanted dead or alive, I'll get the reward either way, and dead is easier. Now draw."

"I'm shot bad," Jake said

"Lucky for you, the wound is not on your shooting hand.

"We need a doctor," Bart demanded.

"If you outdraw me and kill me, you can head for Cheyenne and find yourself a doctor, and if I win, you won't need a doctor. Now draw."

Joshua stepped back ten feet, his eyes watching both men "I'm going to draw at the count of three unless you choose sooner. I reckon none of us knows just how quick the other might be and shortly some of us still won't know."

"You can't just shoot us. What kind of man are you?"

"You raped two helpless young women. What kind of men are you?"

Joshua's hand dropped to the butt of his Colt. "I'm going to start counting. One...two,"

Jake went for his revolver. As it cleared his holster, Joshua fired once, twice. The shots rang true and the outlaw stumbled and fell backwards into the snow, his shot fired harmlessly into the sky. He lay motionless. Joshua turned to the second man. Still on the ground, the second killer's revolver was in his hand as Joshua fired. Bart stared blankly at Joshua for a moment before falling silently into the red stained snow.

"You'll never get the chance to touch another woman with your filthy hands."

Joshua checked all three men, ensuring they were dead. He brought his horse to the cabin, saddled the dead men's horses and loaded the three bodies on them. He would collect a nice reward for these three fugitives, and he would use the money to continue his hunt for other despicable low life like them.

****

Joshua led a caravan of three dead men lying across the saddles of their horses and an increasing number of onlookers as he proceeded down the streets of Cheyenne to the sheriff's office.

As Joshua swung from the saddle in front of the office, a crowd of twenty or thirty people had gathered. Questions came at him from all directions, but all that Joshua said was "I'll explain it all to the sheriff and he can answer whatever he chooses."

As Joshua finished tying the last horse to the hitching post, the sheriff came from the office and leaned on the rail. "Looks like you've been busy."

"Sure have, Sheriff. These are your three bandits that robbed the National Bank. They are also the three on these wanted posters." Joshua removed them from his pocket and handed them to the sheriff.

The sheriff looked them over. "The Sagebrush gang, that's pretty impressive, Marshal.

"Not marshal any more, Sheriff, I resigned from that job a few day ago. I'm eligible to collect the reward."

"You shouldn't be taking the law into your hands like that. That's what I'm here for."

Joshua struggled not to make a scene. He carefully worded his statement. "I was going on a hunch, Sheriff. Didn't want to waste your time."

The sheriff was not amused. "It's my job, and next time, I'd appreciate it if you'd notify me of any mass killings you're about to do."

"I took whatever action was needed, Sheriff. I'm not interested in the politics of this city. I just want my reward."

"Don't worry, I'll make sure you get it. Be here tomorrow morning and I'll have it ready for you."

Joshua left. The sheriff was busy ordering a deputy to deliver the bodies to the undertaker.

Joshua had hoped he would feel better once he had disposed of the three men, but the anger and emptiness remained inside him. There should be a feeling of rejoicing now, but instead he found the heart empty...his soul aching...and the yearning for life gone. His inner most being was still calling out for Jennie.

Chapter 30

The following morning, Joshua stopped by the sheriff's office to pick up his reward for the Sagebrush gang. Seeing a rankled sheriff doling out the reward made the morning unusually enjoyable for Joshua. There would never be enough he could do to even-out the wrong, caused by the sheriff, but everything helped.

Joshua planned the remainder of the day saying good-byes. He would be gone an indefinite period, if he ever returned. His future was empty--no plans, no dreams, only one day at a time.

Joshua's first stop was the Gazette to see Thomas. Thomas quickly closed up shop and offered Joshua a drink at the nearby saloon. Thomas purchased two mugs of beer and they found an empty table near the back.

"I should do things like this more often," Thomas said. "I get too tied to that darn Gazette and I don't leave enough free time to enjoy the better things in life."

"I know what you're talking about. I had this confound idea that I needed to be spending all my time chasing the bad guys, when I should have been home loving Jennie, the good one."

"Where you headed?" Thomas asked.

"How do you know I'm headed anywhere?"

"You never stop by to chat. There is always a reason and I assume you're leaving and stopped to say good-bye."

"I'm that obvious?"

Thomas nodded as a smile appeared. "You are."

"The Dakotas."

"Any reason?"

"Yeah, I think there's a lot of low-life there, and I'd like to rectify some of that. The other reason, it's not here. Not a constant reminder."

"As a friend, Joshua, I don't think either reason is a very good one. The first one, where you're going, I'm concerned you're only going to find trouble. The second one, Joshua, you're avoiding something that you will eventually need to deal with, not run from. Stay around here and find something, Joshua. Go out to the Richardson ranch and work for Joseph for six months or a year, or come in here and work for me at the Gazette for a while. Face the hard times with those you know and care about you. Up there you're going to be alone, the nights will be longer, and time will become endless. Please heed what I'm telling you, Joshua. I'm your friend."

"I appreciate the advice, Thomas. I really do, but this is something I have to do. There is another reason I'm headed that way. Two of the robbers I brought in yesterday raped two young women that I found along the road when I was looking for Jennie. They're devastated, particularly the young teenage girl, and I want to tell them the two maggots are dead and everything will be all right."

"I see. That's a just reason, and I do hope it helps them heal from such a horrendous act. Still, Joshua, you could return after you see them and not go on to the Dakotas."

"As a friend, Thomas, I'll be frank with you. You're trying to change my mind and me, and the only one who could do that was Jennie. My father couldn't. It's within me to be what I am. The bad news for you, Thomas, is that you have a son just like me. Mark and Matthew wanted to go with me. I said no, but it's not going to stop him. At some point the itch will take over unless

231

Mark finds a woman like I found Jennie, and even then it'll take a while to finish scratching that itch."

"I know. Maybe I'm practicing on you so I'll be prepared to deal with Mark."

"It probably won't help."

"I suppose, but as a father I have to keep trying. Nothing personal, but I don't want him following your path."

"Maybe I need to leave. It might settle his wings. He won't be watching me and getting ideas. I hope he doesn't follow my path either."

"I do wish you the best of luck, Joshua."

Both stood and shook hands. "Thanks, and thanks for being such a good friend," Joshua said. "I was at a total loss when I first arrived. You saved me from the wolves."

"I was glad I could help, but you would've survived just fine on your own. That's what you are, Joshua, a survivor."

"Strange, I don't feel like one."

The two friends parted ways. Joshua wondered if it would be for the last time.

****

After the conversation with Thomas, Joshua decided to avoid saying good-bye to Mark and Matthew. He did not want to influence their young minds any further. He believed it would not change their destiny, particularly Mark, but there was no sense adding fuel to the fire.

The next visit was the Richardson ranch. Joshua knew this would not be easy, but he had to say good-bye. They deserved no less.

When Joshua arrived at the ranch, Joseph was working on the buckboard. He waved and called out, "Be in, in just a minute," and continued his work.

Before Joshua could dismount, Hallie came onto the porch. "So glad to see you, Joshua," she said as she came down the porch steps. "I was afraid we might not see you for awhile." She proceeded to give him a long, tight hug.

"Why would you think I wouldn't come around?"

"You seemed quite upset when you left the last time. We were afraid you might be high-tailing it off somewhere and we wouldn't get to see you."

They climbed to the porch, her arm around his waist. "Actually," he said pulling the door open for her, "I'm headed north to the Dakotas."

Her face showed disappointment, but she remained steady. "I'm not going to ask why. I know you have your reasons and I'm sure you don't want any lectures."

"Thanks, Hallie. I do appreciate that."

Margaret came from the kitchen with a cup that had steam rising from it. "Joshua," she said cheerfully. " I'm glad I didn't frighten you away."

"Never, Margaret."

Margaret set her cup down and hugged Joshua. "I suppose we're not just lucky that you stopped by for any other reason than to sit a spell."

"He's leaving for the Dakotas, Mother," Hallie said.

"Long trip, Joshua, especially this time of year," Margaret replied, her face tightening, showing her concern.

"I know it's not the wisest decision."

"It's not for any of us to question, Joshua. I've done some serious thinking and I realize we all need to do what is best for each of us. We're all different. You've taught this old woman a lesson," Margaret answered. Joshua felt a little bewildered. Maybe the good-bye was not going to be so bad. He had expected more questioning or perhaps interrogation about his trip, especially from Margaret, but it sounded like she was supporting him, or at least without condemnation.

Joseph had come into the house. Hallie quickly informed him of Joshua's plans.

Joseph nodded and quietly stood by, trying to analyze the situation. He was probably confused like Joshua, expecting fire, but not even seeing smoke.

Joshua assumed that Hallie and Margaret had had a discussion concerning him and decided not to question his plans and wishes. It made Joshua feel much better that he could leave without any conflict or unsettled issues. He remembered how it felt when he had left home for the army and then his return after the war. It was not a feeling that he wanted to duplicate. It would have been difficult for him, but also for those he was leaving behind.

"I'll keep an eye on the place," Joseph offered.

"I'll sign it over to you and you can sell it and keep the proceeds, if you don't mind."

"You don't think you'll want to return to it someday?"

"No. I can't go back."

Joseph did not push the issue further, nor did Margaret or Hallie.

With needed paperwork signed, Joshua glanced to the big clock on the wall and then back to the three loved ones. They were all aware of him looking at the time and without any word stating so, each came forward to say good-bye.

Joseph came forward first. "Be careful. I don't want you taking any unnecessary risks. We want you back. You're family, and we want to see you from time to time."

Hallie hugged him for a long time. "I've lost a sister," she said, "I don't want to lose my brother." Joshua could tell she was crying as she held him.

"I'll be careful, Hallie. Thank you for making my life here in Cheyenne a memorable one. You and Joseph are such wonderful, unselfish people. I wish the best for you."

"Promise you will come back and see us."

"I will. I only plan on being gone six months or a year at most." Joshua was troubled by his remark, knowing he was uncertain what his future plans would bring.

With that promise, Hallie released Joshua, but continued to grip his hands. As she stepped back, Joshua turned to Margaret. She was smiling, but her eyes were glossy with tears.

Margaret hugged him and whispered in his ear, "Come home safe to us, son." She pinched his cheek playfully and stepped back.

They all followed him to the porch. He walked down the steps and mounted his horse, waved, shouted, "Good-bye and thanks for everything," and rode away. It was an empty feeling, but he just couldn't stay. Maybe someday he would feel different. He actually hoped so.

Chapter 31

$\int$oshua left Cheyenne in mid-December. The journey to the Black Hills would be long and cold. There was always the danger of Indian uprisings, road agents and probably most dangerous--a northerly winter storm. He knew it was the wrong time of year, but still something kept pushing him onward, not allowing him to delay or postpone his trip. When in the army, he would hear the foghorn on the Mississippi River, bellowing its warning of danger in the dark foggy waters ahead, yet it seemed to beckon him like a mysterious sultry woman of the night.

Travelers had lessened considerably for the winter. Most men were not fools, Joshua thought. In the beginning, the weather was giving him a break; the sun shone, glistening on the snow that lay from earlier storms, and the temperature, although cool was warmer than most December days. The day was quiet except for an occasional crow calling to his friends and the crunching of snow beneath the horses' feet.

By bringing a second horse, Joshua hoped to speed his journey and arrive at a small stop-over settlement near Horse Creek the first night, and being in Chugwater by the second day. If the roads or weather worsened, he would have to adjust accordingly. As the day progressed, he would occasionally pass freight wagon trains heading north. The influx of people in the gold country to the north required a constant renewal of supplies.

Joshua's plan was to detour his trip and go to the Fuller ranch. He wanted to tell them the good news that the two men that had raped the young women were dead. He was sure it would help ease the family suffering.

Joshua arrived the first night at the Goodwith Place along Horse Creek. He fed his horses and put them in a stall in the barn. He had arrived after supper hours so all they could offer him was hardtack and jerky. He graciously accepted and headed to his sleeping quarters behind the house. It was a small shack that had a small potbelly stove in one corner and, even when fully stoked, beyond a few feet, rendered itself useless on a chilly night. Earlier arriving travelers took almost all the cots, so Joshua had to make due with a cot at the far end away from the stove. By morning, Joshua concluded that if faced with the situation again, he would choose to sleep with the horses in the barn. They would give him more warmth than the useless potbelly stove.

Joshua got an early start. His head and body ached from the cold night, hard cot, and the fellow bunkmates' smelly feet and their snoring. He made note that if he traveled this road again; he would try to find different quarters to stay. He cursed at his inner voice that told him to travel in the middle of winter.

The weather was beginning to become a concern for Joshua on the second day. The sun had disappeared and the sky continued to darken with heavy, layered clouds. As of yet there were no storm clouds but he worried it might soon change. He had about twenty-five miles to travel for the day if he was going to arrive in Chugwater by nightfall.

His stop in Chugwater, coming south after burying Jennie, was still very painful and vivid in his memory. He was not sure how he would react once Chugwater came into view, but there was really no way to avoid the small town with the weather worsening. Joshua did not want to face a northern winter storm without shelter.

It was late afternoon when the high plateau dropped down along the Chugwater creek and the outline of the community lay ahead. Joshua was anxious to arrive in town. Chugwater became a haven for a weary traveler after the two long days of travel and the previous night of misery At least for now, the agony of remembering Chugwater was somewhat subdued by his exhaustion.

After taking care of his horses which had also gone through a long, grueling two days, he found a room at the same hotel where he had stayed on his prior trip through Chugwater. He ate at the same eatery and found himself going by the same saloon after eating. Joshua was beginning to question his reasoning for doing such a thing, but inside he knew why. He just did not want to admit it. The young woman in the saloon that seemed different from the others had intrigued him. She, in some remote way, reminded him of Jennie. He did not know why she did, but she did. Maybe he was stretching his thoughts to bring Jennie back into his life. Maybe that would help, he thought, if another woman reminded him of Jennie. He scolded himself for even thinking such thoughts. There was only one Jennie.

Still Joshua stopped and stared into the well-lit window of the saloon. He did not see the mysterious woman and gave a sigh of relief. Feeling a little disappointed, yet thankful, he returned to his room. Before entering through the hotel door, he looked up and down the almost empty street. A cold wind was picking up and it felt like snow. He questioned whether he would be able to leave town in the morning. He went to his room. The room was not at all fancy, but it was warm and the bed was soft. He immediately fell asleep.

Joshua awakened to a dark, heavy, overcast morning. The wind rattled the window of his room. Snow flurries were just beginning to fall. He would have to wait a day, maybe more, until the storm blew over. It was not his plan, yet he really did not have a plan or schedule. He decided to make the best of being stuck in Chugwater. He had breakfast and ordered up a hot tub of water to soak away the aches and refresh his weary body. He spent the rest of the morning staring out his hotel window. He had his noon meal, and then returned to his room. By evening, he was beginning to have cabin fever. He ate supper and methodically went to the familiar saloon. It was rather full with all the stranded travelers. The smoke was so thick is burned Joshua's eyes and he struggled to keep from coughing. Joshua assumed most of the men were freight drivers after seeing several freight wagons lined up and down the street. When the weather broke, he would have company for a distance until he could break away from the slower wagons. Joshua was about ready to leave when the mysterious woman appeared at the door of the saloon. She was dressed in a dark full-length dress, her hair up with a plumed hat on top. She looked young, perhaps late twenties. Her brown eyes sparkled with delight as she proceeded through the throng of tantalized men. The bartender acknowledged her as she walked by. He called her "Katie."

Joshua was curious about Katie, but the bartender was busy, and bumbling men surrounded her. Maybe tomorrow, he thought, if the sky doesn't clear and I'm unable to leave for another day.

Joshua awakened to a second day of snow. The wind had died down and the snow was much lighter, but he chose to wait one more day. He had a long two-day ride from Chugwater to the Fuller ranch, and being stranded along the desolate trail was not a very appealing thought.

While eating breakfast, he asked the waiter if he knew a woman by the name of Katie. The man smiled. "Of course I do. I work for her. She owns this place and half the town."

"Really? I suppose she owns the saloon a few doors down."

"Sure does. From the moment you rode in, she was in your life and wallet. She owns the stable where you probably have your horse. If you are staying at the hotel, she owns that, this eatery, the saloon and if that isn't enough, she owns the house for gents at the end of town."

"How did this all come about?"

239

"When they found gold in the Dakotas, Katie, being a clever woman, came up this way from Denver and built an empire here knowing there would have to be layover stations along the way. I guess she still owns a good piece of Denver too."

"So how did she accumulate all that wealth?"

"Not for me to say, but rumors have it, she started it all from being a madam in Denver. Dealt in high-level clients with lots of money. She's a pretty one."

"She is."

"You got an interest in her?" The waiter smiled.

"I saw her the other night in the saloon, and she didn't fit there. Kind of got my curiosity up. Nothing beyond that."

"She looks soft, but she is anything but. She has hired guns out there keeping things in order. Just a little warning to be careful."

"Thanks, but I plan on being on my best behavior and when the snow stops, I'm leaving and if I come back, it'll be because I'm passing through."

****

Next morning, the sun returned and Joshua left Chugwater, heading easterly toward the Fuller ranch. The morning was cold, but his head was clear. He began to think about the joy the Fuller family would feel once they learned of the rapists' deaths.

It was early afternoon on the second day that Joshua spotted the Fuller ranch house in the distance. He was very glad to see the ranch, since he had become concerned that he might become snow-blind with two days of sun reflecting off the snow-covered ground. There was hardly anything else to see except the glistening white snow.

Elizabeth was in the corral working with a young foal. She spotted Joshua and immediately led the foal to the barn. Joshua waited for her. He certainly did not want to share the good news of the rapists without her being present.

Elizabeth came from the barn and hugged Joshua. "I'm happy to see you. I wasn't sure if you'd come back this way."

"I'm never sure which way I'm going sometimes. I was headed north and decided to swing by the ranch and visit some good people."

"Thanks. That's very kind of you."

As they ascended the step to the broad porch, Martha and Julia, cloaked in shawls, came onto the porch to greet Joshua. Joshua's gaze immediately fell upon Julia. He had been concerned for her well-being since he had left the last time. She smiled at him, but the haunting look still prevailed on her face. He was sure his news would renew her spirit and return to her the dreams of a young girl.

After the greetings, Joshua went inside with the three women. Martha immediately set about fixing something to eat, while Elizabeth and Julia served coffee. Once they had Joshua seated at the kitchen table, they all sat down and watched him eat a fried chicken leg and potato salad.

"You said you were headed north. How long will you stay here?" Elizabeth inquired.

"I was thinking a day or two if no one minds."

"Yes, we mind. You have to stay longer than that. Father won't be back until tomorrow," Elizabeth insisted.

"Maybe a little longer," Joshua responded.

"I would hope so," Martha added.

"So where are you going up north?" Elizabeth asked.

"The gold fields in the Black Hills. Maybe even north of there."

"Prospecting?" Elizabeth inquired.

"No. I don't think that's the likes of me. I resigned as marshal and I'm working on my own to see if I can find some bad guys that need to be taken out of circulation." Joshua kept glancing at Julia. Her eyes were on him, but he was not sure if she heard a word he was saying. Joshua chose to hold off telling his news until Syd returned. He wanted all the family to hear it together.

"Sounds to me you're in no particular hurry," Martha said. "You'll stay until after Christmas?"

"Oh, no, definitely not that long, but thanks for the generous offer."

She smiled. "We'll see. You're not out of here yet."

She was larger in stature, but she was sounding a lot like Margaret, Joshua concluded.

"You said Syd was gone for a couple days. Any problems?"

"No, not that I'm aware of. The ranchers and locals get together around this time of year, and then again in early May to discuss problems like livestock markets, feed, water and such things like that. What I believe is the main reason for the meetings, is to get away from the women."

Joshua laughed. "I would imagine being neighborly out here is important. If it weren't for neighbors, I guess coyotes would be about all there would be to keep one company."

"Definitely. Sometimes it feels that way. As much as I love it here, it can get lonely. Every couple of months we try to get together with neighbors and have a little gathering. The winter can make it tough, though."

"I'm sure. Winter storms can change plans rather quickly. I was stuck in Chugwater for a couple days with the storm." Joshua leaned forward. "I hate to be rude, but if you folks don't mind, while it's still daylight, I think I'd like to take a walk out to Jennie's grave."

"Certainly." Martha said.

Joshua bundled up and walked to the family cemetery. He kicked some of the snow away and knelt beside Jennie's grave. "It's been awhile," he whispered. "I still miss you so much. I don't think that'll ever change."

Joshua knelt for several more minutes remembering their times together. It still seemed impossible she was gone. It was as though he expected her to walk up behind him and put her arms around him as she used to do. A warm tear rolled down his cold cheek. He left it. "I'll come by tomorrow," he said, rising to his feet. He looked around him. "When spring comes, it'll be beautiful here, Jennie. I think you'll like it."

Joshua returned to the house. Julia was in the kitchen, helping her mother. Elizabeth was preparing to go outside to do some chores. Joshua offered to help Elizabeth. It would give him a chance to see how Elizabeth and Julia were doing. From a glance, he could see the difficulty Julia was having, but it appeared Elizabeth was doing quite well recovering from the ordeal, and yet a person might be hiding their true feelings. He knew that about himself. It just seemed easier, sometimes.

They started by gathering eggs from the chicken coop. "I hate the idea of keeping the chickens penned up," Elizabeth said, "but there are just too many varmints around here. We're not the only ones that like chicken." They laughed.

"Jennie and I had a few chickens. Actually, they were Jennie's. She nurtured them. She was a very intelligent woman, yet she loved the simple life. She always said that kind of life allowed one's mind to be free."

"That sounds about right," Elizabeth said, placing the eggs on the back porch. "Time to milk the cows now," she said, heading to a nearby pasture. "Sometimes I go for a ride, letting out my thoughts and ideas. They flourish. It's a wonderful feeling. A person begins to feel they can do anything their heart desires."

"Are you doing okay, Elizabeth? You know..."

"I think I'm getting better. I still have my moments. I worry so much about Julia, though. She is having such a hard time."

"I've noticed. I worry about her, but you too. I know it had to be horrible."

The conversation stopped as they began herding the two cows towards the barn. Joshua wanted to tell Elizabeth the good news, but was determined to wait for Syd's return. As strong as Elizabeth showed on the exterior, he was sure she still hurt inside. She had also just lost a husband. He wanted to hug her and tell her that everything would be okay, but he knew he could not be that person.

****

Syd returned the next afternoon. He was cold and tired, but remained his cheerful self. "What a pleasant surprise seeing you here, Joshua. Staying awhile, or passing through?"

"Passing through. Your lovely, but persistent wife is trying to convince me to stay until after Christmas, but I need to get moving."

"And where would that moving be to?"

"The gold camps in the Black Hills."

Syd's eyebrow raised. "Panning?"

"No, just looking for murders and outlaws."

"Martha said you gave up your badge."

"I did. I felt too restricted with it. I think I can do more good on my own."

"I know it's all good intentions and I commend you for that, but be careful, Joshua. You're a good man."

"I know your concern. I'll be careful."

"Good."

"How'd the ranchers meeting go?"

Syd leaned back in his chair. "Mostly good. There is some concern that good land is being swallowed up by outside investors. They seem to be aiming at land with water supplies, and that could be a problem if it continues, and they decide to take advantage of their situation."

"Does sound like it could be serious, alright."

"Jeb's got a spread about twenty miles from here, and is going to do a little traveling to see who is buying and how they're getting the land. He has a couple sons who can look after the place while he's gone."

"Too bad people are trying to get rich quick at the expense of good people."

"Fortunately, they are few in number out here. I always believed people were inherently good. God started them on the righteous path, and then the devil intervenes and puts the temptations in people's path. The strong ones reject those temptations, the weak ones don't."

244

Joshua was not certain that most people were inherently good. He had seen too much riff-raff, including the Harrison brothers, to agree with Syd, but saw no reason to challenge his belief.

Supper was served. Julia appeared with a quiet meekness as though blending with the furniture. Joshua sat and stared at the fine china in front of him. He could never remember eating in such elegance. Joshua concluded that the cattle business was quite lucrative. "Such a magnificent setting, Martha. I hope this is not for me?"

Martha laughed, holding her napkin over her mouth. "It is a pleasure having you here, Joshua, but we always use our best for Sunday supper."

Joshua was surprised with her answer. He realized he had lost track of time since he had returned home and found Jennie missing. "I forgot what day it was," he answered, feeling somewhat embarrassed. His eyes traveled around the table. Martha and Syd were smiling; Julia was staring down at her plate with only sadness for an expression. Elizabeth's eyes were riveted on his face, carefully absorbing each word and each expression of his. He smiled and shifted nervously.

After dinner, the three women started to rise. Joshua raised his hand. "May I have everyone's attention for a moment? I have some news I wanted to share."

Everyone sat down. He had everyone's anxious attention. It was the first time he had seen Julia looking up since she had been seated at the table. Joshua felt his palms sweating from nervousness as he rubbed them together. The mood of the table was about to change.

"When I left here, I returned to Cheyenne. It was there that I discovered the two men that had attacked Elizabeth and Julia were members of an outlaw gang." Martha and Elizabeth gasped. Julia's head dropped. Joshua understood everyone's feelings, but when he had finished telling them the rest of the story, he knew it would lift their spirits. Joshua continued, "They robbed a bank in Cheyenne, and I got wind of where they were held up. I tracked them down, and they resisted arrest. The two men plus a third member are all dead. They will never bother anyone again."

Syd quickly responded, "That's good to hear. What a relief."

Martha was watching her two daughters, "That is good news, Joshua."

"Yes, it is," Elizabeth added, however, her voice was strained and her eyes were filled with tears.

Julia never looked up, but her body shook and Joshua realized she was crying. An initial disappointment filled Joshua, but he began to realize it would take time to absorb the news. He was sure it would eventually help restore happiness to the whole family.

Shortly, the women excused themselves and began clearing the table. Syd brought Joshua into the front room. "Sorry I can't offer you a cigar. Never liked them and never had them around. Tomorrow I can give you a shot of whiskey. Mother would not be happy partaking in the stuff on the Lord's Day." He smiled. "The best woman a man could have. Thirty-two years."

"Definitely a long time."

"Long time, but more important, they were good years. A person can spend an eternity, but if they're not good, what are they worth?"

"No need convincing me." Joshua took a deep breath. "Our years were short and I know as a marshal I was gone far too much, but we were in love." Joshua paused. Syd remained quiet, waiting for Joshua to collect his thoughts. "I miss her a lot," Joshua continued, his voice becoming raspy. "I don't know what to do. I'm going crazy without her."

Syd leaned back in his chair. "I wish I had an all-knowing answer, but honestly, I'm lost for words. I'm just an old man with little wisdom to offer. I think the best is stay close to those who care. That'll be where your strength will come from in the days ahead."

Joshua nodded in agreement, but for him, being alone was what he wanted. It made it easier to remember Jennie and be alone with her. He had clearly said more than he wanted to say. He needed to change the subject.

Joshua cleared his throat. "It looks like Julia is still troubled. Maybe the news of the death of her attackers will help once she has time to think about it."

"I sure hope so. I pray time will begin to heal her. She was always weak and timid. The horses were always her life, but she won't go near the stables now. Just sits around the house with her head hung. None of us can get through to her. We all feel guilty for what happened. We sent her with Elizabeth and her husband, Frank, hoping she would spread her wings rather than be bunkered down here on the ranch. Elizabeth said it did seem to help some, and then this terrible thing happened to her. Of course we all regret we insisted she go." Syd paused, shaking his head sadly before resuming, "If we had only known."

"The problem is we can't live on hindsight. We all have those regrets on our decisions, and I'm not sure it will ever go away. My mother-in-law, Jennie's mother, bless her, says one has to forgive to release the pain...I can never do that. What they did to Jennie...Never."

Both men sat quietly, each filled with sorrow.

Martha had been standing in the doorway, listening to the two men's conversation. She watched the two men, strong in so many ways, now finding themselves helpless in grief for the ones they loved.

****

By the next morning, Joshua had decided he was ready to move on to the Dakotas. He would leave the following morning. The weather was good for traveling and he would rather grieve alone. His reason for coming by the ranch was to deliver the good news of the rapists' death, and he had finished that. He could not imagine what else he could do to help the family with their problems, especially when he was carrying his own. Perhaps they were only dragging each other down.

The family was disappointed with his news of leaving so soon, but no one tried to change his mind. He wondered if they realized the sorrow of each was not helping anyone.

Joshua spent much of his time at Jennie's grave. He was not sure when, if ever, he would return. As usual, memories began to flood Joshua's mind. He could almost hear her laughter, feel her touch, and her soft gentle consolatory dying words.

"Oh, Jennie, life is so hard without you." The anger and pain began to swell in him. "I'm going to make all the low life pay for your death. Every one of them had a hand in it. Every one of them. I will hunt them down. I know it will never bring you back to me, but it's all I can do." He took a deep breath. "I love you, Jennie. I always will."

****

The following morning, Joshua said his good-byes and headed north towards an unknown future.

Chapter 32

Joshua Parker arrived in Lead during a wind-driven snowstorm. The street was empty of people as the blinding snow whirled down the street. Joshua located a stable and took care of his horses, and then from directions given, found a nearby hotel.

The hotel was a two-story building. From what Joshua could tell, it was one of the few two story buildings in the camp. The clerk was a grizzly faced, large man who eyed Joshua suspiciously. "Cash up front," he growled. "Plan on being here long?"

"A few days perhaps. At least until this storm passes."

The clerk laughed as though he had an 'I gotcha.' "That may be spring, mister, and spring here isn't until June, maybe July." He regained his serious composure and rubbed his chin whiskers. "Where you from?"

"Primarily Cheyenne."

"Hmm."

"Sheriff's office around here?" Joshua asked.

"Down at the far end of town." He pointed the opposite direction from which Joshua had arrived. "Little office with the jail in back. The mean ones they haul over to Deadwood." He paused, then grinned as he spoke, "or shoots 'em." He laughed. "Get all kinds around here, you know."

"I'm sure."

"Got business here?"

"Yup." Joshua took his key. "Which room?"

"Three. End of hall." The clerk watched Joshua ascend the stairs, his face reflecting disappointment that Joshua had not shared any further information.

Later, when Joshua returned downstairs, the clerk was sitting in a chair, reading the newspaper. He eyed Joshua over his paper. Joshua nodded to the clerk and left. The storm had not let up, and there was no indication it would in the near future. Snow was beginning to drift and pile up against the buildings. A freight wagon rolled by as Joshua headed out into the storm. It was good to see that he was not the only fool out in the storm.

Joshua found the sheriff's office, a small building at the end of the street, butted up against the incline of a hill. Joshua kicked some drifted snow aside and opened the door. The room smelled musty and the air was clogged with cigar smoke. An older man sat behind a desk, his feet resting on top of it. The small room had an empty gun rack behind the desk, a potbelly stove to one side with a coffee pot on top, and two empty chairs. There were no windows. A burning lantern hung from the ceiling offering the only light. There was a small door with a hinge lock at the back near the desk. Joshua noted the Lead office was of similar appearance to his old office.

"Morning, sheriff," Joshua said, stepping inside and knocking the snow from his coat and hat.

"Good afternoon, young feller," the old gent greeted him. "I'm just keeping an eye on the place. You're probably looking for Deputy Danson. He just went across the street to the Buckhorn to grab a bite to eat." The man gave a toothless smile. "He may be there awhile, I reckon. He's got an all-fired hankering for the waitress, Miss Jennie. She's a pretty one."

A chill raced through Joshua and a lump lodged in his throat. It was like a dream of many years past with a lawman falling for a girl named Jennie.

"Thank you. Excuse me." Joshua quickly turned and left the office. It was like some strong force pulling him across the street to a dim lit restaurant. A crude sign hung on the eatery with the lone word, 'Buckhorn' painted on it. Joshua knew he was being irrational, but the yearning for a moment to reappear from his past, completely devoured his reasonable thinking. The battering storm around him seemed distant and insignificant.

Joshua pushed open the door. The eatery was about twenty by thirty feet with ten tables crowded inside. The room was plain, but looked clean, which was hard to find in a mining camp. An open door led to the back where the clanging pans told Joshua it was the kitchen. Most of the tables were empty. Three men in suits sat at a table to one side. Another man, perhaps a gambler, sat in a back corner facing the door, his nervous eyes moved continuously about the room while he ate. Sitting alone in the middle of the room facing the kitchen was the deputy.

Joshua presumed Jennie was in the kitchen. He looked back to the deputy. How foolish, he thought, sitting in a public room with his back to the door. Lawmen were continual targets in places like these. Moreover, just down the road, the famous Bill Hickok was killed. Love was obviously in the way of common sense.

A young woman appeared from the back. Joshua held his breath with anticipation, but she did not look like his Jennie. He felt relieved, yet disappointed. He knew there was only one Jennie, and he was foolish to think there would ever be another. Guilt swept over him as he stood at the door, staring at her. Why did he keep looking for another Jennie?

Jennie's eyes caught sight of Joshua. She stopped and stared at him. Joshua thought that perhaps it was his abnormal expression. However, the stare was significant enough that the deputy turned to see what or whom she was staring at behind him. Jennie smiled as though realizing her obvious stare, and hurriedly began servicing her steaming plates to the three men. After placing the plates on the table and a cordial conversation, she headed back to the kitchen, hurriedly glancing at Joshua.

"Please be seated," she said, motioning with her arm sweeping around the near empty room. "I'll be with you in a moment with some hot coffee."

Joshua suddenly realized how long he had been standing at the door. He removed his hat and headed for the deputy's table.

"Sorry to bother you, Deputy Danson," Joshua said as he stood across from the deputy, purposely blocking the kitchen door to ensure he had the deputy's full attention. "I'm new to the area and need to get some information."

"If I can help you I reckon so. Have a chair. You don't mind if I keep eating?"

"No, please do." Joshua noticed the plate had perhaps two bites left, and one swipe with a piece of bread.

"So what is it you need from me? I don't give out any free nights sleep in my jail."

"No, not at all. I'd like to take a look at any wanted posters you have and perhaps if you know the whereabouts of any of the people on the posters."

"You a bounty hunter?" the deputy asked, looking appalled at the thought.

"Some people might say that."

"And what do you say?"

"I think I'm a guy trying to even things up for the good people who are trying to abide by the law."

"Then why don't you get one of these," the deputy remarked, pointing proudly to his badge.

"I had one for some eight years as a U.S. Marshal. I felt I could do more without it."

The young deputy hearing the words U.S. Marshal quickly changed his attitude. "U.S. Marshal, huh. Sounds like you gave up a great job."

"Not always. You can create a lot of enemies. I know all too well. And speaking of enemies, let me give you a little advice. If you're going to be wearing a badge, someone, for one of many reasons, might want to put a bullet in you. I came in here and you

252

were sitting with your back to me and never knew I was there. You're lucky I wasn't the one that wanted to take down a badge."

"I know you're right. I'll keep that in mind from now on. I just figured I was a nobody and wouldn't matter to anyone."

"If you have on that badge, you're someone that matters to somebody. Never forget it. Now, about the posters I wanted."

Jennie appeared at the door and the conversation took an awkward lull. Jennie smiled as she passed. "I'm getting the coffee."

Both heads turned to follow her. She returned with the coffee. "As I promised," she said, pouring coffee for both men. "Had a chance to look at the list?"

"List? What list?"

"Sorry, the menu, the list of what we serve."

"Oh. No, I haven't. The coffee and what you might recommend."

"Not the coffee." She laughed. She brushed her reddish curls from her forehead. "Well at least it's hot. Bart just had some venison stew and he's still alive. Find any slugs, Bart?"

The deputy acted pleased that he had been included in the conversation. "Perhaps the stomach is feeling a little heavy." Jennie laughed, pleasing Bart, who grinned from ear to ear.

"I'll give it a try. Could eat a bear I'm so hungry."

"You want bear, we got that, too. Got it before hibernation. Fat as the circus lady."

"I'll stick with the venison. Bear might put me in a bad mood."

"Coming right up. I'll bring you boys some more coffee." She quickly returned with the coffee and left.

"Quite the lady," Joshua remarked.

"Yeah," was the only reply from the deputy.

Joshua knew what that meant. He thought about putting Bart's jealousy at ease, but decided it might help the romance if he left that jealousy twang inside a bashful Bart. It might provoke him to begin courting Jennie, rather than sit there like a helpless babe. He did sympathize with the deputy. He had plenty of his own troubles getting a start with his Jennie.

"So what about information on any men you might think is a problem around here?"

"I reckon you walk into any saloon, flophouse, or brothel from here to Deadwood, and you'll find one of those. Sheriff Roscoe over at Deadwood told me to only deal with what comes to me and don't go looking for trouble. I'm kind of glad you're here though."

Joshua nodded. "I'll do my best to not interfere with your job. I'll just go about my business and then one day I'll be gone.

"Okay."

Jennie brought the venison. "Good luck, stranger, with your meal." She laughed and returned to the kitchen.

Bart rose. "Better get back. Sometimes old Gus gets strange ideas."

Joshua nodded and set about his stew.

Chapter 33

𝒮he wanted poster read, 'Jasper Collins, Wanted Dead or Alive, Murder of Stage Coach Driver: Nebraska, Murder of Railroad Agent: Nebraska'

"Are you sure it was him that you saw around here?" Joshua asked.

Deputy Bart glanced at the poster again. "I'm positive, Marshal. It's been awhile though. Maybe a month ago. I know at the time I thought he looked like trouble. I just never paid any attention to the posters."

"Sounds like he's gone, but I'll check around and keep my eyes open for him. The varmints move around and he may come back."

"Like I said, we're busy enough without looking for trouble."

"I'm sure and I understand. When I was the only lawman back in the earlier days of Cheyenne, I had the same situation. The only problem is they eventually become trouble. It's their nature."

Joshua returned to his hotel room. The storm was breaking, and by morning, he would have a chance to begin scouring the saloons and brothels in search of Jasper Collins and any other wanted criminals in town.

When he entered the hotel, grizzly was standing at the desk. "Find the sheriff's office okay?"

"Yeah, thanks."

"Were they able to help you?"

"Sure did." Joshua continued to the stairs.

"Staying long?"

Joshua stopped and turned. "I think I will be here awhile. Especially with the friendly people here at the hotel."

"Really...a...well, thanks."

Joshua tipped the brim of his hat. "You're welcome."

****

Joshua began his rounds through the saloons, dance halls, flophouses and whorehouses. Each was always busy every time he entered one. In the saloons, the poker tables were always full and each had women roaming from table to table. Yet with all the patrons packed inside, he did not recognize any from his collection of posters or from memory.

It was day five in Lead and Joshua was not making any headway. Perhaps his belief that the mining camps here in the Black Hills were filled with wanted men was not true. He wondered if word had spread through the camp, who he was, and they had left. Another potential problem, if word was out who he was, his health was definitely at risk. He would stay another day or two in Lead. He would check with Deputy Bart in the morning for any new posters. He decided to have a drink at one of the saloons. He had spent all his time looking in them but never indulging in a shot of whiskey or glass of beer.

Joshua returned to his hotel that night having consumed too much alcohol. It was against his rules about drinking too much in public. He needed to start obeying his own rules and not just be giving advice. He knew it was too dangerous, yet he had to relieve his mind of the constant torment of not having Jennie waiting for him at home after completing his job.

The next morning, Joshua was slow to rise. The sun was shining through the small dirty window. He crawled from bed and splashed cold water on his face. It was his last day in Lead unless someone crawled from beneath a rock. He needed to get out and start looking. As he descended the stairs, he hoped Grizzly was not at his desk. The clerk got on his nerves on a good day. He didn't see Grizzly. He hurried towards the door.

The pestering clerk's voice sounded behind him. "Good morning, Parker."

The voice sent a chill through Joshua and echoed in his aching head. "Good morning," Joshua answered back.

"You're looking a little peaked this morning."

"I'm fine. Thanks for your concern."

Joshua hurried outside, reminding himself that this time tomorrow he would be gone.

The sun was shining, but the air was still frigid. There were more people on the street than Joshua had seen in the total five previous days. Shop owners were busily shoveling snow from their shop entrances. A log wagon rolled down the street, and another wagon was being loaded with supplies. The cold air cleared Joshua's head. He was angry with himself for his stupidity the night before, consuming so much alcohol. He had to regain control.

As Joshua approached the sheriff's office, he noticed the door open at the restaurant across the street, which seemed unusual to him with the weather so cold. He entered the sheriff's office and found it empty. The chair behind the desk was tipped over. Joshua was trying to comprehend what had happened when a shot rang out.

With revolver drawn, Joshua started outside. A woman's scream came from the restaurant. Joshua moved quickly across the street to the eatery and with revolver ready to fire, moved through the open door. Deputy Bart was on the floor, grasping a bloody left shoulder. Jennie was hovered over him, crying. A man stood at the other side of the room with his revolver in hand. Joshua immediately recognized him as Jasper Collins, the killer on the wanted poster.

Jasper was yelling at Deputy Bart, his revolver waving wildly. "Get up and face me and stop hiding behind a woman's petticoat." He suddenly became aware of Joshua's presence. "Who the hell are you?" he shouted and pointed his revolver toward Joshua. Joshua fired first, hitting Jasper. Jasper fired back, his bullet hitting the doorframe next to Joshua's ear. The room became a tunnel with only Jasper and Joshua. Joshua's gun was blazing, firing three times more into Jasper as he was collapsing to the floor. He moved towards the fallen victim, his revolver aimed at the head of Jasper. He kicked the motionless body to see if there was any response. The body remained still. Joshua picked up the dead man's revolver.

Joshua looked around the restaurant, ensuring there were no friends of the outlaw. He turned to the injured deputy; Jennie was already helping Bart to his feet and sat him in a chair.

"How stupid of me to let him get the draw on me," Bart moaned.

"Don't blame yourself," Jennie replied as she looked at his wound. "You were just trying to protect me and you didn't know he would draw on you."

"I should have come more prepared, isn't that right Marshal?"

"You'll learn."

"You're a marshal?" Jennie asked.

"No, I used to be one."

Bart smiled. "Well at least we found the varmint you were looking for."

"Sure did. I was about ready to give up, but snakes always come out to bathe in the sunshine."

"Maybe more will show up," Bart added.

"You never know. Word gets out about this and one of two things happens, they run and hide or they come looking for me, or maybe you. Remember that, Deputy."

Jennie took charge. "You two stop your jabbering. I need to clean the wound and get him to a doctor.

Joshua grinned as Jennie led Bart away. Bart looked back over his shoulder and smiled. It took a gunfight to get those two together, Joshua concluded. Love takes many paths.

****

Joshua decided to swing by a couple saloons and check for other wanted men who might have come out of hiding. It was his last day in Lead. He knew Deputy Bart would be out of commission for a couple days.

The saloons were not as busy as usual. He guessed with the better weather, everybody was returning to their normal routines, so Joshua decided to take advantage of the emptier halls and have a couple drinks. He knew he was making a mistake before he started, but for a short time, it helped bring Jennie closer--her kiss at his lips, her fingers touching him softly, and her words whispering to him. She only lived in his fantasy now, and he did not want to let go of her.

The afternoon passed, and darkness had spread over Lead before Joshua left the dingy saloon. He had drunk far too much. He had known it for hours, but he let the numbness come and wash over the painful emptiness.

As he made his way down the darkened street towards the hotel, he sensed somebody was following him. He turned with hand on the butt of his revolver and pulled it from the holster. His hand missed its grip and the Colt fell uselessly in the snow. Panic griped him as he looked at his revolver and then stared into the near empty street. There was no one behind him. His survival instinct had misfired. His precision draw had failed. He was risking his life, letting himself fall into this condition. If he continued, it would get him killed. Next time, there might be someone behind him. Maybe he wanted to end his misery. He wiped off his revolver and placed it back in the holster. He returned to the hotel. Fortunately, Grizzly was not working and Joshua did not have to encounter the man, in his condition.

Next morning, Joshua was up early, even with his nagging headache, and was heading out of the hotel. As expected, Grizzly was there. "Are you leaving?" was all Grizzly could ask as Joshua hurried past.

"Yes," was the only reply Grizzly received.

Joshua went by the sheriff's office before leaving, and found Bart proudly displaying his injured shoulder with his arm in a sling. Jennie was close by and very attentive to her heroic patient. It gave Joshua a good feeling seeing the loving couple, a feeling he had severely missed in recent weeks.

The day was still young, and Joshua was riding the short distance to Deadwood.

Chapter 34

𝒜s soon as Joshua entered Deadwood, the sense of danger prevailed. It was almost a smell of ruthless degradation. Joshua carefully eyed both sides of the street as he rode slowly into town. It was towns like Deadwood that inherently attracted the worst of mankind. Joshua had seen the wagonloads of gamblers, prostitutes and scavengers coming through Cheyenne, heading for the mining camps like Deadwood. In addition, he knew killers, outlaws, road agents and thugs filled the road to the camps. The newly inhabited camps in outlying territories provided opportunities for the worst of society, and it provided a safe haven due to limited law enforcement.

Most of the snow on the street had been worn away, leaving the rutted wagon tracks. Joshua was surprised at the multitude of businesses that filled the streets. As expected, the street had an abundance of saloons, brothels and eateries, but there were also cleaners, clothiers, barbershops, bathhouses, drug stores, flophouses, hotels, a telegraph office, a newspaper and printing shop, and a sheriff's office with a jail next door. The main street was primarily wooden structures, some with a second story. Off the main street, tents were often the only protection from the weather. The early afternoon was bustling with activity as Joshua passed by. Women hung from their windows, beckoning to the passing men below. A Chinese man and woman hurriedly moved along the street, each carrying baskets of laundry on a yoke over their shoulder. A peddler called from the back of his wagon, selling his cures-all potion. Most people were busy, but there were also the elements standing along the crude wooden walks watching and obviously waiting for their opportunity. Joshua anticipated he would be busy here in Deadwood.

Joshua stopped at the sheriff's office. He wanted to check in with the sheriff. It was in part being respectful, but the law could also be helpful. Even from the outside, it was obvious the sheriff's office and jail in Deadwood was much larger and more elaborate than Lead. Joshua was sure there they had a much larger need here.

Before entering the sheriff's office, Joshua stopped and observed the surrounding area to see who might be watching him. He always faced the danger of recognition from his prior days as marshal.

The office was busy. Five men were huddled together in the middle of the room in apparent serious discussion. They stopped and looked in Joshua's direction when he entered.

"Sorry for interrupting. I can come back later."

"No, we're done," a large man responded. He had a large bushy mustache that fell below his jawbone. He wore a sheriff badge on his coat. "Okay Frank and Delmo, get going," he said, moving to his desk and sitting on the corner of it.

Two of the men grabbed rifles from the rack and left. The other two remained near the sheriff. "What can I do for you, mister?" the sheriff asked in a demanding tone.

"Good morning, Sheriff. My name is Joshua Parker. I'm up from Cheyenne where I used to be the U.S. Marshal, but since retired. I'm up here looking for some rowdy types, and I was wondering if I could look at your wanted posters, and to see if you had any idea if any of them might be around here."

"From what you're saying, I guess that would make you a bounty hunter. Never took a liking to your kind. I usually found they weren't much better than the ones they were chasing. What would make you give up a respectable profession to become a bounty hunter?"

"Personal."

"You got yourself in trouble?"

"No. I was going to leave it as is, but since you're being persistent, I guess I'll fess up the whole story. I put away a couple brothers and killed the third one. They escaped from Laramie and came looking for revenge. I happened to be away from home on an assignment, so they kidnapped my wife and killed her. Like I said, it was personal."

"Sorry about your wife, Joshua. That's a darn right terrible thing that happened. It's my job to know what's going on around here. This is not a clean town. So are you up here looking for those brothers?"

"No. I've already found them and they're dead. I just decided to rid society of more low life."

The sheriff's face scrunched up with concern as he listened to the anger in Joshua's voice. "There's a lot of respectable folk here, and there are a lot that I wouldn't trust with a red cent and certainly not my life. Just be sure you know the difference. I don't need a killing spree around here. Now maybe we can start again." The sheriff extended his hand.

"I'd be glad to, Sheriff." The anger that had been building in Joshua began to ease.

"I've got a wagon load of posters," the sheriff said. One of his men was already retrieving them. "I try to look at them, but I have so many troublemakers to deal with here that I don't have time to worry about posters."

"Your deputy in Lead mentioned you wanted him to deal with problems as they arise."

"You mean Bart? Nice young fellow. Someday he'll make a fine lawman, but honestly, he's wet behind the ears. I worry he's going to get himself killed. I just got word he up and got himself wounded by some gunslinger."

"I know. I was there."

263

The sheriff eyed Joshua curiously. "What's your name again?"

"Joshua Parker."

"So I'm guessing you're the fellow that saved my deputy's hide. Well I owe you a big thanks. Now what else do you need from me?"

"Any places in particular that you think I should be looking?"

"I guess most anywhere to be honest. They all operate on the edge of the law, but for the type you're trying to track down, I'd check the Strike Saloon. A Jeb Parson owns and runs the place. I can't prove anything, but I think it's a front, or at least a hangout, for some of the bandits that are robbing the Treasure Coaches. They're the wagons leaving here full of gold. If you can help with that, it would relieve a big headache for me."

"Definitely sounds like a place that needs to be checked out. I'll see what I can uncover. Also, can you recommend a hotel?"

"Recommending a hotel around here is like recommending a choice on how to die, by hanging or being shot. I guess I would pick The Harper down the street a short distance. You can get a hot bath there and I here they use fresh, clean water." The sheriff smiled, pleased by his humor. "Also, there's a stable behind the hotel. It's close enough for convenience, yet far enough to keep the smell away, or at least on calm days."

"Okay, Sheriff, thanks for your help."

"My pleasure and good luck."

Listening to the sheriff, Joshua knew Deadwood would keep him busy. That's what he needed to keep his mind off his own problems. He found the Harper Hotel and the stable. He spent the remainder of the afternoon checking the layout of the town. It appeared that for every man working for his money, there were two, in one way or another, trying to take it away. The brothel doors and windows often had women enticing men to come inside, and the streets were busy with men selling wares from the back of their wagons. Dance halls and saloons often had loud music playing inside, and barkers outside offering poker games, exciting entertainment and women for their patrons.

As evening approached, Joshua had supper and returned to the hotel with a bottle of whiskey. One drink to soothe the nerves. Tomorrow would be a busy day. Joshua pulled the tin cup from his saddlebag and poured a small portion of whiskey into it. He began laying out his plan for the next day. He supposed he would start with the Strike Saloon. Not wanting to show his hand, maybe he could work his way inside the road agent process. If the sheriff were right about the place, it would be nice to help bring down the whole robbery and murdering operation at one time. Jennie would be proud of him. If she could only be here to see the good he was doing.

"For you, Jennie. Always for you." He poured another cup of whiskey, but this time to the top of the cup.
****

The noises from the street below awakened Joshua. He peered outside through the small window. It was late. He searched for his watch. It was ten. He fell back on the bed and looked over at his half-empty bottle of whiskey.

"Oh," he moaned, "What am I doing?" He knew he had to keep a clear head. Staying alert was essential at a time like this.

Joshua splashed cold water on his face and prepared for the remainder of the day. He headed straight for the dining room in the hotel. The tables were empty. It was the nicest public dining room he had been in for some time. A nicely dressed man came out from the back. "Looking for something to eat?" he asked.

"Yes, and coffee, please."

"Okay. I have some eggs left and some salt pork."

"Sounds good. Thank you."

Joshua had his breakfast in a quiet surrounding. He watched the lobby from his vantage point, but there was little activity at The Harper.

After his breakfast, he headed down Main Street for the Strike Saloon. It was a dimly lit establishment, with rustic tables and bar cut from logs. Two men were standing at the far end of the bar. Two poker games were going--one with four men and the other had seven players. The table with seven had two players who looked like professionals. Usually professional gamblers would find tables where they were the lone wolf preying on the others. Joshua wondered if the two gamblers were working the table together. The second table of four players seemed more attentive to their private conversation than they were to the game. All four of the men were rough looking and did not seem very congenial.

The man behind the bar strolled toward Joshua. "Yeah, what can I get you?"

"I'll have a beer and don't make it half foam."

"The bartender glared at Joshua, then poured the beer. He set the beer down, splashing some of it on the bar. "That'll be twenty-five cents."

Joshua placed the money down. "Thanks." The bartender looked curiously at Joshua as though it was the first time he had heard the word. "Any tables open?" Joshua asked jerking his head toward the tables.

"I can get you in that one," he responded, nodding toward the table with seven players.

"That table looks a little crowded, how about the other table?"

"It's full."

"Full. It only has four players."

"I said it's full." He walked away.

There was no doubt in Joshua's mind which table he needed to penetrate. He just was not sure how he was going to do it. The bartender controlled the saloon, and Joshua suspected he controlled much more. Joshua stayed for another hour and then left. He would try another day, he thought. He did not want to move too quickly and create any suspicion.

Chapter 35

For the next three weeks, Joshua moved in and out of the Strike Saloon every day or two. He began to sit in on the open poker game, watching who came and went from the room and who they talked to while they were there. The four men came and went, and occasionally other men joined them at their table. The bartender was the only one that spoke to the table and they spoke to no one else.

It was February when Joshua had just sat down at the open poker table at the Strike, and a small man in a business suit and derby hat came into the saloon. He looked out of place and acted very nervous as he went directly to the bar. There was a short exchange of words between he and the bartender, then he quickly slipped the bartender a note and left. The bartender turned his back and read the note. He turned back. The four men at the private table were watching. The bartender nodded. Joshua hung around the saloon for another three hours, then left.

Joshua returned to the hotel with a new bottle of whiskey. He knew the danger he was taking by bringing the bottle to his room, but he was sure he had learned his lesson on controlling his drinking.

The afternoon of the following day, still carrying a hangover, Joshua left his room and went to the dining area. He drank coffee until evening and then returned to his hotel room. The following morning he awakened early and went downstairs for breakfast.

"Feeling better today, Sir?" the waiter asked.

"Much better, George," Joshua replied, embarrassed by his previous day's condition.

"Good." George smiled. "Got some really good hash this morning."

"That sounds good. I'm starving."

George immediately left for the kitchen. Joshua looked around the room. Most of the tables were full. As usual, the clientele in the dining room were not the type he would find on any posters. Most appeared to be businessmen, many dressed in suits, and a few men with women, presumably their wives who were dressed in proper street attire.

The miners would be busy working their claims, some victoriously finding gold, some not, but at the end of the day, each cold and exhausted miner would find their pockets soon emptied by the businessmen, spending on the essentials to live and any left, picked away by the gamblers, prostitutes, and thieves.

George returned with the steaming hash and more coffee. "Hear about the robbery yesterday?" George asked.

"No. What robbery was that?"

"The gold wagon that left here yesterday morning got robbed about fifteen miles out. They're saying it was over one hundred thousand dollars in gold. They killed two guards and wounded two. Pulled it off without a hitch. Word just came out this morning."

Joshua whistled. "I understand that's not the first time."

"It sure isn't."

Joshua needed to see the sheriff to get the details, but he wanted to be careful not to let anyone see him coming and going from the sheriff's office. He would have to wait until dark.

That evening, after ensuring no one was watching, he went to the sheriff. The sheriff was sitting at his desk, his chin in hands leaning on the desk. He sat up when Joshua came in.

"Evening, sheriff. You look a little tired."

"Tough couple of days." The sheriff leaned back in his chair. "I guess you heard the news?"

"The robbery. Yeah, I did."

"Have any information or ideas?"

Joshua shook his head. "I thought I would check with you."

"Not much that's useful. I'm hearing there were six to eight of them waiting in ambush. They caught the guards by surprise, for the sake of me, how, I don't know, and killed two guards before they even saw the bandits. They loaded up some pack mules with the gold and left. I sent a couple deputies out, but they lost the bandits' trail on the rocky terrain southeast of here."

"Obviously well planned."

"Always is. You see anything suspicious yesterday?"

"No." Joshua was not going to tell the sheriff his predicament and that he had never left his room the day of the robbery.

Joshua resumed his usual observation of the saloons. His drinking worsened. He would have a drink or two at the saloons, and then return to his room with a bottle. Days and nights began to become blurred.

March arrived, and he had made no progress towards solving the gold wagon robberies or finding any killers in town. His stay in Deadwood had become a waste of time, and more troubling, it had dragged him deeper into a hole. He continued to drink more, and Joshua had stopped observing or watching for outlaws or any suspicious activities at the Strike Saloon.

One morning after a two day drunken binge, Joshua left the hotel and was heading to the Strike Saloon. He had convinced himself to stop the drinking and get back to the business that he had come to Deadwood for in the first place. He came upon two men in the middle of the muddy street who were harassing a young Chinese wash girl. She carried her laundry in baskets on a yoke that rested on her shoulders. The men were laughing while pushing her around. She staggered to maintain her footing with her heavy load. One man grabbed her broad rimed hat and tossed it on the muddy street. "Oh, so sorry," he said laughing. "Let me pick it up for you." He turned, stepping on the hat. "Whoops," he said, then picked up the muddy hat and jammed it on her head.

Joshua watched the revolting incident, his anger growing, but he was hesitant to help. It might blow his cover. He could see the bartender from the Strike across the street watching the carnival atmosphere in front of him. The helpless girl toppled and fell to her knees, but maintained her laundry baskets on her shoulders. She kept pleading, "Please, mister, please."

The torment continued. Joshua was bursting with anger. How could he just stand there? His whole reason for life now was to rid things like this from happening. Without any further thought, he stepped from the wooden walk into the street. "I think that's enough, boys."

The men stopped and looked at Joshua. They were obviously surprised that anyone would stop the fun they were having. "This is none of your business, stranger," the ringleader of the two said angrily.

"I think it is." Joshua moved to the frightened girl and helped her to her feet. She hurried down the street as fast as she could. Joshua and the two men stood facing each other. Joshua had no idea of the drawing and firing abilities of the two men, but an even more perilous situation he faced was his own ability to draw and fire his weapon in his stupored condition from all the whiskey he had consumed over the last few days.

The tension grew as the two men and Joshua stood ready to draw at the flinch of the other. "Do it," Joshua stated firmly. One began to slowly back away. "Do it!" Joshua demanded. The man stopped.

"We're just having some fun," he said, fear in his voice.

"Now I'm having fun," Joshua said in a sinister tone. Joshua was not worried about the frightened man doing the talking. From the corner of his eye, he continued to watch the ringleader as he slowly moved further away from his cohort and out of view of Joshua.

The ringleader suddenly went for his revolver. Joshua was amazed at the speed and ease that his revolver cleared its holster. He fired, the man grunted and fell as his revolver, having just cleared the holster, fell harmlessly to the ground. The other man stood frozen, his eyes staring at Joshua in horror.

"The next time something like this happens, you'll be joining your worthless friend." The man nodded and left with his dead friend still lying in the street.

Joshua looked towards the Strike door. The bartender had disappeared. Joshua figured he had lost any chance of getting on the inside of the road agents, but he still felt good. He had done the right and noble thing.

The sheriff and deputy were there before Joshua could move. "What the damn hell is going on here?" the sheriff spouted.

"Take me in, Sheriff," Joshua quietly said to the irritated sheriff.

"Damn rights, I am. You got some explaining to do."

The sheriff ordered the deputy to take care of the body, took Joshua's revolver and led him back to the office. The sheriff slammed the door. "Now what was that all about on the street out there?" The sheriff emptied the revolver, opened his desk drawer, shoved Joshua's revolver inside and slammed the drawer shut.

"I was protecting a young Chinese wash girl from harassment by a couple no counts. They were getting out of hand."

"And you had to kill one of them?"

"He drew first. They were mad I had stopped their fun."

"That's not what I asked."

"He drew first."

"I knew you'd be trouble for me. I have enough to deal with, without you trying to single handedly make everything in this country right. You can't do it, Joshua. You're walking the line on staying within the law." The sheriff's anger softened. "I know you know that's why you gave up your badge."

271

"Lock me up for twenty-four hours, Sheriff."

"I might lock you up and forget you're there. You're going to push me too far one of these days."

"I appreciate your concern for me, Sheriff."

"Yeah, you and everyone else around here." The sheriff turned to the deputy sitting at another desk on the far side of the room. "Lock this varmint up. Put him in the cell with Henry. The two crazies should get along fine."

The deputy had a smirk on his face as he led Joshua to one of the three cells in back. The first cell had an ornery looking drifter who looked up from his cot and snarled. A big scar lay across his grizzled face. He definitely had a social issue as he snarled hatefully at the two men. The second cell was empty and Joshua presumed the sheriff did not put him in the second cell to get even with Joshua. The third cell had a frail, older man who looked like he had not bathed or shaved in ten years.

"Henry, got you some company," the deputy said with a delighted voice. Henry grumbled and turned his back to the deputy and Joshua. "An old prospector," the deputy said.

"I guess he'll talk my ear off," Joshua commented sarcastically.

"Little warning," the deputy remarked, "he gets to howling sometimes. Talking to his coyote friends I guess."

The cell door closed, echoing through the small room. The keys jingled as the deputy left the room. The jail door closed behind him with a thud. Joshua looked at his two cellmates. If he had to choose, he figured he had the better of the two. Perhaps the sheriff was looking out for him.

The jail remained relatively quiet during the day. Scar face in cell one snored, groaned a lot, and occasionally shouted for food and something to drink.

Henry sat with his back to Joshua, mumbling. Joshua tried to ignore him, but the persistence of his mumbling began to feed Joshua's curiosity and he tried to decipher Henry's speech. The words 'sacred Indian grounds', 'don't go', 'gold', 'so much gold', 'kill me', kept repeating in Henry's mumbling.

Later, Henry began to rock, and the more he rocked, the louder he mumbled. Something out there had frightened him. What did the old prospector see?

"Henry, tell me what you saw? Maybe I can help."

"Voices of the Spirits."

"Voices. What'd they say?"

"Voices." Henry began to howl, low at first, but the howling grew louder. There had been no warning.

A voice from the first cell rang out, "Give me a gun so I can shoot the stupid idiot. Choke the bastard."

Henry continued howling through the night with obscene shouting responses from scar face in the first cell. Joshua knew that there would be no more information from Henry for the rest of the night, and certainly no sleep. He believed everything Henry had said earlier was only the ravings of a mad man.

By morning, Joshua was ready to leave. The howling of Henry and the angered responses of scar face were almost more than he could take, but he had remembered the words of the sheriff, "lock him up for twenty-four hours." He still had several hours to go.

The sheriff came in late. He look despairingly at the maniac in cell one and then made a casual stroll to cell three. "Heard the coyotes were circling last night. Think you're ready to get out, Parker?" He held up his keys.

"How about me? You can't keep me here forever," scar face shouted.

The sheriff very purposely turned to face the prisoner. "You want a bet on that?" The sheriff turned back to Joshua. "Well?"

"I'm ready," Joshua remarked."

The sheriff smiled, "I thought you'd be ready."

Once they had reached the outer office, the sheriff addressed his lone deputy in the office, "John, will you run down to the telegraph office and see if anything has come in on our friend in the back. I'm tired of feeding him."

"Gladly, Sheriff. He gives me the creeps." The deputy left.

The sheriff turned to Joshua, seriousness on his face. "Why the night in jail? You on to something?"

"I don't know, Sheriff. Maybe. The Strike Saloon has some seedy characters like you mentioned. There is one table in there that only about a half dozen men can sit at it. Usually the same four. The bartender controls who are allowed to sit at that table and I can't seem to get close enough to hear anything."

"So what do you think they're up to?"

"Maybe nothing, but something came to mind last night as I listened to Henry's howling."

The sheriff chuckled. "It can get pretty bad. I haven't decided what to do with him. Anyway, go on."

"The day before the gold coach robbery, I recall a fellow coming into the Strike. He was rather unusually dressed and out of place for that saloon. He wore a suit and derby hat. Anyway, he came in, acting nervous, went straight to the bartender. They talked quietly for a moment, he handed the bartender a note and left. The bartender read the note and nodded to the private table of men. Nothing else happened that day that I know of."

The sheriff shrugged. "What about the next day?"

Joshua hesitated. He did not want to tell the sheriff he had been drinking and lost a day. "Sorry, Sheriff, I was a little occupied and didn't come back for two days."

"Occupied. With what, a whore? That sounds like a good clue. Why didn't you go back?"

"Personal, Sheriff."

"You were on a drunken binge, weren't you?"

Joshua did not answer.

The sheriff took a deep breath. "Alright, where do we go from here? It sounds like an inside job, which I always suspected. To be honest, I was concerned that one of my deputies was rotten. I feel a lot better about that now."

"Who coordinates the shipments?" Joshua asked, removing his hat and tossing it on the desk. His sandy bushy hair fell onto his forehead.

"The mining companies and the freight company."

Different mining companies, but the same freight company?"

"Yeah. I see what you're getting at."

"Who's the freight company and where are they located."

"Johnson Brothers. End of town."

"Anymore shipments soon?"

"We never know until one or two days ahead of the shipment. They try to keep it quiet."

"I'll see what I can find. One last question, Sheriff."

"What?"

"Who did I kill yesterday?"

"Nobody knows. His partner seems to have left the territory."

"Okay, I guess I'll do some checking around about those robberies, but I need my revolver."

The sheriff pulled the holster and revolver from the desk drawer and handed it to Joshua. "See if you can do a better job keeping your weapon in the holster."

"I'll try, but honestly, Sheriff, he drew first."

"After you incited him. I'm not stupid, Parker."

Joshua touched the brim of his hat, nodded and left the office. The cold air felt good on his heavy head after the night from hell.

While Joshua was having biscuits, gravy, salt pork and coffee, he decided he would have to push harder to get inside the gang. He was still concerned where he now stood with the bartender from the Strike after the shooting incident. He might be facing a slug in his forehead when he entered the saloon. Suddenly the breakfast was not settling well. His future was about to take a dangerous course. A drink would settle his nerves, but he knew somehow he had to resist.

Chapter 36

As soon as Joshua finished his breakfast, he headed straight for the freight company. The business had a dozen wagons of assorted sizes and a corral of draft horses to pull the wagons. There were two men working around the grounds, but it looked like no one was in charge. There was certainly no well-dressed man with a top hat, and no place where he might be found.

"Anybody else around?" Joshua asked.

"Nope," one of the men answered bluntly, and went back to forking hay into the feeder trough.

"Where's the office?"

"Ain't here."

"I can see that. Where would I find it.?"

The worker leaned on his pitchfork handle and stared in disgust. "For a stranger, you sure ask a mighty lot of questions. If I tell you, maybe you'll leave and quit asking questions and nosing around?"

"That would be very hospitable of you."

The man snorted. Without pointing, he nodded. "The place you're looking for is above the bank. It's not written on the outside so if you get lost don't come back here."

"Thanks. It has been a real pleasure," Joshua said with a cordial nod.

The man snorted again and resumed his pitching hay.

Perhaps the smell of horse dung all the time does that to a person, Joshua thought.

Joshua located the bank and found the freight office upstairs. It was a small two-room establishment. The outer room had two desks. A man was sitting at one desk, while the second desk was empty. The door to the second room was partially open and Joshua could see a portion of the other room. He could see a much larger desk, but could not see if anyone was sitting at it.

"Can I help you?" the lone man asked, remaining seated.

Although the greeting was not particularly friendly, Joshua thought, it outdid the one he had received from his co-worker at the stables.

"I'm looking for work."

"We need guards."

Bet you do, thought Joshua. The ones that are still alive probably took off.

"What's the pay?"

"You working now?"

"No," answered Joshua.

"More than your current pay."

Friendly bunch, Joshua thought.

"Kind of dangerous, I reckon," Joshua replied.

"Reckon so. Got any references."

"I'm new in town."

"Need references."

"My mother's dead."

"Funny guy." The man stood up, went to the back office door, and opened it. "I've got a drifter out here looking for work as a guard, but he's got no references."

"We need references with all the problems we're having."

"I told him that."

A second man appeared behind the man at the desk. It was the little guy with the derby hat from the Strike. He did not have his hat on, but it was him. Joshua stepped to the side. He

277

hoped the derby hat man did not recognize him. The front office man returned to the front, closing the door behind him.

"I reckon you heard the boss?" he said with a matter of fact.

"Who was the other person in the room?"

"The man raised an eyebrow. "You mean, Frederick, the bookkeeper?"

"So he can't hire me?" Joshua said to try to deflect any suspicion.

"Not hardly." The man laughed. "He couldn't get you a glass of water without getting permission." The man laughed again. "Hire you," he mumbled as Joshua grinned and walked to the front door and left.

Joshua hurried from the building. It was coming together. The bookkeeper supplied the information of the gold shipments to the bartender, and then it was given to the bandits. Somehow, he had to report his findings to the sheriff without creating suspicion.

Joshua was also beginning to rethink Henry's ranting. Maybe he had seen something that frightened him. Maybe he had stumbled on to a hideout where they stored the stolen gold shipments.

Joshua purchased some paper and returned to the hotel. He carefully laid out his finds and thoughts. He knew where the sheriff usually ate. He would watch for him leaving the office for the evening meal and give him the note.

The street was in a shroud of darkness when the sheriff left for supper. Joshua was waiting near the eatery when the sheriff approached. They nodded and Joshua slipped him the note.

"Let me know what you think?" Joshua whispered to a surprised sheriff.

"Okay."

"My hotel room. Room six."

The sheriff strolled on into the restaurant.

It was noon the following day when the sheriff came to Joshua's hotel room. "It looks like you have something, Joshua."

"I think we need to set up a fake shipment, Sheriff. We have to hope the bookkeeper is the only rotten apple within the freight lines. You'll have to set it up with the boss at the freight company. I hope that it can be set with only the bookkeeper getting wind of it. Maybe we can ambush the ambush. I still want to try to get inside the gang. Give me a couple days and meanwhile see what you can set up with the company boss."

"I'll get with the freight boss. Are you sure, you're okay? You're not going to have a relapse on me, are you?"

"I've put the bottle away. Any idea on how we can communicate?"

"I do." The sheriff smiled. "I have a good lady friend. She works about town. Every other day I'll have her come to your room exchanging messages. I don't think she'll arouse any suspicions. Her name is Helen."

The sheriff left. Joshua waited a half-hour and left. He immediately headed for the Strike Saloon. The day of reckoning had come. He wondered if he would be leaving the saloon upright or carried out.

When he arrived at the Strike, he started for his normal poker table.

"Hey, drifter," the bartender called out. Joshua looked his way. The bartender motioned for him to come over. Joshua took a deep breath and headed his direction. His burning question was about to be answered. "Buy you a drink?" the bartender asked as Joshua leaned on the bar. Something was coming down.

"Sure, I'll have a beer." Joshua's body eased slightly.

The bartender poured the beer and set it down in front of Joshua. "You looked pretty handy with the revolver the other day. Where'd you learn to use it?"

"Hired it out over the years."

"Law looking for you?"

"No, I can't say they are. I'm careful. I always say, you're not breaking the law if you're not caught."

The bartender grinned as he listened. "I like your thinking. What's your name?"

"Joshua will do."

"Okay, Joshua, you're in here a good deal of the time so I assume you're not working."

"You could say that."

"Interested in some work?"

"Perhaps."

"It pays well."

"Breaking any laws?"

"Not if you don't get caught." The bartender grinned.

"What if I say, yes?"

"Let us know where we can contact you and wait."

"How about an advance?"

The bartender opened his safe below the bar and removed a stack of bills. Here's fifty dollars. You run out on us and you're a dead man."

"Not to worry. I'm at the Harper. By the way, what should I call you?"

"Like the others. Boss. That way there's never any confusion." Boss smiled.

"The information is well taken. I think I will partake in a game of poker." Joshua started for his usual table.

"Why don't you join the boys over here?" Boss said, pointing to the private table. "Men, Joshua wants to join you."

They glanced up showing little interest and never spoke. Joshua sat in one of the two empty seats, waiting for the next game. He carefully eyed each man. Their physical appearances were different, but they had one common look. They all looked hard, perhaps without a soul. Joshua swallowed hard. He concluded he must have the same look or he would not be sitting at the same table. It was not a good feeling.

The biggest differences that Joshua discovered playing poker with the private table was that talk was a rare commodity, and the money flowed more freely. Apparently, their jobs paid well, too.

Towards late afternoon, Joshua left the Strike, grabbed a quick supper from the hotel dining room and returned to his room.

Later in the evening, a knock sounded on the door. Joshua pulled the revolver from its holster and moved quickly to the side of the door. He wondered if it was word from Boss with a job already.

"Who is it?" Joshua called out.

Joshua was surprised to hear a soft woman's voice. "It's Helen."

Joshua removed the chair from the door and opened it. A mid-thirties aged woman with a bright red gown stood in the doorway. Her brown hair folded neatly into a bun on the back of her head. Her smile was pleasant and her eyes glistened with vibrantly.

Joshua stepped back. "Good evening, Helen. Come in."

They stood for a moment looking at each other. Joshua was feeling awkward. Helen spoke first. "The sheriff never said how handsome you were, but I suppose though, he doesn't really care." She laughed.

"You know why you're here?" Joshua asked, avoiding her sense of humor.

"Is this a brush off? I'm not used to something like that. Yes, I know why I'm here. I just thought we could pass the time, since I'm supposed to hang around here for an hour."

"I'm sorry. You are a very attractive lady. You could jingle any man's spurs."

"What a smooth talker."

The words hit Joshua like a rock. Jennie had said those same words to him the first time they had met. He took a deep breath.

"I'll write a note for the sheriff."

"Take your time. I can't leave early. I have a reputation to keep you know."

Joshua looked up and smiled. "I understand. Relax."

Helen was true to her word. She stayed for over an hour. As she stood at the door to leave, she stared into Joshua's eyes. "Joshua, I've been around. I've seen eyes of desire, fear, anger, all kind of eyes, but I worry about you. Your eyes are so sad, almost lost. Do what you need to do, but let your heart find some happiness."

Joshua never answered. Helen kissed him on the cheek and left. The door closed with a final thud. She had read him well, but he also knew he would have to continue his waywardness...at least for now.

****

When Sheriff Bowling received Joshua's note, he immediately contacted Harold Tillman, owner of the freight company. In their private meeting, the sheriff explained what he knew and that the company's bookkeeper was suspected of being an informant for the road agents. They quickly set about a plan to end the outlaws' domination of the roads.

They decided to send a false shipment and wait in hiding to catch the road agents by surprise. They hoped Joshua working inside would be able to supply information with their numbers and location of the robbery. They would make sure the bookkeeper would know the details of the shipment.

The next night Helen arrived at Joshua's door with a note from the sheriff. The excitement began to build as Joshua read the note. It would all be ending soon--good or bad-- it would be ending soon. He looked up at Helen.

"Good news?" she asked. "I wish I could get you that excited."

"Never give up hope. Sometimes it's all we have."

"I won't."

After Helen spent her hour, she left. "Next time," she promised as she kissed him on the cheek.

Two days later, Joshua received a message from the boss. There was a meeting the next afternoon at two. Come to the Strike. It was coming down. Joshua's body began to tense with anticipation. He wanted a drink. His hand rested around the bottle. "No," he said aloud, "too much is riding on me." His hand released the bottle.

The next day, Joshua arrived at the Strike near two o'clock. Two men were guarding the door to the saloon.

"The saloon is closed," one of the men said in a gruff tone.

"He's the new guy the boss hired," the other remarked.

They stepped aside to allow Joshua through. The saloon had a half dozen men present. They were sitting quietly, only a couple of the men were in conversation.

Shortly, the boss strolled in from the back. "Gather around men," he stated matter of fact. He paused, waiting for complete attention from all the men. "Tomorrow there is another gold shipment headed for Cheyenne. There is supposed to be in excess of one hundred fifty thousand in gold on this shipment. The shipment is leaving Lead about six tomorrow morning. We're going to greet them at Hollow Pass." Boss held up a map of the area. "They'll probably be there around noon. We'll make our escape up the draw about a half mile before the pass. Bill and Kansas, ride out and notify the boys that I want the pack mules in place before seven. No slip-ups, men. A couple more heists like this and we can divide it up, and each head in their own direction with a tidy sum."

The crowd broke up and some started to leave. Joshua headed for the door. "Hold it," Boss called out. Joshua stopped. A chill raced through him. Something was not right. "There is a tradition with us," the boss said as he came to Joshua's side. "The new guy spends the night before a heist here at the saloon. A little precaution we like to take. You can bunk out in the back tonight."

Joshua nodded. His mind began to swirl. How could he get the information to the sheriff? He found his bunk in back and wrote the information down, hoping that somehow the opportunity would arise that he could pass the information. He returned to the front and waited as the time ticked away. His chance to pass the information was becoming bleaker with each passing minute.

By evening, Joshua lost hope of passing on the information. He was never going to find an opportunity to slip out from the constant surveillance and deliver the message. Suddenly as though being in a wonderful dream, a familiar face appeared in the doorway. It was like sunshine on a dismal stormy day. Helen, in all her color and brightness, entered the saloon as though she owned the place. She moved through the saloon with a sensual drama that any theatre would be delighted to present, playing to each man, sitting on laps, rubbing against them, whispering in their ear, all the while moving closer to Joshua. When she arrived at his table, she slid into his lap. She smelled so sweet and felt so good against him; he wished he were in his room.

"Hello, good-looking," she said, pushing her breasts to his face. Joshua heard a couple whistles and shouts. She pressed her cheek to his mouth. "Whisper sweet nothings to me you big hunk of a man."

Joshua's hand ran beneath her petticoat. He hoped she had a garter belt on. She did. He slipped the note under her belt, while nibbling her ear.

Helen jumped up. "Well aren't you ready. Your place or mine?"

"Sorry, I need to stick around here."

"I guess it's your loss," she said, squeezing his cheeks and bending so he could have a vivid view of her breasts. "There'll be no more free feels for you."

Helen finished her sweep through the saloon and left. She did a masterful performance. Joshua wanted to give her a standing ovation.

****

Sleep evaded Joshua, so when the boss rousted him long before daylight, he was ready. "Are the rest coming here?" Joshua asked.

"No, we have a place to meet outside of town. A large group of horsemen leaving town together might create suspicion.

The early morning felt particularly cold and dark. The streets were empty as they moved through town. Joshua noticed the sheriff's office was dark. Oh please, Helen, he thought, I hope you didn't let me down.

Three miles out of town, Boss reined in his horse. "We'll wait here," he said. Shortly riders began to arrive...five...six...seven...and then ten in total, including the boss and himself. The men with the pack mules had not arrived. That would mean at least twelve road agents. Joshua wondered if the sheriff had prepared for so many bandits. Shortly, two men arrived with four pack mules. Boss stood up in the stirrups and motioned to the men, "Okay, let's move out."

They traveled quietly, only the sounds of hooves and occasional snorting from one of the horses split the silent mountain air. When they arrived near the pass, Boss raised his hand. "Kansas, Frank, Pete, stay here and when you hear gunfire move in from the back. The rest are with me. We'll move in from the front and side."

Joshua tried to play out the scenario. Where would the sheriff and his men lie in wait? The two groups might run into each other.

Soon Boss raised his hand. They had a view of the pass from here. It would be only a matter of time now. Joshua saw Boss glance at his watch. Joshua wondered if time seemed endless to him, too.

Joshua's hair bristled. The distant rumbling of the freight wagons broke the silent air. The sound steadily became louder as the moment drew near. Then the wagons appeared out of the fog like a ghostly mirage. Four large draft horses pulled each of the two wagons. A driver and a shotgun sat on each wagon. There were six riders accompanying the wagons.

The lone rumbling of the wagons was suddenly pierced by a shot that rang out from the rear, and then another. Boss shouted, "Those damn fools. I told them to wait for me. Come on." With a surge, he spurred his horse forward. All of the others followed. Joshua fell to the rear. He noticed the driver and shotgun on each wagon had dropped into the wagon and considerable gunfire came from the wagon itself. The men on horses had dismounted and were firing from the opposite side of the wagon from the onslaught of the bandits. Obviously, the guards and the men on the wagons were prepared for the attack.

Because the road agents were busily focusing on the wagons, several horsemen arriving from the front, which included the sheriff, surprised them. Joshua began firing from his position. He could see three rider-less horses, which meant three men were on the ground. The gun battle continued as the bandits were suddenly taking gunfire from every direction. The outlaws, finally realizing their hapless situation, began surrendering.

Joshua rode alongside the sheriff. "It looks like you've got yourself a pretty good haul."

"It worked out darn well, I'd say." The sheriff was all puffed up like a peacock. His face was alive with a smile that ran from ear to ear. "And we didn't lose one person, only a couple minor wounds."

They counted the number of road agents they had taken prisoner and the number dead. "There are at least three men missing, including the boss," said Joshua, once he heard the count.

"Probably read the ambush early and got out while they could," the sheriff surmised.

"I'm guessing they're heading straight to where they have all the stash from the other robberies. They'll divide it up and get out of the territory in a hurry. If we don't find them before they leave, we may never find them."

"We can see if they've left any tracks," the sheriff said.

"Good and I'm thinking they might take the pack mules with them. Where's Henry?"

"I still have him locked up for his own protection."

"I think if he's turned loose, he might lead us to the gold. I really think he knows where it is. He was frightened, but he's still a prospector and I'm sure he'll go back if he has the opportunity."

****

286

The seven prisoners were taken back to town and put in jail, and the three dead men were sent to the undertaker. The sheriff released Henry and his mule, and then the sheriff, Joshua and four deputies waited for Henry to leave town. It did not take him long. Although Henry was old and frail in appearance, he moved like a deer avoiding a grizzly. The lawmen stayed as close as possible as they moved through gullies, dense undergrowth, around buttes and along streambeds. They followed him for three hours when suddenly Henry changed his behavior and began to move cautiously forward, before finally hiding behind some rocks. Obviously, the old man had become frightened, but something brought the prospector to this place.

"This has got to be it," Joshua said excitedly. It must be down that ravine."

With revolvers drawn, the lawmen moved in quickly on the bandits. Their sudden appearance caught Boss and four other bandits busily loading the gold onto six pack mules. They had already filled their saddlebags.

"Good afternoon, Boss," Joshua said.

Boss looked up. "You rotten stupid bastard! You could have been set for life."

"Sorry to disappoint you. The sheriff made me do it."
****

The following morning, Joshua stood in the sheriff's office. "Your reward is quite large, Joshua. Any plans for it?"

"Actually I do have some plans. I want a third to go to Henry, but give it to him in small portions though. I'm worried he might do something stupid with it. I know you can't take rewards, but give yourself a nice administrative fee for watching the money. Fifty-fifty sounds about right."

"A very generous thing you're doing, Joshua."

"I guess I better get going."

"It was a pleasure having you here. I thought for a while you were going to be the death of me, but you proved me wrong. Those boys in the back will be hanging once the judge gets here."

"Good. Keep a close eye on them until they are swinging. I would hate to see any of them get loose. It would create a bad situation."

"I sure will."

Joshua returned to his room and packed. He made himself comfortable waiting for a visit. It was not long when a knock sounded.

Joshua went to the door. "Yes."

"It's me. Open the door."

Joshua opened it. Helen stood there as he had expected, but she did not look like the Helen as he had expected. She was not wearing one of her bright flamboyant dresses or the bright lipstick and rouge. Instead, she wore a soft blue dress with soft lace around the neck and wrists, yet she still showed just enough of her well-formed body to tantalize any man.

"Wow!" Joshua exclaimed. "You are a ravishing beauty, Helen."

"Thank you. I decided to change careers. I've saved a little money."

"You can't imagine how happy I am for you. I knew underneath all that fanfare flare was a fine refined lady ready to burst forth."

"Our long talks inspired me, Joshua. I will forever be grateful. I also wanted to tell you I'd be much happier if you'd rethink your future. I want you to get rid of all that sadness and hate, Joshua. It won't bring your Jennie back and the good heart you have can do so much good for others."

"I hear what you're telling me and I'll try to do my best. Maybe this time I can climb out of this hole I'm in."

"Please keep trying." Helen rubbed her hands gently across Joshua's face.

"I will. Now Helen, I want to share something with you." Joshua reached into his saddlebag and withdrew a stack of money. "Your share of the reward. I want you to have it."

Helen's eyes became large, and her mouth fell open. "Joshua, are you sure? It's so much."

"I am absolutely sure. Without you, we probably would have never captured the bandits. You did a marvelous performance and I can say you did a great job of tantalizing me that night. You deserve this money."

"The performance for you was personal and I enjoyed every moment of it. Thank you for this and for being kind to me. With this and all your kindness, my life has definitely changed." She kissed him on the cheek, and then her lips moved to his. After considerable time, she slowly released her lips from his. She smiled. "I could have taken you in a heartbeat."

"I know, but now it's time for me to go."

"When the time is right, I want you to come back here and make me a happy woman."

"I think you have always been a happy woman, Helen."

She smiled. "I suppose, but walking arm in arm with you could make me a great deal happier." She started for Joshua's lips again, and then stopped. "I'm going to wait when I know it'll be special for both of us."

"Thank you, Helen."

****

"As they passed the front desk, the young clerk called out, "Is that you, Helen?"

She turned towards the clerk. "The name is Miss Dashing, Herman."

"Yes, Miss Dashing. You look lovely."

"Why thank you," she answered as she left the hotel, her arm tucked into Joshua's arm.

Once outside, she turned to Joshua. "I'm not sure it's lady-like to hug a man in public." She smiled. "But if it's not, I'll revert to my old life for a moment."

Joshua took her into his arms and squeezed her. When he released her, he took her soft delicate hand in his and bowed, kissing it lightly.

"Oh my, thank you, Mr. ..."

"Parker, ma'am."

"Thank you, Mr. Parker."

"Have a good day and a good life, Miss Dashing. I hope I have the pleasure of seeing you someday not too far in the future."

"And the same to you, Mr. Parker. I mean it. I would be so disappointed if we were not to pass ways again."

Miss Dashing smiled and walked away. Joshua watched as she passed along the street while men's heads turned to have a better look. Wherever Miss Dashing goes and whatever she makes of her life, she'll have men eating from her hand, Joshua thought, shaking his head...and I suppose I could be one of them someday.

When she had disappeared from sight, he threw his saddlebag over his shoulder and headed for the stable. He could not wait to get out of Deadwood. The environment was not good for him. If he was going to keep his promise to Miss Dashing, he needed to be somewhere new to make his start.

Chapter 37

$\mathcal{J}$oshua rode along the creek that would lead him to the Fuller ranch. It was mid-April and most of the snow had melted, with only hidden patches along the tree-lined road. The warm spring breeze felt good against his face. It was the best he had felt in six months. He had helped capture a dozen road agents and killers in Deadwood and in the process, he had helped Helen rethink her life. Now it was his turn to change his life as he had promised Helen...or Miss Dashing. He was excited to see the progress of Elizabeth and particularly Julia. Three months had passed since he had been to the ranch, and he was confident that once the reality of the rapists being dead had set in, the Fuller women would be well on the way to recovery. In addition, he was anxious to visit Jennie's grave. He could tell her all the good news that he had bottled up inside him. It would make her happy, and besides, spring was always her favorite time of the year. She always said how life renewed each spring with the blossoms, flowers and grasses. The cold dreary winter was gone. Maybe spring would renew his life, his hopes and aspirations.

The ranch house came into view above the foliage along the stream. Joshua spurred his horse into a gallop. He almost felt like a child heading for the swimming hole on the first day of summer with the building of excitement. With all that had happened between the family and him, a closeness had developed, and he was sure they felt the same way.

As Joshua rode past the corral towards the house, he saw Syd coming out of the corral gate. He turned and rode back to greet Syd. Joshua dismounted and shook Syd's hand enthusiastically. "Good seeing you again, Syd."

"Glad you're back. Everyone will be happy to see you." A forced smile came to his face. "Are you back to stay?"

Joshua wondered if he had offended Syd the last time he had been at the ranch. Something was not right with the elder Fuller.

"Just might. One never knows with me, I guess. How is the family?"

Syd's face was pale and his eyes dull. "Joshua, I've got bad news." He took a deep breath. Joshua felt a cold chill race through his body. Syd's words were forced and uncertain as he spoke, not like his usual self-assured voice. "Julia...our dear, dear Julia...is gone."

"What? What do you mean gone? She ran away?"

"No. She's dead, Joshua. She took her own life." Tears welled up in Syd's eyes.

"I don't understand. What about the good news about the filthy men being dead? Didn't that help? I don't understand. When?"

"Early March." Syd wiped his eyes with his large brawny hands. "She never got any better. She just seemed to become more depressed. We all talked to her. Nothing seemed to help her. She no longer cared for anything, including life. She couldn't get rid of the nightmare."

Joshua's head was spinning. Julia could not be gone. She was so young and had so much life ahead of her. "I'm having trouble grasping it, Syd. I...I had such hopes returning this time and finding her better."

"I was the same way. I was just sure she would start getting better, but she didn't. One morning, a cold dreary March day, she disappeared. We searched for her everywhere we could think of. All the horses were still here so we knew she had to have gone on foot. Then..." he stopped, his voice choked up. "Sorry," he whispered.

"I understand, Syd. Take your time or if you'd rather not talk about it."

"No, I need to. I found her at the bottom of the ridge north of here. She had jumped."

"Maybe she had accidently fallen."

"I wish, but I'm sure she jumped. We found a letter later saying she could not go on living any longer. She could not live with the horrible nightmares and memories. She wanted to be left alone."

"I'm so sorry, Syd. I was so sure."

"I guess we all were. I don't think Martha and Elizabeth were as surprised as I was. Maybe it's something women know and understand better. I'm angry with myself because there seemed to be nothing I could do. I was helpless."

Joshua walked a few feet away, staring off into the distance. His hopes for his own recovery rested on finding the Fuller family doing well, and they in turn would lift his spirits and he might find the ellusive, shifting winds of happiness. If he stayed now, the deeply rooted sadness that filled the Fuller home would only drive him deeper. He had counted on Julia's recovery to be the key that opened a new life for him. Now her suicide was like a knife cutting into his dream of a new life with happiness...a dream that had given him hope.

Joshua turned back to Syd. "I can't stay, Syd. I know I'm not being a decent person for what I'm about to do. I know you and the family would never turn your backs on me, but I can't stay. I can feel the overwhelming sorrow of Julia's death pulling me down. Not the sorrow from you, but from me. I've been trying to climb out of the bottom, and I thought I could here. But now, I can feel me slipping back, falling deeper into the muck, and it's going to destroy me. I need to leave for me, but also for you and the family too. I can't allow my misery to fester here with you. I would like to offer my condolences to the family, and then I must go."

"Perhaps you should leave now. I hope they haven't seen you yet and I think it would be best if they didn't. I know you want to go to the graveyard. Do, but please leave from there."

Joshua nodded. "I'm sorry for Julia and I'm sorry for my behavior."

Syd never answered.

Joshua led his horse to the nearby cemetery. A few feet away from Jennie's grave was the fresh dirt of Julia's grave. "I'm sorry, Julia. I wanted it to be better for you." He knelt by Jennie's grave. "Jennie, I wanted to start my life again with the blooming of spring. But I can't right now. I pray someday soon. I love you, Jennie. You must know that. You have such a healing kindness to you, take Julia under your care. Why am I saying that? I know you already have. Bye for now, my darling."

Joshua mounted his horse and once again headed into a future with no windows...only darkness.

****

Elizabeth watched Joshua ride away. Tears rose in her eyes. She had hopes of him staying...dreams of a future. She had only lost her husband ten months ago, but she had found love for a man who was now riding away. Each time he left, she wondered if she would ever see him again. Perhaps she was being foolish; she wondered if he could ever love another woman other than the one lying in the grave so near her window. She knew love was no guarantee, but she was not about to give up on Joshua yet. "Lord, please bring him home, physically and in spirit," she whispered as she wept. "I know I can help mend his battered heart if he would only let me."

Chapter 38

$\mathcal{O}$ver the next year after leaving the Fuller Ranch, Joshua Parker roamed through Wyoming, eastern Montana and western Nebraska. As the year progressed, he spent less time searching for the wanted criminal elements and more time lost in the dregs of whiskey and rye. He would lose track of days on end; drinking, and then trying to regain sobriety. After days of not leaving his room, management would kick him out into the street.

Joshua had tried his hand at being a cowpuncher in eastern Montana, but after a month, left. He thought about searching for a friendly face--Helen, the sheriff in Deadwood, the Fullers, Tom, or his family in Cheyenne, but he could not allow himself to show up in his condition. He had always been a proud man and he could never imagine arriving at their doorstep begging for help.

It was early May when Joshua rode into a small town in western Nebraska. He had only a two-dollar gold piece to his name. Perhaps it was enough for a night for his horse at the stable, a cheap hotel room and something to eat. However, he knew whiskey would come before eating. He had gone without the numbing of the whiskey for five days and the craving was there.

Fighting his dilemma, Joshua stood on the wooden walk, watching people busy with their lives. Each seemed to have a purpose, something he did not have. The town was a farming community with a church, general store, a small saloon, an eatery, stable and feed store. It was a typical quiet farming community that Joshua had seen throughout the west.

For no particular reason, Joshua began watching a farmer nearby loading grain and supplies onto his wagon. The man stopped for a moment, removed his hat and wiped his brow with his sleeve. Joshua was not sure why, but the farmer looked familiar. He studied the man, trying to place him. Maybe, he thought, and removed a stack of wanted posters tucked away in his saddlebag. Slowly he thumbed through the thirty or so posters. He stopped. An old poster from some ten years prior had a picture that resembled the farmer. He was older looking as expected, but it was a good resemblance. The poster read, 'Wanted for Murder, Dead or Alive, $1000 reward, Derrick Colby, Murdered government worker, Arkansas.'

Joshua called out, "Derrick Colby." The farmer looked up and quickly back down. That's him for sure, thought Joshua. The farmer hurriedly finished loading his buckboard and left, going east out of town. Joshua watched for a while, mounted his horse and headed out of town following the wanted killer. Looks easy, thought Joshua. All he had to do was overtake him a short distance out of town on the empty road to ensure no problems from the locals, and then escort him to Scottsbluff. The farmer did not even appear to have a weapon. It would be an easy thousand dollars. He could live off that for some time.

About a mile out of town, Joshua caught up with the wagon. He rode alongside. "Derrick Colby?"

"I'm Lewis Baxter. You got the wrong person." He looked very nervous as he continued to hurry his wagon along.

"No, I have the right person." Joshua pulled out the poster and flashed it to the farmer. "It does say, dead or alive, so I would hope you decide to come along peacefully."

The wagon stopped. The defeated man lowered his head. "It had been so long, I thought everything was going to be okay."

"How long?"

"Twelve years. Can I say good-bye to my wife and children? It's about another mile. I have to let them know what happened to me."

Warning bells went off in Joshua's head, but he felt obligated to allow a man to see his family before he was hauled off to prison, or perhaps hanged. "Sounds reasonable." They continued along, Joshua riding alongside Derrick Colby.

"So what happened?" Joshua asked. "You don't strike me as a cold blooded killer."

"I'm not. Twelve years ago after the war, government carpetbaggers moved into Arkansas. My wife and I had a small farm. We had a two-year-old son. We were struggling with me being off to war for so long. The war had created so much hardship for everyone. The carpetbaggers began to confiscate what little livestock and meager possessions we had. We would die of starvation without our animals and I had a family to feed. They would laugh at our begging and did everything under the sun to humiliate us. In a moment of rage, I shot the government man. We had to run, leaving everything behind. They ended up getting everything in the end anyway and I lost my life and destroyed my family's life. Perhaps you finding me is for the best. I've lived in fear of this day for twelve years."

The wagon pulled into a road leading to a small farmhouse and barn. Half dozen cows wandered in the field nearby. The chickens scattered as the two men approached and a half dozen pigs were in the pen by the barn. A pleasant looking woman came from the house. Her clothes were old and dreary, but even they could not hide her shapely body or her hidden beauty. Two small children stopped playing beside the house and ran to greet their father and stranger. A teenage boy remained standing in the doorway of the house.

Lewis Baxter climbed from his wagon and moved slowly towards his wife as though trying to find the right words to tell her that he was going away for a long time, perhaps forever. As he spoke to her, she closed her eyes and clenched her teeth, and then she started to cry with a mournful sound. Her voice was pleading, "No, Lewis, oh Lord, please let this not be true." Lewis put his arms around her. The children, not understanding what was happening, clung to their mother's waist.

Joshua had dismounted and was standing nearby. He felt sorry for the family, but the law had been broken. A man was dead, however evil he may have seemed. He was following orders in his own sadistic way.

Without warning, the teenage boy who had been standing in the doorway appeared some twenty-five feet away from Joshua, holding an old musket rifle. Joshua found himself surprised and unprepared. He had been too involved in the sorrowful good-byes of the rest of the family. The rifle pointed directly at him. Joshua cursed for becoming too lax and allowing a young teenage boy to get the upper hand on him. A mistake only inexperience should have made.

Lewis realizing his son was holding a rifle on Joshua, shouted at his son, "No, Gordon, no. Don't even think about this. I will not have my son being hunted like me." Swiftly, Lewis moved between his son and Joshua. Joshua knew he should seize the opportunity, but he could not imagine shooting a young boy, whose only fault was trying to protect his father. Joshua just hoped that the father would resolve the tense moment.

"Gordon, you're smart, mighty smart. Think this through. You shoot him and somebody is going to come looking. They'll figure out who I am and decide I was the one who killed this man since I'm a wanted killer. What have we gained? Nothing."

Joshua doubted Lewis' reasoning whether anyone would miss him and ever come looking, but he was not going to intercede in Lewis' great speech.

"Besides, Gordon, you kill someone, the remorse is horrible. I know, son. I know.

Gordon slowly lowered his rifle. He began sobbing. Lewis pulled his son to him and held the boy. "You did the right thing, Son," Lewis said as he wept with his son. "The choices are not always clear, but you made the right one. I need you to take charge, Son, and be the man here. You'll have to take care of your mother and the little ones. I don't know what is going to happen to me."

Lewis stepped back from his son and faced Joshua. "I'm ready, mister."

Joshua carefully eyed each member of the family. The little ones might never remember their courageous father, the teenage son would have to become a man overnight and miss the wonders of youth. The wife would lie alone at night and not have a husband to share their happiness and sorrows together. How painful he knew that was. The law could be cold, blind, and without feeling. It did not have a soul to know when something was right or wrong, just words.

"Lewis, do you have anything that would indicate that you were Derrick Colby?"

"I don't know. I don't believe so. I tried to clear myself of the name and person."

"Father, the rifle," Gordon said. "The initials DC are etched into the butt of the rifle."

"That's right."

"I'd like the rifle please."

Lewis handed Joshua the rifle.

"I'm taking this." Joshua mounted his horse. "Lewis, grow a beard. You folks have a good day." He tipped the brim of his hat and rode away as the entire Baxter family stared in disbelief. As Joshua turned on to the main road, the family with tear-filled eyes began hugging each other. They had received a precious gift from a stranger...a second chance.

Mrs. Baxter, tears running down her cheek, held her husband's face in her hands. "I think you'll look very handsome in a beard."

Joshua wanted to rejoice. For the first time in a very long time, his heart felt light and free. He realized a family united with love is a very powerful force and can deal with most anything thrown their way. Others survive pain and tragedy and still keep their heads up and live life with purpose. Why was he so different? Was he weaker? Surely he had the strength to survive. A good friend had told him so. Things were about to change. He had received a gift from a loving family...a second chance.

Chapter 39

Collinsworth Hershel Kingsley was born to a banking family from St. Louis, Missouri. Almost from the first day of birth, he had been a rebellious child. When he reached sixteen, he robbed his family's vault of money and jewels and headed west. He immediately purchased a revolver and began practicing his draw and firing every day and night. His confidence grew as he progressed westward and he was getting the itch to test his skill with his forty-five caliber revolver.

Collins found a poker game in an old rundown joint just inside the Wyoming border. An old drifter sat across from Collins. Collins noticed the old Remington forty-four in the old man's holster. It was old, large and clumsy. Collins scoffed as he ran his fingers over his smooth sleek Colt 45. He smiled. The old drifter could never match his speed and accuracy. The drifter was old and his revolver was old. He was young and his revolver new. This would be his first test. He knew he was fast. He would begin building his reputation tonight.

The game proceeded into the evening. Collins was losing and the old drifter was holding his own. The money did not matter; it was the humiliation. The next time the old Remington dealt, Collins would accuse him of cheating and call for a duel.

As the moment approached, Collins felt his hands perspiring, his body twitching. As his cards lay on the table before him, Collins shouted, "You're dealing from the bottom of the deck, old man." Collins went for his Colt. The drifter with cat-like quickness flipped the table onto Collins, knocking him to the floor, while his Colt fell harmlessly to the floor and out of reach. He reached for the revolver, but a booming voice cut him short. "I wouldn't, you poor excuse for a man." Collins looked up. He stared at a large, bulky, old Remington barrel pointed at his head. The drifter picked up the Colt. "Nice looking piece of metal. Perhaps it needs someone who is man enough to use it. Get up!" He stuck the Colt in his waistband. Collins rose. The drifter grabbed the young slinger by the collar and led him to the door. He shoved Collins outside. "You better hope we never meet up again. Now get your young butt out of here."

Collins mounted his horse and rode away. He swore he would never be embarrassed again.

****

Joshua Parker once again passed through the gate that led to the Fuller house. He was nervous. It had been over a year since he had rudely left the ranch. Maybe they would turn him away. He would not blame them.

As Joshua dismounted, he noticed Syd approaching from the house. His eyes were hard and dark. Joshua was concerned there was more bad news.

"Hello, Joshua. It's been sometime, stranger."

"I know it has, Syd. Far too long. I've been feeling bad for the way I treated you and the family."

Syd ignored the remark. "I'd like to take a little walk. You feel like joining me?"

"Sure." They began to move away from the house and toward the corral. "Has everything been okay here, Syd?"

"I suppose. We're all still having a hard time trying to let go of 'what if' about Julia."

"I understand that completely. I've found it just takes a long time to accept that one does the best he can and that's all he can do. I still fight it."

Syd nodded, and then changed the subject. "So what are your plans, Joshua? Are you going to stick around this time?"

"I thought I would if the family would have me?"

"Joshua, you know I've got high regards for you and I'll always be indebted for what you did for my girls. My problem, Joshua..." Syd stopped and faced Joshua, his feet set, "is well, it's that Elizabeth has a fixing on you. She's never really said it, but it's the way she talks about you, and the way she acts when you come around and when you go. And there lies the problem for me. I can't continue to let my lone remaining daughter's feelings be yanked like a spirited horse on a bit. It's not fair to her, Joshua."

"I'm sorry. I didn't know."

"Understand, I'm not saying you have to be courting her, but I just can't allow you to come and go and keep messing with her heart. I'm asking you to keep that in mind. If you choose to stick around, good, and I'll be glad to have you. If you decide to take off again, you won't be welcome back. I don't mean to be hard and cold, but my daughter is too important to me."

Joshua listened to everything Syd was saying. He had no idea that Elizabeth had feelings towards him other than their friendship. He still wondered if Syd was misreading his daughter. He did understand how his coming and going was upsetting to the family. He had given little consideration to their feelings...only his. With a clearer head now, he was beginning to realize how he had never considered other people's feelings in his wild escapades. It had been that way all the way back to Iowa. He wanted to stay at the ranch, but he feared he might suddenly fall back to his old ways. He felt he had truly changed, seeing the Baxter family and their unity. He wanted that. He no longer had that desire for the thrill of the hunt. And to hear Elizabeth had feelings for him actually felt good. Would Jennie approve? He knew she would want him to be happy. She had always been that kind of person.

"I want to stay, Syd. I'm a different person now. It was just a short time ago, I was at the bottom, and there was no light, no feeling of life, and no hope. Then I met a family that had very little in possessions and they had lived in fear for years, but they were on top. They didn't live as individuals wallowing in their own sorrow; they lived as a loving family unit always caring for each other. I watched them that day as I was about to destroy them, yet they held together. I saw them that day, and I felt them that day, and I changed that day. They changed me. It was a revelation of sorts. I've come a long ways since then."

"Good to hear that, Son. I think it'll be good for you and I know it will be for the family and me. Now, I have a couple women waiting inside, chomping at the bit to get their hands on you."

Syd slapped Joshua on the back and they headed for the house. Joshua no longer needed that pouch of tobacco to look casual; he was anxious to go inside and start his new beginning.

Except for a concerned glance at Syd, Martha and Elizabeth were all smiles when the men entered the house. Each gave Joshua a welcoming hug.

"Welcome back," Martha said leading him to the couch and directing Elizabeth next to him. Elizabeth's face reddened at the obvious maneuver by her mother.

After everyone was seated, Joshua was the first to speak. "I must apologize for my rude behavior the last time here. It was very wrong of me and I offer no excuse for my actions. I only considered myself and without any regard to a wonderful family that was in mourning. I'm truly sorry."

The two women were dabbing their eyes with their kerchiefs and even Syd inconspicuously wiped his eye with his hand.

Everyone sat quietly for a short period. Syd broke the silence, "Joshua is planning on staying with us. We hope for a very long time."

"Yes I am, if everyone will have me."

The entire family quickly voiced their approval.

The conversation lasted into late afternoon. The two women excused themselves and went to the kitchen to prepare the evening meal. Although Joshua knew it would eventually come up, he was relieved that no one inquired into what he had been doing the past year.

Joshua decided to visit Jennie's grave and excused himself. It had been some time since he had visited her and he was anxious to tell her that things were looking better. He actually could see some brightness in his future, and it felt good, very good.

After a heart filled talk with Jennie, Joshua returned to the house in good spirits. Maybe he had at last found himself.

After supper, Syd led Joshua into the front room. Syd placed two glasses on the table and held a bottle of Jack Daniel whiskey in his hand. "Care to partake in a glass of fine whiskey?"

Joshua looked at the bottle, then up at Syd. "I'm sorry, Syd, I can't. It's Sunday."

Syd laughed. "Son, you're confused. It's only Thursday."

Joshua's face was set. "For me, it's Sunday. Everyday will be Sunday."

Syd showed surprise, and then gathered his thoughts. "Okay. You know, I could use a good cup of coffee right now. How about you?"

"Sounds good, but Syd, I have no problem if you wish to have some fine whiskey."

"Okay, I'll remember that, but tonight I think I would like some coffee."

Both men laughed and headed for the kitchen.

As the men were finishing their coffee, the women joined them. After some conversation, Syd leaned forward. "I was thinking, Joshua, since you're sticking around, I need to start showing you our setup here. I figure you need to start earning your keep."

"That would be great," Joshua quickly responded.

"Okay. Tomorrow morning, breakfast at five-thirty. On the trail by six-thirty."

"I'll be ready. Sounds exciting." Joshua turned to Elizabeth. "Would you care to go for a little stroll with me on this fine spring evening?"

"I would love to join you." Her face glowed.

As they walked through the garden, Elizabeth discussed the garden. "Mother loves her garden. Other than the stables and the horses, this was Julia's favorite place. Julia always wanted to be where it was quiet and she could be alone. Even before the horrible incident, she struggled with life. I think that eventually she would have taken her life even if the incident had not happened. It just made it happen sooner. I know that may sound terrible, but that's what I believe. I try to spend time with mother in her garden. I know she enjoys talking to someone out here and showing them things. I think this is her healing place."

"How are you doing, Elizabeth? You've been through so much, with Julia, your husband and you went through the same terrible ordeal Julia did."

They had reached the garden swing and sat next to each other. Joshua felt a chill as their bodies touched in closeness.

"One day at a time, I guess. It has not been easy, but I think I'm doing good."

"I'm sure it's been difficult, so much in such a short time. You seem to be doing so well though. I'm happy for that."

"I'll be fine. I inherited my folk's fire for life. Poor Julia never had that fire. Life was so hard for her. She always just existed. It made it extra hard on everybody because it was not easy for the rest of us to understand what she was going through."

"After Jennie's death, I think I may have known how Julia felt. My fire had gone out. Maybe that's why it was so difficult for me when I heard of Julia taking her life. I knew how she felt."

Elizabeth rested her hand on his hand. "I think your difficulty was you were always in control of your life and when that control was removed so tragically, you didn't know how to

306

respond. From what I've seen, I believe you have that fire, perhaps it was just out of control like a wild fire."

"This last year, it certainly went out of control."

"It was bad?" Elizabeth squeezed his hand.

"Since Jennie's death, I have not been a good person, especially during this last year."

"What changed you? What made you come back and start again?"

"A family. A single family that stood together, faced their problem head on and looked to the future with hope. Their love and unity was overwhelming. I almost destroyed them, but then what I saw in them, shot through me like a lightning bolt. I can't even explain it. My head began to clear itself of all the hate and woeful feelings I had for myself. I began to realize your family had the same power, but my mind was always filled with such muck that I couldn't see anything. Jennie would have been very disappointed in me for the way I acted."

"I'm happy you changed. I'm glad you're back."

Joshua without a thought, leaned forward and gently kissed her. "I'm happy, I'm back, too."

Elizabeth brushed his cheek with the back of her hand. "I'm glad."

****

Breakfast came early as promised the next morning, but with a clear head, Joshua was ready and excited for the day. Syd had been right, they were riding out before six-thirty. The sky was partially cloudy, the sun warm and the grasses lay green across the land as far as the eye could see.

"A perfect day," Joshua declared as they moved away from the buildings.

"Days like this make everything worth it. As you probably noticed, Martha has her garden and she manages the chickens. We have a dozen hogs and I keep about a dozen horses. The rest are cattle, mostly longhorns. I did purchase a few white-face Herefords that come out of England. They're a nice looking animal, but I need to see how well they adapt to the Wyoming terrain and weather."

"How many cattle do you have here?"

"Up to five hundred before heading them off to market. The weather has a lot to say how many I have. The winter can take quite a few, and then I have to deal with water shortages, grass shortages. Many variables out here can make or break you. You also have to deal with the trail drives, rustlers and the market itself. Today I want to check on the water reserve. Of course, with the spring melt and rains, the water will be plentiful now, but I hope to get an idea where we will be by fall, before the fall rains and winter snow arrive. If we get a heavy snow, it makes for a difficult winter-feeding. If it doesn't snow enough, the water supply comes up short. Rarely do we get a happy medium."

Joshua knew and understood what Syd was saying, but it still brought the reality of a rancher's life to the forefront. His small spread of a dozen cattle and three horses were not in the same category as the Fuller spread.

When they returned to the house, it was early evening. The horses were put away, Joshua and Syd washed up and sat down for supper.

"It was a great day, Syd. Thanks."

"Better save the thanks. You'll wonder if you made the right choice when I put you to work, and I guess that'll be tomorrow." Syd laughed and the others joined in.

Chapter 40

"Joshua, could you ride to town with me to pick up some supplies?" Elizabeth moved closer to him. "Besides, I haven't seen much of you all summer with father keeping you so busy."

"Sure. I'd be glad to if your father doesn't mind."

"It was his suggestion to ride shotgun for me. I need a big strong man to lift some sacks for me."

"Okay. I need to mail a couple packages anyway."

Joshua had been at the ranch for nearly four months and he was finding each day more enjoyable than the previous. He was healing. The anger and pain were subsiding. Although Jennie would never leave his heart, he had developed a love for Elizabeth and he knew someday they would be married. He had found that ellusive happiness that had been avoiding him since Jennie's death and it was a wonderful feeling. The wandering days of aimless drifting were over.

****

Collins Kingsley headed north after his humiliating incident with the drifter. Each day, his anger festered inside him and with each mile that he traveled north, he became more determined to prove himself with a gun. One day he would cross paths with that drifter and savor a satisfying revenge, but for now, he needed to find a reputable gun to bring down and begin proving his worth. He wanted to become so well known that his family in St. Louis would hear of him. The day would come and it would be soon. There would be no more waiting.

****

Elizabeth and Joshua arrived at a small community several miles from the ranch.

"Go on to the freight office and send your packages, Joshua, and I'll leave the order at the general store. I want to stop by the clothiers and maybe buy some frilly things. Maybe you'd be kind enough to load the supplies while I shop for awhile."

"Only if you promise to buy the frilly things."

They smiled at each other.

"For you." Her words sent a tingle through him.

Joshua wanted to kiss her, but remembering his conversation with Miss Dashing, he grasped her hand and kissed it.

"My, my, aren't we the gentleman."

"I try."

Joshua headed for the freight company, stopping shortly to gaze at Elizabeth who was standing at the storefront watching him. They smiled and waved bashfully and went about their business.

Joshua delivered his two packages and headed for the general store. Elizabeth was already gone. "Good morning, Edward," Joshua called out to the owner of the store. "I guess Elizabeth placed an order with you a while ago."

"Sure did, Joshua. I'll be finished with it here, shortly. So how are things going at the ranch?" he asked as he continued working.

"Very well now, but I guess we'll have to wait and see what winter brings." Joshua began carrying some of the supplies to the wagon.

After several trips, Joshua loaded up the last of the supplies and left the store. "Have a good day, Edward," he called.

"You too, Joshua. Say hi to the family." Edward responded with a wave.

"Who is that fellow?"

The voice startled Edward. He had been busy and had not noticed anyone else in the store. The man stepped from the shadows.

"That man that just left?" Edward asked, nodding his head in the direction of Joshua.

"Yeah."

"His name is Joshua Parker. He's hired on at the Fuller ranch. Word has it, he used to be a U.S. Marshal down in Cheyenne."

"Really, that's quite impressive. A marshal, huh?" The stranger watched Joshua load the last of the supplies then turned back to the storeowner. His voice was very precise when he spoke. "My name is Collinsworth H. Kingsley. You might want to remember that name to tell you grandchildren someday that you saw me."

The confused storeowner watched Collins stroll from the store with a swagger of confidence.

Collins had been waiting for this opportunity. He could feel the adrenalin begin to rush through his veins. What better way to build his reputation than kill a marshal.

Elizabeth was leaving the clothiers, excited that she had purchased a new dress, frilly as promised. She saw Joshua standing by the wagon, waiting for her. She smiled and waved. He waved back. How handsome he looks, she thought. Her total thoughts were on Joshua with her eyes fixed on the man she loved. Then movement behind Joshua caught her attention. It was a man facing Joshua with a threatening stance, his hand resting on his revolver.

"Marshal Joshua Parker," the man called out.

Joshua turned, trying to locate the voice. The stranger drew his revolver. Joshua catching a glimpse of the stranger drawing his revolver, reached for his Colt. Two shots rang out. Joshua's revolver was still in the holster as he fell back against the wagon and slumped to the ground. Elizabeth screamed as she watched in horror at the shooting before her. She dropped her package and ran to Joshua lying on the ground.

"Joshua! Joshua! "She screamed. She dropped to her knees, and rested his head and shoulders on her lap. "Don't leave me, please," she pleaded. His eyes were dark and distant. She looked up, but the gunslinger was gone. His voice barely detectable, whispered, "Jennie, I'm home." She felt his hand grasp her arm and then the hand fell to his side. "Oh, Joshua, please don't leave me. I love you," but her lover did not hear her words. Once again, tragedy had left Elizabeth with a broken heart as she held Joshua tightly in her arms.

****

Hallie Richardson held a small package from Joshua. She excitedly called for her husband, "Joseph, come here. Hurry. It's a package from Joshua."

Joseph rushed into the house. She was opening the wrapped package. "Oh my Lord, Joseph. Look at all the money here." She held up a large handful.

"I'll be darned. What'd he say?"

"Let's go to momma's room, and I'll read it there. She'll be so glad to hear from Joshua. Praise the Lord. Praise the Lord," she kept repeating all the way to momma's room.

Hallie stuck her head in the door. "Momma, are you awake?" Hallie whispered.

"Yes. Come on in, dear," Margaret answered.

Hallie hurried to her mother's bed. "Momma, we got a letter from Joshua. I brought it in here to read it."

"I had almost given up on that boy," she whispered. Please read it."

Hallie opened the paper and began to read, "*Dear Mrs. Peterson, Hallie, and Joseph.*"

Margaret interrupted, "I could never keep that boy from calling me Mrs. Peterson." She chuckled. "Go on, dear," Margaret said, motioning with her frail hand.

"*Dear Mrs. Peterson, Hallie and Joseph, I pray this letter finds my loved ones well. I know it has been a long time. I am sorry for being so inconsiderate. I am doing well. I am working at the Fuller Ranch where Jennie is buried. They are very nice people. I hope one day before too long I can come and visit. I think of you often. I was fortunate and received some extra money. Use it as you wish. Your Loving Family Always, Joshua.*"

Joseph squeezed Hallie's shoulders as she wiped her eyes. She waited for a moment for her mother to speak, but instead Margaret lay there, staring at the ceiling.

"Momma, you okay?" Hallie asked.

"Such a blessing," Margaret replied, her head turning to face Hallie and Joseph. "The two of you with such love and happiness and my new grandbaby, Jennie. And now Joshua finding peace and happiness and can be where he can watch over our Jennie. The table is set and now whenever, and I know it to be soon, the good Lord gathers me in his arms, I can leave this world with a light heart and soul."

Hallie took her mother's hand. "I know, Momma. All our hearts are lighter now."

****

Lewis Baxter watched his neighbor ride away. His wife, Malinda came to his side. "What did Bernard deliver?" she asked.

"A small package." He looked more closely at it. "I'll be," he spouted, "It's from that kind fellow that was here, Joshua Parker. Let's go inside and open it."

The couple anxiously sat at the table across from each other. Lewis carefully opened the mysterious package. As he pulled the contents out, the couple gasped. Wrapped in the letter was a large amount of paper money.

"Lewis, can that be real?"

"It looks like it is. But why?"

"Read the letter," Malinda said excitedly.

Lewis nodded. He opened the first paper and was startled by what he saw.

"What is it, Lewis?"

Lewis did not answer immediately, but just stared.

"Lewis, what's wrong?"

Lewis handed the paper to his wife. His hand was trembling. Malinda looked at the paper and gasped. It was a wanted poster for Derrick Colby. Across the top, '*Wanted Dead or Alive*' had a bold line through it and above in bold letters was written, '*Dead.*'

The couple stared at each other. Lewis opened the next piece of paper. "It's a letter." He handed it to Malinda. "You read better than me."

Malinda took the letter and began to read.

'*Greetings to the Baxter family. Praying this letter finds everyone well. You have noticed the money enclosed. It is five hundred dollars. I split the reward money for Derrick Colby. I hope this can be of some help for you. Lewis, buy your beautiful wife a new dress and some fancy things. You will appreciate it as much as she will, I am certain of that. Be sure to give your children a good schooling and have many books of knowledge and adventure around home for them to read. For you, Lewis, you already have the greatest gift--your loving wife, a courageous son, and the contagious laughter of small children. Watching your loving and united family overcome such overwhelming challenges, left me with new hope. My life has changed now because of you and your family. I thank you. As you can see from the poster, Derrick Colby is considered dead by the law. This should help ease some tension and uncertainty in your life. Your old musket and my word was the proof I gave them. With thankful Regards, Joshua Parker. P.S. Lewis, be sure to grow a beard.*'

Lewis smiled as he rubbed his stubbly chin. "Advice well taken, Joshua Parker."

Lewis and Malinda came together in a long and tearful hug, until finally; they called the children to the house to share in their celebration.

Chapter 41

Collinsworth H. Kingsley stood in front of Miss Dashing's Saloon in Deadwood in the Dakota Territory. His reputation had grown since the killing of the marshal in Wyoming. Men now feared him. He had power now. He was convinced that his father, with all his money, did not have the power that he now possessed. In fact, he thought, perhaps he would return to St. Louis to confront his family and watch them shudder with fear. He was in control. He deserved their respect just like the others. He smiled. The thought delighted him.

A woman's voice suddenly interrupted Collins thoughts. "You handsome young stranger, why are you standing out here by yourself?" The sensual woman stepped forward and slid her arm into his.

Collins had been startled by her sudden arrival and it made him angry that he had let his defenses down momentarily. "Who are you?" he growled, pulling away.

"You can call me, Helen," she answered. "Don't you like women or are you the type that likes to rough them up a little? I like a little roughness now and then."

The question caught Collins off guard. "Yes. Yes, I like women as long as they know who's boss."

"Good." She smiled. "I have a room next door."

"You don't look like one of those whores," he remarked, eyeing her attire.

"Perhaps I'm not. Maybe just a spirited woman with an uncontrollable curiosity for a young handsome man. I bet you could give a woman plenty of pleasure."

"Of course, you're right. Many women desire me. I get this all the time. Don't think you're the only one."

"I'm sure, handsome. I'm sure you do. I heard you earlier inside, telling of your many thrilling quests with your gun, and one was a marshal. How thrilling. I saw all the men how they watched you with respect and hovered in fear. That excites me." Her arm slipped back into his. "Well?"

Collins did not pull away this time. "I sure as hell wouldn't want to disappoint a woman with such good taste, now would I."

"Okay. What are we waiting for, handsome?" Helen said with a giggle.

"Absolutely. Lead the way and I'll give you the time of your life. I promise you'll never forget me."

"I'm sure I won't."

They walked next door to the Dashing Hotel. Helen stopped outside. "Let me go in first and clear it with the desk clerk. It's a very reputable establishment." She went inside, spoke with the desk clerk, and then motioned for Collins.

Collins proudly followed Helen. He felt very superior as he strolled by the jealous looking clerk, who was eyeing him with resentment.

Collins followed Helen to her room. The room was lavishly done with a definite woman's touch. However, Collins gave little time or thought to the room. This woman was far more intriguing.

When he turned, she was watching him. "You like?" she asked.

"The room?"

"I don't give a hoot what you think of the room." She moved closer, sliding her arms around him. "Me, silly." She began to moan as she nibbled his ear. "What do you think of me?" She playfully stepped back.

"I think you know."

"I can feel your strong confident manliness, but you got all that bulky stuff getting in the way. Why don't you get rid of it and I'll start disrobing. What should I call you in the heat of the moment?"

"My name is Collinsworth H. Kingsley."

"My, that's quite a tongue twister when I'm all worked up. How about big man?"

Collins had never had a woman like this. She was such a beautiful, well-bred woman. A real woman and she wanted him. His fire was raging and she was stoking it with each passing moment. He could do with her as he pleased. He tossed his hat and coat to the padded bench. The gun belt was next. The need for her was growing. He pulled off his shirt, boots and pants. He looked up to see the naked woman that he was about to ravage in bed. His mouth fell open. He reached for his gun, but it was not there. Panic set in as he stared down the barrel of a Schofield revolver.

"What the hell is going on here?" he shouted.

Helen held up a poster...a wanted dead or alive poster for Collinsworth H. Kingsley. "Well, it's this way Collinsworth H. Kingsley, your reputation precedes you. You may be fast with your hand, but you're a might slow with your head. Word has it here that you quick drew a marshal by the name of Joshua Parker. He was my very good friend. In fact, he had several friends here. You see, one of the disadvantages of carrying around a reputation, people begin to dislike you."

"You can't just shoot me. The law will hang you. I'm an unarmed man. "

"Helen ripped her garment, exposing her upper torso. "You attacked me, you beast. I had to protect myself. Oh, and you should know, Joshua Parker was a very good friend of the sheriff here in Deadwood. I wanted you to know this before you died. In fact, he had a lot of friends between here and Cheyenne.

We've all been waiting for you. It would be a shame if you left this world not knowing. I'm sure an Elizabeth Fuller will be glad to hear you're dead. She was also a friend of Joshua Parker and sent out the information everywhere to keep an eye out for you. You see what is happening here? You've made the friends of Joshua Parker damn mad."

"Don't shoot me. I can change. I'm still young."

His pleading only antagonized Helen more. "Wasting your time, Collinsworth H. Kingsley. Justice needs to be served and there are a lot of people that are anxious to start celebrating."

Helen Dashing fired the revolver once, twice, three times. She looked at the despicable man on the floor. "It was all I could do for you, Joshua," she said, crying. "I wish there was more." She cleared her throat. "Okay, Sheriff, you can come in now."

The door opened. Helen fell into the sheriff's arms, sobbing.

****

Elizabeth Fuller stood at the foot of Joshua Parker's grave. She wept. "I fulfilled my promise, Joshua. Your killer is dead. Justice has been served. I just wish I felt better in my heart. Take good care of him, Jennie. I know now that this was how it was always meant to be."

Elizabeth walked away. Life would go on. It always did, even when the heart felt like it would never mend, because she had the fire. She would survive, and perhaps one day, happiness would return.

About the Author

Al Patrick, the youngest of four children of Sam and Josie Patrick, was raised on a ranch in South Boulder Valley in the shadow of Old Hollow Top Mountain of the Tobacco Root Mountain Range, southwest Montana. He attended grammar school in a small three-room schoolhouse in a small community of Cardwell that had fifty students in eight grades, and later graduated from Whitehall High School.

During the summers in his early years, he had few opportunities to mingle with children his own age. He used the hillsides, creek bottoms, and the wide-open countryside for the magical playground that stretched his imagination. He used this childhood world to build on storytelling skills which followed him into adulthood by writing short stories for his young children.

In 2007, Al completed and published his first novel, *"Silent Hawk"*. It was well received, and upon numerous requests for more, Al decided to write his second novel, *"Justice Beyond The Trail's End"*. Both novels are based on the old west era in the mid 1800's.

Al currently writes from his home in San Leandro, California. He is married to his life-long love, Bonnie. They have three wonderful children: Shannon, Robert, and Paula. They have been blessed with four beautiful, loving grandchildren: Haley, Hannah, Violet, and Quentin.